DRAKIN

The Story of Raiya

A Novel by James Harrington

Drakin

The Story of Raiya

ISBN:
978-0692057070
First Printing:
January 2018
<u>Cover Art:</u>
Brett Warniers
Rick Chandler
Hanna Hymel
<u>Editing:</u>
Eric Klingenberg
Copyright © January 2018, James Harrington

Drakin
The Story of Raiya

"Command, we're in position. Approaching target!"

"Roger lieutenant."

Lt. Rich Ye checked his Geiger counter as it clicked, "Command… radiation levels here are much higher than normal… This thing is reading a level… good God, this is close to where Chernobyl was about 10 years ago!"

"That confirms our initial readings, Lieutenant. Proceed to the crash site."

"Copy that."

The new Ford F150 pickup truck plowed through the rubble and debris with little issue. Lt. Ye kept his eyes focused on the road in front of him, desperate not to blow a tire. He held the wheel as straight as he could.

Another voice appeared behind him, "This is incredible… hard to believe that a few days ago, this was Manhattan…"

Rich looked over the edge of the crater. The dust and smoke made it difficult to see too far, but in the distance, he could make out smashed buildings and debris that had been ripped from the ground. The impact of the meteor had caused an unbelievable amount of devastation and it was likely that New York would never be the same.

"I hear you Mike, but Hiroshima was in as bad a shape and they were able to rebuild. Come on, let's keep moving."

Drakin
The Story of Raiya

The two men donned white and gray radiation suits that sparkled in the sun. They had been anxious to see for themselves just how big the meteor was, but they had to be cautious. The way down inside the crater was steep and the truck was having a hard time navigating the debris.

Roughly halfway down, the pickup began to jolt violently. Lt. Ye pressed on the breaks, "That's as far is it goes. We're on foot now."

Mike stumbled over a piece of debris as he stepped out of the back. Rich grabbed his arm to keep him upright, "Easy buddy… you don't want to fall and risk tearing your suit."

Mike nodded, "Thanks!"

He quickly straightened up the silver suit and continued walking, "Didn't NASA see this coming? You would think…"

"They did…" Rich replied, "but there was no way to stop it. You saw the news. They threw nukes, remote satellites, and several other things to knock it out. No matter what they did, it just kept on coming. It was like nothing even made a scratch!"

He quickly looked over the debris before he spoke, "Hey, at least they saw it in time to evacuate the city. We saved what counts."

"I hear you… I mean look at the size of that thing!"

"It's a wonder it didn't do more damage…"

The black meteor looked like a giant cannonball from a pirate ship. It sat prominently in the center of the crater. The impact hadn't caused as much as a crack in its shell. Several burn marks remained from where the U.S. Military had made a valiant effort to shoot it down. Smoke and steam emanated from the surface.

"Mother of God... How big do you think it is, Mike?"

Mike squinted as he measured with his eyes, "Six... seven stories, about seventy, eighty feet tall? I'm heading around to the other side. I want to get an idea of the total mass of this thing..."

"Roger that," Rich replied. "Be careful and keep me posted."

"Wilco."

As Mike headed in the other direction, Rich examined the surface of the meteor, "Command... this is odd... This thing is perfectly smooth. That shouldn't be possible."

All he got in response was static.

"Command?"

"..."

"Someone, respond!"

"..."

Rich tapped on the radio, "Mike, are you there?"

The static became even worse.

Gotta be the radiation... "God damn radio!"

He sighed and turned back to the meteor, "Now what?"

Maybe it was the way that the sun was shining, but something on the side of the otherwise smooth surface caught Rich's eye, "What the heck?"

Drakin
The Story of Raiya

There was an odd-looking symbol covered in dirt roughly four feet to the right of where Rich was standing, "What is this?"

He stepped closer to it and brushed the dirt away, "Command… if you're reading this… There's some kind of symbol here. It… it looks like a circle with a triangle in the middle… almost looks like a planet with clouds etched in. Command… I think it's now pretty evident that this meteor is not a natural phenomenon… Could be a derelict satellite from another world… or an actual spacecraft…"

"…"

"Could it really be…?"

Rich bent down at his knees and ran his finger over the triangle, brushing as much dirt off as he could. As his finger reached the upper-most tip, the triangle flashed blue. *What the*…

Rich didn't know what to make of it. What had he just activated? He didn't have long to think as it flashed a second time, then a third, and then a fourth. There was a loud crumbling sound as the entire side of the meteor collapsed into dust.

"Command, something's happening. I'm not sure how, but I think I just activated… something."

Rich took several steps back as a massive dust cloud engulfed him, "Command… Come in, damn it! I'm now convinced this thing is alien in origin… likely some kind of spaceship?"

As the dust cleared, Rich could see something odd in the opening that had been created, "All right… I can't be certain, but I think I see

Drakin
The Story of Raiya

something here that might be alive… There's five… maybe six giant reptilian creatures here."

Rich strained his eyes as the dust continued to clear, "I'll be… Command, I don't believe this, but they… they look like dragons! Honest to God dragons! They have wings, long curved horns from their heads, hand-like claws… but they don't look bipedal. This is incredible."

As he stepped closer, Rich could hear a sound like the purr of a mighty lion. His shoulder brushed against the wall, causing another crumbling sound. A small rock dropped from the wall and struck the ground. It made a small popping noise, like the sound of a ping-pong ball hitting the floor. It was faint but audible nonetheless.

Rich held his breath as, to his shock, one of the dragons began to stir. The massive black lizard, resting atop the other five as though he were protecting them, opened its eyes. Dust fell from his head and neck as the beast came to life.

Rich quivered as the yellow and green eyes bared down on him as though they were piercing right through his chest. The dragon spread its wings and stretched as it stood up.

He flinched as it began to speak, "Shreork terroj ein wroon!"

Rich's breathing became irregular. The menacing look on the creature's face was unnerving, "Command… I think it's trying to communicate."

"Teoric wge vcara!"

Drakin
The Story of Raiya

"Definitely sounds like it's trying to communicate!"

Rich spread his arms as a sign of peace and nervously smiled at the beast, "On behalf of the people of Earth, I'd like to welcome you to our planet. My name is Lieutenant Richard Ye. Can you understand me?"

The dragon's eyes narrowed, "Shorac torren terensa!"

Rich had no idea if he was making any sense. Likely he wasn't, but what else could he do, "You landed in one of our cities. We called it Manhattan."

The dragon appeared to be confused by Rich. After a few moments of silence, it managed to speak, "So we made it... We live again... I thought our slumber would be eternal."

Rich took a step back, "You... how can you speak our language?"

The dragon arched its neck as it stood up. It was a massive beast, easily the size of one of New York's smaller towers, "My mind has abilities far beyond your comprehension. Hearing only a few conjugations of your language was more than enough to grasp the basics of such a primitive form of communication."

A cold feeling came over Rich. He wasn't certain that he was safe any longer, "So... why did you come to Earth?"

The dragon stepped off his still-sleeping companions and stood over Rich looking straight down at him, "It was not by choice, I can assure you. The few of us you see before you are all that

Drakin
The Story of Raiya

remains of my people. For countless rotations of our sun, the drakeas and cenizals lived together in peace. We lived in harmony with our planet and with each other. However, as time went on, those pathetic creatures grew to view us as a threat. We were... an ecological disaster, as they called us. We consumed too many resources and infringed on their lands. Over time, they developed advanced cognitive abilities, including telepathy and telekinesis."

The dragon closed his eyes and released smoke from his jaw, "They started hunting us down. Mass genocide became a crusade to protect their world. My kin and I are the only ones they failed to destroy. We resisted every attack, every torture... all of it. We survived."

Rich slowly stepped away from the dragon, "So you are the last of your people... the drakeas?"

The dragon nodded, "I suppose the translation in your language is 'dragon'. A fitting name, I suppose. For the crime of existing, we were imprisoned in this vessel and flung into space by the most advanced of the cenizal practitioners. For ten thousand rotations, we have slumbered... waiting... hoping that we would find a planet suitable for us. Though not conscious... we did experience moments of... horrific disembodied thought..."

The look in the dragon's eyes was clearly one of disdain as it glared at Rich, "You... tell me what the atmosphere of this planet is."

"Nitrogen Oxygen?"

Drakin
The Story of Raiya

"Similar to our world… but not exact… this will take some adjustment… still, it is better than we could have hoped for."

The dragon sniffed the air as a look of disgust came over it, "This is disgusting. The air here is horribly polluted… what has happened to this world? What have you done?"

Rich shrugged, "You landed in downtown Manhattan. This was one of our cities. A lot of people lived here."

"I see…" The dragon replied in an intrigued tone. "A megalopolis then… So, your people are responsible for all this damage."

"Kind of…" Rich said defensively. "For years we didn't know what kind of damage we were doing. We've only recently realized it, but we've made efforts to repair the damage. We've made significant…"

The dragon huffed as it spoke, "I think I might be able to help speed the repairs along."

"How?" Rich asked nervously.

The dragon smiled as its eyes rolled over red. In a flash of teeth, blood, and intense pain, Rich found himself in the dragon's mouth, impaled on several teeth. The pain was paralyzing. He tried to scream, but his voice was completely drowned out by the blood pooling in the back of his throat. He couldn't even breathe.

One violent thrust of the dragon's neck sent Rich's dying body flying into the air. It landed on the dragon's tongue and disappeared as the beast clamped its jaws together. A rumbling sound emanated from the its stomach as it began to work

Drakin
The Story of Raiya

again after countless years of slumber. "Such a pathetic creature… is that the infestation we now have to deal with?"

Finally, the dragon turned to its companions, "Brothers, sister, awaken! After ten thousand rotations, we have finally been awakened. It is time for us to rebuild the home that was stolwn from us!"

🜲

Mike stood on the far side of the meteor, unaware of what was going on. He was attempting to take measurements as he slowly paced around the side. Most of his equipment was working, but he couldn't get through to command. Every time he tried, all he got was static, "God damn it, someone respond, please? This thing is massive!"

Once again static was his only reply.

"Command, hello? Hello? Can anyone here me? Someone respond!"

"…"

"Seriously what the hell? My lot in life that my equipment fails now of all times!"

At that moment, Mike heard what sounded like crumbling and the growl of a lion. He looked up to see a massive lizard holding onto the side of the meteor, looking down at him menacingly, "Holy shit… what...?"

The massive, mustard-yellow-colored creature with red eyes jumped off the meteor and roared as its massive jaws opened. Mike screamed as he tried to turn and run, "No… no… Jesus, no! ACK!"

Drakin
The Story of Raiya

The beast thrust its neck forward, caught Mike in its jaws and bit down hard. Blood spewed everywhere. Mike didn't get a chance to scream as he watched the red liquid spill from his ripped skin. The pain was paralyzing as the lizard took hold.

The beast opened its mouth, letting Mike loose before clamping down again. Mike went motionless as the pain overpowered him. He didn't even have a chance to close his eyes before the world went black. Silence was all that remained.

Drakin
The Story of Raiya

10 years later...

"Please… please… if anyone is home, please open the door!"

"What in God's name?"

Ben shot straight up in bed. The hysterical sound coming from the next room echoed throughout the house. Loud banging and a woman's frantic cry filled the room as he jumped out of bed.

Ben was no stranger to uninvited guests at their door. In fact, he had a bolt gun right next to his nightstand for just such an occasion. He quickly grabbed it and made his way to the door.

"Ben, what is it?"

Ben turned back and looked at his wife, "Stay here Linda, I'm going to find out. Better not be another shake down."

He pressed a small button on the wall next to the doorway before he stepped out into the living room. Light quickly flooded the hall, letting the voice outside know that she had gotten their attention.

The banging immediately ceased and was replaced by a faint sobbing, "Please… help me…"

The sound made Ben a lot less apprehensive as he gripped his rifle and opened the door. He quickly stepped back and aimed the gun. The indicator on the side screamed as the gun immediately came to life.

Drakin
The Story of Raiya

14

The scene outside his house made Ben's old heart ache. A woman with dark hair and extremely pale skin looked at him lifelessly. Her face and neck looked horribly thin like she hadn't eaten in a long time. Water dripped down the hood of her sweatshirt. Her breathing was labored and she was clearly sick, "Please..."

Ben kept the gun trained on her, "Stay back... We don't welcome drifters here. What do you want?"

"Please help me..."

Ben shook his head, "No way, you're not coming in here. I've seen this before... I know what you have. That illness... it's Dragon's Bane if I ever saw a case!"

"I'm not looking for shelter, sir..."

"Then what do you want?"

Before she could respond, Linda appeared between them, "For goodness sake, Ben. Put the gun away! She's not going to hurt anyone."

Ben lowered the gun so that it wasn't pointing at his wife, "Linda, she's ill. We can't let her in here! It's not..."

Linda ignored him and looked at her sympathetically, "You poor dear, do you want some food?"

The woman shook her head and let out a deep, labored, sigh, "Please... take her..."

"Who?" Linda asked.

The woman opened her sweatshirt and stepped forward. Linda gasped at what she saw. The woman was little more than a skeleton. Her bones protruded through her thin skin. If she did have

Drakin
The Story of Raiya

Dragon's Bane, it was further along than any victim she'd ever seen.

Cradled in her impish arms, was a small black bundle, "My baby… please… save her. Spare her the… life I lived…"

The woman's weak arms looked like they were about to collapse. They trembled and her strength vanished as though she were holding something incredibly heavy.

Linda quickly grabbed the baby from her before her arms gave out, causing Ben to panic, "Linda, we can't!"

"Hush you!" Linda replied sternly. "Dragon's Bane doesn't get transmitted to infants, you know that!"

Ben fell silent, allowing Linda to return her attention to the woman at the door, "Sweetie, can we get you some food or…?"

Before Linda could even finish her question, the woman's eyes fluttered and she began swaying to the left. It was as though the woman's remaining life had gone with the child. Her arms dropped, her shoulders slouched, and she became completely lethargic.

The woman let out one last sigh as she collapsed on the ground, "Thank… you…"

Linda cradled the child in her arms as she leaned down and extended her right hand to the woman's neck, "Miss…? Miss?"

Ben watched as she gently adjusted her fingers, "Is she alive?"

A sad look appeared on her aging features as she pulled her hand away. She looked up at Ben

Drakin
The Story of Raiya

with tears in her eyes and shook her head, "No…
Poor thing, it must have taken everything she had
left just to get here."

Ben knelt down next to his wife, "It's just how
things are these days… We'll need to burn her
body. We can't let the Dragon's Bane spread."

Linda nodded, "Yeah, I guess so."

At that moment, a faint sound came from
inside the bundle, causing the elderly couple to
flinch. Ben took the bundle from Linda and
opened it. His eyes narrowed, "A girl?"

As more of the little baby's skin appeared,
Ben's eyes widened. His face went pale as he shot
to his feet and looked at his wife, "It… it's a
monster!"

Linda stood up next to her husband and
looked at the child, "What the…?"

"We have to get it out of here!" Ben shouted.
"We have to take it into town. We'll leave it at the
orphanage and…"

A tender feeling in his right hand stopped him
mid-sentence. The baby's little fingers had
reached out and grabbed his index finger. She
looked up at him innocently. Her odd eyes made
him speechless.

Linda smiled, "Oh Ben, look at that. She likes
you."

Ben closed his eyes. He knew what she was
about to ask and dreaded every word, "Ben…
can't we keep her here? You know the life she'll
have at the orphanage."

"Linda, she won't replace Teagan."

Drakin
The Story of Raiya

Linda shot Ben an angered look, "I know that you old fool! Nothing could ever replace our daughter, but this baby needs a place to stay and we still have all of Teagan's old things. We should be able to provide for her without much trouble."

Ben watched silently as Linda took the baby from him. He had a look of defeat on his face. When his wife made up her mind about something, it was impossible to change it.

Linda cradled the baby in her arms as it cooed happily, "Ben, the day our daughter left to fight in the Red War, do you remember what she said?"

"Yes…" Ben replied. "She said that she wanted to do her part and help protect our people."

"I remember…"

"Teagan did her part, maybe we can honor her memory by protecting this baby? I think that's what she'd want."

Ben took one more look at the child and frowned as he turned away, "Someone else might be looking for her… she can stay with us for now, but if someone comes…"

"I know, Ben… I know. We'll have to give her up. That's fine."

Thunder cracked outside as Linda closed the door, "It's a deal."

"This could be very bad."

Linda waved at Ben in disregard, "Oh stop it. You worry way too much, what is the worst that could happen?"

Drakin
The Story of Raiya

The baby flinched and began to cry as the thunder echoed in the distance. Linda tightened her arms to bring the child closer to her, "Shh... no, no... it's okay. You're safe now... shh..."

New Framingham
Westcon Territory
Formerly Massachusetts

Drakin
The Story of Raiya

Chapter I

"Unbelievable… thirty years of this shit… wonder how we've been able to keep this up for so long."

As Jagger pulled his jeep onto what was once Route 9, he reached over to the dash and activated the radio. A tired-sounding voice appeared over the speaker, "This is Matt Lowry, WPR hourly news. Today the Second Battalion, Eastern division, rendezvoused with the Third Battalion outside of New Washington beneath the third parallel in district 5. They were successful at warding off the dragon advance. Casualties were estimated at 30%. However, initial reports estimate that at least six dragons were downed in the fight…"

Jagger sighed. *Why do I even bother listening to this? It's never good news, just a constant reminder that we're all fucked. Every time those beasts attack, we're pushed a little closer to extinction.*

"In other news, Captain Suen Luli of the Eastern Coalition Air Corps was awarded for…"

Click.

Jagger turned the radio off. He knew the typical song and dance of the news source. They'd tell the bad news first and then deliver some good news which would be played up to be more important. He understood why things were done this way. Morale was very important… especially when it was hidden from no one that humanity was losing the war quite badly.

Drakin
The Story of Raiya

The jeep drove under the remains of an old overpass that had long since collapsed. It maneuvered gently around the piles of debris. Jagger had spent a lot of time rebuilding and refurbishing his truck. He wasn't about to get it banged up. Once it cleared the debris, he pressed the gas and picked up speed.

A sign on the side read 'Now Entering Natick.' Jagger had been told stories about how that whole area used to be lively with stores and restaurants for people to enjoy. He was too young to remember any of this.

The Red War had been going on for years before his birth, and Natick had been laid to waste while he was still a young child. Now all that remained was rubbed and maybe some salvageable equipment buried in the dirt.

The jeep rounded a large piece of concrete that, at one time had been the side of a storefront. This was usually Jagger's marker to find his way back home. As the jeep hit the open road, a loud noise cut through the air. *Shreeeee!*

Jagger hit the brakes, "Wyverns… shit! One of those days…"

Jagger quickly put the car in park before reaching behind the passenger seat and grabbing a large bolt rifle. A dark shadow passed overhead as he checked the cartridge battery. The indicator light jumped from red to blue, showing a full charge. *Good… let's do this!*

Jagger jumped out of the jeep, brushed a few strands of his long, brown hair out of his face and aimed the rifle. The first wyvern he saw was

Drakin

The Story of Raiya

flying low overhead. He ducked down behind the large piece of rubble that he had passed a moment ago. His gray eyes followed the target. He watched and waited… waited until he had lined up a clean shot, and pulled the trigger. Three large, positively-charged, bolts flew from the barrel. Two shots hit the large beast, sending it falling from the sky. *I've gotten too used to taking down drakes. I used to be able to hit with all three shots!*

Sparks of blue electricity flashed through its body as it hit the barren ground. The wyvern's skin was too thick for the bolts to do any real damage. They only stunned it, but it was enough to give Jagger the advantage.

He quickly ran to the wyvern, pulled a large machete from his belt, and jabbed it into the only vulnerable part of a dragon's body; the eyes.

The blade destroyed the creature's left eye and plunged into its brain. The dying wyvern let out a painful cry as it tried to dislodge the blade. It was a gruesome sight that Jagger had grown used to. He'd been trained for a long time to show no mercy.

Every time he had to watch this scene, he remembered back to the first one he'd killed during his training. He remembered that it had made him sick to his stomach. Seeing a creature suffer like that seemed cruel, but every time he was about to look away his drill sergeant would stop him and force him to watch, "They're lethal to the very end. Turning your back on one now could be the biggest mistake you ever make."

Drakin

The Story of Raiya

'The biggest mistake.' It was something that he'd never forgotten.

The wounded beast slowly ceased movement as death overtook it. Jagger placed his foot over the beast's snout and pulled his blade from its head. Redish-purple blood spewed from the wound as Jagger cleaned his weapon.

As Jagger finished working on the blade, he turned to head back to his jeep and grab a few supplies. The snout of a second wyvern was in his path. *Oh shit...*

Somehow the beast had used its partner's death screams as a cover, holding Jagger's attention long enough to sneak up on him. The beast smiled, "Hope you taste good!"

Jagger frowned, "This is one meal you're going to have to work for."

Jagger gripped the blade at his side, knowing he'd never raise it in time. He waited for the wyvern to lunge. This was likely it, "Bring it on... you ugly freak!"

As the wyvern took a step towards him, a black blur appeared in its path. It shrieked in surprise upon realizing that it had become outnumbered.

Jagger blinked as his eyes adjusted to the new player. They were completely clad in black robes from head to toe, making identification impossible. A gray backpack was strapped tightly to their back. Whoever this was, they moved with lightning speed.

The wyvern snapped at the robed figure, only for it dodge out of the way and grab the small

Drakin
The Story of Raiya

dragon by the neck. The stranger held the wyvern in a headlock as it struggled to get out. Jagger watched as it hissed and roared, "Damn… this guy is good!"

"Let go, bitch or I'll tear your heart out!" the wyvern snarled.

Female… okay, well that's a start, Jagger thought as he quickly moved to grab his bolt gun.

No amount of thrashing could shake this stranger lose. Her hands were locked tightly around the wyvern's neck. She spoke in a voice that was barely more than a whisper, "No… you won't…"

To Jagger's utter shock, she jerked her arms, causing the wyvern's neck to sharply turn to the side. The sound of a loud snap caused the wyvern to go limp.

The skeletal structure and bone mass of even the youngest dragons were considerably thicker than humans. Their muscle tissue was also incredibly strong. No human being should possess that strength. It was a physical impossibility.

Jagger watched in amazement as she let go of the beast, tossed its head to the side, and turned to confront him. He put on a friendly smile and nodded nervously. *Careful Jagger, she looks like she's ready to kill you.* "Thanks."

He couldn't see most of her face under the hood, but her yellow eyes almost looked like they were glowing. Her voice was deep and very quiet when she spoke. It was almost a whisper and difficult to hear, "It was stupid of you to leave your car. A jeep can outrun those beasts and they always hunt in pairs, at least."

Yup… definitely a woman. "It didn't seem that dangerous. Wyverns can't breathe fire, so it's easier to fight on foot, especially if there's only one. I didn't see the second, and I'm usually not caught off guard like that."

"One stupid move… all it takes."

"Words of Wisdom."

"Why did you fight?"

"Instinct I guess."

"I see…"

The figure stared at him for a moment. To Jagger, it felt like he was in the middle of drill inspection back at Westcon command. Her eyes darted up and down for a moment before she abruptly turned and began walking away.

Jagger called after her, "Wait!"

The figure stopped but did not turn and did not respond. Jagger took a few cautious steps towards it, "I owe you one for helping me. Do you need anything?"

"No."

"Really? Nothing?"

"No… not unless…"

"Yeah?"

The figure paused for a moment. Jagger waited as she slowly turned around. Her hood was down as though she were looking at her stomach, "I haven't eaten in a few days… I could use some supplies. Do you have any?"

Drakin
The Story of Raiya

Jagger smiled, "No, but my town is nearby. Hop in, I'm heading for New Framingham. There are plenty of shops there."

"A… town?"

"Yeah, you'll be able to find anything you want there."

"I… I'm not sure…" the figure replied in a nervous whisper. "I don't typically do well around large groups of people."

Jagger looked at her oddly, "Well… It's the only major hub in this part of old New England after Boston and Worcester were destroyed. The survivors moved out here and established a fortified city in the only nearby area with buildings left standing."

"Boston and Worcester… they were both destroyed?"

Really? How could she not know about this? "Yeah, for almost six years now, where have you been?"

"Away…"

"Away?"

The robed woman climbed into the jeep and rested her gloved hands on her lap. She turned and watched as Jagger grabbed a saw out of the back, "Yes… I've been wandering the country since my grandparents were killed by an elder dragon. That was roughly ten years ago. I don't have access to a radio so…"

Her eyes narrowed as Jagger walked over to one of the fallen wyverns, "Wait… what are you doing?"

Drakin
The Story of Raiya

Jagger looked down at the saw, "I'm going to get their teeth."

"Why?"

"Dragon teeth are flame-resistant. They can be melted down and used to make armor, weapons, walls… all kinds of different things. They're worth a fortune if you can get them."

He placed the saw on the nearest wyvern's mouth and began to run the blade across its gums. Blood stained his hands as he struggled to make conversation, "So… you're a nomad?"

"There a better way to live beyond city walls?"

"Not really…" Jagger chuckled as he removed the upper jaw. "Okay… well let's see, ten years huh?"

"Yeah."

"All right so I can fill you in on the Red War, but what do you know so far?"

The girl shrugged, "Not much… From what my grandparents told me, the dragons first appeared in New York… After decimating Manhattan, they flew east and were seen weeks later heading towards Siberia. The five of them disappeared for about five years. When they reappeared, there were many… many more of them and they continued to multiply."

She leaned on the roll bar of the old jeep as Jagger threw the teeth into the back. He then quickly wiped his hands and went to work on the second wyvern, "They were immune to conventional weapons and were too fast for nukes to work… not for a lack of trying… obviously."

Drakin
The Story of Raiya

Jagger looked around the barren wasteland that used to be Wellesley, Massachusetts and nodded, "Obviously… is that it?"

"No," the woman replied stoically. "I heard that countries were toppled by the onslaught of the dragons… Even the U.S. Government retreated. I heard the president's speech, vowing to return and retake the land lost to the dragons… That was three days before he and his chiefs of staff were all killed. The remaining world leaders set aside their differences and formed into two governing bodies; the Eastern and Western Coalitions. They established regional governors, but the cities and settlements themselves are largely self-governed… That's all I know."

Jagger nodded as he removed the second wyvern's jaw, "Sounds like you've heard most of it. The problem was that most weapons couldn't penetrate a dragon's scales. Missiles didn't work, bullets didn't… some armor piercers did, but they're rare. Eventually, we developed electrostatic shock weapons and super-focused lasers that could burn a hole through them, but by then…

Jagger let out a deep sigh as he spoke, "… by then, it was almost too late. Humanity had been reduced to nearly 2 billion people."

"You're losing the war…" the woman said in a whisper.

Jagger grabbed a bottle of water from behind his seat and poured some over his hands. The cool liquid rinsed away the dragon's blood and soothed his skin, "Don't you mean we're losing?"

Drakin
The Story of Raiya

"Sure…"

Jagger got behind the wheel of the jeep and started it up. The engine came to life and caused the entire car to vibrate. He pulled back on the break and allowed the car to wheel forward.

The stranger eyed the dash, "Your car's engine sounds different. They're usually louder."

Jagger smiled, "They're usually falling apart. I spent years working on this one."

"Impressive."

Jagger kept his eyes on the road, though he occasionally looked up to make sure that the sky was clear, "By the way, I'm Lieutenant Jagger Bishop, Westcon Security."

No response.

"What, you don't have a name?"

"…"

"All right then…"

Jagger couldn't be certain, but he thought he detected an annoyed sigh before she spoke, "…Raiya if you must know."

"Raiya, that's an unusual name."

"I'm an unusual person."

Jagger nodded, "Yeah, I believe that just from watching you."

"Whatever you say," Raiya replied in a disinterested tone.

Jagger released a deep breath as he watched the debris pass, "So… those were some nice moves you pulled back there. You must be pretty jacked to snap the neck of a dragon. That was amazing."

Drakin

The Story of Raiya

"It's not that hard if you know where the joint is."

"Maybe you could show me?"

"Doubtful, you also have to be really fast…"

"Oh… too bad."

As the jeep picked up speed, Raiya struggled to keep her hood up. It acted like a sail, catching the wind that blew past her face. As it was pushed back, small flashes of her skin appeared. She grabbed the sides and forced them forward, holding the hood down over her face.

Jagger had his eyes on the road and could only see her out of the corner of his right, but what he saw left him with more questions than answers. Her skin was tanned, but her pigment appeared to have a greenish hue. The strands of hair he saw looked like they were a dark olive color. Maybe she dyed it somehow? *Yeah right, where would she get some dye out here? You're probably just seeing things.*

It was a reasonable thought. He never really had great lateral vision. However, as the hood flew back a second time, he quickly glanced over to confirm what he initially saw. His eyes caught sight of her skin's odd complexion. There was no doubt that something was off about her. Who or what was this girl? *Dragon's Bane? There hasn't been a confirmed case of it in a few years…*

"Are you okay?" he asked.

"I'm fine… why?"

"Your skin… it's… pale."

"So what…? It's just how I look."

"All right."

Drakin

The Story of Raiya

Drakin
The Story of Raiya

Chapter 2

Jagger pulled a right-hand turn after passing by a large building next to the Foss Reservoir. At one time, the building had been a massive living quarter for the families and people who worked in the area. It had long since been reduced to rubble.

The jeep headed up an old concrete ramp that had somehow remained fairly intact. The walls were cracked and were black from dragon's fire. The columns were largely intact except for the burns.

Jagger remembered the first time he'd taken this route. He'd previously avoided the road, but it was getting late and he wanted to be back before nightfall.

The jeep turned onto another road where a smashed sign lay on the right-hand side. It was crimson with a black border and white lettering which read 'Fra…ingham State University.'

Moments later, they approached a massive metal wall that had been built from scavenged debris and discarded sheets of steel. A huge iron gate stood at the end of the road. Behind it, Jagger could see intact buildings and large trucks lining the side of the street. He was home.

The jeep pulled up to the gate and stopped. As Jagger pressed on the horn, he noticed Raiya turn to the side and pull on one side of her hood. Her chin disappeared behind the dark cloth.

Is she really that worried? Maybe bringing her here wasn't a good idea.

Drakin
The Story of Raiya

His thoughts were interrupted by a voice from the other side of the wall, "What do you want? Identify yourself or you will be fired on!"

"Lieutenant Jagger Bishop, reporting back from patrol. Let me in, asshole!"

"Sorry, sir," the voice replied. "You know the rules."

"How could I not? It's the same damn thing every single day; I go out, do my job, come back, you yell out 'identify yourself,' and then finally let me in."

"And you're always surprised when I do it. You should expect it by now. Hold on a sec."

Jagger looked over at Raiya as he let out a deep sigh, "Sorry, this should only take a few minutes."

Sure enough, the gate opened and a stout man with a scruffy beard came out carrying a bolt gun. The man pointed his weapon at the jeep as he looked Jagger over, "How was your patrol, Lieutenant?"

"Fine, mixed it up with a couple of wyverns. Nothing out of the ordinary. How was guard duty, John?"

John kept his gun trained on the jeep with an annoyed expression, "It's sergeant to you, buddy! Oh, you know… peaceful and quiet. Nothing fun… or profitable."

"I hear that…"

"Who's this?" John asked, beckoning towards Raiya.

"A civilian. I found her out wandering in the old Natick area."

"A nomad, you mean."

"Yeah, so?"

"Nomads don't think like us civilized folk."

Jagger rolled his eyes, "John, she saved my life out there. I got ambushed by a wyvern."

"You let yourself get jumped?"

"I know… first time for everything… Anyway, she killed it before it got too close."

"That a fact, huh?"

"Yeah… look, she's just looking for something to eat. I owe her that much. She won't be any trouble."

John eyed the girl suspiciously, "Why are you hiding your face, you sick or something?"

"The sun hurts my skin…" Raiya replied.

John's eyes narrowed as he looked at her and then glanced at Jagger, "All right… Well, Jagger, your word is good enough for me. I'll let her in, but you're responsible for her. I'll notify command. If she puts so much as a toe out of line… you know…"

"I get it," Jagger said in an annoyed tone. "It'll be my ass that they throw out. Understood."

John stepped away from the jeep, "All right, – Let them pass!"

The gates opened wide enough for Jagger's jeep to pass through. It moved forward as Jagger tapped on the gas, "There see? No big deal."

Raiya turned and looked at Jagger from beneath her hood, "Thanks…"

"No worries. Just don't cause any trouble. These people tend to be jumpy around strangers."

"Yeah… I know…"

Drakin
The Story of Raiya

"Oh?"

Raiya turned and looked forward as the jeep passed through the gates, "Let's just say this isn't the first time I've tried to get into a city. People aren't very accommodating."

Jagger nodded, "Well... you can't really blame them. Dragons aren't the only thing out there that's a threat."

"Sure..." Raiya replied as she rubbed her arm.

Jagger looked down and noticed a rather large scar on the small part of her wrist that had been exposed, "Where did you get that?"

Raiya flinched and immediately hid her gloved hand under her robe, "Human raiders."

"You're kidding."

"Nope."

"So, you tussled with a dragon, but it's humans that actually managed to hurt you."

"Yup."

"That's kind of sickeningly ironic..."

Raiya turned away, "I don't want to talk about it."

"Okay."

Jagger sat back as the jeep passed by several massive trucks at the entrance. They were a dark green color with numbers and military insignia.

Raiya eyed them suspiciously as they passed by, "I've never seen trucks that huge before... at least not intact."

"Well, these are..."

A loud siren cut through the air and pierced Jagger's ears. People immediately came running out to the trucks. A small group of men in uniform

Drakin
The Story of Raiya

split up and got behind the wheels. Loud roars emanated from the engines of each one as they were started and moved into position near the gate.

"What's this about?" Raiya asked.

"It's what I was about to say. Those trucks are for evacuation. What you're seeing is a weekly procedural drill the local militia does in case of a dragon attack."

"You have an evacuation procedure? Smart…"

"Yeah well, when Hartford fell, most people couldn't get out of the city quick enough. They were roasted alive around their own homes by dragon fire. Since then, plans have been put in place to prevent a repeat. Now, most settlements have escape vehicles and procedures for civilians to follow."

The jeep picked up speed as it passed through the military encampment, into the civilian sector. The militaristic area acted as a second wall to the city. It sat behind the makeshift ramparts and surrounded the town. Only a barbed, chain-link fence stood between the two areas.

Raiya gasped as they entered the town. She hadn't seen anything like it since she was a child, "This is…"

The jeep passed by intact buildings with windows that hadn't been blown out. There were no burn marks or melted debris. Trees with actual green leaves were flourishing next to sidewalks, whose pavement had not been smashed. It was as though she had traveled back in time to before the Red War, "This... how is this possible?"

A prideful smile stretched across Jagger's face, "Impressed?"

"Yes..."

"We're one of only a handful of cities in the Western Coalition that haven't been pillaged by the dragons. We were able to set up laser citadels before they got here. Since then, we've successfully beaten off every dragon attack."

"So all this... it's original. The dragons never got this far?"

"Nope, these buildings have never been attacked."

Jagger turned the wheel, pulling the jeep into the parking lot of a nearby shop. It was a two-story brick building with a large window out front. The window had been painted with red lettering spelling the name 'Jerry's.' He put the car in park and turned to Raiya, "This is the best place around to get some food."

Raiya nodded, "Thanks..."

She got out of the car without another word and headed for the entrance. Her gloved hand reached for the door, only to be blocked by someone else's. She looked up to see Jagger pulled the door open, "I haven't eaten today either, can I join you?"

"If you must."

"Probably not a bad idea... I am responsible for you after all."

"Don't remind me..."

Drakin
The Story of Raiya

Inside was a small bar on the left with at least four people propped up on stools. The bar was clearly not part of the original room, given how out of place it looked against the tanned wall. Several small chips of dark wood were missing from the surface. Raiya figured they'd salvaged it from an actual restaurant outside the city.

Two of the patrons at the bar were hunched over a plate of food, the others stared blankly at mugs of brownish liquid. Their clothes were torn and covered in soot. The stench of stale booze rose from their seats.

The casualties of war... she thought as she watched them. *The people left behind by those that have died, forced to endure a life of misery and loneliness. I know that look all too well.*

The sound of juvenile laughter interrupted her thoughts, "What the..."

The sound had come from the next room over. A makeshift wall had been constructed of old pieces of wood and brick that separated the restaurant from the bar. It wasn't a perfect seal. Small slits of light escaped right where the wall and ceiling met.

Raiya moved to the small opening in the wall that acted as the doorway to the actual restaurant. Five small wooden tables with at least two chairs apiece took up most of the floor. There were also five booths lining two of the walls, giving the place a cluttered feel.

A family of five with three young children sat at one of the booths in the opposite corner. The children were standing up in their seats, looking around while their parents tried to get them to sit and enjoy their meals. Everyone had a smile on their face. It was a completely stark contrast to the next room over.

Raiya didn't know how to handle this. A bunch of passed-out drunks at a bar was one thing. She was used to seeing that, even on the frontier. This was something different. She froze, not entirely sure what to make of it or how to react.

Raiya stood, staring at them for a few moments. Jagger stepped in next to her and followed her gaze, "Something wrong?"

"No," Raiya replied.

"You sure?"

"Yes, it's just… It's been a long time since I've seen children playing like that."

"That so?"

"Out on the frontier, they're usually huddled in fear in some dark house. Usually, they're missing a parent… if they have any at all."

"Must be hard."

"It is."

"I know that family, their name's Foster. Would you like to meet them?"

"No."

"You sure?"

"I am, what good could come of it?"

Jagger looked like he still had something on his mind. She braced herself, waiting to hear whatever the question may be when a voice appeared behind them, "Hey Jagger, hungry?"

Drakin
The Story of Raiya

The uneasy look disappeared. He smiled and turned to see an older lady with blonde hair smiling at him from behind. The portly woman had a clean white apron on with a notepad in the front pocket. He nodded as he spoke, "I'm starving."

"You going to be able to pay for it this time, right?"

"Really, Mariam?" Jagger replied. "You're still sore over that one time I asked for a tab? I paid you within a week. Come on, give a guy a break. Times have been tough."

"They're tough all over, sweetie. Jerry doesn't like loans or debts. He certainly gave me an earful the last time I gave you a tab."

"Don't I know that?" Jagger replied as he looked at Raiya. "Don't worry, Jerry will have nothing to complain about this time. Lucky for me, I've brought in enough of a haul to pay not only for my meal, but my friend's here as well."

"A new friend for you, Jagger?"

"Yeah, I met her outside the town. She helped me kill some wyverns."

"I see."

Mariam looked at Raiya with suspicious eyes but spoke with a kind voice, "You always this talkative, sweetie?"

"Do you always call everyone sweetie?" Raiya replied dryly.

"Every chance I get," she said with a chuckle, ignoring Raiya's tone. "Take a seat anywhere you want. I'll be by with some water for you."

"Any chance of getting a beer?" Jagger asked.

"Sorry, this week's supply run didn't have any."

"Two weeks in a row…"

Mariam reached out and rubbed Jagger's arm, "It'll come at some point, just be patient. I'll put some aside for you when it comes in."

"Right…"

Mariam smiled, "We do have some of Jerry's blood booze if you're interested?"

"No way! I don't know what's in that stuff and frankly, I couldn't see straight for days last time!"

Mariam laughed, "All right then. Have a seat."

Jagger followed Raiya to the nearest booth. She abruptly dropped into the seat opposite him, "I'm not letting you pay for my meal."

"How are you going to pay for it then?"

"I have some wyvern's teeth too."

Jagger frowned, "Come on, I still owe you for saving my ass."

Raiya looked at him for a moment. Her hood was strategically placed so that no one could see past her chin. The dark lighting of the restaurant didn't help. The glow of her yellow eyes cut through the darkness, giving her an eerie appearance.

Mariam came over a few minutes later with a pair of menus and glasses of water, "All right you two, take your time."

As she stepped away to bring a refill to the Fosters, Jagger looked over the menu, "What's your pleasure?"

Drakin

The Story of Raiya

Raiya held the menu up in front of her face as she scanned the page, "Not in the mood for anything that came from a bird… I eat too much of that."

Jagger frowned, "Yeah well… sadly beef is hard to come by these days."

"What about the mutton?" Raiya asked, looking at the menu.

"Mutton… yeah, one of the few things I haven't tried yet."

Jagger lowered his menu and leaned back. He watched Raiya for a few moments. She quickly blocked his gaze with her menu. He pretended not to notice as he spoke, "So Raiya, what's the deal with you?"

Raiya lowered her menu, "Excuse me?"

"How long have you been on your own?"

Raiya slowly placed the menu on the table. Questions about her past were an annoying subject that she saw no value in. She sighed, deciding to indulge him for the time being, "You really want to hear this?"

"Yeah."

Raiya twisted her lips, "Since my grandparents were killed in an attack… ten years ago."

"Oh, I'm sorry."

"They were good people, but I got the feeling that they looked at me as a bit of a burden…"

"So how did you survive?"

Raiya fidgeted her fingers as she spoke, "At first I just scavenged for whatever I could find. Then a group of nomads took me in. They taught

Drakin
The Story of Raiya

me how to fight, how to stop a dragon, how to survive…!"

"Sounds like a tough life."

"It was mine to live."

"Sorry."

"What for?"

Jagger looked at her for a moment. It looked like he was trying to carefully word his answer, "That you had it so rough."

"It was my life. I've lived it well. I neither want nor need sympathy."

"Fair enough," Jagger replied as he shifted uncomfortably in his seat. "My family died years ago too. We lived in Foxboro and were there when the dragons hit. I got separated from them and placed on a different transport… I never saw them again."

"Couldn't they still be alive?"

Jagger smiled, "After all this time? You'd think I would've found them by now. No, likely they were in one of the transports that the dragons took out. We made it all the way here and… well as soon as I was old enough to shoulder a weapon, I joined the Western Coalition and became a scout."

"So, you've had one too…"

Raiya didn't get a chance to complete her sentence as her hood was pulled back.

"Boo!" Apparently, the Foster's oldest girl had snuck over, hid in the booth behind Raiya, and grabbed her hood.

Raiya yelped as the light revealed her face. She tried to cover it with her arms, but it was too late. The incident had drawn the attention of everyone in the room. Her arms simply didn't hide enough and she had no time to grab her hood.

Jagger's eyes widened at what he saw. Raiya's face and hair were exactly the colors he thought he'd seen out of the corner of his eye. Her skin was a flesh tone, but it had a green hue to it while her hair was dark olive in color. Her hair had been done up in a bun with only a small section of bangs coming down to her left cheek.

Her eyes were shaped like those of a human, but the pupil looked more like that of a cat… or a dragon. The outermost part of her iris was a dark green that faded into yellow around the pupil. They were bright and definitely glowing.

Her ears were noticeably prominent. The hood had kept them pressed against her head, but now they stood out completely. They were sharp and slanted so that they pointed outwards to either side. They were notched near the tip, almost giving the illusion of two separate lobes. The rear ones were longer and slightly curled upwards.

The most striking thing about Raiya was her face. Reptilian scales covered her forehead and ran down the bridge of her nose to its fairly pointed tip. They also ran the length of her forehead and down her temples, where they disappeared behind her ears, only to reappear on the sides of her neck. A small row also ran under her neck to her chin. Her cheeks, thin nostrils, eye sockets, cheek, and jaw bones were the only areas that actually looked human.

Drakin
The Story of Raiya

If her human features were to be trusted, she couldn't have been more than eighteen or nineteen years old. Though almost alien in her appearance, she was strikingly pretty.

Jagger sat back, not knowing what to make of this. His jaw hung open as his eyes studied her appearance, "Wh… what are you?"

Raiya looked at him with sad eyes, "I…"

"Aiiiiyyyeeeee!" The little girl let out a high-pitched screech. "Mommy, Daddy, a monster!"

Mr. Foster got up and walked over to the table, "Miranda, that is not nice! –I'm really sorry miss, my daughter is…"

Then he saw Raiya's face, "What the hell? – Jagger, who is this? Did you bring someone into this town with Dragon's Bane?"

Jagger's eyes darted between her and Mr. Foster, "She… saved my life when I was on patrol. She said she was hungry, so I brought her here."

"To infect us all with Dragon's Bane?" Mr. Foster demanded.

"Does that look like any form of Dragon's Bane you've ever seen?"

"Then what is she?"

"What business is it of yours?" Jagger demanded. "I don't appreciate your tone. No one's done anything wrong, so back off. Don't start something in front of your kids…"

Chick-chick!

The sound of an old-school shotgun appeared behind him. No doubt Jerry had heard the commotion and come to break it up. This was

Drakin

The Story of Raiya

nothing new. People had been on short fuses for years and heated disputes were commonplace. A poke of Jerry's shotgun to the back was usually all it took. Jagger couldn't even remember Jerry ever actually using the gun.

He turned, expecting to see Jerry pointing the gun at either him or Ed. To his shock, Jerry was pointing the gun at Raiya, "Jerry?"

The angry look on his old face gave Jagger the chills. Jerry had been forced to break up many a violent brawl over the years. Jagger himself had been on the working end of the shotgun before, but Jerry never got angry over it. He'd also never pointed the gun at someone who wasn't directly involved.

His eyes glared at the young woman on the other end of the barrel, "Get out of my place, freak!"

A hurt look appeared in Raiya's eyes as she stood up from the table with her hands open. Jagger stepped in front of the gun with a glare that would have burned a hole through someone with less nerve, "Jerry, what the hell, man? She saved my life out there. She's not here to hurt anyone. All she wants is something to eat!"

"You know that for a fact, do you?" Jerry demanded. "When'd you meet her?"

"Well… today…"

"Yeah you know all about her then, don't you? Get out and don't come back! Nomads are bad news, especially sickly ones."

"Jerry, are you out of your mind?" Mariam said as she stepped out of the doorway. The look

Drakin
The Story of Raiya

on her face was more anger than surprise. "This poor girl looks like she hasn't eaten in days. What harm would it do to let her eat?"

"Plenty!" Jerry snapped. "She's scaring the customers, and look at that face! She's sick with something, all right."

"Jerry put the gun down before…"

"I don't want her here. Stay out of this. –I'm asking you one last time to leave!" Jerry shouted, refusing to lower the gun.

Raiya looked at the anger in Jerry's eyes. She then turned and looked at the Fosters. The mother was keeping the young children back, the father's expression matched Jerry's, and all three of the children had fearful looks on their faces. She frowned and slowly pulled the hood back up over her face, "I didn't come here to cause trouble. I'll be going."

She quietly stepped around the group and headed for the door. A hot tear fell from her eye as she walked out past the jeep, and headed for the main gate of the town.

This was all too familiar. Most of the time it was at the gate of a town. A guard would see her and turn her away. On the rare occasion that she did get in, she was often discovered and forced to leave… sometimes by the point of a knife.

"Raiya, wait!"

She didn't bother responding. She knew who it was but didn't want to deal with him.

"Raiya, come on. Please?"

"Go away."

Drakin
The Story of Raiya

"Raiya, not everyone here is like that. I'm sorry that happened."

Raiya stopped in her tracks and turned to look at him. The yellow in her eyes burned like fire, "Oh really? They're not, huh?"

She quickly threw back her hood so he could clearly see the mixed look of anger and sadness, "Do you know how many times I've been called 'monster', 'freak', 'leper', or 'abomination?' It happens so often and it's been happening since I was a child!"

"Raiya, I…"

"When I was a child, other kids wanted nothing to do with me. They called me the dragon girl. The few that would actually play with me were quickly herded away by their parents… They were very cruel."

She clenched her teeth and quickly wiped her eyes to prevent any more tears from falling, "It didn't get any easier when I grew up. People were afraid of me. They'd either threaten me or form a lynch mob. Do you have any idea how many times I had to run and hide out of fear? 'Maybe this time will be different. Maybe these people won't be so bad.' I say that each time, and each time it blows up in my face."

The harshness of her voice, combined with her sad words, stopped Jagger in his tracks. Her typical cautious whisper had been replaced with an angered tone. For the first time, he was hearing her voice at full volume. He clearly didn't know what to say to refute her words, "I'm sorry… it must have been…"

Drakin
The Story of Raiya

"No, you know what? I'm tired of it. I'm better off on my own. These people don't want me here, so I'm not going to stay. Thanks for showing me the city. I appreciate you trying to get me something to eat, but I really need to be going."

Jagger sighed, "Raiya, it's getting late. The sun's already starting to come down. You'll be a sitting duck out there."

"I'm used to it."

"Why don't you come stay with me?"

"What?"

"At least until tomorrow. Then you can disappear if you want."

Raiya took a few steps closer to Jagger and looked into his eyes, "Why?"

"Why, what?"

"Why are you being so nice to me? Would you be so eager to help me if I wasn't a girl?"

"What the hell is that supposed to mean?"

"I think you know what it means. Are you attracted to me or something?"

Jagger took a step back, "Huh?"

"Are you attracted to me?"

Jagger sighed, "I've barely even seen what you look like. You saved my life and you look like you could use a break. Yes, I would make this offer if you weren't a girl. Christ, I had made the offer before I'd even seen your face!"

Raiya lowered her eyes as her attitude became more apologetic, "You're stupid, you know that? You don't even know me. I could slash your throat in your sleep."

Drakin

The Story of Raiya

"I'm a good guy. If you cut my throat, I'll die a good guy, but I'm also a good judge of character. I don't think you're on the level where you'd kill someone who opened their home to you. I have a feeling you're better than that."

Raiya looked toward the city gates. In the distance, she could hear the howls of ravenous coyotes and other creatures she couldn't identify. It was true, being outside the city at night was dangerous. It was even more so when on foot.

She let out a defeated sigh and turned back, "Well I suppose I'd get a similar reception from the local shelter… I guess you're right. It's too late for me to find shelter and make up a camp."

"Where do you usually sleep?"

"Mostly in abandoned buildings where I can hide and keep myself covered. Any place where no one would find me."

"So, what do you want to do then?" Jagger asked.

Raiya glanced at the exit one more time before speaking, "All right, but tomorrow I'm gone. No whining, no fuss, got it?"

"Got it."

Drakin
The Story of Raiya

Chapter 3

Raiya kept quiet during most of the trip. Her encounter at the bar had left her bitter and unwilling to say much. She watched as small houses, surrounded by trees, lined the road on either side. Her eyes focused on a group of kids playing an odd game with a ball and sticks.

She quickly forgot her sour mood as she watched them. They stood in the shape of a diamond in the middle of the road as one help up the stick and swung when the ball was thrown.

"What are they doing?" Raiya asked.

"Playing baseball."

"Baseball?"

"You've never heard of baseball?"

"No."

Jagger smiled, "It's an old game that the U.S. loved from before the war. Each player tries to hit the ball as far as he can. Then they run to each point of that diamond. When they make it back to the first one, they score a run. The team with the most runs wins the…"

"I get it."

"Oh… okay."

Raiya's lips curved into a frown, "Your people live like there is no war going on. It's unnerving."

"I know… but you have to understand… we've got bad things happening all around us. The reality is that we're all more than likely going to die a fiery death. It's just a question of when."

"Right."

Drakin
The Story of Raiya

"Well we already know that, but no one outside of the military need to be reminded of that fact. The only way any of our people can live any form of a happy life is if they aren't constantly reminded of it."

"Willful ignorance then…"

"Pretty much."

The jeep pulled past the residential neighborhood. The lush green trees became less and less as they approached a large building. Judging from the arched windows and architecture, it was likely used as a factory at some point. The bricks were crumbling and the windows looked decrepit. Even so, there were several lights shining from them.

The jeep turned into a small parking lot off to the side. It slowed to a halt next to an old sedan that looked like it hadn't moved in years.

Raiya looked up at the old building, "You live here?"

Jagger nodded, "Yeah. It's not much, but these places have been known to withstand dragon attacks better than most others. The old brick buildings don't burn down."

"No, the bricks just get really hot and become an oven."

"True," Jagger admitted, "but at least you've got a chance to get out."

"If you say so."

They got out of the jeep and headed for the door. Jagger pulled a small black fob out of his pocket. He waved it over a pad on the side of the door. The indicator beeped and the door unlocked.

Drakin
The Story of Raiya

Jagger's home was the first door to the right on the second floor. The stairway was black rot iron and spiraled around a thick pole.

Jagger pulled out his key and unlocked the door at the top of the stairs. The light snapped on inside as he dropped his bag on the counter.

Raiya's eyes blinked as she looked around. There were guns and various bits of technology everywhere. Otherwise, the apartment looked like something most young men would live in. A couch that had seen better days was the main piece of furniture in the living room. The coffee table was covered in gun parts. The kitchen had a small diner-style bar with two stools leaned against it. A few pictures hanging up on the exposed brick walls were the only decor.

Raiya focused on one photo in particular. It was a beach scene with a younger Jagger standing with a girl that had similar hair and eye color. She was clad in a red and blue bikini with ties on the hips.

Raiya's eyes narrowed as she examined the photo, "Old girlfriend?"

"Sister," he replied.

She turned and looked at him oddly, "Really?"

"Yeah, we got along better than most siblings. She was my partner in crime… my best friend."

"I see. What happened to her?"

"She was in Hartford."

"Oh."

"Yeah. Didn't even stand a chance. I went looking for her, but there was nothing to find."

"Sorry."

Drakin
The Story of Raiya

Jagger shrugged, "It was a long time ago. I won't say I got over it, but… well you know, I've moved on."

"Gotcha."

They were interrupted by a gentle knock at the door, "Jagger are you home?"

Jagger instinctively pulled out the laser he kept in his belt and pointed it at the door. Raiya's eyes narrowed, "I think it's your friend Mariam."

Jagger lowered the gun and went to the door. Mariam stood on the other side with a sympathetic smile and a bag at her side, "Sorry to just drop by…"

"You're always welcome, you know that," Jagger replied.

She raised her right hand to offer Jagger the bag, "Well I brought you some food. Jerry was way out of line at the restaurant today…"

Then she caught sight of Raiya, "Oh good, you're still here. Sweetie, I'm sorry for what happened. Please don't judge us too harshly. It's been a hard life and some of us are not as welcoming to outsiders as we should be."

"I'm used to it," Raiya replied.

"I'll bet. So, I was hoping to give you both these. I didn't know what you were in the mood for, so I brought over some of Jerry's sheep burgers."

Jagger smiled, "Thanks, I really appreciate that."

"No problem, sweetie," Mariam replied. "Now since I've given you these, I'd better get home. My man isn't too happy if I get home too late."

"Good luck."

"Thanks, I'll need it."

Jagger took the bag and closed the door as Mariam turned away. Raiya looked at him oddly, "Do you always answer the door with a gun in hand?"

"No, not always. Just usually after dark… and honestly, your story about people coming after you in mobs got me a little jumpy."

"Uh huh."

Jagger cleared off his table before emptying the bag's contents. There were two plastic boxes that were warm to the touch, utensils, and small containers of sauce.

Raiya's eyes dilated as she looked at the food, "Amazing that people can still produce sauce like this."

"A lot of it is homemade, but we do still have some bits of civilization intact. They're just not as easy to come by."

Raiya sat down and ripped open the box that Jagger placed in front of her. Her throat made a faint growling sound as she bit into the burger. The juices from the meat ran over her tongue, causing it to tingle, it was as though time had frozen in place. She looked down at the burger and began fiercely devouring it.

Jagger's eyes widened as he watched her eat. Her four front teeth on both jaws looked human, but the rest looked incredibly sharp, "I guess it really has been a while, hasn't it?"

Drakin

The Story of Raiya

Burp!

"Yup, definitely a while," he quipped.

Some of the juice from the burger ran down the side of her lip, she quickly licked it up with an unusually long and pointed tongue, "That was sheep?"

"Yeah. Jerry uses different seasoning to fool you into thinking it's beef."

"The man has some skill. Too bad he's a jerk."

Jagger shrugged as he picked up his own burger, "He's just an old school hard ass. Once you get to know him, he's not that bad."

"If you say so."

Jagger ate down his burger and then looked at Raiya. She returned his gaze with an annoyed expression, "Do I have something on my face?"

"No."

"Something wrong?"

"No… I've just never seen anyone like you before."

"Not the first time I've heard that."

Jagger sucked down a deep breath as the scene fell into an awkward silence. Raiya's gaze did not make it any easier. Her glowing yellow eyes stared at him as though saying that they weren't going to move until he did.

"All right, this way. Your bedroom's over here."

Raiya got up and followed him down the only hallway at the back of the apartment. On one side stood a bathroom, built out of the brick wall. Two bedroom doors lined the hallway on the opposite side.

Jagger pointed to the first door, "Here you go. This one is yours."

Raiya stepped through the doorway and looked around. The entire room had been white-walled. The brick was covered up, giving the room a homely feeling. A queen size bed sat in the middle of the room with a nightstand on either side. It was little more than a mattress propped up on some wooden beams, but it looked comfortable enough. There was also a small wooden chest at the end of the bed for storage.

Raiya looked at him oddly, "This… is pretty big to be a guest room."

"Yeah, both bedrooms are the same size," Jagger replied with a yawn.

"And this is what a single person gets?"

Jagger's eyes narrowed, "No, this is what a member of the Westcon security force gets."

"Why?"

"The average life expectancy for someone who does my job is five to ten years, max. Those who take on this job are given a little extra. Call it appreciation."

"I see…"

"What?"

"Nothing."

"Go ahead," Jagger insisted. "You can say it."

Raiya let out a deep sigh as she spoke, "Just seems like this extra space could be used… you know?"

"You mean for refugees or dissidents?"

Drakin

The Story of Raiya

"Yeah."

"Well, they often are. When we get a group of refugees coming in, we're often asked for volunteers. Usually, I'll take in a few people until they can find better arrangements."

"All right…"

Jagger yawned as he turned away, "I'm going to call it a night. Do you need anything?"

"No… but…"

Raiya bit her lip and lowered her eyes as she turned to Jagger. Her demeanor was one of someone who was struggling or perhaps in pain. Her conscience was wrestling with something she wanted to say, that was obvious.

Jagger watched her carefully as she squirmed, "What?"

"I… never really thanked you for taking me in."

"You don't have to."

"Well… thank you anyway."

Jagger nodded, "No problem. You know, you never really answered me before."

"About what?"

Raiya turned her back to him, pushed her hood back, and undid the bun on the back of her head. To Jagger's shock, her hair was quite a bit longer than he originally thought. It reached all the way down to the small of her back as it fell.

An even bigger surprise was waiting for him on her head as she turned back around. His eyes widened at the two large protrusions coming out of her hair. "You have horns?"

Drakin
The Story of Raiya

Two inch-thick horns protruded from the hairline on either side of her forehead. They looked almost exactly like dragon horns. They spread out from her forehead and wrapped around the side of her skull, barely above her hair. The tips curved and slightly stuck out in the back, "Yeah. I've tried grinding them down and sawing them off, but it hurts too much. So now I just cover them with my hair."

"What are you?" he blurted out.

"That's the question you asked earlier, isn't it?"

"Yeah."

Raiya sat down on the bed and shrugged, "To be honest, I have no idea."

"Huh?"

"My mother was pregnant with me when the dragons attacked our home. She was injured as she fled Richmond. After the city fell, she made it all the way to Philadelphia."

"The Richmond attack... led by one of the Five Dragon Lords and one of the worst massacres of the war."

"What do you know about it?"

Jagger shrugged, "Not much I'm afraid. I wasn't there. Most of what I heard came from reports later on."

"Tell me."

"Okay well, the attack was launched by five dragons. Two wyverns, one beta dragon, and one dragon lord. The city put up one hell of a fight, killing both wyverns and sending the elder packing, but nothing they did could push back the dragon lord. The death toll at his claws alone was beyond words."

Raiya frowned, "Yeah… well after that fight… I was told that my mother lived long enough to hand me off to an old couple. They told me that she had dragon's bane… I guess that's why I look like this."

Raiya leaned against the wall as she tried to get comfortable, "So do you know anything else about the dragon?"

Jagger sucked down a deep breath, "Well… there is currently a pretty massive reward out on that dragon's head. They're asking any mercenary or dragon hunter group to keep their eyes open for a black dragon with yellow eyes and red tips on its scales."

Raiya smirked, "No merc in their right mind would be stupid enough to try and go after one of the dragon lords. It's an automatic death sentence. I should know…"

"Why?"

"Because I'm hunting it."

Jagger's eyes widened, "What the heck? Are you serious?"

"Yes."

"Why?"

"It murdered my mother... and probably my father. I want it dead," Raiya said through clenched teeth.

"How are you going to kill it?"

"I'm still working on that. I've been coming up with new ideas about how to fight it."

Drakin
The Story of Raiya

"You're going to get yourself killed," Jagger said.

"No… I'm not going after it without a plan. I've been tracking it since I was old enough to get out on my own. It's a blight on this world that has to be stopped. You and I both know it."

"True… well, sadly I don't have any other information for you. By the way, how did you find out about your real parents?"

"I looked up my mother as soon as I was old enough… and put two and two together about my father. Maybe I'm wrong, maybe he's out there somewhere. I don't know… and I somehow doubt I ever will."

"He might still be out there. I mean it's not impossible."

Raiya rolled her eyes, "An optimist in this day and age, truly a rarity… and an annoyance."

"I do my best. Good night."

"Yeah, night."

Jagger closed the door behind him as he left the room. Raiya kept her eyes fixed on it until she heard the soft impact of his own door closing. *Well, here I am… stuck in a stranger's home, in a town where I clearly would not be wanted. Probably best if I just leave before everyone wakes up.*

Raiya frowned as she looked down at her slender body. "I guess I really did need some food."

The relief of finally being able to sleep in an enclosed space was extremely comforting. She

Drakin
The Story of Raiya

quickly stood up, pulled off her robes, and tossed them on the floor next to her. Her undershirt and loin cloth quickly followed it.

She turned to the side and sat down on the mattress. The soft sheets made her skin itch for a moment before it became accustomed to the fabric. She curled up and wrapped herself in the blankets before resting her head on the pillow.

Raiya's head and neck had to adjust to the cushion. At first, she wasn't certain that she could sleep. Then her body slowly settled into the gentle caress of the blankets. *I'd forgotten what this… felt like.*

Her eyes fluttered and she quickly fell asleep in a level of comfort that she hadn't known in years.

🕇

What is wrong with you man?

Jagger lay in bed looking at the door. *She'll be gone tomorrow morning before you even wake up, just you watch. She'll probably make off with half your guns too. That's considering she doesn't kill you in your sleep.*

Jagger sighed as he pressed his head into his pillow. *It was the right thing to do and worth the risk. The poor girl looked like she needed to get back to civilization and I get the feeling that she hadn't eaten in days.*

Jagger closed his eyes as he stretched out. *Eh… we'll just see what happens tomorrow.*

He rolled over a few times and looked at the wall. He pictured her curling up under the sheets of his spare bed. *For such a weird creature, she*

Drakin

The Story of Raiya

was very pretty. She's pretty sharp too, read me right away.

Jagger's thoughts had drained him enough that he could finally lose consciousness. *See you tomorrow... maybe.*

Chapter 4

Jagger's eyes shot open to the ear-piercing sound of an alarm in the distance. His room was almost pitch-black except for a small orange hue coming from behind a curtain. He jumped out of bed and ran to the window. Not sure what to expect, he quickly pulled back the curtain and peered out onto the town.

To his horror, a building that was a few blocks away had been set ablaze. A large dragon was circling it with its head angled down towards the ground. The high-pitched scream of the dragon's roar hurt his ears worse than the alarm. He quickly got dressed and ran down the hallway to Raiya's room, "Raiya, you still in there?"

"Yes."

He quickly flung the door open to see that she was already dressed. "We've got to get to the gate. You need to be evacuated while I get to the command post! We're under attack."

"I'm ready, let's go."

She opened the door and joined Jagger in the hallway. The building shook, causing debris to fall all around them. Fearful screams could be heard from the other apartments as they reached the door.

"Another dragon?" Jagger asked.

"Maybe more… the wyvern and drake class dragons tend to attack in packs… but…"

"What is it?" Jagger asked as they continued running.

Drakin
The Story of Raiya

"They don't usually attack at night… and that didn't look like a wyvern or a drake."

"How can you tell?"

"It was too big, its roar was too deep, and the way it flies… smaller dragons have to continuously flap their wings to remain airborne. Older dragons have longer wings and can hang in the air like a bird of prey."

"So… what are we dealing with?"

For the first time since he met her, a look of fear appeared on her face. Though it wasn't cold, goose bumps appeared on the parts of her skin not covered by scales, "I think we may be dealing with an elder dragon. If so… we're fucked…"

"Great. All anyone's ever been able to do is drive them off…"

The two made their way to Jagger's jeep and hopped in. The engine roared to life as he slammed it into reverse. Raiya turned and pointed above them as she hopped into the passenger's seat, "Look out! Wraith class!"

They both looked up to see Jagger's home set ablaze. The brick walls resisted the flames, but the windows blew out and fire spewed from them. The whole building was quickly transformed into a massive inferno.

Jagger could hear the screams of the people in his building and hit the brakes. Raiya looked at him oddly, "What are you doing?"

"Can't you hear them? We've got to go back!"

"We can't," Raiya said stoically.

"Seriously? There are people still in there. Families with children…"

Drakin

The Story of Raiya

"I know that," Raiya replied sternly, "but you can't help them. They're already dead. Dragon fire is much hotter than any fire you've ever dealt with. If you get too close, it'll kill you in seconds."

Jagger closed his eyes and slammed his fist on the wheel as the painful screams were quickly silenced, "Damn it…"

"Sorry… there wasn't anything you could've done."

WREEEEE!!

As the voices vanished, Jagger spotted the large dragon crawling across the blackened building. Its eyes reflected in the fire as the beast jumped into the air. It grabbed two other people who had just emerged from their apartments and crushed them in its grip.

They didn't even have a chance to scream as the dragon grabbed them and tossed them aside. Its claws were incredibly powerful.

"Can you shoot a gun?" Jagger asked.

"What?"

"Can you shoot?"

Raiya nodded, "Sure… Anything up to a rifle."

Jagger pulled the jeep out of the parking space and put it in drive. The tires squealed as he reached behind his seat and grabbed the bolt gun, "Here, we've got to try to draw it off."

"Draw it off?"

"There's a lot of innocent people nearby. If we don't do something, they're going to die. I'm asking you… will you help me?"

Drakin
The Story of Raiya

She looked at him suspiciously, "You're asking me for help?"

"Yeah, will you?"

"… Yes?"

Jagger nodded, "All right, let's do this…"

Raiya grabbed the gun and turned around in her seat. She peered through the small scope that was seated just above the barrel. The scene was reminiscent of a sniper, trying to carefully line up his shot.

Jagger revved the engine to draw the dragon's attention. It was still dark and hard to see anything. His bolt gun didn't have a night vision scope. He could only hope that Raiya's eyesight could handle it.

Raiya switched on the power converter and lifted the gun over the roll bar as it came on. She remained motionless, except for a few wrist adjustments.

"What are you waiting for?" Jagger shouted as she lined up her shot.

"Shh!"

SCREEEEEEE!

"I think we already got his attention," Raiya said as she aimed.

"When you get a shot, take it!"

"One second… just a little closer… a little closer… Come on you son of a bitch…"

Raiya pulled the trigger and sent three pulses flying towards the shadow. The black silhouette of the dragon immediately turned blue as static charges flew through its body. The beast seemed

Drakin
The Story of Raiya

almost paralyzed as the electricity flowed through it.

RAAAWRRK!

"I think we just pissed it off," Raiya said as she fired off three more shots.

Little by little, the dragon began to slow its approach. It was as though someone had attached weights to its wings. Each thrust was labored. It had to lower its head with each thrust. The dragon was clearly in pain as it struggled to keep pace.

After two more shots, it gave up and flew off into the clouds. Raiya threw her fist into the air, "Got it!"

"Yes!" Jagger shouted. "Good job!"

As Raiya sat down, her advanced hearing detected fearful screams coming from the left. The sound was coming from where the burning building stood, "Jagger, we've got to go over there."

"Where, to the main compound?"

"Yes."

"The elder dragon is still there, are you crazy?" Jagger demanded.

"Yes, but I can hear voices over there as well. They need our help. Some of those voices are children and trust me, that dragon won't spare them."

"You can hear that?" Jagger asked.

Raiya pulled the green hair back and pointed to her elongated right ear, "What do you think?"

Jagger smiled, "So now you care?"

"Contrary to seemingly very popular belief, I am not a monster," Raiya shot back. "I may not

Drakin
The Story of Raiya

really want to get involved in everything that's going on, but I don't want to see people die, especially not kids."

"Good answer."

Jagger turned the wheel hard to the left, causing the jeep to swerve. Its tires whined and screeched as the car slid across the old pavement. He pressed on the gas the moment it righted itself, causing the engine to rev even louder. *Christ, the old girl is going to need a tune-up after this one.*

The massive flames grew larger as they approached the burning building. As they reached the clearing, they saw a massive dragon dodging around the laser citadels that had been set up on the walls protecting the city. He moved gracefully each time they fired like he was taunting them with a dance.

"Why aren't they all firing?" Jagger asked as his eyes scanned the wall at the edge of town. "There are supposed to be six in total. I only see three."

Raiya pointed to a few small plumes of smoke, "Something tells me they were taken out before they had a chance."

"Shit! This isn't supposed to be possible."

"It never is…"

Two more wyverns appeared and drew the attention of the laser cannons while the elder dragon continued its work. The citadels were doing their jobs, but the dragons had them outnumbered.

Drakin
The Story of Raiya

Jagger watched the scene unfold and frowned, "This isn't looking good. We're not going to last long!"

The terrified screams brought them both back to the field. A small family had been caught in the dragon's sight. The three children huddled with their parents for protection, as if that would do them any good. Every time they tried to run out of the square, the dragon would swoop in and push them back.

"He's toying with them," Raiya said through clenched teeth.

"What?"

"I've seen this before... Some of the elder dragons are known for being sadistic. They'll taunt and torment these people until they either get bored, or the family begs for death."

Anger flashed through her eyes as the horrific scene continued to play out, "Not this time... Let me out."

"What?"

"Let me out, I can help them!"

"You're serious?"

"Trust me."

Jagger thought she was insane. How was she going to help them without getting eaten or becoming human jerky? He was about to refuse when she locked eyes with him. Despite her appearance being that of an eighteen-year-old girl, her eyes showed a level of determination and maturity that he had not seen previously.

"I hope you know what you're doing," he said.

Drakin
The Story of Raiya

Jagger hit the brakes, causing the jeep to screech to a halt. Raiya nodded and jumped out, "I'll be just fine…"

She marched quickly towards the family. Her face was a mix of stoic and angered expressions. She'd faced down dragons before, but nothing this big. On the surface, her stance was pretty bad-assed, but Jagger couldn't be sure if it was genuine or a ruse.

She reached under her cloak and slowly pulled a blade from a concealed sheath on her leg. It measured at least twenty inches and was completely covered in blood. She lowered it to her left side and clenched the grip.

The dragon's ears perked up as her feet crushed the burnt grass. He looked up and saw her coming towards him. The beast hissed and moved in to attack, "Finally… someone bold enough to challenge me."

Jagger grabbed his gun as Raiya stepped fearlessly into the dragon's path. She stepped around the family so that she blocked the dragon's view of them.

This was where she would make her stand. She stood with her hands on her dagger. Her feet were roughly twenty inches apart, and her knees bent. Her eyes were burning with the same yellow fire she'd used on Jagger the day before.

She turned her head to the side and was clearly surprised when she saw who the family was, "Fosters…"

Drakin
The Story of Raiya

Mr. Foster looked up at her, "Please… I'm sorry for what I said, please help us."

"Don't move, stay behind me and you'll be safe. I promise."

Mr. Foster nodded, "Thank you."

The dragon ceased its descent a mere six feet from the ground and stared at Raiya, "You bear the appearance of a human, yet your eyes are telling a much different story. How intriguing."

Raiya stepped forward menacingly, "Leave this town, now, and I'll let you live."

The dragon chuckled, "You are brave young one, stupid, but brave. Clearly, you deserve such beautiful eyes, but you're in over your head."

The dragon landed and spread its wings. She couldn't see it as easily in the moonlight, but now that it was on the ground, the fire and artificial light lit up the beast's scales. Its hide was bright red in color, and its wingspan was far more impressive than any other dragon she'd ever seen.

The shock hit her, causing the hair to stand up on the back of her neck. She'd completely miscategorized this dragon. He wasn't an elder at all. Raiya was face to face with one of the Five Dragon Lords. It wasn't the one she was hunting for, but there was no mistaking it close up. *Oh shit…*

An elder dragon would have been nearly impossible to kill. Her plan was to simply ward it off or distract it long enough for the Fosters to get away, but one of the dragon lords would not be susceptible to any of her strategies. It definitely wouldn't be scared off by a single human. There was nothing she could do now, but that was not about to stop her.

She immediately looked over her shoulder at the Fosters, "Run, now! Don't look back!"

The family scattered, heading towards the group of people that were running to the gates. The dragon roared and tried to give chase, but Raiya stepped in its way with her blade pointed at its throat. Its eyes were full of malice as she stared it down, "If you're so tough, why leave?"

The dragon could have easily just knocked her over and gone after the family, but Raiya was betting that its pride and ego would not allow it to ignore a challenge. She stiffened herself and kept the blade pointed.

The dragon smiled as it curled its neck back and looked at her. Its lips curved into a hideous smile, "You really think you can take me on? I've lived for thousands of years. Am I to be slain by such a pathetic creature?"

"Pathetic or not, I'm not letting you hurt them."

Raiya's voice successfully hid her quivering nerves. As the dragon regarded her, she began to question why she was even doing this. *These are the people who called you 'Monster.' Why risk your life for them?*

At that moment, the dragon was hit by three blasts from a bolt gun. The mighty beast roared and shook its head back and forth as the static charges broke away from its body.

Drakin
The Story of Raiya

Raiya turned her head to see Jagger pointing his gun at the beast. It growled and attempted to charge at him, "Pathetic wretch!"

Raiya immediately jumped between them, "No!"

Now him, I have reason to defend.

Once again, the dragon looked at her, "Do you really wish to meet your end so quickly? Very well… though it seems such a shame to destroy such beautiful eyes. If you will deny me my prey, then you will take their place!"

The dragon thrust its head forward and opened its mouth. Its tongue curled back and flame spewed from its lower jaw. It spread across the pavement like napalm and engulfed Raiya.

🦇

Raiya crouched down on the ground as the flame struck her. Jagger could only watch helplessly as she was consumed by fire. His eyes widened as she disappeared into the flame, "No!"

He raised the bolt gun and completely unloaded the cartridge into the dragon's side. The bolts hit the thick scales on its skin and sparked for a few moments before disappearing. The beast flinched but appeared otherwise unharmed.

He lowered his gun, suspecting that he'd be next, "God… I'm sorry."

The flames eventually died down as the dragon recoiled its neck. Jagger expected to see a fried corpse where Raiya had once been. No human could have survived that blast. Dragon fire had been measured at almost four thousand Kelvins.

Drakin
The Story of Raiya

Unbelievably, as the flame disappeared he saw Raiya. She was still crouched in the same position she had been a few minutes ago. Steam poured off her body, which was trembling as though she were cold. Her clothing had been completely disintegrated by the flame, but her hair and skin appeared unharmed. She looked up at the dragon angrily. Her lips were curled back, revealing clenched teeth. Her eyes burned with intense rage.

The dragon growled and took a step back, "It's not possible!"

He brought his face in close to her and sniffed the air, "You... those eyes and your scent... it can't be..."

The dragon raised its head and let out a deafening roar. The two wyverns in the distance responded with their own call. Surprisingly, they turned and flew off into the distance. Someone ignorant of the situation would have guessed that they had been scared away.

The remaining dragon flapped his wings and took off, "I'll leave you to consider your fate... for now, but this is not over. We'll see each other again."

Jagger wanted to take another shot. If he could just get one clean hit, then maybe he could bring the dragon out of the air. He struggled to reload as the dragon quickly faded into the night sky when a voice called to him, "Jagger... Jagger, please help me! I'm burning up! Please... I can't stand the pain! Jagger, it burns!"

Jagger dropped the gun, grabbed the half-full water bottle and an old jacket out of the back of the jeep and ran out into the clearing. Raiya was still steaming and frozen in her crouched position. *Poor girl, it must be painful to even move.*

"Please… please help me…" she said as her voice began to die down to a whisper. Her body trembled even harder.

The moment he reached her, he quickly emptied the bottle over her head, shoulders, and legs. The cool liquid steamed as it touched her, but she immediately stopped shaking and let out a deep sigh, "Thank you…"

Jagger only had half a bottle left. He poured the rest of it over her head, allowing it to drip down and cool her off, "Are you okay?"

"I think so? What happened."

"I don't know. You should be toast right now. Somehow the flames didn't hurt you."

"How… is that possible?"

Jagger shrugged, "The dragon seemed just as shocked as you were."

Raiya's eyes fluttered. Her breathing slowed, but she was still steaming. Jagger carefully touched her arm to see if she was still burning, but her skin was back to its normal temperature. Her eyes slowly closed as her head fell forward.

"Raiya, are you okay?"

No response.

Jagger quickly touched her neck to see if he could find a pulse. The skin on her neck was scaly and somewhat rough. It wasn't quite as rough as sandpaper, but the toughness of it was likely why she survived the flames.

Drakin
The Story of Raiya

Jagger wasn't sure what he was looking for. Did her heart beat like that of a normal human or a… whatever she was? He pushed his fingers into the side of her neck and closed his eyes.

A beating sensation pushed against his fingers as they found the artery in her neck. *Phew… she's still alive.*

Jagger ran his hand under her back to pick her up. He immediately noticed something odd; her spine was covered in solid, boney, plating.

He turned her over to see squared plates running the length of her spine. They started at the base of her skull beneath her hairline and got bigger as they traveled to the middle of her back. The largest ones were about two square inches in size and continued to run to her tailbone.

At the bottom of her lumbar curve, the plates spread to her hips. Jagger thought it looked like she had a tattoo above her butt, something his father used to refer to as a 'tramp stamp.'

Her hands were now also bare as the gloves had been burnt away. For the most part, they looked like normal human hands. However, her fingernails were thick, dark brown in color, and extremely sharp-edged. They looked almost like claws.

He quickly covered her over in his jacket and carried her to the jeep. After placing her in the passenger seat, he pulled the lever on the side, allowing it to slide backward.

Thankfully the jacket was long enough that it covered all the way down to her knees. He quickly strapped the seatbelt around her. It was damaged and burned from previous dragon attacks, but it would at least keep her from falling out.

Jagger quickly jumped behind the wheel and headed for the gates. A large crowd was waiting for him at the entrance. The trucks had lined up, ready to evacuate, but were sitting idle.

Jagger's eyes narrowed and the hair stood up on the back of his neck. They stepped forward like an army ready to charge as they approached his jeep. He slowed to a stop and looked at them. He'd seen mobs before and knew what a group of panicky people could be capable of.

Without making any sudden moves, Jagger lowered his right hand to his belt. His index finger found the grip of his bolt pistol. He hoped he wouldn't need it, "What is this?"

Jerry stepped forward with his shotgun in hand, "We've never been attacked by anything more than a couple wyvern. You bring that nomad freak into this town and an elder class dragon attacks a few hours later? You can't expect us to believe that's a coincidence."

Jagger put the car in park and stepped out, making sure the sidearms on his belt were visible, "What are you saying, Jerry? You accusing me of something?"

"Just stupidity for bringing her here," Jerry replied.

"I don't think I like your tone, Jerry."

Jerry raised the gun so that it was pointing at Jagger's jeep, "I don't give a fuck whether you like it or not. No way is she not responsible for bringing those dragons down on us!"

"Jerry… Jerry, wait!" a voice called from the crowd.

Mr. Foster appeared with his family close behind him, "Jerry, that woman… –Raiya was her name?"

Jagger nodded as Mr. Foster continued, "Jerry, she saved my family. That dragon was going to kill us, but she distracted it so we could escape! We wouldn't be here if it wasn't for her. She fought the damn thing!"

Jerry turned slightly so his shotgun was facing Jagger, "So maybe she didn't know. Maybe she drew them here. Look at her, she's clearly connected to them! Bet they picked up her scent and came for her."

"You don't know that!"

"Don't I? Elder dragons are a rare sight, especially around here. So, either she called them here or they were looking for her. Either way, she brought them down on us and that makes her a danger to the town!"

"Yeah, that's right," another member of the crowd called out.

Jagger clenched his jaw as more shouts exploded from the crowd. This was quickly turning from a fleeing group into a lynch mob. He placed his right hand on the pistol on his belt. It was an old Springfield 1911 with a nickel finish, but it still packed a .45 caliber punch, "Put the rifle away, Jerry."

Drakin
The Story of Raiya

At first, Jerry didn't move. He kept his eyes trained on the unconscious woman in Jagger's jeep. It wasn't clear what was going through his head, but Jagger didn't take any chances, "Jerry, put the fucking rifle down!"

Jagger wrapped his hand around the grips of the pistol, ready to draw it. This was going to get ugly real fast if Jerry didn't back down. The two glared at them for a moment before a voice shattered the tense atmosphere, "Stop it!"

Jagger turned to see that Raiya was awake, "I swear I didn't bring them here. I've never tried to hurt anyone. I don't want to cause any more trouble... I'll leave."

"Jagger needs to go too!" another member of the town shouted.

At that point, even Jerry looked worried, "Jagger's just a fool who brought the wrong person into town. We don't kick people out for that!"

"We do when they get people killed!"

Scattered anger turned into mass outrage. This was about to get violent. Jagger could feel his blood begin to boil. What could he do now? His choices were to stand and fight, at which point more people would be killed, or leave. He also had to consider Raiya's well-being. If he put up a fight, she'd likely get hurt too.

His eyes fixed on Jerry, "See what you started? Hope you're happy now."

Jerry nodded as he lowered his gun, "This isn't what I wanted... even so, they're not wrong.

Drakin
The Story of Raiya

Get her out of here, Jagger. Don't make things get ugly."

Jagger sighed as he jumped behind the wheel of the jeep, "You'd best report this to Central Command... otherwise, you'll be short a scout."

"Isn't that your job?"

"Go fuck yourself, Jerry."

"So, this is the thanks we get?" Jerry asked. "We take you in, we treat you like our own, and for what? So, you can put us all at risk for some freaky lizard-girl tail?"

That was it. Jagger felt his face go red. He stepped out of the jeep, balled a fist and struck Jerry on the right side of his jaw. The older man staggered back a few steps before recovering and attempted to attack. Several people stepped in to try to defuse the situation.

Mr. Foster stepped out in front, "Hey, hey! Stop it you two!"

Jagger stepped back and slammed his fist into the side of his jeep, "Jerry, you pompous son of a bitch!"

"Get out or I'll throw you out."

"You don't have the authority!" Jagger replied.

"If he doesn't, we will!" someone else in the crowd shouted.

Jagger let go of the pistol and pointed at Jerry with his left index finger, "I'm a nice guy... so I won't say that I hope that you get what you deserve for your behavior... but... If that day comes, I hope you treat the people who come to help better than you treated her."

Drakin

The Story of Raiya

"Hey, what about his guns and jeep! Those are our…"

Jagger pulled his 1911 from its holster and pointed it at the crowd, "Property?"

The crowd fell silent. When it became obvious that no one was about to play the hero, Jagger nodded, "Yeah they were… but most of them would still be in pieces if I hadn't taken the time and cost of repairing them. Everything I have here is coming with me."

At that moment, he drew the second pistol from his belt, "Or does anyone have a problem with that?"

"Keep them," Jerry replied as he raised his own gun. "Keep the bolt gun too. Just get out of here and don't come back."

Jagger nodded and dropped the newer pistol back in its holster. He stepped back and got behind the wheel of his jeep, "Fine."

He put the jeep in drive, but kept his foot on the breaks as he looked up, "One of these days Jerry… just you wait…"

"Last chance!" Jerry replied as he aimed the shotgun.

"All right, all right. We're going."

Mrs. Foster ran over to Raiya as Jagger started to pull the jeep forward, "Thank you… thank you so much."

Raiya looked at the woman with eyes full of surprise and sympathy, "You're… welcome."

"I'm really sorry for how we treated you."

Raiya nodded as the jeep slowly pulled away from them. Jagger kept his hand on his gun as they slowly approached the gate. Any one of the angry faces they passed by could easily turn violent in an instant. He would have to move quickly if one of them tried to attack.

Most stood with their arms crossed while others held flashlights or other weapons. They all stood completely still as the jeep passed by.

The small truck slowly approached the main entrance on the edge of town. The black bars slowly moved out of there way, allowing them into the open darkness that was the outside world.

The moment the jeep cleared the crowd, he hit the gas. The wheels of the jeep screeched as it picked up speed and disappeared into the night.

Chapter 5

Raiya didn't look at Jagger, how could she? The fool had just lost his home for defending her against an angry mob. He had basically just paid a huge price for being kind to her.

It technically wasn't her fault, but that was of little comfort. Raiya could deal with being exiled from a town. That was a regular occurrence for most nomads, doubly so for her. The real sting came from knowing that such unreasonable anger and paranoia had now hurt someone else.

The headlights clicked on as the town faded behind them. A light that Jagger had attached to the roll bar also came on, partially illuminating the open cabin. The light was slightly yellowed, indicating that it may soon need to be replaced. It wasn't strong enough to illuminate the exterior of the jeep. It reached the floor, but only enough so that Raiya could see the outlines of her feet. The light gave the scene a rather sinister look.

Raiya shifted uncomfortably in the seat. The jeep wasn't exactly the safest mode of transportation and its open cabin left them exposed to the elements. Dragons didn't typically attack at night as their eyesight wasn't very good in the dark, but that didn't make her feel any better, "May I ask where we're going?"

"Dunno," Jagger replied.

"You're driving pretty fast. You must have some idea."

"Yeah, away from the city."

"I see… and when we're far enough away?"

Drakin
The Story of Raiya

"Then I was going to ask you."

"Me?"

"Yeah, you've been out here a while. Is there a nearby encampment or something?"

Raiya shrugged, "Like I said, I've been wandering ruins for years. I tried to avoid the cities and large settlements. As you can see... for obvious reasons."

"How do you get by?"

"I hunt for food, salvage supplies, and try to maintain some level of hygiene."

Raiya lowered her eyes as the jeep once again fell silent. An uncharacteristic feeling of remorse came over her, "Look... for what it's worth, I'm sorry this happened. You can let me off up the road and probably go back and talk to them..."

"No, I can't," Jagger replied. "This was a solid break. I'm really fed up from dealing with their bullshit. Besides I'm not just going to dump you off on the side of the road to fend for yourself."

"My life since I was a child. I'm used to it."

"I'll bet."

"So, I take it then you want to tag along with me?"

"If you don't mind."

She did mind. She'd already cost this young soldier a lot. The idea of having to look out for a city boy while trying to fend for herself wasn't a pleasant one.

Jagger let out a deep sigh before she could object, "The dragons destroyed everything I cared about. They turned my friends against me and killed my family. As long as they continue to

Drakin
The Story of Raiya

fight, we'll never be safe. You want to go after one of their elders. Just answer me one question."

"Sure."

"You're serious about killing it?"

"Yes."

"Then you've got yourself a partner."

Raiya's eyes narrowed, "What?"

"I'm going with you."

"Oh really? Do I get a say in that?"

Jagger smirked, "No."

"Jagger, the ruins, and the frontier areas are much different from the town you lived in. It's a rough life and frankly, I don't think you know what you're asking."

"I do. Trust me, I've killed my share of dragons… and other threats to the town."

Raiya's lips twisted as she eyed Jagger. She had seen him fight dragons and knew he could reasonably handle himself, but he was still a city-dweller, "I… no, you know what? Absolutely not. Drop me off and get yourself to the nearest town. I'm not going to be responsible for getting you killed."

"You won't be."

"So you say."

Jagger frowned and glanced over at her, "How long did it take you to get this far north?"

"What difference does that make?" Raiya demanded.

"Must have taken months."

"Yeah so?"

"How are you ever going to catch that dragon lord if you can't keep up with him?"

Drakin
The Story of Raiya

Damn it… Raiya thought to herself. He was right. At the very least, she needed transportation. "What's stopping me from stealing your jeep and leaving you stranded while you sleep?"

Jagger smiled, "The same thing that kept you from killing me in my sleep or stealing it earlier."

Raiya crossed her arms and looked out into the night, "Fine…"

"Partners, then?"

"Until you piss me off."

"All right."

Jagger unhooked the bolt pistol holster from his belt and offered it to Raiya, "Here, you may need this."

She took the gun and slowly inspected it. Jagger turned and glanced at her momentarily, "You know how to handle that?"

"It's been a while, most of the pistols I get to see are broken and usually won't fire. I haven't held a functional one in a long time. Still… I think I did all right with your rifle."

"True, but pistols are a bit different."

"I know. I can handle it."

For the most part, the pistol looked like the Springfield that Jagger had on his other hip. No doubt it had been modeled to look that way. However, the sides bulged out more with an indicator bar built in just above the grips. There was no ejector and no hammer either.

"What do you think?" Jagger asked. "I customized that myself."

Raiya placed it on the console next to her, "I think it's a little barrel-heavy. Hard to aim…"

Drakin
The Story of Raiya

Jagger looked hurt as he continued driving. Raiya saw it and forced a partial grin, "But it should do the trick. I doubt I'll use it much anyway."

"Well it's better to have it and not need it, you know?"

"If you say so. Where are we going anyway… partner?" Raiya asked with a grimace.

Jagger smirked as he glanced down at her bare legs, "Well first we need to find you some clothes. It's too hot for you to keep wearing that jacket… and frankly, you're a little… exposed."

Raiya looked down to see the jacket opening low on her chest, as well as riding up on her legs. She quickly closed it and pulled the ends down as far as they could go, "What, don't like what you see?"

"I didn't say that… it's just…"

"Maybe you should just keep quiet for now. You talk way too much. Keep it up and I may just feed you to the Dragon Lord as bait."

The look on Jagger's face told her that he wasn't certain if she was serious, "Okay fine, I'll keep it to a minimum."

The sound of a low growl, mimicking that of a lion made Jagger stiffen up, "Sorry."

Raiya sat back, "But yeah… I do need some clothes. Any ideas?"

"As a matter of fact, yeah," Jagger replied. "The old Natick Mall is up the street here. It's been pillaged, but if we're going to find anything for you, that'll be the place."

"How long ago was it attacked?"

Drakin
The Story of Raiya

Jagger shrugged, "It was abandoned six or seven years ago. I don't know when it was actually attacked."

"And you think we'll find anything wearable there?"

"Worth a look."

Raiya sighed as she thought about the moldy, bug-ridden cloth they'd likely find. It wasn't ideal, but what other choice was there? "Fine... let's go."

Another ten minutes up the road, Jagger turned the jeep into a building that was surprisingly still standing. It had several large blast holes and appeared to have been the scene of a battle.

"Here?" Raiya asked.

"Yup."

"Is this wise?"

Jagger looked at her oddly, "What do you mean?"

"City boys..." Raiya said softly. "You've got a lot to learn about living outside the cities. Places like this are best avoided. Usually, raider clans or... or worse hide out here. Going in could be suicide."

Jagger frowned, "I've driven by here several times and never seen anyone. Besides, we're going in there armed."

Raiya looked at the building as an ominous feeling came over her, "I don't like this..."

"Either this or you're going to have to get used to walking around with no clothes."

Drakin
The Story of Raiya

"What about those stores?" Raiya asked, pointing to the collapsed strip malls on the opposite side of the road.

"They were completely pillaged long ago. The people of New Framingham conducted trips out this way. They took everything that wasn't already destroyed."

"Then how do you know there's anything left in the mall?"

"I don't, but it's the one place we never went."

"Why?"

Jagger pointed at the roof of the old mall, "Look at the place. It's one thing to raid a small store, but something that huge is a different story."

"All right... I still think this is a bad idea."

For the most part, the building was either a solid brick or concrete gray. Raiya squinted in the dark, trying to make out the writing on the side of the buildings, "I've been curious... what's Crate and Barrel? Was that like a place that had storage supplies?"

Jagger chuckled, "You'd think so. It had some storage stuff, but it was more of a store that sold décor, furnishings, and kitchen supplies. It was pretty good from what I was told."

A second later, they passed by another part of the building that was suspiciously shaped compared to the previous ones. Through the burns, this one appeared to be painted yellow and red, "Jagger... what's a cheesecake?"

Drakin
The Story of Raiya

"It's a type of pie. A dessert that's supposedly very thick and very sweet. I've never had one though."

"And they needed a whole factory to make them?" Raiya asked suspiciously.

Jagger burst out laughing, "Hahahaha, no!"

She frowned and flashed him an irritated look, "What's so funny?"

"You're just kind of cute with questions like that."

"Excuse me… cute?"

"Yeah, what?"

"Cute is what you call a small child or a baby. I'm neither!"

"Maybe not, but your curiosity…"

Raiya made stabbing gestures with her fingers, "Just shut up and answer the damn question."

"All right… no, it's not an actual factory per se. It was a restaurant and a pretty good one from what I was told. Apparently, they were well-known for their cheesecakes, so that's where the name came from."

"All right…"

Jagger pulled the jeep into the bottom floor of the garage and parked it against the interior wall. Raiya smirked, "What, you afraid your precious jeep is going to get rained on?"

"Or get stolen… or seen by a dragon."

"Good point."

Jagger turned the car off and locked it. The bolt gun was in the back waiting for him. He quickly switched out the cartridges and picked it up.

Drakin
The Story of Raiya

Raiya pulled her pistol out of its holster and reached inside the jacket, instinctively looking for her blade, "Fuck!"

"What?"

"My dagger…"

"Did you leave it in the apartment?"

"No… I had it when I confronted the dragon lord," Raiya insisted.

"It must have been destroyed when you got hit with the blast."

"Maybe…"

"I still have no idea how you survived that, but I seriously doubt anything you had on you would have survived."

Raiya buttoned the jacket together and raised her pistol, "Maybe we can find a blade while we're in there?"

"We can look."

They slowly approached the entrance on the far side of the Cheesecake Factory. Bits of paper that were burned on both sides and shards of metal littered the ground in front of the entrance. Jagger kicked in the remains of the glass door that had once been there. The metal frame immediately collapsed and a few shards of glass shattered across the floor.

Raiya stepped in front of him with the pistol at her side and proceeded into the darkness. Her vision was near perfect and despite being in complete darkness, she could usually find her way. This was different than what she was used to, however. She wasn't outside or in an area where even a little light shined through.

Drakin
The Story of Raiya

"There's a flashlight on that pistol," Jagger said, pointing to the red button under the barrel.

He then activated the large one on his rifle and shined it through the door. The hallway lit up as the two lights came on. A smashed escalator appeared at the end of the hallway. It had clearly been knocked down during a dragon attack.

Raiya quickly pressed the red button. A beam of white light shot through the darkness from the barrel of her gun. It wasn't much, but at least she could see where she was going.

She quickly walked to the end of the hallway. It opened up into a massive atrium with an upper and lower floor. Abandoned stores lined the walls on either side.

Raiya looked at the hallway opposite her. There was also the pathway to the right which led down the atrium. "Where do we go?"

Jagger pointed with his rifle, "Take a left. There should be more stores down that way."

"All right…"

Raiya quickly turned the corner and looked down yet another dark hallway. She flashed the light over some smashed wooden stalls and a collapsed crosswalk from the upper level. "This place looks like it must have been something in its prime."

"Yeah, kind of wish I'd seen it. Who knows, maybe they'll rebuild it after the war."

"You still think there's a chance you'll win?"

"You don't?"

Raiya shrugged, "Like I said, I just want that dragon lord's head. Whatever happens after that is not my concern."

She looked at the first outlet on the right. The doors were left standing open and broken mannequins were strewn about on the floor. Various pieces of clothing covered the inside. Most were badly stained, ripped, and completely unwearable. None of it was still hanging up at all.

Raiya picked up the first shirt she saw. It was full of massive holes. She held it up in front of her face and watched as the tears got bigger. The weight of the wet areas was too much for the worn-out fabric to hold. It smelled of mold and had several bugs and black spots on it, "Um... I think this was a clothing store, but I don't think..."

The sound of debris falling nearby made her flinch. She turned around and pointed her bolt pistol in that direction. Her yellow eyes scanned the darkness, "Did you hear that?"

"What?"

"Something moved..."

"Yeah so? It was likely a bird or a raccoon or something."

Raiya took another step forward into the darkness. There was another sound off to the right. She turned in time to see a foot disappear into the darkness, "No... That's no animal... someone's here with us."

She quickly looked back at Jagger, "These people are either nomads or canbans. Get behind me."

Drakin

The Story of Raiya

Jagger stepped behind his friend and aimed his rifle into the darkness, "I'm familiar with nomads, but what are canbans?"

Raiya kept her eyes forward and gently shifted them to either side. If she was frightened, she wasn't showing it, "I'm not surprised you haven't heard of them… Very few people that encounter them get away. They're nasty creatures."

"Creatures?"

Raiya nodded, "Creatures… trust me. Nomads simply wander the lands attempting to build a home for themselves. Canbans… take what they want and destroy the rest. It doesn't matter what it is; food, water, tech… if you have it, they'll kill you and take it. What's worse… some of them have become so desperate that they've gone feral and have even resorted to cannibalism. Hence the name."

"I can't believe anyone would have lost that much of their humanity."

"Believe it," Raiya replied. "I've seen it myself. It's not pretty."

Another scampering sound echoed through the room. This time, both of them turned and looked back the way they came.

"You heard it too?" Raiya asked.

"Yeah… I think it might be time for us to go…"

"No… we can't…" Raiya said in a low voice.

"Why not?"

"Because we've been seen… we're being stalked."

Drakin

The Story of Raiya

"What?"

Raiya slowly turned her gun in the direction where she was certain that an ambush was waiting for them, "Behind the rubble… over there."

Jagger shivered as though the temperature had just dropped several degrees, "Great…"

Raiya held her gaze on the rubble, "Don't worry… it'll be okay."

There was another sound off to the left. Raiya's ears perked up as her head turned, "Go… back to the entrance as fast as you can."

"And leave you here?"

"I'll be right behind you."

"All right."

"Now, move!"

Jagger took off running. He looked back a few times as they neared the opening. Raiya was right on his heels, brandishing her gun behind her. They were a mere hundred feet away from the door. If they could at least get to the jeep, they would be safe.

Raiya could feel the breeze on her face. *Come on… come on…*

All hope was dashed when six people appeared in front of them. They were all wearing ragged clothing, some of them had attached metal plates to their outfits. They all had some kind of scarring or tattoos. There was a sinister air about these people.

Raiya eyed them carefully. *Could they be canbans? I've never heard of any this far north… still…*

Drakin
The Story of Raiya

Jagger raised the rifle and rested his finger on the trigger. The sudden stop caused Raiya to collide with him, forcing his body forward and knocking him off balance. He dropped the rifle as he struggled to stay standing.

Raiya's feet shuffled to stay level as Jagger quickly reached for the gun, but a long knife appeared in his path. Raiya looked up to see one of the odd-looking people glaring at them. *Oh shit…*

No matter which way they turned, there was no way out. Raiya and Jagger were surrounded. The man with the knife stepped forward and brandished his blade close to Jagger's throat, "You have trespassed into our land."

Raiya pointed her gun at the man, "Back off!"

The two stared at each other for a few moments. Neither appeared to be deterred by the other's threats. It wasn't until Jagger raised his hand that either of them moved, "Raiya, lower the pistol… please."

Raiya looked at him for confirmation. He nodded, "It'll be all right."

Raiya hesitantly lowered the gun to her side but did not drop it. She was not about to surrender her only defense, especially not with a knife at her friend's throat.

"What do you want?" the man asked.

"We didn't know this area had been claimed," Jagger replied. "Sorry for the mix-up. Let us pass and we'll leave you in peace."

"Not gonna happen…" Raiya whispered.

Drakin
The Story of Raiya

"I'm afraid I can't allow that," the man replied. "If we simply let you leave, who's to say you won't come back with others? Who's to say you won't lure dragons here?"

"Told you…"

Jagger sighed, "All right, look, we're just trying to find her some clothes. We got attacked by a dragon and thrown out of our city. We've got nothing and nowhere to go. What do you want from us?"

The man looked at one of his comrades and then back at Jagger, "A dragon attack? You mean the one in Framingham?"

"Yes," Jagger replied.

"We saw him fly overhead. That was a dragon lord. How did you survive?"

Jagger shined the light on Raiya. The people surrounding her took a step back in shock. The darkness had veiled most of her features, but now they could be seen clearly. She glared at Jagger angrily as he spoke, "She has some kind of ability to resist dragon fire. We don't know how, but when the dragon saw that she was immune, he withdrew."

One of the other men walked up to the leader and whispered in his ear. The leader turned to the side and nodded, "This confirms what we witnessed from outside the city. We were wondering why the dragon withdrew."

"Well, now you know."

He watched them for a few moments, clearly trying to decide what he wanted to do with them,

"Very well. You will come with us. Our elder will decide your fate."

"Wonderful…" Jagger replied.

Chapter 6

Jagger and Raiya were escorted out of the mall to a small encampment up the road. A large brick building that looked like it had once housed offices stood in ruin. Several small tents and shanties stood around it with fires that were no bigger than embers. The ceiling had collapsed and there were no windows. It wasn't very impressive, but it was perfectly defensible.

Jagger surveyed his surroundings looking for any possible means of escape. He would have to be quick and figure out how to signal Raiya to be ready, which was likely impossible.

Raiya's eyes also appeared to be scanning her surroundings. The look on her face told him that she wasn't having any luck either. Anything flammable had long since been burned out, thus dragon fire would have little effect on the walls. The roof was collapsed in such a way that there was enough of it left to provide protection against an aerial attack. The windows were numerous, but most were narrow slits in the walls. Not wide enough to squeeze through.

The only entrance he'd seen was heavily guarded. It looked like he was stuck for the time being. *Well great...*

"This place is a fortress," Jagger whispered.

Raiya nodded as she pointed to the burn marks on the brick "By the looks of it, the building has a history of dragon attacks."

Drakin
The Story of Raiya

"We have endured here since the fall," the leader replied as they approached a makeshift gate. "Wait here."

Jagger stood with his arms crossed as the leader of the group disappeared inside. He let out an impatient sigh, "How long before they kill us?"

"No idea."

"You haven't dealt with these guys before?"

"Nope."

At that moment, he noticed another two of their captors roll the jeep up next to the building. *Oh fuck...*

One of them, a younger man got out and looked at it from the front, "Nice ride!"

"I'll be getting that back when we leave, just so you know."

He took a threatening step towards Jagger, "If you leave."

At first, it looked like he was going to try something. The man's fists were balled at his side, ready to go. A sudden growl made him flinch. He turned to see Raiya glaring at him.

"Not worth it," the man said as he turned away.

The leader came back out a few moments later and beckoned to Raiya specifically. "The elder would like to see you."

Jagger stepped up next to her, silently telling him that she was not going in alone. The leader frowned, "He only asked for her, not you."

"He comes, or I don't cooperate," Raiya replied.

Drakin

The Story of Raiya

"You know I could have you both executed right now, right? It's not a smart move to piss us off."

"Don't care."

This was an odd demand for Raiya. Up until that point, she'd done nothing but hurl insults and threats at Jagger. Why now was she refusing to be parted from him? Was it possible that she was finally looking at him as a partner and not some random idiot?

Unlikely. Jagger thought to himself. *It's probably just strength in numbers.*

The leader looked at Raiya for a moment before turning and giving Jagger the same studious glare, "All right... fine, just know that you're being watched. Make any move against our elder and it will be your last."

He then turned to the side, beckoning them forward, "Please."

The inside was not as Jagger had expected. He thought the place would be a crumbling mess like the mall. Much to his surprise, the inside had been renovated enough to actually pass as suitable living quarters. The collapse in the ceiling had cut all the way to the bottom floor. Most of the damaged areas had been removed and jagged edges had been sawed down. Catwalks and makeshift staircases had been added to allow passage between each section.

Could these people actually be the savages Raiya was talking about? They seemed way to organized and well-equipped. This didn't seem like a savage group at all. They were definitely paranoid, and who could blame them? However, Jagger was more comfortable now that he wasn't dealing with canbans.

They stepped through the first room which looked like it had been some sort of a reception area at one point. There was a bright orange hue coming from the next doorway. It seemed to flicker off the walls and was accompanied by a loud crackling sound.

A fire pit? Jagger thought to himself as he was pushed into the next room.

The main chamber took up most of the interior. From the ground floor, Jagger could see all the way up to the ceiling. Oddly, there were no chairs in this room. Only small pads surrounded a massive fire pit. The flame was easily seven feet in the air.

Under normal conditions, most people would consider a flame that large to be dangerous. However, these nomads appeared to have dug the pit deep and wide enough that they were able to control it.

An old man sat on one of the pads on the far side of the flame. He remained motionless, like a statue. His eyes glowed as though they were on fire themselves. If he weren't sitting in front of a flame, Jagger would have thought his eyes were just like Raiya's.

Now that they actually had some light, Jagger could see his captor more clearly. The man pushing them forward's right cheekbone was horribly scarred. His brown hair was down to his neck and hung loosely around his face. His face

Drakin
The Story of Raiya

displayed a calm expression and his voice was tempered as he spoke, "A little further, keep moving."

"Are you a canban?" Jagger asked.

The man chuckled as he pushed Jagger forward, "If I was, you probably wouldn't be alive right now."

"Good to know."

Jagger and Raiya were led over to where the old man was seated. His clothes were almost completely made of animal skin. His face looked worn and tired with deep wrinkles. Unlike the other man, he had no burns, but a terrible scar stretched over his left eye.

He sat next to an old-style radio with a cassette player on it. Most radios had been converted for use with the universal frequencies of the coalitions, but not this one. Oddly enough, this one was playing music.

Jagger had heard similar music off an old jukebox at Jerry's. The style was known as Rock and Roll. It was incredibly up-tempo and the man singing almost sounded like he was shouting.

As Raiya approached, the man suddenly came to life with a warm smile. His hands slowly parted as he beckoned them to sit down with him.

Raiya took a few steps closer and slowly dropped down to her knees. Jagger stood behind her, refusing to take a seat. The old man smiled, "Peace, child. You are in no danger here."

Jagger looked back at the leader he'd been speaking to, "Is that why we were threatened with knives and brought here against our will?"

Drakin
The Story of Raiya

The man frowned, "I apologize for that treatment. However, you did violate our territory. I'm curious as to what exactly you were looking for?"

"Clothing," Raiya replied. "My robes were burned away when…"

"When we were attacked by a dragon," Jagger said, finishing her sentence.

"You survived a dragon attack?" the man asked inquisitively. "I take it you're from New Framingham?"

"Yes."

The man sighed and turned to the leader, "Eric, take her to our seamstress. See if she can find this unusual young lady something suitable."

Eric stepped forward, "It will be done."

He moved closer, but Jagger stood in his way. Jagger said nothing, but he made it very clear that he wasn't about to let Raiya be taken out of his sight. He stood like a statue, refusing to yield.

The elder sighed, "We're not going to accomplish anything as long as we don't trust one another. Young man, I give you my word that she will not be harmed and will return to us as soon as she's been given the dignity of some proper attire."

Raiya stood up and placed her hand on Jagger's shoulder, "It's okay… I'll go."

"You sure?"

"I can take care of myself, don't worry."

"All right."

Drakin
The Story of Raiya

Jagger nodded as he stood aside, giving her a clear path to Eric. She stepped past Jagger and nodded, "Shall we?"

Jagger kept his eyes on Raiya as she left the room. Despite the friendly demeanor of the elder, he didn't trust them. There was no way to be certain that she was safe.

"She will be fine. There is no need to worry," the old man said.

Jagger turned back to the old man sitting by the fire. The man extended his arm in a gesture of welcome, "Please, join me. Permit an old man the luxury of a few questions while you wait."

Jagger hesitantly sat down and leaned against a piece of the broken wall behind him. The elder was reminiscent of a tribal shaman. He smiled and nodded as Jagger relaxed, "Thank you."

The man looked away with a content smile and swayed to the music, "I love rock music, don't you?"

"I never really thought about it," Jagger replied.

"No?" A surprised look appeared on the old man's face. "Didn't they have any music in New Framingham?"

"Well they did, but…"

"I can't imagine life without it," the elder interrupted. "I was just a little kid when this song came out… John Parr… Restless Heart… a true classic."

"Never heard of it."

"No? I suppose you've never heard of *The Running Man* either?"

Drakin
The Story of Raiya

"Nope."

The elder sighed, "Kids these days... it was one of the best action movies to come out of the 80s. You don't know what you've been missing."

This was going nowhere fast. They'd been captured, separated, and were now at this crazy old man's mercy. More than anything, he wanted a way out of this, but all the guy wanted to talk about was ancient movies and music. Granted it was better than an execution, but Jagger had more important things on his mind, "Who are you?"

"I go by many names," the elder replied whimsically as though he were mocking Jagger. "My friends call me Mason. Everyone else just refers to me as 'elder', 'gramps', 'fossil', 'old geezer who blabbers too much', things like that. How about you?"

Jagger feigned amusement as the flames danced on his face, "Just one name I'm afraid, Jagger."

"No family name?"

"Bishop."

"Ah, after the clergy of old... Well, Jagger Bishop," Mason replied, "what about your friend there? She's certainly an unusual creature."

"Her name's Raiya."

Mason nodded, "Equally unusual..."

"Yeah, I have to admit I was surprised at how... casual you've all been about her appearance."

Mason smiled, "My boy, we've seen many oddities in the past few years. Between dragons, people deformed by years of conflict, and horrible abominations resulting from radiation poisoning, a girl with scales is not about to shock us. She's more of a curiosity than anything else."

"Makes sense, I guess…" Jagger replied.

"Anyway, what brings you out here?"

"We were kicked out of our home up the street in New Framingham."

"Why?"

Jagger looked over to where Raiya had disappeared, "Because of the dragon attack. The people there turned into a paranoid mob. They thought that she brought the dragons down on us. I was blamed for bringing her into town earlier that day."

"Why did you?"

Jagger shrugged, "I was out on patrol earlier in the day when I was attacked by a pair of wyverns. She appeared out of nowhere and saved me from being eaten."

"So, you two had just met."

"Yeah."

"Yet you brought her back to your people?"

What was he getting at? Was this guy trying to blame him for what had happened? "I owed her one."

"Is that the only reason."

Jagger let out a deep sigh, "She's a young woman… heck, she looks like she's only about eighteen. She said she was hungry… and… well look at her, she's wicked thin."

"You took pity on her."

"Yeah… I mean no... Look, she's just a kid."

"How old are you?"

Drakin

The Story of Raiya

"… Twenty-three."

Mason laughed, "My boy, you are way too young to be calling an eighteen-year-old a kid. She's an adult, just as you are. Young adults maybe, but adults all the same. Still, I can appreciate your attitude and your actions."

The air around them seemed less tense now. Jagger was pretty certain he wasn't going to be killed, but he wasn't sure what lay ahead of him.

Mason sat back and closed his eyes as he continued, "So now that you're on your own, what is your plan? Are you looking for a new place to live?"

"Are you offering?" Jagger asked.

"Would you accept if we did?"

Jagger smiled appreciatively as he shook his head, "Thanks, but no. Raiya's hunting a dragon. It seems like she has been for most of her life. I doubt anyone could convince her to give it up. So, I promised that I'd help her."

"Just like that?"

"Well yeah," Jagger replied. "I can't go home, what else am I going to do?"

Now it was Mason's turn to shrug, "So you're going to just go around killing dragons?"

"No. We're looking for one in particular… a dragon lord."

"Why?"

"It killed her parents."

"I see…" Mason said as his welcoming smile turned to a sorrowful frown. "No one has ever killed a dragon lord, much less survived the

Drakin
The Story of Raiya

encounter. What makes you think that you two stand a chance?"

"It's the reason she doesn't have any clothes," Jagger replied. "The dragon that attacked New Framingham was a dragon lord. I don't know what it was doing there, but she fearlessly confronted it and…"

Jagger hesitated. Even he could not explain what he saw when the dragon attacked. She was alive and unharmed when she shouldn't have been. How could he explain it? Would this man even believe him?

"What is it, what happened?" Mason asked.

"I don't really know… The dragon attacked her with its fire breath. She should have been disintegrated or turned into a lump of coal but… she wasn't. Her clothes and gear were burned away, but she was fine. Even the dragon was surprised. So much so that it flew off."

"And they kicked you out for that?"

"Yeah."

A stern look appeared on Mason's face, "They had a viable defense against a dragon lord and they decided to banish it. Fools."

"Tell me about it."

"So, what do you make of her?"

Jagger again looked in her direction, "I don't know. I mean she doesn't even know… I have a theory… but it's absolutely insane!"

"Tell me."

Jagger couldn't believe the words were leaving his lips, even as he spoke them, "If I had to guess… she's infected with Dragon's Bane and this is the result?"

"Yet she seems perfectly healthy."

"Well… maybe a rare mutation?"

"Maybe…"

A faint sound behind them made Jagger turn. Raiya quietly stepped out from behind the curtain. She was dressed in a pair of jean shorts and a brown top that looked like it had been fashioned by animal skin with a small hood. Hand-carved wooden earrings that clipped to her lobes were draped on her ears and a fancy dagger hung from the nylon belt around her waist.

Jagger stood up as she approached. A faint smile appeared on her face, "Well…?"

"Well what" Jagger asked.

"Do I look… okay?"

Jagger smiled, "You look very okay."

"Wonderful…"

"How do you feel?"

"They're comfortable, but I feel a little… exposed…"

"Exposed?"

"I'm used to my old robes that concealed… more."

"I think you'll be fine," Jagger replied.

"All right."

She stepped closer to the flame and looked at Mason, "Thanks."

"No problem," Mason replied. "Now that we know your size, I'll have a few sets of what we can spare put in the back of your jeep. As well as food and supplies."

Drakin
The Story of Raiya

A surprised look appeared on Jagger's face, "Thanks, that's… really generous."

"You're hunting a dragon lord. No one has ever managed to kill one. Most people just avoid them as much as possible. However, I have a good feeling about you two. If you can kill one… it might be enough to turn the tides of this fight."

"What are you talking about?" Raiya asked.

Mason's eyes returned to the flame. "The dragon lords are aptly named. They are the leaders of the dragon horde and the only ones who have been impervious to human attack. Most people don't think that they can be killed anymore. Should one of them fall, it will show humanity that there is still hope, and it should be enough to shake dragon morale. Who knows, it may even unite the factions."

Jagger frowned, "That's a pretty high hope. No one's really tried to work with the coalitions in years."

"Let an old man dream."

Raiya frowned, "I'm sorry… I'm not doing this to start a revolution and I'm not doing it to save humanity. This dragon butchered my family. I want its head."

"Yes, I suspected as much," Mason replied dryly. "However, we still stand to benefit from such a victory. So, we have a common interest here."

Mason stood up and stepped back from the flames, "I don't think anything more need be said tonight. You two look tired. Why don't you rest here? You can start out again tomorrow morning."

Drakin
The Story of Raiya

"Might not be a bad idea," Jagger replied, looking at Raiya.

Raiya shrugged, "Fine with me."

Mason clapped his hands together. The sound echoed through the room and summoned Eric to the scene, "What is it?"

"Show them to one of our empty rooms."

Eric looked surprised, "What?"

"They'll be leaving in the morning," Mason replied. "For now though, they're spending the night."

"Is that wise?"

"It'll be okay."

"As you wish."

Eric led them to a nearby room, off the main area. It was fairly dilapidated and the only pieces of furniture were a pair of twin-size beds.

"You can spend the night here," Eric said.

Jagger looked around and nodded, "Thanks, this will be fine."

"Better be… just don't cause any trouble, all right?"

"Right," Jagger replied as Eric slid the ragged curtain hanging over the door closed.

Jagger turned and looked at Raiya, "Friendly guy…"

Raiya watched the door for a moment, "Suspicious guy… he's smart."

Jagger yawned and stretched his arms, "All right… well, we've still got a few hours before sunrise. Let's get some sleep."

"I'm not tired. You go ahead. One of us should stand watch anyway," Raiya replied.

Drakin
The Story of Raiya

"You sure?"

"Yeah."

Jagger pulled his legs up on the second bed and laid back. He breathed in relief as the mattress cushioned his spine. His eyes fluttered and slowly closed as he passed out of consciousness. *Didn't think it would be this comfortable.*

Raiya kicked off the new shoes she'd been given and sat back on the bed. "Jagger?"

"Yeah?" Jagger replied, not opening his eyes.

"Are you serious about coming with me?"

"Yeah."

"Why?"

"Helping you helps humanity… and honestly, despite your cold exterior… you're nicer than anyone I've met recently."

Raiya scoffed and concealed a partial grin on the left side of her face, "I barely smile or say anything."

"True, but you put your own life on the line to save those people."

"Maybe… I guess I just saw something in those kids… I didn't want them to grow up like I did."

"So that's why I'm sticking around. Is that a good enough reason?"

"I guess… I still think you're a fool though."

Jagger nodded, "I'll take that as a compliment."

"You would."

"All right well, let's just try to get some rest. Something tells me we've got a long road ahead and we'll probably want to start out early."

Drakin

The Story of Raiya

"I agree."

Drakin
The Story of Raiya

Chapter 7

Raiya's eyes opened the next morning to the sound of trickling water. She stood up and suspiciously looked over to a small alcove in the wall. *It's not raining out… what is that noise?* "Jagger?"

No response.

"Jagger, is that you?"

A moment later, Jagger appeared in the doorway, wrapped in a towel. "Raiya, they have running water here. Honest to God running water! The shower was luxurious. You should try it out!"

"Trying to tell me something?" Raiya asked in an accusing tone as she crossed her arms.

Jagger shrugged, "Just that there's an awesome shower in the next room."

Raiya rolled her eyes, "Fine, get out of my way."

She jumped out of bed and went into the alcove. There was no curtain, but the shower was recessed into the wall enough that the view from the door would be obscured. She quickly disrobed, hung her new clothes on a white hook that protruded from the orange wall on the left and turned the nob to make the water flow.

Jagger quickly dried off as he listened to the water turn on and then looked at his clothes. The jeans were stained, not badly, but would still need to be cleaned soon. His shirt was in better shape. It was black, so any stains wouldn't show as easily. He put his pants on and then threw the shirt over his head as the water turned off.

As the shirt dropped over his head, he got a clear view of Raiya stepping out of the shower. Her clothes were under her left arm while she used a towel that was left in the stall to dry her hair. The green scales flowing down the sides of her neck continued all the way down to her ankles. They converged right at her waist and completely covered everything below it.

His eyes widened and he quickly turned away, "Whoa!"

Raiya stopped in her tracks, "What?"

"You're naked."

"Yeah, so? Isn't that how you wash?"

Jagger stuttered as he spoke, "Well yeah, but…"

"What, you don't like girls?"

Jagger turned back around and glared at her, "No, it's just… ah, never mind!"

Raiya sighed and wrapped herself in the towel, "First of all, you've already seen me. Secondly, if we're going to be partners, you're going to need to get used to this. We're not always going to have the opportunity to clean and when we do, there may not be places to run and hide when we get undressed."

"Got it."

"So, is that going to be a problem?"

"No."

"Good."

Raiya dropped the towel and got dressed as Jagger looked out into the main complex. The fire had long since died down and was little more than embers. Mason was no longer there, nor was Eric. There were a few people walking around, but none of them paid him any mind as they went about their work.

Raiya stepped out next to him as she finished adjusting her shirt, "Spying on our hosts now? Naughty…"

"Hosts that brought us here against our will… better safe than sorry."

"Good morning," came a familiar voice from around the corner.

Raiya turned to see Eric staring at them, "Are you ready to go?"

Jagger nodded, "Sure."

"All right then, please follow me."

Eric led Jagger and Raiya outside. Their jeep had been loaded down with a few changes of clothes, some tools, and a bag of food that was on the back passenger seat. It looked like they would have enough provisions for a long trip.

Mason was standing next to the old truck, "It's been a long time since I've seen one of these…"

He touched the faded blue stripes over the orange circle and nodded, "1989 Islander Edition Jeep Wrangler… with a custom winch on the front. You should have seen these in their prime."

He smiled as he turned to Jagger, "So… where are you off to?"

Jagger looked at Raiya for an answer. She shrugged and turned to Mason, "Unfortunately I don't really know. I tracked the dragon to Massachusetts and then the path went cold. It's like he disappeared. I wandered around for weeks before I ran into Jagger. I figured we'd head southwest."

"Why south?" Mason asked.

"The dragon that attacked New Framingham went that way."

"Hm... A sound plan indeed... however I would advise a different path."

"Oh?"

Mason handed them a small paper. On it was a map with written directions, "I would go to Fort Charleston, if I were you."

Jagger slouched against the jeep, "Charleston... are you out of your mind?"

Raiya looked at Jagger inquisitively as he continued, "The last bastion of the United States Military force... are you kidding me? What in God's name would we gain from going there?"

"Knowledge," Mason replied.

"Wait, I'm confused..." Raiya interrupted. "What is Charleston?"

Jagger turned to her, "Fort Charleston is not part of the Western Coalition. After the fall of Washington and the Norfolk Navy yard, the United States withdrew its forces to Charleston. The Eastern U.S. forces vowed to hold the city no matter what. They fortified it, kept their navy nearby, and openly defied the President's order to retreat."

"And they're still there?" Raiya asked in shock.

"Yeah... After the president and joint chiefs of staff were killed, they became emboldened.

Drakin
The Story of Raiya

The fools dug their heels in and referred to themselves as the Last Bastion of the United States. They still fly the flag, still have their remaining citizens abide by U.S. law, and no matter how badly they get beaten by dragon attacks, they stubbornly refuse to retreat."

"So, they're zealous fools with a martyr complex… great…"

"Some might call them patriots," Mason said in a scolding tone. "They've kept much of the dragons preoccupied in the west."

"At the cost of how many lives?" Jagger shot back. "I respect their ideals… but they've been attacked so many times that their city has been repeatedly reduced to rubble and their people are destitute. There is no logical reason for them not to join the Coalitions. Instead, they'd rather just waste resources."

Mason huffed as he spoke, "Regardless of your feelings, they are the ones who cured Dragon's Bane and then shared their findings with the coalitions. They've also developed most of the new defenses we now use."

Jagger lowered his eyes, "That's true… I guess."

"So why do we want to go there exactly?" Raiya asked.

Mason smiled as he looked at her, "You openly defied a dragon lord and survived the encounter. Aren't you curious as to why?"

"No."

"You're lying," Mason said in an almost amused tone.

Drakin
The Story of Raiya

"Think so…?"

"I do. If you want to defeat that dragon… what flows through your veins might hold the answer. If you knew what abilities you truly possessed, but had not yet tapped into, it's possible you may gain a significant advantage. It's worth investigating."

"Not interested."

Jagger bit his lower lip and let his teeth scrape against the skin before he spoke up, "Raiya… I think he's right."

"Do you?" she asked in an accusing whisper.

"We need every advantage we can get. Going up against that beast as we are would be stupid. Figuring out your abilities and why you have a… reptilian complexion might help."

Her yellow eyes flared as she gazed into his. He felt a chill run down his spine as he smiled nervously, "Maybe?"

Mason's eyes darted between them as he spoke, "The doctor that cured the Dragon's Bane lives there. He's a skilled scientist specializing in microbiology and genetics."

"Wait… are you talking about Dr. Ian Castillo?" Jagger asked.

"Yes."

"I'd heard he was a madman with some… questionable ideas about genetics and purity."

"Ideas?" Raiya asked.

"Yeah…" Jagger replied hesitantly. "He was initially investigated by a medical ethics committee before the dragon attacks. His experiments were… unorthodox to say the least.

Drakin
The Story of Raiya

He believed that he could… breed the perfect human being. His hope was to essentially breed a human that would be impervious to illness. At least that's what people were told…"

"But it wasn't the truth?"

"Not entirely. His research also had military applications. He was quickly found to be in violation of the Geneva Conventions and his research was shut down."

Mason nodded, "I know he's… not the most ethical person out there, but he's probably your best chance."

Jagger looked back into Raiya's eyes, "Maybe?"

She held her gaze for a few moments before shaking her head, "Whatever, let's just go then."

Jagger turned and beckoned her into the jeep, "All right, let's go. –Thanks for the supplies and shelter. It made all the difference, Mason."

"No problem," Mason replied.

At that moment, Eric came to life, "Father…"

Mason looked at him for a moment, before turning back to Jagger. His eyes seemed desperate to hide a feeling of agony as he spoke, "I have one last favor to ask…"

Jagger looked at him oddly, "Okay?"

"Would you take my son with you?"

"What?"

Eric stepped forward, "I've been hunting wyverns since I was able to walk. I know how to fight and take care of myself."

Mason sighed, "He's young and impetuous, but you may find him useful. He wants to get out and see the world."

"No..." Raiya replied.

Jagger nodded, "Yeah, I'm afraid I have to agree. It's going to be a long trip. Chances are we're probably not going to come back from this in one piece."

"I figured you'd say that," Mason replied in a sly tone. "Since he really wants to do this... I'm prepared to offer you something in exchange for taking him."

"I can't wait to hear this..." Raiya said in her normal whisper.

Mason picked up a small pack that was sitting in front of the jeep. It was large and almost a perfect square. He opened it and showed it to Jagger.

"Z cell Power cartridges?" Jagger asked as his eyes lit up.

"I noticed your car's power cell was running low," Mason replied. "We replaced it with a fresh one and here are three more for you... provided you take him along."

Jagger eyed them suspiciously, "Why would you give us something this valuable?"

"We have no use for them. Our weapons are as conventional as they come. We extracted these from a convoy that came under attack some time ago. Figured we'd use them to barter at some point."

Raiya and Jagger exchanged glances for a few moments. Both were waiting for the other to say something. When it didn't happen, Raiya closed her eyes and turned away. The look on her face was one of defeat.

Jagger took that as permission for him to make the decision. He took the pack and turned to Eric, "Say goodbye and mount up."

"Already done," Eric said as he jumped into the passenger seat of the jeep. "Let's get going."

Jagger got behind the wheel and looked over at Raiya. She stood next to the passenger's side and glared at Eric emotionlessly, "You're in my seat…"

Eric's eyes went wide and he immediately jumped into the backseat like a scolded little boy, "Sorry!"

Raiya didn't respond and simply moved to reclaim her seat. The moment she was comfortable, she leaned over to Jagger, "If we're going to pick up a new passenger every time we stop somewhere, then you'll need a bigger car."

"I know…" Jagger replied.

Eric leaned forward from the back, "So we're heading south?"

"Sit back and be quiet…" Raiya replied.

Jagger smirked as the car pulled away, "This should be fun."

Mason could be seen waving as he shrank in the rear-view mirror. Raiya unfolded the map and carefully looked over the directions, "Okay… if I'm reading this right… we should head due south… Does this road… I-95 South still exist?"

"Some of it…" Jagger replied. "It's been years since I tried to take it. There are long stretches that were blasted by dragon fire, tank wheels, and weapons. Still, there should be enough for us to figure out where we're going."

Raiya tapped on several points on the map. It looked like she was counting something. Her eyes narrowed as she moved the map closer to her face, "Jagger… that's almost a thousand miles away. Can we even make it that far?"

"What do you mean?"

"I mean won't we run out of gas?"

A faint chuckle came from the back seat, "Gas? What decade are you living in?"

"Come again?" Raiya said as she raised her claws.

Eric sat back defensively, "What I mean is… cars don't use fossil fuels anymore. After dragons began attacking our sources of fuel, we had to find alternatives."

"And those are?"

Jagger pointed to his bolt gun, "They're essentially larger versions of the cartridges used to power our bolt guns. Most cars have had their engines converted to burn on hydrogen. The old radiators were pulled out and replaced with a special device that collects moisture from the air and converts it into fuel."

"Let me guess… the cartridge powers that device?" Raiya asked.

Jagger nodded, "Yeah that's right, and they last for roughly ten thousand miles."

"Nice I guess."

Drakin
The Story of Raiya

"Yeah, they power almost everything these days. That's why we couldn't refuse Mason's offer."

"I figured…"

Jagger turned his attention to their new passenger as Raiya fell, "So Eric, what's your story?"

Eric looked up with a confused expression, "My story?"

"Yeah. You're tagging along with us, so we might as well get to know each other."

"Fair enough," Eric replied. "Where to begin… well, I was born in Montreal before it got attacked. My mother died a few years ago. My father pretty much took charge and moved us all as far away as possible. We thought we'd be safe with the Western Coalition, but even they took a beating."

"So, what have you been doing since?"

Eric shrugged, "A little of this… a little of that… Mostly just trying to stay alive. Nothing too bad, you know?"

Okay… he's hiding something. Jagger said to himself.

WREEEEEEE!

Eric's eyes went wide, "Wyvern!"

"I don't think so," Jagger replied.

Raiya's eyes scanned the sky. She remained completely emotionless as she searched for the dragon, "It sounds… bigger…"

The jeep moved past a grove of burnt trees into an open field. A large black beast appeared

Drakin
The Story of Raiya

from behind the trees and closed on them.
Jagger's eyes widened, "That's a beta class!"

Eric looked at him oddly, "Beta?"

Raiya nodded, "It's a younger adult dragon.
This could be bad..."

No sooner had she spoken when two wyverns
appeared out of the trees and flew in behind it.
Eric turned around and watched the dragon as it
quickly gained on them. His neck slowly began
bobbing in sync with the wings as the dragon got
closer, "Slow down."

"What?" Jagger called back.

"I said slow down, let it get closer!"

"You're insane!"

Eric leaned back and placed his hand on
Jagger's shoulder, "Trust me!"

"You better know what the hell you're doing!"
Jagger yelled as he took his foot off the gas.

Raiya eyed the needle on the odometer as it
quickly dropped, "You guys are crazy..."

The jeep began to slow to a crawl, allowing
the dragon to get in close. Eric resumed moving in
sync with the dragon and waited, "Just a little
more... a little more..."

He waited until the dragon was so close that
they could feel its hot breath. It was almost
nipping at the bumper when Eric smiled,
"Gotcha!"

Eric jumped from the back of the jeep and
landed on the dragon's neck. Using impressive
agility, he quickly wrapped his arms around the
beast and scurried around so that he was facing
forward. The dragon broke away from the jeep

Drakin
The Story of Raiya

and attempted to buck Eric loose. The two wyverns flew in close, attempting to aid their leader.

Jagger jammed on the breaks and grabbed the bolt gun, "We've got to help him!"

Raiya grabbed the dagger from her belt and jumped out of the passenger's side. She had barely waited for the jeep to stop before she began running back towards the dragons.

Jagger watched as Eric fought through the violent jolts as the dragon began an uncontrollable descent. Before it could land, he reached behind his back and grabbed a pair of daggers from his belt. Using all his strength, he plunged the foot-long blades into the dragon's eyes.

The mighty lizard let out an agonized scream as it hit the ground. There was a loud thud that was followed by a cloud of dirt and ash. Half blinded, Eric stepped off the dragon's neck and retrieved his blades.

As the dust settled, he swung the blades around and stabbed them into the dragon's skull, "Die, you fuck!"

Eric once again drew back his daggers as a shadow passed over him. A wyvern loomed above him with its front claws out, diving for a kill shot, "Shit…"

Eric raised his blades out in front of him. If they connected, he likely wouldn't survive. Just as the wyvern was coming in for the kill, three white and blue bolts struck its black hide. Its body gyrated as sparks fled the scales.

Drakin
The Story of Raiya

Raiya darted out in front of him and drove her blade into the wyvern's chest. The force of the impact sent the wyvern flying backward before it crashed on the ground. Raiya landed on top of it and pressed her dagger even deeper until blood spattered everywhere.

She withdrew her blade and smiled as she turned to look at Jagger. Bolts flew from his gun, shocking the wyvern as they struck. It let out a mournful cry as it fell to the ground. Jagger dropped the rifle and removed his 1911 from its holster.

The stunned wyvern looked up at him with malice in its eye, "My death means nothing… your kind shall fall!"

Jagger pointed the pistol at the wyvern's eye.

BOOM!

ERRREAAAAAAK!

BOOM! BOOM!

The young dragon ceased all movement. Jagger nodded as he turned back to see Raiya approaching. A smile appeared on her left cheek, "Nice moves, partner…"

"Thanks."

She daintily brushed up against him as she walked by in an almost seductive manner. Jagger looked at her oddly. *The heck was that about?*

She then approached Eric, "Way to almost get yourself killed, kid."

"Kid?" Eric scoffed. "Are you kidding me? I'm twenty-one, how old are you?"

"Wouldn't you like to know."

Drakin
The Story of Raiya

She pushed past Eric and drove her blade into the beta dragon's mouth.

"What are you doing?" Eric asked.

"These teeth are apparently worth a lot to people in the cities. We've got three sets here."

As Raiya went to work, Eric turned to Jagger, "Can you fill me in on the whole classification thing?"

"You mean you don't know?"

"Not really. I know we call the small one's wyverns, but that's it."

Raiya sighed as she pried the teeth from the beta's mouth, "You start off with the infants. They're called hatchlings... They're lethal in about six weeks. At that point, they become wraith class."

Jagger nodded and took over as Raiya began pulling at a loose tooth, "Wraith class goes on for about five or six years. They can't stay in the air long and can't fly very fast, but they typically hunt in packs or attack single targets. After that, we get to wyrm class. They're bigger, faster, and they are fast both on the land and in the air."

Raiya pulled hard, releasing the tooth from the bloody gum, "Ah... Then we go to the drake class. They're adolescents by then. These ones can breathe fire or are at least starting to learn how to... though they're not very good at it. Usually, they can't aim, they can't hold a blast for long, and they can't do it while flying. Often, they're as much a danger to themselves as anyone else. Next up are the beta and alpha dragons.

Drakin
The Story of Raiya

These are the adult classes. By this point, their scales have fully hardened."

She grabbed another tooth and pulled, "They're not able to breathe fire from the air, but they're incredibly destructive from the ground. Next are the elder class dragons. They're tough... really tough. They breathe fire in flight, they have wings large enough to glide through the sky and they are incredibly fast. Finally, we have the dragon lords. Almost no one who's encountered them has survived. It's said there's supposed to be five of them; a black one, a red one, a green one, a yellow one, and a gray one. The black one is my target..."

Jagger looked at her oddly, "Aren't you forgetting one?"

"Huh?"

"The Dread Lord."

Raiya's arms dropped to the side as she turned to face Jagger. The hiss of air passing over her teeth signified annoyance, "Oh please... he's a myth and nothing more."

"Are you sure?"

"Jagger, rumors of a dragon patriarch are ghost stories spread by idiots who spent too much time in the sun. There have been five confirmed dragon lords. The idea of a sixth one that supposedly dwarfs the rest... someone would have seen it by now."

"I've heard stories about him," Eric said. "He was supposedly the first dragon to awaken on Earth. They say he's gone mad with power. Even the Five Dragon Lords fear him."

Drakin
The Story of Raiya

"Fairytales," Raiya said in a dismissive tone. "Everyone knows that there were only five dragon lords. If this sixth one exists and he's so powerful, why doesn't he come fight? With his help, this war would be over in no time."

"Well... okay, you've got a point there," Jagger admitted.

"Exactly... let's just focus on reality and get moving."

"Right..."

Fort Charleston
United States Remnant
Territory
Formerly South Carolina

Drakin
The Story of Raiya

Chapter 8

"How many cartridges are left?"

Eric looked behind the seat, "Two... I don't think the bolt gun will be much good after that... unless you think you can beat a wyvern to death with it."

Jagger sighed, frustrated with how bad things were going, "Three wyvern attacks and a beta team... are we just unlucky?"

"In fifteen hours?" Raiya asked. "I'd say pretty damn lucky."

"All right good point."

She quickly looked at the map, "How much further..."

Boom...

All three of the jeep's occupants looked up.

"Did you hear that?" Eric asked.

Boom... boom!

Jagger nodded, "Sounded like gunfire."

Within a few minutes, the jeep passed over the old Mark Clark Expressway. Eric's eyes widened as he sat forward and thrust his right index finger in front of them, "Look!"

A massive wood and steel wall stood at the end of the road about five miles away. An American Flag could be seen flying in the distance. Two dark spots were visible, circling a large building protruding from behind the wall.

As they moved closer, the small spots began to take on shape. Both appeared to be dragons.

"They're under attack!" Jagger shouted.

Drakin
The Story of Raiya

Eric sat back and watched, "From what I've been told, they're constantly under attack. This is nothing new. The dragons send out a small party to constantly keep the people there on edge."

"It's just two wyverns…" Raiya replied. "If that's all it takes to keep them on edge…"

A third spot appeared in the sky. Its movements were more mechanical and it appeared to be going after the other two. Jagger squinted to try and get a better look. The small spots became larger and took on more defined shapes, "I'll be…"

"What is it?" Raiya asked.

Jagger peered at the large machine that was dogfighting with the wyverns. It was dark green with multiple armaments on both wings and what looked like a transparent circle that was holding it in the sky. The distant sound of a loud mechanical engine echoed over the land.

"What is it?" Raiya demanded.

"A military gunship!" Jagger replied.

"A what?"

"A helicopter… they're held in the sky by massive spinning blades. I've never actually seen one."

Raiya squinted and watched as the gunship unleashed a volley of machine gun fire on the nearest wyvern. The young dragon instantly exploded in a cloud of blood. The flying machine then turned on the other dragon and did the same. The second dragon let out a surprised cry dodged the machine gun fire. After the chopper missed, a missile launched from the wing, striking the beast

Drakin

The Story of Raiya

dead on. There was a massive explosion followed by smoke as small pieces of debris fell from the sky.

As the smoke cleared, the gunship slowly descended behind the wall. Raiya sat back and folded her fingers together, "Impressive."

Eric's eyes narrowed, "They've got that kind of tech and they're not attacking the dragons?"

"They have it, just not enough to do any real damage," Jagger replied. "From what I've read, we used to have hundreds of those things."

The jeep approached the seemingly unending wall. A dark gate stood at the end of the road. Unlike the one in New Framingham, this one was solid so that no one could see inside. Two men dressed in green military uniforms stood on either side of the road. Behind them was a barrier and a small guard shack.

"Halt!"

Raiya flinched and quickly pulled the hood over her head as they were signaled to stop. She kept her eyes facing forward, refusing to move. It was like she had been turned to stone; she was emotionless and completely impervious to outside stimuli.

Jagger stopped the jeep as he'd been instructed. The nearest guard stepped forward. He was a young man in a green uniform with a black helmet. The old American banner on his arm was unmistakable; he was part of the Marine Corps. The soldier first looked at the jeep before addressing its driver, "Identify yourselves."

Drakin
The Story of Raiya

"Lieutenant Jagger Bishop… this is Raiya and Eric, they're nomads," Jagger replied.

The soldier eyed them suspiciously, "Sir, you're a Westcon soldier?"

"Yeah."

"Do you have any identification?" the soldier asked.

"No."

The soldier continued to eye the group, "What would a Westcon soldier be doing with a pair of nomads?"

"These are my friends. They've helped me get this far."

The guard nodded, "I see… well… sir, what's your business here?"

"It's very important that we see Dr. Castillo."

The soldier scoffed, "You came all this way to see that… to see the doctor? May I ask why?"

Jagger turned to Raiya. Her head turned slightly towards the guard. As he caught sight of her eyes, the man stepped back, "Dragon's Bane?"

"No," Jagger replied. "She was born this way. We'd like to find out why. He's probably the only one who can tell us."

"Sir, I think you may be placing too much faith in the man," the guard said before quickly turning back to the post. "But it's not my place to say. Stay put, I'll radio this in."

Jagger waited patiently, fully expecting to be turned away. As soon as the guard was out of earshot, he turned to Raiya, "They're not going to let us in."

Drakin

The Story of Raiya

"You think?"

"All this way for nothing."

Eric shrugged, "Hey at least we got some things to trade. If they won't let us in based on her, maybe we can bribe someone."

"That's… actually not a bad idea," Raiya admitted.

Jagger quickly surveyed the soldiers standing nearby, "I somehow don't think these guys would go for that. They seem kind of… fanatical?"

"I suppose you'd have to be to maintain a posting here," Eric said.

Raiya frowned, "I told you this was stupid… I never wanted to come here in the first place. Now we're way off the trail of the black elder dragon. I'll have to start all over."

"It's not like we haven't been killing dragons," Eric chimed in.

Raiya clenched her fists, "I don't care about pathetic wyverns… I'm hunting a dragon lord. I've already had to wait years to find him. Now…"

A grinding mechanical sound turned Jagger's attention away from the conversation. He glanced over to a nook in the wall where a surveillance camera was nested. It turned a little more to the left and seemed to focus on Raiya.

Jagger lowered his eyes, "Well look, maybe we could…"

"Open the gate!" the group heard a nearby soldier yell.

The guard came back out to them with a surprised frown on his face, "It looks like the doctor wants to meet with you. You can go in, but don't go beyond the first checkpoint. A representative of the provincial government will be there to meet you."

"Thanks," Jagger replied as he put his truck in drive.

"Good journey," the soldier replied as he tipped his helmet.

The truck slowly pulled under the massive archway which served as a crosswalk for soldiers. Raiya pulled her hood back and stood up in the jeep as the city came into view.

Jagger looked at her oddly, "Maybe you should keep your hood up."

"Why?"

"We don't want to draw any more attention."

Raiya shrugged, "No I'm good. I want to actually see this."

Smoke filled the sky over the city, casting a large shadow over the land. Smashed debris and rubble littered the streets, yet somehow the buildings were still standing. Burns and scorch marks painted the taller towers black. However, the windows were somehow still intact.

Row upon row of tanks, personnel carriers, and combat trucks lined the streets, clearly ready for any attack that came through. The few open fields that hadn't been burnt out had been converted to training grounds for recruits. Other soldiers marched up and down the streets in perfect formation with their units. Their faces were almost as emotionless as Raiya's.

Drakin
The Story of Raiya

Raiya looked depressed as she watched two soldiers walked by; one boy and one girl. They looked like they were siblings and kept close to each other in the marching ranks. They were very young, even younger than she was.

Jagger leaned over at Raiya as the jeep continued forward, "You okay?"

"Yeah, why?"

"You look upset."

"No… not really … just…"

"What is it?" Jagger asked.

Raiya looked around and nodded to the clearing, "Where are all the people? This is nothing like New Framingham. All we've seen are soldiers. Where are the children? Is everyone in this town part of the military?"

Jagger's eyes quickly darted around the scenery. Raiya was right, there was nothing but military encampments as far as he could see. There was no other sign of life.

Jagger pressed on his breaks as Raiya sat down, "There's the first checkpoint."

A small building that almost looked like it was poking out of the ground appeared in front of them. It was little more than a one-story doorway that didn't appear to lead anywhere. A red flag stood on either side of the entrance.

Eric's eyes narrowed as he looked at the structure, "A bomb shelter?"

Jagger shrugged "Maybe it was at some point?"

"Why do I suddenly feel like we just willingly walked into a cage?" Raiya asked.

Drakin

The Story of Raiya

Jagger nodded, "Glad I'm not the only one."

A man in a blue uniform with several colorful patches on it waited for them. He had pale skin and wore a helmet that blocked anyone from seeing his hair. Jagger pulled up and put the truck in park. The soldier eyed the group suspiciously.

His expression gave Jagger a bad feeling, but he tried to remain as cordial as he could, "Is this the checkpoint we were told to stop at, soldier?"

The soldier's eyes focused on Raiya, narrowing as they looked at her horns. He made no effort to hide his inspection as his eyes traveled down her face, chest, stomach, all the way down to her toes. He remained silent, not even acknowledging the rest of the group.

At first, Raiya pretended to ignore him, but his stare was becoming intrusive. She crossed her legs in a seductive manner and looked at his nametag, "What, you see something you like... Lieutenant Rollins?"

Lt. Rollins stiffened as his eyes returned to the group's faces. "Huh? Oh um... My apologies ma'am. Lieutenant Jeffrey Rollins, at your service. I was ordered to make sure that you received a proper welcome and introduction to our city."

Jagger nodded, "Lieutenant Jagger Bishop... formerly of the Western Coalition."

He then turned and pointed to his companions, "This is Raiya and Eric... um..."

"Eric Fausten," Eric added.

Drakin
The Story of Raiya

Rollins turned and beckoned them to the check post door, "Good to meet you. Please follow me."

"What about my jeep?" Jagger asked.

"Don't worry about it. Just leave the keys. We'll have one of our boys take it to the depot."

"The depot?"

Lt. Rollins smiled, "Our techs will give it a tune-up and a little TLC while you're here. You won't even recognize it."

It looked as though someone turned on a light in Jagger's eyes as he jumped out of the seat, "Wow thanks."

"Just hope it's still in one piece when it's time to leave..." Raiya whispered.

"Well... great now I'm going to worry the entire time. Thanks a lot!"

"No problem..."

Eric got out of the back and pulled his shirt down over the dual dagger sheath on the back of his belt, "Are we going to see Dr. Castillo now?"

"Regrettably, the doctor is indisposed at the moment," Lt. Rollins replied. "He asked that I give you a proper reception and tour of our facilities. He requests that you enjoy what hospitality we can offer for today."

"He can't even be bothered to meet with us?" Raiya asked.

"Unfortunately, the doctor is unable to. He's a busy man, but he's offering you food and rest under our protection until he can meet with you. You'll have full access to a menu of different items, a shower, and bedrooms for your use."

He frowned as his words became almost sarcastic, "I'm sure you're very busy out in the wastelands, but I would ask your indulgence for a little while."

"Fine…" Raiya replied unenthusiastically.

"We are guests here, Raiya," Jagger added. "Try to remember that."

"Try to remember that I can still kill you in your sleep if you don't watch it," Raiya whispered.

Lt. Rollins pushed a small button on the panel next to the door. There was a low beep as the heavy door opened behind him. The next room was little more than a downward-sloping hallway with a large metal arch at the entrance. Red and green lights flashed from the top of it.

Lt. Rollins beckoned them forward, "Please step this way. We just need to do a security check."

Jagger sighed as he pulled his pistols out and placed them on the metal table next to the arch, "I want these back."

Lt' Rollins nodded, "When you leave, they'll be returned."

Jagger stepped through the arch without incident and proceeded forward. Eric was next. He ignored the bin and kept his daggers concealed as he stepped through the arch. To Jagger's surprise, it didn't go off. He quickly looked over at Lt. Rollins for a reaction.

The lieutenant was looking at the keypad on the side of the archway. His expression was still emotionless.

Drakin

The Story of Raiya

Eric smiled and winked as he turned around and stood next to his companion. Jagger whispered out of the side of his mouth, "How?"

"Dragon bone… no metal."

Jagger nodded, "Of course."

Raiya pulled her own dagger out and looked at it before looking at Lt. Rollins and showing him her clawed fingers, "One scratch on this and I'll do the same to your eyes."

"Is she serious?" Eric asked.

Jagger nodded, "I wouldn't doubt it."

Lt. Rollins didn't respond, despite clearly being affected by her remarks. She passed through the arch without incident. A devious grin appeared on her face as she walked past Jagger, "Don't worry, my claws are sharper than those daggers anyway."

Lt. Rollins came around the arch and beckoned the group forward, "Please follow me."

He opened the door behind the archway which led to a downward escalator. The group lined up behind him and took their turn getting on.

Raiya hesitated as she stepped forward, "What is this?"

Jagger offered his hand as she stepped on, "They're mechanical stairs. This way we don't have to walk all the way down."

She ignored the hand and peered into the darkness ahead of her, "Why is it such a big deal to walk down?"

"Dunno… maybe it's a long way?"

"We also use this as a service entrance," Lt. Rollins said. "We couldn't rig an elevator down here, so instead we put this in. It's not much, but it makes carrying heavy supplies down here a little easier.

Everyone stood in darkness as the escalator took them down the underground passageway. There was nothing remarkable to look at. The tunnel was drilled out of solid rock, obviously very quickly. The walls were rough, but wide enough for the group to pass through without having to duck.

Recessed lighting in the floor and ceiling came on as they reached the base of the passageway. A glass door stood about twenty feet away as the group stepped back onto solid ground. A small keypad rose from a hidden recess next to the door with a red light on top.

Lt. Rollins input his key, and then pressed his thumb against the red light. The light turned green and made a buzzing noise. It slowly began to recede back into the ground as the doors opened.

Raiya's eyes widened as the group was led into a massive underground cavern. The whole thing was illuminated by recessed lighting. To the left, there appeared to be offices, control consoles, as well as a network of tunnels and rooms, each with specific labels on them, detailing their purpose. One had a red sign on it that read 'science division.'

Why can't he just take us there? Raiya thought to herself.

To the right were large gardens, enough trees to make up a small forest, and row upon row of what looked like wheat and corn. This was a

Drakin
The Story of Raiya

perfect setup for Fort Charleston and explained how they'd been able to survive.

People in special gear tended to the plants. Some were pruning leaves while others focused on turning the soil. An overhead irrigation system provided rainwater to the plants.

Lt. Rollins smiled as he turned back, "Welcome to the American Remnant Force's Central Command."

Raiya stepped forward and looked at the forest in amazement, "How is this even possible? Was all this here before the dragon attack?"

Lt. Rollins beckoned them to a small lift with yellow handrails. Once they were all aboard, Rollins pushed the 'down' button. He turned and looked out at the forest, "It took us almost ten years to do this. When the war first began, we did everything we could to create sustainable resources that would allow us to hold our position. After losing field after field of crops to a dragon attack, we decided to attempt to create an alternate option."

He pointed up to the ceiling, "We began using our military equipment and ordinance to carefully carve out a massive cavern under the city… a sub level if you would. Once we had the cavern built and stabilized, we added full spectrum, recessed, fluorescent lighting to keep plants alive. Environmental controls keep the plants watered and the temperature just right. We then moved our engineering and science divisions down here and carved out full facilities for them to use."

Drakin
The Story of Raiya

"How do you keep this place running?" Jagger asked.

"It's a combination of solar energy from recessed panels on the surface, but also large fuel cells like the one that powers your jeep. Our cells are rechargeable, and thus we have an almost inexhaustible power supply."

"Why haven't the coalitions ever thought of any of this?" Jagger asked. "Our forces still try to keep soldiers fed with farms above the ground. They just do the best they can to fend off dragon attacks."

"We have shared our technology with the coalitions," Rollins replied. "However, things like this take considerable time and resources, and aren't always possible."

"Do the civilians live down in those tunnels?" Eric asked.

"No, they live on the surface. There simply isn't enough space to accommodate them down here."

Raiya's eyes narrowed, "Where do they live exactly?"

"Well technically there are no civilians here," Rollins said. "We each serve a purpose to aid in the military effort."

"Yes… I saw your child soldiers on the surface," Raiya said in a low voice.

"Such is the reality we live in. It's not something we ever wanted to do, but as we're running short on soldiers, we've had to call up a few younger recruits. However, to answer your question, the civilians live in small encampments that are closer to the shore."

Rollins continued to beckon them forward, "Come, we have rooms set up for you in a place that may make you feel more comfortable."

He led the group to the other side of the cavern where another lift was waiting. The yellow handlebar was in its raised position, waiting for them to board.

Rollins got everyone on and flipped the switch to bring them up to level two where an elevator was waiting, "So Jagger, what's your story?"

"My story?" Jagger asked

"You said you were former Westcon. Never heard of anyone leaving their post."

"He didn't leave his post," Raiya hissed. "He was forced out."

"Oh, excuse me," Rollins replied defensively.

Jagger nodded, "Raiya saved my town. She fought back a dragon and forced it to flee."

"So, what happened?" Rollins asked.

"Paranoia happened… a mob accused Raiya of bringing that dragon down on our town because of… well just because of how she looks. I was also blamed because I brought her into the town. It didn't even matter that she'd saved them from the damn dragon. So, we left New Framingham."

Lt. Rollin's eyes widened, "New Framingham? Shit…"

"Yeah, why?"

"Jagger… you mean you don't know?" Rollins asked.

"Know what?"

Drakin

The Story of Raiya

Raiya placed her hand on Jagger's shoulder. This was a scene she'd been witness to many times before. Rollins sighed and gave Jagger a sympathetic look, "We lost contact with New Framingham about 8 hours ago. Our scout fighters arrived on the scene roughly thirty minutes later. All they found was rubble, ash, and a lot of burnt bodies. We didn't detect any survivors."

Jagger leaned backward. He looked like he was going to be ill and fall off the lift, "They're all dead?"

"It looks that way…"

Eric frowned, "I'm sorry man… –What about the surrounding areas?"

Rollins took his helmet off, revealing short, brown, hair. He scratched his head as he looked at them, "No report of any attacks outside of the city. It looks like the attack was fairly localized."

Jagger turned to Raiya, "Could they have been looking for you?"

"Maybe…" Raiya replied. "After the way that dragon lord reacted. He probably went back and reported what he saw…"

"And they attacked in force… Jerry… that son of a bitch was right."

A hurt look appeared on Raiya's face, "I'm sorry…"

The lift reached platform two, where Rollins tapped on the wall panel. The up arrow lit up momentarily as the door opened. The group filed in as Rollins turned to the keypad on the wall.

Eight small circular buttons were recessed into the cold steel plating. The bottom one read 'CC',

Drakin
The Story of Raiya

which Raiya assumed meant 'Command Center,' while the one next to it read 'G.' The others were labeled with numbers going up to six.

Jagger remained silent as Rollins pressed the '6' button and the doors closed. Raiya kept her eyes on him as the sounds of working machinery filled the small chamber. Though she maintained a stoic outwardly appearance, inside she felt horrible. Were they right to fear her? Had she somehow brought the dragons down on those poor people? Was she responsible for ruining Jagger's life?

Raiya's heart sank as she was forced to ask herself the question she feared most; did Jagger blame her? She wouldn't blame him if he did.

Her left cheek flinched slightly as she watched him, fighting back a tear. Clearly deep in thought, Jagger was worlds away. Likely he was burying the people he knew, metaphorically speaking. She bit down hard on her lower lip as her chest began to ache. *I'm sorry.*

It had been years since she'd sympathized with anyone. She'd seen many people cut down, but they weren't people she knew or cared for. Most of them were like the people of New Framingham that cursed and scorned her.

Jagger was different, he'd stood up for her, defended her, and even gone along with her despite not being asked to. He never once grimaced at her appearance, nor did he make any comments about it other than genuine curiosity. She'd only been around him for a few days, but he

Drakin
The Story of Raiya

was her friend. She actually wanted to be there for him.

The sinking feeling inside made her sick. She hated it. No doubt this was the downside of having a partner or letting someone get too close. Eventually, it would wind up hurting.

Ding!

The elevator opened on the sixth floor, interrupting Raiya's thoughts. Rollins stepped out and beckoned the group forward. Jagger's jaw dropped as the group stepped into the room, "Whoa…"

In front of them was a massive suite overlooking the city. They were a few stories up above the ground. The windows looked out on the city on all sides, giving them a view of everything. The furniture looked brand new and was actually clean. In fact, everything was clean. It was all white with black accents. The floor was white and black tiles, the countertop was black granite, and while the chairs were white, the padding material was black.

In the middle of the room, on a large table, was a meal that looked big enough to feed ten people. Jagger's mouth watered as he looked at the massive spread. Everything from a roasted chicken to beef, to meats that Jagger had never even seen before had been prepared for them.

Rollins nodded, "This is where you'll be staying for the duration of your visit. We hope that you'll enjoy your time here. Food has been prepared and an assortment of clothing has been left in each of the rooms. Feel free to help yourselves. Something is bound to fit each of you."

Jagger turned back to Lt. Rollins, "This is how you treat every random wanderer who shows up at your gates?"

"Absolutely not," Rollins replied. "This was at the personal request of Dr. Castillo himself, otherwise you likely wouldn't have made it through the front door."

"How does he know about us?" Raiya asked.

Rollins shrugged, "The man has access to the city surveillance system. With the CSS, you can literally see anything going on throughout the fortress. No doubt he saw you pull up and took an interest in your... appearance."

"No doubt..." Raiya replied.

SHOOOOOOOOO!

"What was that?" Eric asked as he ran to the window.

"F-18 fighters. They're returning to base, likely from a counter-attack on the dragons that tried to give us trouble."

Jagger turned back in surprise, "You have an airfield here?"

"No such luck," Rollins replied. "We have a small landing pad for choppers and transports, but nothing a fighter could use... no, they're going to the *Truman.*"

"The *Truman?*" Jagger asked.

Rollins pointed to the window on the opposite side. Both Eric and Jagger peered out to see where the fighters had gone. There, they could see what looked like a massive flat field that had been attached to the nearby dock with a building sticking out of one side.

Eric looked back, "What you mean that dock is a runway?"

"That's no dock," Jagger replied. "That is an aircraft carrier."

"Wait… that thing is an actual ship?"

Rollins nodded, "Yes sir, the *USS. Harry S. Truman,* CVN 75, Nimitz class U.S. Naval carrier… probably the last of her kind."

Eric's eyes were wide as he pressed his face against the glass in awe, "You mean people made ships that big?"

"Yeah."

"Can she sail?" Jagger asked.

"She hasn't in a few years, but she's quite capable of it," Rollins replied. "I don't know for certain… but think our naval brass are too worried about sending her out at this point, given that she's important to the city's defense. Right now, she serves as headquarters for our military command and our airfield. A lot of our older officers feel safer on her than they do in our command center."

Jagger's eyes narrowed as he watched the fighters land, "I thought planes couldn't land on a docked carrier?"

Rollins smiled, "You know your history, very good. It's true, a conventional jet fighter couldn't perform the landing while their carrier was at anchor. The ship can't meet the wind-over-deck requirement. That's why most of our planes have been replaced with vertical takeoff and landing

Drakin
The Story of Raiya

fighters. We've also installed special turbines on the sides of the flight deck to generate the necessary wind for the fighters that don't have that capability."

"I see…"

Rollins stepped back into the elevator. He pointed to a small panel on the wall that looked like the old radio in Jagger's jeep, "If you need anything, please don't hesitate to call us. In the meantime, try and relax. Dr. Castillo is a busy man, but he's punctual. He'll be by to see you early tomorrow morning. Sleep well."

"Are we safe up here?" Eric asked.

Rollins nodded, "Perfectly. This entire building is concrete with fireproofing to reinforce the exterior. The windows are ballistic glass with a flame-resistant coating. This place took on an elder dragon's flame and is still standing, so don't worry about it."

The elevator door closed as the group sat down to eat. Eric smiled, "Well at least they're treating us okay."

Jagger nodded, "Yeah but I don't think we should stay here a second longer than we have to."

"Are you all right?" Raiya asked as Jagger sat down in one of the chairs.

"I can't believe it… New Framingham had over two thousand people living there and the dragons just… just…"

Raiya sat down next to him, "I know…"

"Jerry, Mariam, John… everyone's gone. I just can't believe it. They took me in when I fled to them from my home. I was the only one to make it. I can't believe they're all gone now. It's just…"

"I'm really sorry Jagger," Raiya said as her voice cracked.

Jagger looked up at her, "What's wrong?"

"Nothing."

Raiya was a bad liar and she knew it. The look in Jagger's eyes told her that he didn't believe her, "Tell me the truth."

Raiya sighed, "You can say it. I won't get mad."

"Say what?"

"That Jerry was right about me. That it's my fault everyone's dead. Had I never gone to your town, they'd all still be alive."

Jagger reached out and touched the clawed finger of her right hand. "Look, it's not your fault. You can't help who or what you are. All you wanted was something to eat. That's not a crime."

"Jagger's right," Eric interrupted. "Besides, you don't know that they were looking for you. They attacked once before they noticed you were there, right?"

"Yes…" Raiya replied.

"Well, then likely they just wanted to finish what they started. If anything, you just postponed them from getting wiped out sooner. New Framingham isn't the first town to fall, you know? There's no reason behind why or when the dragons attack."

"That doesn't make it any easier."

Drakin
The Story of Raiya

Jagger nodded, "No I know… it never does. Just look… this was not your fault, it wasn't my fault, it wasn't anyone's fault."

"Well… except for the dragons," Eric said. "I'm pretty sure we can justify blaming them here."

Raiya looked into Jagger's eyes, "Are you okay? I know that's a lot to take in."

"I'll be all right. Why don't we all just get some food, huh?"

"Sounds good."

Chapter 9

Jagger laid back on the firm mattress. He'd taken up residence in the bedroom closest to the window. If a dragon planned on attacking the city, Jagger wanted to know about it. Despite Lt. Rollins's assurances, he didn't feel particularly safe high up in a building. He'd seen dragons accomplish what should have been impossible and had learned to expect anything.

The suite was essentially a massive living room with a kitchenette off to the side and a bedroom in each corner. He wasn't certain that he could sleep, so he watched the city lights as they flickered on and off. He'd never seen anything like it before, not even in New Framingham. This was a massive city, a modern miracle that shouldn't still be standing, but thanks to the steadfast stewardship of its inhabitants, they'd managed to make it almost impervious to dragon attacks. Rubble from the old city still lined the streets, and several buildings were damaged, but the city still stood.

Jagger's eyes began to flutter and he could finally feel himself slip into his dream world. The mattress was as comfortable as the one back home. He hadn't slept very well since he'd left and his body was practically forcing him out of consciousness.

A knock came at the door as his eyes closed. He sat up, clad only in a white cotton t-shirt and boxers that he'd found in the drawers, "Come in."

Drakin
The Story of Raiya

Raiya stepped into the room, rubbing her arms. She was wearing a dark nightdress with black lacing on the seams. The outfit hugged her hips and almost seemed like it was made for her.

"That dress suits you," Jagger said.

Raiya's arms were crossed with her hands rubbing her upper arms. Her breathing was slightly erratic. Something was clearly bothering her, but she remained silent as she stood in the doorway.

Jagger looked at her oddly, "Are you okay?"

"It's very cold here…" she replied softly.

Jagger smiled, "You're used to being outside in the heat… and something tells me that your body wasn't designed for cold weather. This place is climate controlled. Given that it's the middle of the summer…"

"I tried using the com to ask them if they could turn up the heat, but no one responded."

"Likely they're all in bed," Jagger replied.

"Probably… Jagger… um…"

"What?"

Raiya lowered her eyes, "The nomads often huddled together for warmth on the rare occasions when we were stuck in cold weather."

"Body heat?"

"Yeah…"

A look of humiliation appeared in her eyes. He knew what she wanted to ask, but clearly, she was having trouble finding the words, "Okay, come on, climb in."

"Really, you sure?"

"Yeah."

Drakin
The Story of Raiya

"Okay… thanks."

Jagger turned over and lay on his side, facing away from Raiya as he waited for her to join him. He could hear a light tussling sound, followed by the sheets tightening as they were lifted. He was about to close his eyes when he felt Raiya's arms find their way around him.

The feel of her body press against his forced his eyes opened wide, "You're freezing!"

She had removed her nightdress and her skin felt like fine grain sandpaper. The texture of her skin didn't bother him, but it was extremely cold. He could feel her head turn to the side, allowing her cheek to press against his back, "Does it bother you?"

"No."

It was a lie. It did bother him. If her body didn't warm up, he'd be freezing all night. It was like trying to sleep while being pressed against a block of ice. His instinct was to try to pull away, but Raiya's rhythmic breathing told him that she was finally comfortable.

His skin broke out in goosebumps. As her arms passed over his, her rhythmic breathing stopped, "Liar… it is bothering you. I can feel the goose bumps."

"It's fine."

"No, it's not…"

"Raiya, really. Get some sleep, I'm sure you'll warm up."

"All right… but if you decide you can't sleep, tell me."

"Okay."

Drakin
The Story of Raiya

Raiya lay on her side with the typical frown on her face, "Jagger?"

"Yeah?"

"The attack on New Framingham… um…"

"It wasn't your fault."

"You keep saying that, but how do you know?" Raiya demanded. "For all you know, they could have been looking for me."

"Maybe, but how is that your fault? Don't listen to what those idiots said to you. You didn't bring the dragon down on them. I know that. When we evacuated, all you could think about was saving those people. You kept them alive longer than they likely would have survived."

"That doesn't make it any easier."

"It wasn't supposed to. I'm just saying that you did what you thought was right. No one can fault you for it."

"Thanks, I guess," Raiya replied.

Jagger felt her body relax against him again. She slowly drifted off to sleep as her body continued to remain pressed against him. Little by little, her skin did warm until it was a normal temperature.

As he began to fall asleep, Raiya unconsciously let go of him and turned over. She immediately began to shiver as her breathing became erratic. *Is it really that cold in here?*

It didn't matter, she was uncomfortable and he needed her in good shape. She needed to be well rested if they were going to have any chance against a dragon lord. He rolled over and placed

Drakin
The Story of Raiya

his arms around her. His body pressed against hers as he leaned over to see if she had woken up.

Raiya's eyes were closed, but a narrow smile had appeared on the corner of her mouth. She was content at least. That was good enough for him. He ran his hand over her hip and reached out for her arm.

Her side raised as she took in a deep breath and let it out slowly. Jagger blinked a few times as he looked at her. *Are you attracted to me?* That question still caught him off guard. It wasn't exactly something that a person just came straight out and asked... at least not so directly. Yet he was lying next to her contemplating those exact words.

There was an opening in the blanket that allowed him a glimpse of her slender body. Yeah, despite the scales and odd boney plates on her back, she was actually very attractive. However, she was a nomad who likely wouldn't survive very long, given what she was after. *Probably best to just keep it to yourself.*

Without another thought, Jagger drifted off into a dream world he was certain that Raiya would soon be dominating. Both of their bodies were warm and they'd both be comfortable... sort of.

I'll be lucky if I don't wake up with a road rash... skin rash... whatever you want to call it.

The next morning, Raiya awoke to the sound of light snoring. The sun was up again and their big day was upon them. Then she noticed that

Drakin
The Story of Raiya

Jagger had apparently rolled over and held her in place to keep her warm.

A faint smiled appeared on her face as she lay in bed. Part of her resisted the urge to move. This was the first time she'd ever slept in a comfortable bed being kept that warm, she liked it until another sensation became apparent.

Right at the bottom of her tailbone, she felt something stiff press against her. *What's this? Oh boy... Someone's having a fun dream... wonder if I'm somehow involved.*

Feeling devious, she slowly arched her back and gently wiggled her butt against his hips. Jagger groaned and turned on his back. She sat up and looked at him, "Was it good for you?"

No response.

She giggled to herself as she got up and headed for the nearby shower. She didn't feel dirty, but she'd gotten into the routine of taking a shower whenever one was available. Who knew when the next time one would be?

The sound of running water woke Jagger. He pressed his eyes closed, stretched, and sat up. *Raiya must have decided to grab a shower.*

Jagger got up and moved to take a look out in the living room. Loud snoring from across the room let Jagger know that Eric was still out cold. The sun was peeking through the window, creating a shadow on the floor in front of him.

To his surprise, Jagger saw that an assortment of breakfast foods including fruit, pastries, and beverages had been laid out for them. He was

Drakin
The Story of Raiya

hungry, but he decided to wait until the others were ready to eat before digging in.

Behind him in the bedroom, Jagger heard the shower stop. He turned and went back in to wait his turn. He could only hope that she had left him some hot water.

He grabbed a towel out of the small closet next to the bathroom as Raiya stepped out. Once again, she didn't bother wrapping herself in one.

This time Jagger didn't immediately try to look away. He just looked at her like he did when she was dressed. Her nipples were fully erect, her breasts seemed very firm, not moving as she walked, and there was no trace of pubic hair anywhere on her, despite her clearly being of age. He began to wonder if her skin could even grow such hair. She had a full head of hair, so who knew? It was either that or he'd have to solve the mystery of how she shaved it off.

She smiled deviously at Jagger, but he pretended not to notice, "Oh good, shower time!"

Jagger got up and picked up his towel. Raiya's eyes narrowed as he briskly walked past her, "What, no reaction this time?"

"Nope."

Raiya frowned, "Really?"

"Yeah, why?"

Raiya's lips twisted like she was pissed off, but didn't want him to know. She shook her head and turned away, "Nothing, just forget about it."

"You sure."

"Yeah, just go."

Drakin
The Story of Raiya

She quickly grabbed the sheet off the bed, wrapped herself in it and marched back to her room. He shrugged the whole thing off and got ready for a shower.

✝

Jagger sat down for breakfast and was quickly joined by his companions. Eric speared a few pastries and quickly began munching on a croissant. Raiya began devouring a slice of bacon.

Jagger's plate was a little bit of everything. He was actually kind of surprised with Raiya. Her plate was almost entirely meat. He'd seen her sharp teeth and figured that she was likely more carnivorous, "Someone likes her bacon."

Raiya looked down at her plate, "What? I've never had this before… it's actually really good."

"Have you tried the fruit?"

"No… to be honest, it kind of makes me sick."

"Really?"

Raiya nodded, "Yeah… I don't know why, but it always seems to make me nauseous within minutes."

They had only been eating for a few moments when the elevator bell sounded and the door opened. A tall gangly man with a white beard entered the room. He spoke with an accent that was clearly not American. Likely this man was from Mid-Western Europe, "Good morning my friends. I trust we all slept well?"

Jagger turned and stood up, "Dr. Ian Castillo?"

"At your service. I understand you wished to speak with me?"

Drakin
The Story of Raiya

"Yes sir, we've got a little bit of a mystery on our hands," Jagger replied as he turned and beckoned towards Raiya.

Dr. Castillo's eyes lit up like a dog's that had just been offered a slab of beef, "Well... well... Yes, I can clearly see what you mean."

The way this doctor was looking at her made her skin crawl, "You're Dr. Castillo? You're the guy we've come all this way to see?"

Dr. Castillo smiled warmly as he extended his hand to her, "Don't sound too disappointed, my dear. I may not look like much, but I helped cure Dragon's Bane and treated many injured soldiers. What can I do for all of you?"

Raiya showed him her clawed right hand at which point the doctor grabbed it and kissed the back of her palm. Jagger stood up next to her, "Doctor, we're hunting one of the Five Dragon Lords. Raiya may be the key to defeating it, but we need to know... why she is the way she is."

Raiya flashed Jagger a momentary look of appreciation for his careful wording as the doctor scoffed, "A dragon lord, you say? You think you can battle one and survive the encounter?"

"We already have," Raiya replied.

"What?"

Jagger stepped forward, "I wouldn't have believed it if I hadn't seen it myself. She stood between a dragon lord and its prey. He sprayed her with dragon's fire and not even her hair was burnt."

"Intriguing..." Dr. Castillo replied.

Drakin
The Story of Raiya

His eyes fixated on her scanning her body from head to toe. Raiya looked at Jagger as if to say, 'make him stop.'

Jagger nodded that he understood and looked at the old doctor, "Can you help us?"

"Of course," Dr. Castillo said enthusiastically. "We'll need to run a few tests and take a few samples of her skin and blood, but it is completely doable."

Dr. Castillo looked at her face, "Those… are the most striking eyes I've ever seen. You'll need to come with me."

Jagger stood up, "I'm going too…"

"No," the doctor replied as his voice suddenly became stern. "I'm afraid my equipment and my lab space have certain environmental requirements that have to be maintained. We can't have a bunch of filthy nomads down there making a mess and contaminating the air. I'm sorry, but I have to insist. Either she comes alone, or not at all."

Jagger shook his head, "I'm not going to…"

"I'll go," Raiya said, cutting him off.

"Are you sure?"

"Yeah, it'll be all right. I can take care of myself."

Jagger's face twisted as he sat back down in the chair. Dr. Castillo looked overjoyed as he clasped his hands together, "Terrific! We'll proceed immediately!"

The doctor beckoned Raiya to the elevator. She hesitantly stepped by him and proceeded through the metal doors. Dr. Castillo nodded and turned to follow Raiya out of the room, "Enjoy yourselves, we'll be back before you know it and I should have information for you."

Jagger turned back to Eric as the doors closed, "Something doesn't feel right about this."

Eric looked up from his plate of food. His face was a mess and his voice was sticky, "What do you mean?"

"I didn't like the way he looked at her."

"It was kind of pervy now that you mention it. Even so, she's unique and he's a scientist. Maybe he's just overexcited. You know how these guys are. They spend so much time in the labs that they don't really develop people skills."

"Maybe…"

Eric sighed as he sat back, "Buddy I don't think we really have much to worry about and we do need his help. Why don't we just let this play out for now and see where it goes?"

"I don't want to take that chance… if something happens to her…"

Eric's eyes narrowed, "Yeah what's your deal man? You act like the two of you are brother and sister. Didn't you just meet her a few days ago? Why do you seem so attached to her?"

Jagger sighed, "I'm not really sure, to be honest. I can't explain it… but I think she might be the key to ending the war. If she can withstand dragon's fire, she might have a chance against the one she wants to kill."

"It's not just that…"

Drakin
The Story of Raiya

"What is it then?" Jagger asked as he slouched back in his chair. "If you've got something to say, spit it out."

"Calm down man," Eric replied defensively. "I'm not trying to attack your character or anything, I just think maybe... maybe you've got a thing for her?"

"Like you said, we've only known each other for a few days."

"So? Love at first sight may be a myth, but instant attraction sure as hell isn't. You've also had two days with no one else around to talk to. I mean in the time I've been around, it's like you've been drawn to her more and more. The fact that you're so protective is proof of it."

Jagger rubbed his forehead, "And what if I am?"

Eric put up his hands defensively and shook his head, "Nothing wrong with that, Jagger. It's just an observation. If that is what's going on, it's something you might want to keep in check. That's my opinion anyway."

"Well keep it to yourself."

"Sorry buddy," Eric said with a smirk. "So, what are we going to do?"

"Keep your daggers with you, I think we're going to need them."

"Not really an issue. Anything else?"

"Yeah... I'm going to try to get out of here and go exploring. We'll see how they react and what happens. If they try to keep us locked up here, we'll know something's up."

Drakin
The Story of Raiya

Jagger got up and pressed the down arrow on the elevator panel. Feint clanking and the grinding sound of mechanical equipment emanated up the shaft from behind the door. He waited patiently as the down arrow light turned off and the door opened.

Eric shrugged, "See?"

Jagger shook his head and stepped inside, "Just be ready… We'll see how this goes."

"No problem," Eric replied as the doors closed.

Jagger was greeted by a fairly spartan lobby as the doors opened a few moments later. He stepped out and surveyed the area. There was no reception desk, no real furniture other than a few seats near the door, and no one to meet him. Two surveillance cameras, one at either end of the hallway was the only proof that the area was guarded. *Why would they need guards? This entire area is one big fortress. If anything does happen, I doubt we could escape on our own.*

Jagger stepped outside where he was greeted by two heavily armed guards. They looked extremely bulky due to the armor and ammo-heavy belts that they wore. *Ah, here we go. This is more like it.*

The one on the right, a young but very gruff looking man with whiskers, turned and looked at Jagger, "Can we help you, sir?"

Jagger nodded, "I was hoping to look around. I wanted to check on my jeep and maybe see the *Truman*?"

Drakin
The Story of Raiya

"You're free to move about the city, but your jeep and the carrier are both in military restricted areas. I can arrange to have someone take you to the jeep, but you may not be able to get very close to the ship."

"All right," Jagger replied. "Please do."

"Yes, sir," the soldier replied as he pulled out his radio.

Chapter 10

If he doesn't stop staring at me, I'm going to gouge his eyes out.

Every time Dr. Castillo looked at Raiya, her skin crawled. "Yes... very interesting indeed. Tell me, my dear, what do you know of your past?"

"Very little... I was able to find some information about my mother before the internet collapsed, but I know nothing about my father. I assumed he was dead."

"Tell me what you know."

She sighed softly as she thought back to her grandparents, "My mother escaped Richmond, but was injured on the way. The people who raised me said that when they found her, she was filthy and covered in blood."

"Did you ever see anyone about your appearance?"

"A few clinics and medicine men. Most of them believe that I have some kind of weird form of Dragon's Bane..."

Dr. Castillo nodded, "Quite conceivably... perhaps a mutated version that somehow altered your appearance, but that is all conjecture at this point."

Raiya touched the scales on her forehead, "Doctor, what is Dragon's Bane? I mean... how do you get infected with it and what does it do?"

"You mean you don't know?"

"I was orphaned at a young age. No one ever really told me much."

The door to the elevator opened to the command center. Dr. Castillo bid Raiya to follow him, "This way."

They stepped out onto the catwalk and headed over to the science division. Dr. Castillo led the way over the metal planking, "It's a good question. To put it simply, Dragon's Bane is considered a disease, but that is not entirely accurate. It does act like a disease, but there is a difference."

"What do you mean?"

Dr. Castillo scratched his head, "Forgive me, I'm getting ahead of myself. A dragon's blood has some interesting properties, not the least of which is its cellular makeup. Their normal blood cells are quite passive and function similar to those of a human. However, their immune system is quite different. Humanity technically has five different kinds of white blood cells that each have a specific function, dragons only have one. I named them 'Parisicytes'."

"What's so special about them?"

"The way a dragon's immune system works is that when the body is infected, these Parisicytes immediately run to the source and begin attacking it. Except unlike human cells they attack a pathogen by attaching themselves to it and becoming a parasite. They use the pathogen as a carrier to procreate, thus creating more of themselves. The pathogen is killed when the new parisicytes reach maturity. They break out of the pathogen like a chick from an egg and they go after other foreign bodies."

Drakin
The Story of Raiya

As they reached the science division, Dr. Castillo reached over to a keypad built out of the rock. It stood in a recessed metal panel next to the door, like most man-made items attached the walls.

The doctor quickly typed in his code as he continued, "Now what do you think would happen if even one parisicyte got into another organism's bloodstream?"

Raiya shook her head, "Um... wouldn't it die?"

Dr. Castillo smiled, "True, a cell can't survive long in an environment that wasn't designed to support it. However, these cells are quite resilient. In essence, they act as a pathogen, attaching themselves to whatever cell they find and begin replicating. As the host's cells begin to die off, the host quickly becomes ill and their body can no longer function properly."

"My mother had it... according to the people who raised me. They say she died soon after giving birth to me."

Dr. Castillo frowned, "Then you were extremely lucky. Dragon's Bane kills its victims very quickly. We're usually talking a year or two at the most. Fetuses don't contract the infection, but they have to be born before dragon's bane attacks the womb or else it will be broken down around them."

"How does someone get Dragon's Bane?"

The door slid open. Dr. Castillo stepped into the next room and turned back to Raiya, "Well that's the intriguing piece. The victim would need to have come into contact with a dragon's blood. Consumption of raw dragon flesh could do it. Being bitten, in rare cases is another way, but most of the victims I've seen were ones that had open wounds. They managed to come into contact with dragon blood, likely from fighting with a wyvern. Fortunately, that is no longer the case. I created a special medicine that, if inoculated at birth, makes human cells impervious to those of a dragon."

The next room was little more than a glass chamber with vents on the floor and ceiling. As soon as the door closed behind them, the room slowly began to fill with mist. Raiya shivered and stepped closer to the center of the small chamber, "What is this?"

"Welcome to decontamination, my dear. The fumes coming out of the vent are a special dioxide that is meant to kill any bacteria. It will neutralize any foreign substance that may be dangerous to my lab."

"Is this really safe?"

"Oh, perfectly safe. I've used it many times, my dear."

"No, I meant for me."

Dr. Castillo nodded, "We've tested it with various other organisms as well. None of them displayed any ill-effects. Relax. It's perfectly safe."

The air was chilly and wet. Her skin began to gleam as it became moist. She hated how it felt, but if this was what it took to get any answers, she was all for it.

Drakin
The Story of Raiya

Raiya began to shiver, attracting Dr. Castillo's attention once more, "Raiya, are you okay?"

"Yeah… It's just… cold…"

Dr. Castillo examined her skin as she rubbed her arms, "Interesting…"

"What is?"

"Well, all lizards on Earth are cold-blooded creatures. Our initial tests on dragons indicated that they have a different makeup. They actually like the cold. Given your appearance… I wonder if you have similar biological traits."

A green light on the wall behind them lit up and a loud fan began sucking the mist from the room. Dr. Castillo smiled, "There, you see? Nothing to worry about."

"If you say so."

The glass door on the other side opened and a robotic voice spoke up, *"Welcome back, Ian."*

"Ah yes, thank you, Lucy. Light on, please."

"What was that?" Raiya demanded in a nervous tone."

"That was Lucy," Dr. Castillo replied. "She's a digital assistant."

"Digital assistant?"

"A talking computer. She can communicate with humans, but it's all artificial intelligence."

"Okay…"

Bright recessed lighting in the ceiling immediately powered on as a young man came out of the next room, "Dr. Castillo, you're back… is this the girl?"

Raiya studied the younger man as he and the doctor spoke. He was older than Raiya and

Drakin
The Story of Raiya

Jagger, but not by much. She guessed he was in his late twenties. He was tall, athletically built, and had short brown hair. She couldn't make out his eye color behind his glasses. Probably someone who spent most of his life buried in books. *He'll be fun to screw with.*

"Yes Andrea, this is the one. Can you get her prepped for examination?"

Examination... what?

"Yes doctor," he immediately turned and looked nervously at Raiya. "Please come with me."

Andrea led Raiya into the room where he had emerged from, "I've... um... laid out a few things for you, based on Dr. Castillo's recommendations. They won't be that comfortable, but they'll keep you covered while allowing us to do our examination."

"What does this examination entail?" Raiya asked suspiciously.

Andrea looked up from the table, "Ugh... it's just like him. He didn't tell you anything about the procedure, did he?"

"No."

"I figured... well, then I should apologize on his behalf. He's a brilliant man, but his bedside manner is severely lacking. It's to the point where he actually calls some of our patients' *specimens*."

"Great..."

Andrea picked up a folded cloth from the table and offered it to Raiya, "You'll need to take everything off and put this on. We're basically going to do a full body scan of you, using an SAT scanner."

"What's that?"

"It's a new innovation we've employed over the past few years. It gives us all the information a CT and an MRI would give us all in one. One scan maps out the entire body."

"Does it hurt?"

"No, not at all. It's really just a very sophisticated camera, nothing to worry about. It's perfectly harmless."

"Okay…" Raiya replied. She had no idea what he was talking about but didn't care enough to find out more. As long as she got the answers she wanted, that was all that mattered.

Andrea nodded, "With your permission, we're also going to take skin, hair, and blood samples. Our hope is to determine specifically what caused your… genetic mutation."

Raiya nodded, "That's fine…"

"Great. I'll be outside if you need anything. Feel free to come out when you're changed."

Andrea immediately turned and left the room. He closed the door to give her some privacy as she changed.

Well at least he doesn't sketch me out. Raiya thought as she unfolded the cloth. At first, she thought it was a towel to wrap around herself, but she quickly discovered that it was a kind of thin dress.

Once she was changed, she tied the gown together, making sure her backside wasn't exposed and opened the door. *Here we go.*

Drakin
The Story of Raiya

Dr. Castillo had vanished, but Andrea was waiting outside for her. His hands worked quickly to finish prepping some of his equipment on a small machine with blinking lights. He turned when he heard the door opened and quickly closed his case, "Oh good, are you ready to get started?"

"Sure…"

"Great, please follow me."

The room had a few tables and looked more like a galley where food was prepared than an actual lab. Everything appeared to be stainless steel or aluminum. Cabinets lined the walls and a large closet stood on the back next to the door. The clean room was on the left where they had entered from. Another doorway with a keypad stood on the right.

Raiya followed Andrea as he entered his code into the pad and the door slid open. The next room was a narrow hallway. The lights were a dim blue color and the walls were lined with transparent drawers.

Each drawer had a label on it that read 'Sample' with a number next to it. Judging by the contents of the ones she looked at, Raiya figured that most of them were dragon parts. She became slightly unnerved when she noticed a few suspiciously human-looking appendages in the cases that were further from the door.

An eerie hum gave the hallway a rather sinister feeling. Raiya always had an uncanny sense of when danger was near and this place was

Drakin
The Story of Raiya

giving her a similar feeling, "Where are we going?"

"Right down the end of the hall is the main lab," Andrea replied.

"So, who are you in all of this, an assistant?"

"I'm sure that's what Dr. Castillo wants everyone to think," Andrea remarked, snidely. "No, I'm a general surgeon… which pretty much makes me the base's chief doctor and medic when people get wounded. Dr. Castillo is more on the research side of things. I do my best to keep my patients away from him. It's bad for their care and sanity. I'm well aware of the reputation he's gained with them."

"You resent him…"

"No…" Andrea said softly. "Well… not really… I just don't like his attitude or how he views people."

Andrea lowered his eyes, "I apologize… I shouldn't say such things. He is a brilliant doctor and it is true that he's saved many lives. It's just hard sometimes. The man has the worst God complex I have ever seen."

Raiya smirked as Andrea opened the door at the end of the hallway, "Here we go. Have a seat on the bed and we'll get started."

Raiya looked hesitantly at where he was directing her. It wasn't a bed. It could barely even pass as a table. It was a sheet of aluminum with a small pillow at one end. No blankets, no mattress, nothing to cushion her or provide her with any comfort. Below it was a set of cabinets that appeared to be attached to the floor.

Drakin
The Story of Raiya

Raiya released a nervous sigh and did as she was told. Andrea nodded, "Thanks, I know it's uncomfortable, but we'll make this as quick as possible."

Raiya nodded as he reached into one of the drawers below the table and pulled out what looked like a large rubber band. She watched as he rolled up the sleeve to her gown and tied it tightly around her upper right arm, "Can I see your wrist?"

Raiya turned her right hand over, letting him see the light green of her skin. He held it close to his eyes, "Well... I hope that your skin isn't too thick... or this could be difficult."

He opened his case and pulled out a small tube. It had long clasps that looked like butterfly wings on either side. His fingers quickly snapped the red cap off. A small needle now protruded from the lower end.

Raiya's breathing became slightly more rapid as he brought the needle close to her skin, "Wait, what is that? What are you doing?"

Andrea lowered her arm and looked at her calmly, "The needle needs to go into your vein in order for us to collect a blood sample. You'll feel a quick pinch, but it won't be bad. I promise I'll be quick, I'm usually pretty good at this."

"Do I have to?"

"No, but we won't be able to tell you much without it."

Raiya bit her lower lip and nodded. Andrea smiled, "Thanks."

Drakin
The Story of Raiya

He was good on his word. The needle quickly pierced Raiya's skin. She winced, but the pain quickly went away.

The moment the needle was in place, Andrea placed his thumb over it. He pressed some gauze under his thumb and grabbed some white tape to hold it in place. Once the IV was in, he inserted a small tube to the other end of the needle. The tube was attached to a splitter that held three empty glass vials.

Raiya watched as the tube went from being clear to a purplish-blue color. Her blood flowed quickly through the tubes into the vials at the other end. When they were full, Andrea detached the pipping and bent one of the wings, "That should do it."

"Can you take this thing out?" Raiya asked. "I... I really don't want it in anymore."

Her breathing became more rapid, causing her pulse to increase. Andrea looked at her with calm eyes, "We'll take it out soon, I promise. We need to leave it for a little while longer, just in case we need any more samples. It's better than having to stick you again. Just hang tough for a little while longer, okay?"

Raiya nodded as Andrea took the vials over to a lab station on the opposite side of the room. His work area had a large white monitor that glowed in the dark blue light. Other equipment also flashed green and red as it worked.

Andrea placed the vials into a large white machine on the left side of the table and turned back to Raiya, "Lay down for me, please?"

Drakin
The Story of Raiya

Raiya did as she was told and laid down on the table. Andrea came over with a file, what looked like scissors, and a couple small sample jars. He carefully clipped a small amount of hair and put it into one of his jars.

Raiya stared at the ceiling as Andrea gently shaved off a piece of one of her scales, "Uh huh… there we go. I didn't hurt you, did I?"

"No."

"Okay good."

"Dr. Wagner, are you quite finished?" Dr. Castillo's voice erupted over an unseen intercom.

Andrea rolled his eyes, "I'm just finishing up, Dr. Castillo! One moment, please!"

Andrea frowned as he looked at Raiya, "Sorry… okay, this is the last piece, please lay back. Try to relax."

Raiya nodded and laid back on the table. Relax? Was that a joke? She couldn't relax, it was neither big enough or soft enough for that. The lights and the beeping equipment wasn't helping either. She did her best to release the tension in her muscles, but that's as far as she was going to get.

Andrea stepped out of the room behind another glass enclosure. He was soon joined by Dr. Castillo through the door on the opposite side. The glass was slightly tinted, but she could still see them both.

"Okay, are we all set?" Dr. Castillo asked.

"Yes doctor," Andrea replied. "I've collected all the samples and we're ready to begin the SAT scan."

Drakin
The Story of Raiya

"Very good. –Lucy, we are ready to begin phase one."

The robotic voice appeared over the speaker, *"Understood, Dr. Castillo awaiting final clearance to begin."*

Dr. Castillo looked at the readout on his panels, "Rotors look good… RPMs are normal… Okay, begin scan on my mark."

He slowly looked up at Raiya, "3… 2… 1… mark!"

"Initiating phase one, now."

The lights in the room flickered on and the room became as bright as day. A light on the ceiling flashed and began spinning in a circle. It looked like a disc. It was dark in the center, but bright at the edges. The spinning became so fast that it turned the room into a small wind tunnel.

Raiya closed her eyes as her senses were overtaken by a mechanical whooshing sound. Strands of her hair twisted and flew out of control as the wind picked up. She began to shiver as it got colder and colder in the room.

"Are we almost done?" She cried out, trying to make herself audible over the machines.

"Don't worry, it's normal for the temperature to drop a few degrees during the scan," Dr. Castillo replied. "Try to stay still."

A few degrees? It's freezing in here! she thought to herself.

"Beginning Phase Two."

Raiya opened her eyes and looked at the ceiling. The lights in the room flickered from blue to red. The glow was now even more sinister than

Drakin
The Story of Raiya

before. The massive disk was now glowing, but was considerably darker than before, allowing her to see. The room slowly returned to its normal temperature as the machines worked.

Raiya let out a deep sigh as the lights slowly began to fade back to blue and the disk ceased motion. *"Scan complete."*

Dr. Castillo and Andrea came out from behind the glass. The older doctor nodded as Raiya got to her feet, "There now, that wasn't so bad, was it?"

I am so killing him later…

Drakin
The Story of Raiya

Chapter 11

Jagger closed up the back of the jeep, "Yes sir, I tell you, they don't make them like this anymore. You know it took me forever to find the parts to fix it?"

Lt. Rollins nodded, "Yeah I know... the old Islander model... classic. You said the same thing three hours ago."

"Well... everything looks good here. All right, can we go see the carrier?"

"Sorry, Jagger. I told you it was off limits. I took you as close as I could," Rollins replied.

"Oh come on, just a peak?"

"No."

"All right then. I guess..."

Beep Beep "Lieutenant Rollins, report in."

Rollins pressed the black button on the side of his radio, "This is Rollins, go ahead?"

"Lieutenant Bishop is to be returned to his room immediately. Dr. Castillo is on his way there now with his report."

"Copy that, on our way back. —You heard him, Jagger. Let's go."

Jagger nodded and climbed back into the passenger's seat of the humvee, "I guess they finished their tests."

The humvee roared to life as Jagger closed the passenger door. The black gate that surrounded the lot where his jeep was parked closed behind them automatically.

Jagger kept his eyes out the window and watched the scene pass by. The layout was very different from New Framingham. Instead of the military installations surrounding the civilian population, the military took up most of the base. Most of the civilian encampments and residences were off to the east. The center and western sides of town were all barracks and hangars for military vehicles and equipment.

The humvee passed over a small pothole, causing Jagger to turn his attention to the left. He looked past Lt. Rollins and saw the residence quarter. Several apartment buildings had been erected on the rubble of whatever had been there previously. There were also several tents surrounding a new building that appeared to be incomplete. They were red and green in color and clearly enough to house only one or two people a piece.

"Can I ask you something, Lieutenant?" Jagger asked.

"You can if you call me Rollins."

"Breaking protocol?"

"Would you rather us just go back and forth saying lieutenant, lieutenant, lieutenant?"

Jagger chuckled, "Okay fair enough… So why do you keep your civilians up here when you have such a large facility underground?"

"As I said before, there simply isn't enough space to permanently house all of these people. Trust me, I wish we could."

Drakin

The Story of Raiya

"So, what if a dragon were to attack those buildings?"

"Remember the tunnels you saw?" Rollins asked. "In the event of a dragon attack breaching our defenses, each compound has escape tunnels carved out underneath them. It's safer than having them scatter above ground."

"Yeah that I agree with," Jagger thought to himself as the screams of the New Framingham residents echoed in his mind. A tear formed in his eye as he watched his friends and neighbors die all over again.

"Hey, you okay?" Rollins asked, breaking him out of it.

"Yeah, I'm all right."

The people passing through the large encampment were completely destitute. Jagger caught sight of one older woman as the humvee passed by. Her face had deep wrinkles and black soot all over. Her stair was emotionless as she exchanged glances with him. Her clothing looked worn out and covered with patches from multiple repairs. Some of her rags looked as though they were a compilation of various torn up pieces of clothing that had been stitched together.

Each tent had a makeshift fire pit in front of it. A small grilling tray hung over each. Many looked like they had various meats and vegetables being cooked.

"Well at least everyone eats okay," Jagger said.

"Yeah, we do what we can to make sure everyone is fed a healthy meal. We have to ration

Drakin

The Story of Raiya

a lot of the crops, but our underground gardens seem to do the job."

"Where do you get your meat?"

Lt. Rollins pointed beyond the residential buildings to what looked like a fenced in pasture with brown fences, "We have a decent herd of cattle here. The dragons have tried to attack it before, but we keep them in the most secure area. Nothing gets through."

"Impressive, you guys seem to have thought of everything."

The expression on Rollin's face seemed to brighten up, "Thanks, it is tough work sometimes, and we don't really get much appreciation for it, but at least we're able to survive."

The building where the group had been staying was a decent distance from where the jeep was kept. It took them almost half an hour to get back. Having to avoid military processions and any patrols going through the area made their trip even longer, but they didn't want to be stuck behind them for hours.

When they arrived, Jagger hopped out and nodded to Rollins, "Thanks for the lift."

"No problem, any time."

Jagger turned and walked past the guards, through the door. The elevator was open and waiting for him on the ground floor. He proceeded inside as the door closed.

The elevator doors opened on the sixth floor. Raiya was standing on the other side with a look on her face that made his blood run cold. Her left eye twitched and her lower jaw trembled as she stared at him.

Jagger took a step back as her yellow eyes burned into his face, "Are you okay?"

"No. They stuck me with needles, put me on a scanner… I was treated like a lab rat!"

"Sorry. You said you'd be okay, I wanted to come with you but…"

"I know that, but… urgh! I just wish you had been here. This whole experience was unpleasant, to say the least."

Jagger nodded, "Sorry, I was hyper-suspicious of what was going on around here. I wanted to make sure that everything was all set for us to leave when we got the information we wanted. I basically tested the guards to see if they'd try to keep us here."

"Did they?"

"No."

"Okay good."

Jagger stepped off the elevator and sat down on a nearby couch, "So what did they tell you?"

Raiya joined him and sat on one leg, "Not much."

"Really?"

"I've been sitting here for over an hour. They said the blood tests would take time. Dr. Castillo disappeared after the initial round of testing, while his assistant continued to poke and prod me!"

She huffed as she sat down next to him, "I really never want to do that again."

"Hey if it helps us…"

"No!"

Drakin
The Story of Raiya

"All right… I just hope we got what we needed."

He turned to her as she sat back, "Are you all right?"

"Yeah, I guess… It just wasn't fun…"

"Did you find out anything at all?"

"Just some things about how Dragon's Bane works."

"And?"

Raiya looked over at Eric's room, "Dragon's blood is lethal if it comes into contact with the human bloodstream. It works like a disease. You should be safe. Most city kids are immune because of the treatments… but someone who's not inoculated, like a nomad, should be careful."

Jagger nodded, "I'm sure Eric already knows. It's fairly common knowledge to avoid dragon's blood."

"Right."

"Speaking of which… where is Eric?"

Raiya shrugged, "He was asleep when I got back. Fool probably put himself into a food coma."

Jagger chuckled, "Yeah he did kind of stuff himself."

The smile disappeared from his face as he looked at Raiya, "Are you okay?"

"You keep asking me that. My answer hasn't changed in five minutes… that was unnerving, but…"

At that moment, the doors to the elevator slid open, "Raiya?"

Raiya grimaced at the sound of Dr. Castillo's voice. He was accompanied by Andrea as he stepped out into the main suite. Jagger couldn't be certain, but he thought he'd heard whispering coming from the elevator.

"Yeah I'm here," Raiya replied. "What is it?"

"Your results are in and… they're… intriguing, to say the least," Andrea replied.

The two doctors sat down in the chairs opposite the couch as Eric also came out of his room. He picked out a seat at the table and relaxed onto the cushion, "What's going on everybody?"

"We've got news about Raiya," Jagger replied.

"Indeed we do," Dr. Castillo replied. "Raiya… I hope you're ready for this. Because I can scarcely believe it myself."

"What is it?" she asked.

Dr. Castillo looked over at Andrea, signaling him to speak. Andrea looked into Raiya's eyes as he answered her, "We tested your blood and took a close look at your DNA. After we got the results… we recalibrated the equipment and tried again. The same results occurred and… they're almost impossible to believe."

"What were they?" Raiya asked as she shifted uncomfortably in place.

"We're not sure how it happened, but according to our results… you're a hybrid."

"Hybrid, what do you mean?"

Dr. Castillo leaned forward, "It means your DNA is only half human. Believe it or not, you're part dragon. There is no mistaking it."

Drakin

The Story of Raiya

Raiya lowered her eyes, "I had a feeling… I guess I was always hoping for some other explanation."

"What?" Eric asked from the back table. "How is that even possible? I mean dragons are huge! How would you… I mean could you even… what the fuck?"

Dr. Castillo scoffed, "What the fuck indeed… Truthfully, it isn't possible. Even if a human and a dragon could somehow… successfully mate, dragon seed is too large for a human egg."

"Then how could she be a hybrid?" Jagger asked.

"Well I have a theory on that," Dr. Castillo replied. "Dragon's Bane doesn't just attack blood cells. It attacks anything small enough for it to use to make copies. In theory… if your mother was at the right time of her menstruation cycle when she became infected… it is conceivable that one of the cells carried the right genetic material from the dragon. When it attacked your mother's egg, it actually wound up fertilizing it. This is only a theory of course, but it happens to fit what we know."

Raiya sat back in despair. She rested her arm on her stomach and closed her eyes. The skin of her eyelids became gloss as her lips formed a disgusted grimace, "So… my father…?"

Andrea nodded, "Is a dragon, all evidence points to it."

"It gets even more interesting than that," Dr. Castillo replied. "We know exactly which dragon too."

Drakin
The Story of Raiya

Raiya looked up in surprise, "Huh?"

Dr. Castillo nodded, "We recovered blood and tissue samples from the Richmond massacre. You mentioned that your mother was present during that tragedy."

Raiya closed her eyes. She went stiff, as though she anticipated being struck. Jagger also braced himself, having a bad feeling about what was to come. *Oh jeez...*

"We compared a sample of it to your DNA... and it's a match. The dragon lord that attacked Richmond... is your biological father."

Raiya buried her face in her hands, "No... No, it can't be... It just can't... Anyone but him... God... why?"

Jagger rubbed her shoulder, "I'm sorry Raiya..."

She flinched and pulled away, "Don't... don't fucking touch me! Everyone just stay the hell away, leave me alone!"

Jagger lowered his eyes as Eric spoke up, "Well that complicates things. I'm sorry Raiya... –Did you doctors find out anything else that's useful?"

Andrea nodded, "As a matter of fact, we did. You mentioned to Dr. Castillo about her resistance to flame... well her skin has a layer of scaling that we believe shields her from burning. It's reinforced by the fact that she can't regulate her own body heat. In other words, she absorbs it from outside sources. When the dragon flame hit her, she simply absorbed the brunt of it."

Drakin
The Story of Raiya

Dr. Castillo nodded and picked up, "We've also noticed that you have a very unique salivary gland under your tongue. While the rest of your glands produce regular saliva, that one produces an extremely flammable fluid. It looks like it has to be manually activated, but we haven't figured out how that works yet."

Jagger's eyes narrowed, "You mean she can breathe fire?"

Dr. Castillo nodded, "Likely she'd be able to do it as well as most of her dragon brethren, if not better as she could focus it easier due to her narrow mouth. The radio images of her front teeth indicate that they're made from a substance that's not unlike flints. So, likely if she can activate that salivary gland, it would function as a flamethrower."

"Wow…" Eric replied. "That's actually kind of awesome."

"Sure…" Raiya replied sarcastically as she raised her face from her hands, revealing a look of absolute disgust. "It's fucking awesome… So, all this time… the dragon that murdered my family… he is my family."

"Not willingly, I'm sure," Dr. Castillo replied.

"Wait a minute, there is something I don't understand," Jagger said. "If she's half dragon, why does she look more like a human?"

"That… I don't know…" Dr. Castillo replied. "Your physical makeup is that of a human, although many of your organs are definitely dragon. If I had to guess, your mother's genes were likely extremely dominant over those of the dragon, but I can't give you a definitive answer based on what we have."

Jagger looked over at Raiya, "So what do you think?"

"I… I don't know…" she replied. "I don't think this changes anything though. I don't care if we're related or not, he murdered my mother and massacred an entire city. He has to be brought down."

Jagger nodded, "All right, then we should probably get going."

Dr. Castillo stood up, "Go? I don't think so."

Jagger looked up, feigning surprise. He'd had a feeling that they would try to prevent him from leaving, but he'd hoped he'd been wrong, "What do you mean?"

Dr. Castillo looked at Raiya, "You really are a miracle of evolution. You could be the answer we need to fight this war. You have all of the dragon's strengths, but you're still human. With your blood, I could find ways to genetically enhance humanity to be able to withstand dragon attacks. Think of it, a whole new race of human/dragon hybrids. With you around, humanity would quickly become obsolete. I'm afraid I can't let you leave. We need to run more tests, take more samples, and study you in greater detail."

"And if I refuse?" Raiya asked.

Dr. Castillo snapped his fingers. At that moment, five soldiers carrying assault rifles filed into the room, "I'm afraid there is no refusal."

Drakin
The Story of Raiya

Andrea looked up in shock, "Dr. Castillo, we can't do this. It's unethical!"

"Unethical?" Dr. Castillo scoffed. "We're fighting a war we can't win, on the brink of extinction and you want to sit here and debate ethics? Are you mad?"

"What about our oath, do no harm?"

"We'll be doing humanity a world of good by continuing our experiments. Think about it, you could be there at the very beginning of the turning point. Are you going to turn that down?"

Andrea sat in silence for a few moments. He was clearly conflicted, but finally, he nodded, "Fine… I'm with you."

Dr. Castillo smiled, "Good boy, now let's get our specimen out of here."

"Yes… doctor…"

He stood up and extended his hand to Raiya, "Please follow me."

Raiya crossed her arms, refusing to move. The guards pointed their guns at Jagger and Eric. Clicks from the rifles indicated that the safeties had been removed.

Jagger and Eric jumped to their feet, only to have the muzzle of a rifle pointed directly at each of their foreheads. Jagger clenched his teeth, "Shit…"

There was no way out of it. No matter how quick they were, there was no way they could dodge a rifle on full auto, let alone several of them.

Raiya finally stood up and nodded, "Fine… I'll go."

"Raiya, no!" Jagger protested.

"Shut up… just get out of here. It'll be all right."

She was lying and Jagger knew it. They'd treat her like a lab rat for as long as they could and most likely euthanize her to get more of the samples they needed. He wanted to help, but with a fully automatic rifle pointed at them, there was nothing he could do.

Jagger sat back with a defeated look, "You son of a bitch… I swear to God…"

Dr. Castillo got up and ignored him, "We'll make arrangements for you to be dumped outside of the city with that junk heap you call a car. I wouldn't recommend that you try to come back. We won't be as hospitable next time."

Jagger kept his eyes locked on Dr. Castillo as the group surrounded Raiya. They slowly backed into the elevator, keeping their guns pointed on Jagger and Eric as they went.

The moment the door closed, Jagger ran up and pounded on it, "Son of a bitch!"

"You were right…" Eric replied. "You knew all along. Did you hear him? He called Raiya a specimen."

"She's not even human to him. As far as that doctor is concerned, she's a means to an end. A new anomaly to satisfy his curiosity."

"I can't believe it…" Jagger could feel his entire face heat up as he turned back, "Three decades of war does weird things to people. You have to be careful if you're going to survive."

Drakin
The Story of Raiya

"Yeah, I see that now… so what's the plan? They're going to kill her… you know that, right?"

Jagger pushed the down button on the elevator. To no one's surprise, it made a buzzing noise, but did not light up, "Yeah I know… For now, we lay low. We'll have to wait for someone to come up here."

Jagger raised the bottom of his shirt, allowing Eric an obscured view of a pistol. Eric's eyes widened in surprise, "What the… How'd you get that in here?"

"They didn't search me when I came back. I had it under the seat of my jeep."

"All right… so you've got your gun and I've got my knives, now what? We're still trapped here."

Jagger nodded, "When someone comes up, we jump them and try to make our escape."

"You think it'll be that easy?"

"Hell no, I'm not stupid. We'll just have to make things up as we go. What choice do we have?"

"I dunno man…"

Jagger lowered his eyes, "I can't let them kill her. If she dies, we'll have no way of stopping that dragon."

"Yeah… the greater good doesn't know a limit. Trust me, I'm familiar with that one."

"All right… let's just wait for now and see what happens."

Drakin
The Story of Raiya

Chapter 12

Night fell and still no one had come to escort them out. Jagger set up next to the elevator while Eric hid behind a nearby chair. They waited and waited for the inevitable. Eventually, someone was going to have to come check on them.

Jagger was extremely tense. He could only imagine what that sick doctor was doing to Raiya. What kind of tests was he performing? How badly would she be hurt? Worst of all, would she still be alive when he found her? It agitated him beyond belief to the point where he was ready to rip open the elevator and climb down the shaft to help her, "I can't stand it anymore... Come on, help me."

"What are you going to do?" Eric asked.

"If no one's coming, then we're going to rip this door open and find our own way down."

Eric walked over to the other side and tried pulling on the opposite door, but they would not budge, "I don't think this is going to work. This thing is sealed shut."

"We need to get out of here!"

"I know, buddy. Believe me, I know... I just don't think it's going to be this way."

At that moment, the sound of gears turning echoed up the shaft. Jagger's eyes widened, "Someone's coming, get back!"

Jagger stepped to the side, turned the lights off, and pressed himself against the wall next to the elevator. Eric dove back behind his chair and waited to see who was coming out. He quickly drew his daggers and held them out in front of him. He eyed the blades carefully as he waited.

The doors slowly opened and a dark figure stepped out. Its head quickly spun from side to side, "Hello? Jagger, Eric, you there?"

The lights immediately came on, revealing that the dark figure was Andrea. He pointed his gun at the doctor's throat as Eric jumped out with his knife. Andrea didn't even have a chance to let out a startled yelp as Jagger grabbed his collar.

Andrea looked down nervously at the gun, "Jagger...?"

"Give me a reason to pull the trigger, I'm begging you!" Jagger said in as threatening a tone as he could.

Andrea raised his hands, showing that he was unarmed, "I'm not here to fight you. As you can see, I'm all alone. Dr. Castillo doesn't know I'm here. They plan to throw you out of the city in the morning or kill you if you try to put up a fight. I don't think the doctor cares what happens."

"This is unbelievable," Jagger said in anger. "This is supposed to be the last bastion of the United States, the land of freedom! This isn't what you're supposed to stand for."

"Dr. Castillo could care less about that," Andrea replied. "He has his own security force that acts independently of the provincial government. The military doesn't even know what he's up to most of the time."

"That figures," Eric replied. "What do you think, Jagger? Do we believe him?"

"Search him," Jagger growled.

Drakin
The Story of Raiya

Eric nodded and lowered his knife. He quickly padded down the white lab coat and khaki pants. After a few moments, he turned to Jagger with his hands empty, "He's unarmed."

Jagger's eyes narrowed, "What do you want?"

"I want to help you get away. Dr. Castillo lost his mind. I'm willing to put up with a lot of ethically questionable behavior, but he's subjecting her to tests that are completely inhumane and could kill her."

"Has he hurt her?" Jagger demanded as he pushed the gun closer to Andrea's left eye.

"No, not yet," the doctor replied nervously. "He's just stressed her out… but I don't know how long we have until it comes to that."

"Why do you care?" Eric asked.

Andrea glared at Eric, "I took an oath against doing harm. I may be a member of the dwindling class, but I still take my oath seriously. I'm on your side here. If you don't let me help you, Dr. Castillo will have you killed and then dissect her."

Jagger nodded, "Good enough… but how are we going to get out of here?"

"I've got your weapons over here in the elevator. I've also got Lieutenant Rollins securing your truck. I'll get you in to get your friend and then get you out of the city."

"Lieutenant Rollins is in on this?" Eric asked, surprised.

"He's U.S. Military, not Dr. Castillo's men. Don't worry, I know him very well. He's with us on this one."

Drakin
The Story of Raiya

Eric's eyes narrowed, "Then why don't we just let the military know?"

"There's no time," Andrea replied. "They don't even know you're here. By the time you got to anyone in the government, it would likely be too late. Raiya doesn't have that much time and frankly… I can't guarantee that they'd help us. Right now, the best thing we can do is get her away from Dr. Castillo."

Jagger lowered his gun, "All right, let's go."

Eric and Andrea followed Jagger into the elevator. The guns were there waiting for them in a small brown sack off to the side. Jagger's customized bolt gun was leaned against the wall as well. He picked up the bolt pistol and handed it to Eric, "I tuned that gun myself. You'll like it."

"All right," Eric replied.

Andrea took a deep breath as he pressed the 'CC' button, "Here we go. This is going to get rough."

"Yeah it is… you better not try anything, or you're dead."

"Got it," Andrea replied with a nod.

The elevator slowly moved down the shaft. Jagger dropped his 1911 in his pocket and clenched the bolt gun in his hands. His eyes were completely fixed on the door, waiting for it to open.

Jagger's feet felt the additional pressure as the elevator stopped on the bottom floor. Andrea nodded, "The command center is staffed by a skeleton crew at night. Thank a manpower shortage. Most of them aren't armed either."

Drakin
The Story of Raiya

"What about the surveillance cameras?" Eric asked. "We were told that Castillo has eyes all over the base! How are we going to keep him from seeing us coming?"

"The power to keep this whole place is absolutely immense," Andrea replied. "Despite what you've been told, it's unsustainable… thus, to prolong our energy, a lot of key systems are shut down at night. It's not public knowledge, but cameras inside the base are among them."

"They just leave the place undefended?"

"What would we need to defend it from? The entire city is completely fortified from nomad or canban, and dragons can't get in here. There really is no point."

"Be ready all the same," Jagger replied.

Andrea nodded, "Right… by the way, how come I don't get a gun?"

Jagger turned to face him, "Get us out of here alive and I'll give you one."

"Fair enough."

The door opened before he could say anything else. Jagger ducked down and crept out of the elevator. The lights everywhere were turned down low, likely to reserve power as Andrea had said. He pressed himself against the wall and slowly moved down the catwalk.

Clank… Clank… Clank…

Jagger ducked into a crevice in the wall at the sound of footsteps. He focused his ears to try to figure out where the sound had come from.

Clank… clank… clank…

Drakin
The Story of Raiya

It seemed to be coming from the other direction, heading towards them. Jagger held his breath, waiting as the sound got louder.

Clank... clank... clank...

A small light illuminated the catwalk to Jagger's left. If he moved even a little, the soldier would see him. He waited quietly as the footsteps on the metal catwalk became louder. A foot appeared next to the crevice, followed by a second one.

A soldier appeared next to Jagger, oblivious to his presence. Jagger jumped out behind him and pointed the bolt gun at his head, "One false move and not even that helmet will protect you. Drop the gun and I'll let you live."

The soldier immediately did as he was told and raised his hands. Eric came out from the elevator and picked up the assault rifle, "Nice piece!"

"Take your helmet off," Jagger demanded.

The soldier again obeyed his command. As soon as the helmet was out of the way, Jagger could see who he was dealing with. It was the kid they'd seen at the gate.

Jagger froze. The look on the young boy's face was one of complete terror. His eyes were welled up so badly that he could clearly burst into tears at any moment.

"Jagger, we can't kill him... he's just a kid."

"I know..."

The boy looked fearfully at Jagger, "Please let me go..."

Drakin
The Story of Raiya

"We can't do that either…" Andrea replied. "If we let him go, he'll warn the others."

"I won't!" the boy insisted. "I swear I won't."

"We can't take that chance," Jagger replied as he pushed a button on the side of his bolt gun.

"No, don't kill me! Please! Ah…!"

Jagger fired a single blast from his rifle. It struck the boy in the chest, illuminating him with electricity for a moment before disappearing.

The boy fell silent. His eyes closed and he quickly collapsed. Andrea caught the young guard before he hit the ground, "You son of… was it really necessary to kill him?"

"He's not dead," Jagger replied, pointing to the boy's chest. "Look."

Andrea quickly checked his pulse and looked back up at Jagger, "How?"

"I adjusted my gun so that the bolt was on the lowest setting… No matter who it is, I don't want any more people to die needlessly."

"I'm sorry," Andrea replied.

With the guard out of the way, the group moved forward. They had to move slowly and carefully mind their footing. The catwalks were designed to make noise to let someone know if there was an intruder.

Jagger was becoming frustrated. He had to fight the urge to just take off running, knowing that there might be other guards nearby. It was tough, his mind was almost completely focused on a single task; save his partner.

The door which read 'Science Division' was a mere few hundred feet away, but it felt like

Drakin
The Story of Raiya

considerably more than that. Jagger took a few more steps and looked down at the keypad, "Andrea, tell me you have the passcode…"

"Of course," he replied as he stood next to Jagger and quickly punched it in. "This is where I work, after all."

Andrea's hands gleamed in the low lighting from sweat. His breathing was erratic and his hands were shaking so bad that he hit the wrong key. He stopped, took a deep breath and tried again.

Jagger narrowed his eyes as he watched, "Hey, you okay?"

"I've never done this before," Andrea said. "I'm a medic, not a commando. My job is to help heal the people who do this. God, my heart is racing and I don't even know if it's from fear or excitement."

"Just relax. You're doing fine."

Andrea nodded as he wiped his forehead and tried one more time, "O…okay… go ahead in."

Jagger kicked open the door and rushed in. He stopped dead in his tracks when he saw several guards lying on the floor. They weren't bleeding and didn't appear to be injured, so he assumed they were unconscious.

The room they were standing in looked as though it had one time been a glass enclosure. The frame was intact, but glass was scattered all over the floor. Whatever had happened to those soldiers, had completely shattered the enclosure.

Jagger took a few steps into the next area, carefully stepping over the bodies. He stopped when he saw the huge mess, "What the?"

Tables had been overturned, medical equipment was strewn about the floor, and even more shards of shattered glass littered the entire room. Still, there were no signs that anyone had been shot, stabbed, or maimed in any way.

Raiya was standing on the other side of the room with her back turned. She was now wearing a gray uniform that looked like it was a military field outfit at some point. Her fists were clenched at her side and she was looking down at something. She looked like a dark statue, completely frozen in place.

Jagger lowered his gun and took a few steps closer. Raiya obscured the scene going on behind her, but it became clearer as he moved in. Crouched behind her on the floor was Dr. Castillo. He had a look of immense terror on his face.

Jagger slowly crept closer, "Raiya?"

"You're late," she replied.

"No shit... do I even want to know how you managed to take out all these guards?"

Raiya smiled, "I told you I could take care of myself."

"I never doubted you. What are you doing with him?" Jagger asked, pointing at Dr. Castillo.

Raiya glared at the old man cowering on the floor, "Tell him what you were planning on doing to me!"

"Raiya, please..." Dr. Castillo pleaded.

Drakin
The Story of Raiya

"Tell him!"

"Raiya, you don't understand. You're a valuable speci…"

"I will rip out your throat if you call me a specimen one more time!"

Dr. Castillo fell silent as she clenched her teeth, "He was going to try to breed me!"

She turned and glared at Jagger, "Do you believe that? He wanted to try something called invitro fertilization with both human and dragon DNA. Just to see if it was possible."

Jagger looked down at Dr. Castillo with a death glare, "What?"

Raiya turned and followed his gaze, "Did you think I'd let you violate me that easily? What gives you the right…?"

Jagger frowned at him in disgust, "You… humanity may remember how you cured the Dragon's Bane… but the truth is that you are one sick fuck!"

"It was a scientific experiment!" Dr. Castillo shot back. "It was for the betterment of the human race!"

"No, it's rape," Jagger replied. "It's disgusting and it's wrong. –Raiya, whatever you want to do to him, go for it. Just make it quick."

Raiya looked down and glared at the man. She was ready to stab him with her claws but seeing the pathetic look of cowardice on his face gave her pause, "It does me no good to kill you. Like it or not, you have done some good."

Drakin
The Story of Raiya

She knelt next to him, extended her right index finger, and jabbed it into his cheek, just below his left eye. The doctor cried out in pain as blood trickled out of the wound. He pressed his hand against it as he looked back up at Raiya.

She stood up and turned away, "The next time you decide to violate someone's life… look at that scar and hope I never find out about it."

Raiya exhaled as she turned back to Jagger, "I'm ready now."

"Good, let's get out of here," Jagger replied.

The city streets were brightly lit as the group made its way to the exit. Jagger moved carefully, trying to avoid the bright lights.

He quickly looked over at Andrea as they ran, "Were those all of Castillo's guards?"

Suddenly a deafening sound that resembled the shrill cry of a raven filled their ears. Someone had set off an alarm.

"That answer your question?" Andrea asked.

The thuds of loud footsteps quickly replaced the alarm as the loudest sound present. Several soldiers scrambled to the scene as spotlights came on. One swept quickly towards the group.

Jagger pushed Raiya over to the side to try to get her out of view, but it was too late. The group was quickly engulfed in a hot, white light.

"There they are!" shouted a voice out of the nearby shadows.

"Get down!" Andrea shouted.

Raiya dropped down next to Jagger and hid behind a piece of rubble. He handed her the

Drakin
The Story of Raiya

assault rifle they'd taken off the guard and clenched his own, "Hold on, this is going to be bad."

Loud gunshots emanated from the direction the voice came from. Jagger waited until the shooting paused and raised his bolt gun. The electric blasts flew from the barrel and struck the nearby building, causing a small amount of debris to fall.

It was all the distraction they needed. Jagger nodded, "All right, come on. Let's get out of here."

Andrea beckoned towards the entrance, "Quick this way!"

"Eric, go!" Jagger shouted. "I'll follow you!"

Eric nodded and took off running, "See you guys outside! Don't get yourselves killed."

Jagger then turned to Raiya, intent on giving her similar instructions. Raiya looked at him and shook her head, "No way, partner. We're in this together, remember? We'll run together."

Jagger tried to protest, "Raiya…"

"No, not this time. Come on!"

"Stubborn… fine!"

Jagger and Raiya jumped up together. Jagger aimed the bolt gun behind himself and fired several shots at the soldiers as they recovered. This time, the falling debris didn't seem to bother them. They were intent on stopping the friends from escaping.

Raiya turned her gun back and squeezed the trigger. A full spray of bullets left the rifle as she continued to run. The soldiers dropped to the ground to avoid getting hit.

Raiya smiled confidently, "See, I told you I could…"

Her voice was cut off by a clanking sound. Jagger turned to see a soldier take aim at him and open fire.

Raiya cried out in panic, "Jagger!"

There was no way he could react in time. If the bullet hit its mark, he was dead. As the gun went off, Jagger's view of it was obscured by a greenish blur. Raiya stepped into the soldier's line of sight, blocking him from hitting his mark.

"Look out…!" Jagger shouted.

A sharp snap cut through the air. Dark red liquid sprayed from Raiya's hip as she jerked backward and to her left. She was knocked back off her feet, "Ah… shit... that kills… Jagger… I need help!"

Jagger stopped dead in his tracks and grabbed her by the arm, "Come on, Raiya…"

"Come… on… Raiya…" she repeated in a barely audible voice.

Raiya's breathing became labored. Jagger had never been shot before, but he had been bitten and knew what penetrating pain felt like. It would quickly spread throughout her body, making it hard for her to move. They didn't have much time. Her eyes fluttered and she quickly became lethargic. Within moments, her legs collapsed and she lost consciousness.

"Raiya?" Jagger yelled. "Hang on, I got you!"

Drakin
The Story of Raiya

He picked her up and continued running as gunfire went off all around them. They were getting closer to the gate, but it still felt like there were miles between them.

Jagger closed his eyes. He knew that if he was going to get hit, it would be then and there. He braced himself for the pain of a bullet. There was no doubt he was about to get hit when a voice called out to him, "Jagger come on!"

A momentary sense of relief poured over Jagger as he arrived at the gate. He was unharmed as not a single bullet had come close, "All right, let's go!"

Andrea looked over as Jagger carried Raiya in his arms. "What happened to her?"

Jagger beckoned with his chin to her bleeding hip, "She jumped in front of a bullet… she saved me."

On the other side of the lot, the gates were wide open. Lt. Rollins stood on the other side with Jagger's jeep, "Come on, come on, move it!"

Andrea nodded, "Let's get going before we all get shot. Don't worry, I'll see what I can do."

Jagger passed by Rollins and nodded, "Thanks!"

He quickly adjusted the back seat to give Raiya a little more space and laid her down. The back of the jeep wasn't very big, so he had to bend her legs. He had to be careful as each time her legs moved, blood poured from the wound.

Andrea pushed the passenger's seat up and crouched down behind it, "Try to keep us on

Drakin
The Story of Raiya

smooth ground. If she's jostled too much, it could make the wound worse."

"I'll do my best," Jagger replied.

Eric sat down in the passenger's seat with his knees close to the dash, "Wait, what makes you think you're coming with us?"

Andrea turned and sat against the side of the jeep, "I was seen. There's no way I can go back now. Let Dr. Castillo worry about the wounded. If nothing else, it'll keep him away from his experiments. Besides, you could use a doctor here with what you're planning."

"That's true… and Raiya isn't going to get better without help," Jagger sighed as he looked at Rollins, "What about you?"

"My place is here and I don't answer to Dr. Castillo. I'll be fine," Rollins replied.

"You sure?"

"Yeah, this isn't the first time I've had to square off against his cronies. I'll be fine."

Andrea looked over at him and nodded, "Thanks, buddy. Now get out of here, I don't think they saw you. Lay low until we're gone."

"Will do, good luck Andy!"

Jagger grabbed the roll bar and pulled himself behind the driver's seat. Lt. Rollins took a few steps back into the darkness, "Good luck everyone."

A few gunshots prompted Jagger into action. He put the jeep in drive and slammed his foot on the gas. The tires squealed as the jeep took off down the broken road. The pungent stench of

Drakin
The Story of Raiya

burnt rubber filled his nostrils as the jeep pulled away.

Eric turned back and fired a few shots at the soldiers that appeared from the gate, trying to buy Jagger a few minutes, "Won't they follow us?"

"No," Andrea replied. "Dr. Castillo has a lot of influence out here, but not even he can requisition something fast enough to catch us. Charleston's resources are too limited to allow him to go off on an insane adventure. Trust me, we're safe… but I wouldn't go back there."

"I don't intend to," Jagger replied. "Not ever, after that…"

Raiya moaned from the back seat as she slowly regained consciousness. Jagger peaked back when he heard her, "Doc…"

Andrea nodded, "I'm on it."

He slowly turned Raiya on her back and carefully pulled her pants off her hip, "Excuse me…"

He carefully inspected the wound as Raiya opened her eyes, "Am I dying…?"

"From a bullet in the hip?" Andrea asked. "I'd have to be a pretty piss poor doctor to let that happen."

He gently pressed his hand around the wound, searching for any sign shatter bone. He felt the protrusion of the bullet against her hip, "It looks like it's a flesh wound… unfortunately, the bullet is still in her hip."

"Can't believe you guys still use those old guns."

Drakin

The Story of Raiya

"We use whatever we can get our hands on. We have bolt guns and lasers, but we save them for dragons."

Jagger nodded, "All right… so what do you need to do?"

Andrea sighed as he looked at Raiya, "We need to stop somewhere so I can operate."

"Not an option…" Jagger replied. "I know your patrols are probably still out this far. It's not safe."

"If I don't get the bullet out, she could get an infection or lead poisoning. Normally that wouldn't be a problem, but I don't have any way of administering a chelating agent. I'm sorry my friend, but this has to come out now."

Jagger bit down on his lip. If he stopped, it would put them all at risk, but if he didn't, they could lose Raiya. Normally, the logic of numbers would prevail in such a situation, but not here and not where Raiya was concerned. Without her, the whole adventure would be for nothing. Jagger had become too protective of Raiya for that. There was no question, they had to stop.

Luck was with Jagger as an old warehouse came into view. An opening had been blasted in the side that was just large enough for the jeep to get through. He turned off the road and headed straight for it, "Hold on… and hope no one's in there."

Eric's eyes widened, "Jagger… uh, Jagger? What are you doing?"

The jeep crashed through the side of the building. Eric screamed, "Holy shit!"

Drakin
The Story of Raiya

Jagger slammed on the breaks and brought the truck to a stop. The tires screeched and the jeep stopped right as it was about to hit a massive piece of concrete. The debris was large enough that it would have destroyed the truck on impact.

In the back, Andrea did the best he could to brace Raiya. Any sudden movements could make her condition even worse. Once the jeep stopped, he immediately jumped out and sifted through the back, "I had Rollins bring some of my equipment out. Hopefully, he remembered… Ah, here we go!"

He pulled out a clean white sheet and placed it on top of the large slab in front of the jeep, "Bring her over here and keep the headlights on."

Jagger nodded as Andrea pulled his medical case out of the back. He jumped out and picked up Raiya from the back seat, "You okay?"

"It hurts a little… but yeah… I'll manage," Raiya replied.

Jagger saw the tears in her eyes and quickly used the bottom of his shirt to wipe them away, "Looks like it hurts more than a little…"

"I said I'll manage… Stop talking and get me over to the cloth before I bleed out."

Eric also came around from the passenger's side and stood on the far corner of the slab, "What can I do?"

Andrea opened his case and looked at his tools, "I'll need you both to hold her down. This isn't going to be pleasant."

"Don't you have any painkillers?" Jagger asked.

Drakin
The Story of Raiya

"If I were in my operating room, I'd administer anesthetic through an IV… as it stands…"

Andrea pulled out a small syringe, "We'll have to settle with good old-fashioned morphine."

He tapped the needle and made sure it was ready, "Okay Raiya, just a slight pinch… though you probably won't even notice."

Raiya squeezed her eyes closed as Andrea went to work. He quickly jabbed the needle into her skin. As the liquid left the small tube, Raiya slowly began to feel better, "I think it's working… it doesn't hurt as much."

"It should help. The pain won't go away completely, but it should make it tolerable enough to keep you from going into shock while I work."

Raiya released a tense breath, "In other words, not quite excruciating…"

"Exactly."

"Great…"

Andrea quickly went to work. He grabbed a small black cylinder from the case and held it up to Raiya's mouth, "You'll want to bite down on that. Trust me… bullet wounds I can cure. Dental work, not so much."

Raiya opened her mouth, allowing Andrea to place it between her jaws. It had a spongy texture to it but was firm enough that she would have a hard time biting completely through.

Andrea looked down at the wound as dark purple blood dripped out, "Okay… are you ready?"

Drakin
The Story of Raiya

"Do I have any choice?"

"Not really."

Raiya nodded as she closed her eyes, "Fuck it, do whatever you have to…"

Andrea grabbed a small scalpel and a pair of tweezers from his case, "Here we go…"

Andrea reached into the wound with the tweezers. Raiya tensed up and released an agonized grunt as Andrea worked. She began to struggle and instinctively attempted to make him stop.

Andrea looked up at Eric and Jagger. The two had horrified looks on their faces. Apparently, neither of them had seen a surgery before.

"Hold her down, but stay out of my light," Andrea commanded.

Jagger grabbed her arms and crossed them over her chest. He pressed down hard enough to keep them in place, but not so much that they impeded her breathing. Eric grabbed her legs. His arms straightened as though preparing for a vicious kick.

Andrea sighed as he placed the tweezers down next to her, "Fuck… I was hoping the bullet would be right near the surface. It feels like its deeper down."

"How bad is it?" Jagger asked.

Andrea pointed at the wound, "The bullet ricocheted off her hip. It's embedded against the bone. This is going to be difficult. Hold her!"

Jagger gripped her arms tightly and placed her head between his knees so that she couldn't thrash her shoulders. He looked down at her with a

Drakin

The Story of Raiya

sympathetic smile. Tears were welling up in her eyes as she braced herself for what was coming.

Andrea picked up the scalpel and looked into her eyes, "Okay, Raiya... bite down hard."

He carefully cut into her skin just above the bullet wound and made an incision down to the opening. The skin separated without much trouble, giving Andrea a little more room to work with.

Raiya's scream was muffled by the cylinder in her mouth, but it was still ear piercing. Jagger winced as he looked down at her. His ears were ringing.

Raiya's face was soaked with tears. Her eyes looked up at Jagger pleadingly. He frowned and shook his head, "I'm sorry... just a little more, okay?"

Blood flowed out of her wound as Andrea worked. Within moments, his hands were completely stained a purplish red color. He picked up the tweezers and inserted them into the wound, "Okay... here we go..."

Pain shot through her entire body as the tweezers passed through her skin, paralyzing her muscles. She struggled to scream through the cylinder in her mouth, "Stop, please stop!"

With one final thrust, Andrea extracted the bullet. "Got it!"

Raiya opened her mouth to breathe more freely, revealing that she had completely bitten through the cylinder with her sharp rear teeth. The pieces fell from both sides of her mouth.

Drakin
The Story of Raiya

Andrea held the bullet up in triumph, "There. That won't be causing trouble anymore! Nasty little thing…"

"Are… we… done?" Raiya asked through a sob.

"I wish… I still have to stitch up this wound or you'll bleed out."

Raiya sighed as she looked up at Jagger, "You're okay?"

Jagger nodded, "Thanks to you… you saved my life again."

Raiya forced a faint smile before the pain could overtake her again, "You're my partner… that's what we do…"

Jagger placed his right hand on her cheek and nodded, "Damn straight."

Raiya's smile widened as she rested her head against his hand. She breathed heavily, trying to absorb the pain. Her body began to tremble as she lay on the slab with an open wound.

Andrea pulled a small needle and thread out of his pack, "All right… this won't heal properly if I don't stitch it closed. You've already lost a lot of blood, so we need to work quickly."

Raiya closed her eyes as her muscles tensed up in preparation for the agonizing pain, "I'm ready."

Raiya's tough façade wasn't fooling anyone and she knew it. If anything, it was more for herself as a way to hold on to her pride. She'd never liked opening up and showing weakness to anyone if she could help it.

Drakin
The Story of Raiya

Andrea threaded the needle and made several small incisions on either side of the wound. He quickly ran the needle through on one side, then did the same on the other. After every stitch, he pulled the wound closed.

Tears continuously fell from Raiya's eyes. The pain was intolerable. She was starting to wish that it would send her into shock. Anything to end her suffering, "Stop… please… I can't take anymore! Please…"

Andrea shook his head, "Just one more incision."

"No… I can't do it. Please stop!"

"I know you're in pain, but you'll bleed out if I don't finish."

"I don't care… stop!"

Andrea stopped pulling the stitches and looked up, "Jagger?"

Jagger adjusted himself so that he was looking straight down at her, "Please Raiya, we can't lose you here."

She looked up at Jagger with a distressed expression. Her eyes showed nothing but pain. She had fought through it but had almost nothing left.

Jagger looked deep into her eyes, trying to help her calm down, "Do it for me."

Raiya grimaced as she closed her eyes, "Fine… for you…"

Jagger looked up at Andrea and nodded. Andrea immediately went back to work. He made the last incision and pulled the needle through. Once the thread was in place, he pulled the wound as tight as he could, "There we go… one last step."

Raiya's body quivered as he tied the stitching in place and pulled a small white bottle from the case, "You guys better hold her tight… this is going to burn."

He popped the cap off the bottle and carefully dripped its contents onto Raiya's hip. The clear liquid spattered on the wound and cleared away most of the blood that was still seeping out. It then quickly began making a sizzling sound as it bubbled.

That was it. Raiya couldn't stand anymore. She let out an agonized cry as the wound went from stinging to burning, "Fuck… fuck… ah… are… we done?"

Andrea nodded as he pulled a square of gauze out of his pack, "We're done. The stitches will fall out in a week or so."

He gently pressed the gauze against the wound and stretched a white bandage around it. He then wrapped the stretchy fabric around her hip, across her stomach, and gently lifted her off the ground to run the bandage behind her. He repeated this process several times until the bandage was strong and tight, "You did great."

"It still hurts…" Raiya replied softly.

Andrea looked up at her, "I know, and it's going to sting. If it doesn't get better in a few hours, I'll give you another injection of morphine. For now, you'd do well to try to get some rest."

"Can she be moved?" Jagger asked.

Drakin
The Story of Raiya

"Yeah, but I'd be careful. The sutures are being held in place by thin cuts and a lot of hope. If she's not careful, she could rip the whole thing open again. This is a deep wound. I don't even really want her walking. In fact, I'd rather her just rest on the ground for a while."

"Not a good idea, buddy," Eric replied. "A patrol could have easily heard all that screaming. We need to get out of here before we're discovered."

"I understand. Then we need to move gently and lay her into the back of the jeep. We also have to keep her legs as straight as possible."

"In other words, hanging out of the jeep," Raiya replied.

"Pretty much."

"No problem," Jagger said as he ran his hands under her shoulders and legs. With a strong grip, he picked her up and carried her back to the jeep.

She looked up at him with a small grin that was all she could muster through the agony, "Don't get any ideas…"

"Never crossed my mind."

He turned and looked at Eric as Andrea cleaned up, "Can you drive?"

"No problem," Eric replied. "What are we going to do with Doc back there?"

Andrea looked up at them, "You can drop me at the next city we pass by if you want, or I could stay with you."

Jagger sighed, "We're going after the Dragon Lord that took out Richmond, you know. We may not be coming back."

Drakin
The Story of Raiya

"I know that," Andrea replied, "but if you do, you'll have dealt a crippling blow to the dragon hierarchy and given our people a major boost in morale. I'd like to be a part of that, even if my job is to basically just close holes that the dragons poke in you."

Jagger chuckled, "You're either really brave or really stupid… then again I haven't even figured out which one I am yet."

"I have," Raiya replied.

Jagger rolled his eyes, "All right Doc, welcome aboard."

"Thanks… so where are we going anyway?"

"New Framingham…"

Eric looked at Jagger in surprise, "What? Why?"

"I need to see what happened… the dragon that attacked when I was there was a lord. I'm willing to bet that it was the same one. I need to know if what Lieutenant Rollins said was true…"

"Why? I thought they kicked you and Raiya out. I figured that's the last place you'd want to go."

"That's true," Jagger admitted, "but our current situation aside, those people took me in. I wouldn't be here right now if it wasn't for them. I owe them at least this much."

Raiya sucked down a deep breath, "I agree… they weren't nice to me… but that might be the best place to pick up a lead."

"All right… New Framingham it is," Eric replied.

Drakin
The Story of Raiya

The jeep pulled out of the old warehouse and slowly turned back on the road. Jagger was in the back, letting Raiya rest her head on his lap. Andrea sat in the passenger seat with his eyes darting around the darkness.

Eric looked over at him oddly, "You all right, man?"

"How do you guys do this?" Andrea asked.

"Do what?"

"Travel in this death trap…"

"What do you mean 'death trap'?" an angry voice demanded from the back seat.

"Jagger… look at us. It's dark, we're out in the open… A dragon could pick one of us right out of the car and we'd never see it coming."

Jagger shrugged, "Hasn't happened yet. They don't usually attack at night."

"Just because it hasn't happened, doesn't mean it can't."

"I dunno Andy…" Eric said softly. "If a dragon attacks, I'd rather be in a car that I can quickly get out of. Doors can jam and enclosed cars can quickly become a furnace."

"That's true I suppose…"

Jagger reached behind the driver's seat and grabbed the bolt gun, "Andy, here."

Andrea took the gun, "Really?"

"Yeah, you've earned it."

Andy turned around in his seat and planted the gun on the roll bar, "Thanks… I'll keep a lookout for now."

"You know how to use that thing?" Eric asked.

Drakin
The Story of Raiya

"Yeah, I've been through basic. I should be able to hit anything that comes at us."

Jagger looked down at Raiya as she struggled with the pain. Every few minutes, she'd adjust in place and let out a soft grunt. Her eyes winced every time.

"How you holding up?" Jagger asked.

"It hurts… badly… but I'll manage," Raiya replied.

"Sorry."

"For what… you didn't throw me in front of the bullet. I jumped in."

"I know… anything I can do?"

"Do we have any water?"

Jagger nodded and turned to the trunk of the jeep, "Yeah, let me grab it."

He carefully moved so that Raiya wasn't disturbed. The water bottles were resting comfortably above one of the ammo cases. He quickly grabbed one and turned back. Raiya grabbed it out of his hand, ripped the cap off, and quickly emptied the bottle into her mouth.

"Feel better?" Jagger asked as she fiercely finished the bottle.

"A little… at least I'm not as parched now."

"That's good."

"It's the blood loss," Andy replied. "You should start feeling better if you keep drinking. Your body is trying to repair itself."

Raiya nodded. "Jagger… I know we're heading back to New Framingham, but…"

"What?" Jagger asked. "Having second thoughts?"

Drakin

The Story of Raiya

"No, not exactly. It's just… You realize that if a Dragon is there, I may not be able to protect you all. I don't think I'll be at one hundred percent by the time we get there."

"It'll be okay. You're not the only one who knows how to take care of themselves."

"I hope so. Dragon Lords are nothing to mess around with."

New Framingham
Westcon Territory
Formerly Massachusetts

Drakin
The Story of Raiya

Chapter 13

The group arrived back in what was once Massachusetts. The sun was just beginning to rise in the distance. They pulled onto the remains of Route 9 and headed west.

The mood was quiet and somber in the jeep as everyone waited and watched the trees. Jagger got the feeling that everyone knew what they were likely going to see, but still waited and watched. The trees were like a relentless wall that would not permit them a view of the city that once stood beyond.

To Jagger, this was like returning to the scene of the crime. He could only hope that maybe someone had survived under all the rubble. Maybe someone was waiting to be found.

Raiya had slept through most of the trip. Her wound wasn't life-threatening but was still serious.

"How's she doing?" Andrea asked.

"She's sleeping. It looks like the color is coming back to her skin."

Andrea nodded, "She lost a lot of blood and her anatomy is very different from what I'm used to seeing... but if her human half has any say, she should make a full recovery."

"Good to know..."

As the jeep passed through what used to be the town line between Natick and Framingham, the trees slowly began to clear. A large tower of dark smoke could be seen in the distance. It climbed

Drakin
The Story of Raiya

several feet into the sky and disappeared in the clouds.

Jagger sat back and sighed, "So it is true…"

"Are we going?" Eric asked.

Andrea looked back at Jagger, "There could still be people alive in there. I was told to prepare for casualties, but the aerial surveillance revealed nothing. So, I was told to stand down."

"Let's go…" Jagger said softly.

The jeep pulled a left onto a side road and approached the massive wall in the distance. It was a familiar sight for Jagger at first. Things changed when more details came into view. Burn marks and holes appeared on the once-mighty wall. Half of it had been completely knocked over. The gate had been smashed and burnt corpses were scattered about the grounds.

Eric drove the jeep through the gates and stopped in front of the trucks. Jagger looked out at the old army vehicles. The tires were melted, the green paint was covered over in black burns, and the cabins had been all but melted, "They didn't even stand a chance…"

Raiya sat up and looked around, "Wow… I didn't think it would be this bad."

Jagger looked at the blood-stained bandage on her hip, "How you doing?"

Raiya nodded, "Better… it doesn't hurt as bad."

"Good… we should probably look around. – Eric, keep driving. Let's get to the town square. Keep going straight."

"You got it," Eric replied.

Drakin
The Story of Raiya

Horrific scenes frozen in time played out before Jagger's eyes as they drove. Burnt husks that had once been human beings were standing, kneeling, and laying in agonized positions. Some had their hands raised, while others covered their heads in a fetal position.

It made Jagger feel nauseous. These were people he'd lived with for a good portion of his life. Seeing them burnt and twisted like this made him struggle against the urge to vomit.

"Hey… you okay?" Raiya asked.

"No, I feel sick," Jagger replied, not looking at her.

Raiya stared at each burnt corpse they passed and rubbed Jagger's arm, "Did I do this? Did I somehow bring that Red Dragon Lord down on them?"

Jagger sat back as he finally regained control, "How? The thing attacked at night. It didn't even attack anywhere near where you were staying."

"No, I mean the second time. Did it come back looking for me? Is it possible that after telling its buddies about me, they decided I was some kind of threat?"

Andy eyed another mound of burnt husks, "Look at that. A family… two children and an adult. This is what happens…?"

"It happened in Richmond," Raiya replied.

"And in Foxboro," Jagger added.

Andy looked like he was going to be sick, "… it'll happen in Charleston too I bet…"

Drakin
The Story of Raiya

"Unless something changes," Jagger replied darkly, "Yeah probably. –Eric, I'm surprised the nomads haven't come by."

Eric kept his eyes on the road, careful not to hit any bodies, "They will eventually. Typically, they don't go near attack sites for a few days. The dragon could always be nearby, but they'll come eventually. They'll check for survivors and bury the dead like they usually do and salvage anything they can use."

An uncharacteristically sad look appeared on Raiya's face. "Unless we find a way to bring down the Dragon Lords, this will be the entire world."

Andy didn't respond as the jeep pulled into the city square. Everything was burnt. The dragon that attacked had done a thorough job of completely going over every inch of space. Buildings had been smashed, anything metal had been melted away. Where there was once green grass and trees, there were now only skeletons and soot. Nothing was spared.

Eric stopped the jeep at the roundabout in the middle of the square. He got out and pulled the seat forward for Raiya. She carefully stood up and stepped over the seat. Jagger jumped out the back with Andrea right next to him.

"I don't see any evidence of a rescue mission," Andy said glumly. "Wouldn't the Westcon have come to look for survivors?"

Jagger shook his head, "We're not much better off than Fort Charleston. The Westcon would have sent a scout plane out to take a look, survey and see if there were any survivors, but it's unlikely they would have set down unless they saw evidence of life."

"And there isn't any…"

"Doesn't look like it," Jagger said. "The dragon did a pretty thorough job."

"I still want to look," Andy insisted.

Raiya stepped forward with a limp, "So do I…"

"All right," Jagger replied. "Let's split up. We'll cover more ground that way."

Eric nodded, "I'll go check the large buildings over by the trucks."

"I'll stick around here," Andy said. "There are plenty of good hiding places to check out and if anyone is still alive, I can set up a treatment camp."

Jagger got back behind the wheel of the Jeep, "Right, we'll meet back here. I'm going to go check the residences. Two hours sound good?"

Raiya climbed into the passenger's seat, "I won't get far with this damn gunshot in my leg. I'll go with you."

"All right."

Jagger waited for her to climb in and nodded to his friends, "Two hours, be safe."

The jeep pulled away from the city square and headed for the building where he used to live. Raiya's eyes focused on the burnt trees and smashed buildings, "Hard to believe… only a few days ago…"

She lowered her eyes and sat back, "This is my reality. This is what I saw when my grandparents were killed. Had those nomads not taken me in... I probably would have starved to death."

"How old were you?"

"I think about eight...?"

"Must have been awful."

"You have no idea," Raiya replied. "I was a little girl... I was starving and went to the gates of some nearby towns begging for food. I even offered to work for it... No one cared, no one helped me. The ones that told me to leave were the nicer ones. I took a fist to the face more than once."

"I thought you said you scavenged."

"I did, but I was still young. What did you think I was going to find?"

Jagger shrugged, "Not much, I suppose."

A look of anger appeared on her face, "I was near death... I could barely move, my stomach hurt, and I was so skinny..."

Raiya placed a hand on her stomach. Jagger wasn't certain if the pained look on her face was for her bullet wound or her memory. Either way, he kept quiet to let her vent, "I finally just collapsed in the dirt and soot. I didn't have any fight left. That's when a group of passing nomads found me. They taught me to hunt, how to fight, and above all, how to survive. I wouldn't be alive today if it wasn't for them."

"Where are they now?" Jagger asked.

"I'd assume most of them are dead. Nomadic groups don't tend to stick around one place for very long. They also don't tend to stay together.

For better or worse, they often go off on their own because a large group of people is a tempting target for a dragon…"

Jagger frowned, "But with the growing number of juvenile dragons…"

"Exactly… lone nomads would get picked off as easily as a group would."

Jagger turned the next corner and came to the building that he used to call home. He stopped the jeep, got out, and looked around. The building was little more than a skeleton. The brick siding was almost all that was still standing.

Jagger climbed the concrete staircase at the entrance and looked down into the pit below. The floor had collapsed onto the lower level, making entry impossible. He didn't even recognize it anymore.

Jagger sighed, "Yeah there's no one alive down there."

He was about to turn and leave when the sound of moving rubbed caused him to turn back. A hand appeared from behind one of the larger pieces of debris. It waved slowly, indicating that its owner was still alive.

Jagger quickly jumped into action, "Raiya, someone's still alive down there!"

Raiya carefully got out of the passenger side and limped over to the doorway. Her eyes widened when she joined him on the stoop, "It's so small… gotta be a child. How do we get down there?"

Drakin
The Story of Raiya

Jagger scratched his head with his right hand, "I… I don't know. If only we had some rope or…"

He quickly turned and looked at the front of his jeep, "Or a winch!"

Raiya looked at him oddly, "What are you talking about?"

Jagger ran back to the jeep and pulled it close to the stairs. He let the engine idle as he got back out. Raiya's eyes followed him as he began pulling a hook and metal line off a large black spool on the front of the jeep.

Jagger tugged until he was confident that he had enough, "I hope this old thing still works."

He flipped the switch on the side of the spool back towards the jeep. A loud cranking sound filled his ears as the winch began to wind the cord back into place. He stopped it and pulled the switch towards him. Again, it turned but this time it unwound the chord.

Jagger smiled as he clapped his hands together, "Awesome, we've got life!"

He immediately wrapped the cord around his waist and used the hook to lock it in place. Raiya touched the cord he'd wrapped around himself, "Are you sure this is safe? This looks like it might hurt."

Jagger nodded, "Yeah if it gets pulled too tight, it could, but I'm only going down one floor."

"All right. What do you need me to do?"

Jagger pointed to the winch, "Pull the lever towards you. That will lower me down. Then when I'm ready to come back up, push it back towards the jeep."

"Right…"

Jagger climbed over the side as Raiya flipped the switch. He was slowly lowered down to the rubble below, "Be right back!"

"Just be careful down there. The ground might not be that stable."

"Will do."

It was a slow ride as the winch wasn't very big, but it got him to the ground floor within a few minutes. He quickly undid the cord and dropped it on the ground as he ran over to the hand. The floor was little more than a few feet of ash and rubble, making it difficult for Jagger to run, but he managed without slipping.

Whoever it was had apparently heard him coming and began to wave more frantically. Their fingers stretched out, searching, hoping that a hand was nearby that would clasp them. The short, thin fingers waved in the air, trying to reach.

Jagger grabbed the hand as he reached the pile of rubble, "Gotcha!"

He quickly knelt down and slowly began to pull large pieces of debris away from the arm. Once the smaller pieces were clear, he went to work on the remaining slab.

"Any luck?" Raiya called from behind.

"No… there's a pretty big piece of rubble down here on top of this person… looks like it was part of the ceiling."

"Can you get it off?"

Drakin

The Story of Raiya

"I'm trying."

"Be careful… if you move it the wrong way…"

"I know," Jagger replied. "Trust me, I'm being careful."

Jagger grunted as he pulled the gray piece of concrete towards him. It was incredibly heavy, forcing Jagger to put all of his weight and rely on gravity to do the rest. The only way to get it to move was by pulling it towards himself and hoping that he could get out of the way in time.

"Don't move," Jagger said.

No response.

"Hey, can you hear me?"

The hand waved in response.

"Are you injured?"

The hand waved more quickly.

Jagger nodded, "All right, I'm going to pull this thing off you. Don't move!"

Jagger leaned back and carefully began to pull. The concrete was even heavier than it looked. After pulling it up high enough, he quickly got on the other side and began to push. The crumpling sound of rocks being crushed under the weight of the concrete filled his ears, "Just a little further… a little more."

The crumpling intensified as the debris from the ceiling began to move freely. The weight was now working in Jagger's favor. He pushed the rock out of the way much easier.

Underneath was a young girl with dark brown hair, wearing a filthy white dress. She was only seven or eight years old at best. Her forehead had

Drakin
The Story of Raiya

a large gash that was bleeding out and her left eye was black. It looked like it had been damaged.

She looked up at him with her one good eye. The expression on her face reminded Jagger of Raiya. It was complete stoicism. She was badly injured, but even that didn't seem to faze her. Her face was completely emotionless.

Jagger recognized her immediately, "Oh my God! Miranda… Miranda Foster? You survived?"

The little girl looked at him lifelessly but did not respond. Jagger smiled warmly, "Can you speak?"

Again, no response. All he got was a blank stare.

"Find someone you know?" asked Raiya.

"Miranda Foster… the little girl who unmasked you at Jerry's."

"Really? Is she okay?"

"No," Jagger replied. "She's badly hurt… I think one of her eyes is damaged… and she won't speak."

"We'd better get her to Andrea."

"All right, I'm coming."

Jagger turned to Miranda, "Can you walk?"

The little girl looked up at him and still refused to speak. Jagger got up and was about to pick her up when she got to her feet. She shook her head with a frown.

Jagger nodded, "You don't want to be carried. Got it."

She followed Jagger over to the wall. He quickly wrapped the cord around his waist and reached out to Miranda, "I know you don't want to be carried, but can I just get you up to safety?" Miranda nodded and stepped forward. Jagger picked her up by the arms, trying to be careful, "All right Raiya, pull us up!"

Raiya pushed the lever back towards the jeep. Jagger felt a quick tug and was lifted up the wall. The cord quickly got tight on his chest as it pulled, but he ignored it. He only had a little bit further to go.

As soon as he was in arm's reach, Raiya took Miranda from him. She grabbed the girl by the waist and placed her on the ground. The two girls looked at each other silently for a moment.

Raiya frowned, "This... is so cruel..."

"Hey um... a little help, please?"

Miranda remained silent as Raiya turned to grab Jagger and help him up. She tugged gently on his arm until he was far enough up to climb.

Jagger pulled himself back onto solid ground as Raiya turned her attention back to Miranda. The massive cut on her forehead was bleeding badly. "Not good... God only knows how much blood she's lost."

Raiya ran to the back of the jeep and grabbed one of Andrea's medical cloths. She bit down on the fabric and cut it with her back teeth. The cloth easily ripped as she pulled on it.

Miranda stood by watching and waiting as Raiya cut the cloth into strips. She remained motionless. Was she somehow not feeling the pain?

Jagger began to wonder if she was completely there mentally. Was it possible that she somehow didn't even realize that she'd been hurt? He wasn't a doctor and had never seen anything like this before. The way this little girl was behaving was creepy at best.

As soon as she had enough straps, Raiya quickly knelt down next to the little girl and wrapped the first one around her head. Blood immediately stained right through the white cloth as she worked.

Raiya wrapped the second cloth around Miranda's head, covering her eye. Just like before, the girl's blood-stained through. Raiya frowned as she looked the poor girl in her one good eye. Her lips mouthed the words 'I'm sorry.'

Miranda came to life and looked up at Raiya. Her blank stare caused Raiya to freeze in place for a moment. Jagger watched from a distance to see what would happen.

A smile suddenly appeared on Miranda's face. She reached up to Raiya and touched her cheek. Her index finger ran across one of Raiya's facial scales. The skin of her hand was cold as ice.

Raiya pressed her hand against the child's and sandwiched it between her cheek and palm. Her eyes filled with tears as she looked sympathetically at the child.

"Everything okay?" Jagger asked as he appeared behind Raiya.

Raiya lowered her eyes and spoke in a whisper, "We... need to get her to Andrea."

"You okay?"

"Don't worry about me, she needs help."

Jagger nodded, "All right then let's start heading back."

He turned to pick Miranda up and place her in the back seat. A fearful look appeared on the girl's face, stopping him in his tracks. She took a step back and shook her head. Jagger knelt down close to her, "Miranda, it's me, Lieutenant Bishop. Do you remember me?"

Miranda didn't respond. Her one eye looked past Jagger to something out of his field of vision. Jagger followed her gaze and noticed that she was looking at Raiya, "You want her to pick you up?"

Miranda nodded. Jagger stood back up and looked at Raiya, "Looks like you've made another friend."

Raiya already looked like she was going to have a breakdown. Her eyes were fighting back tears and she was biting down on her lip to prevent it from quivering, "What?"

"She wants you to pick her up."

Raiya looked at her for a moment and then back at Jagger. A confused expression appeared on her face, "Why?"

"Don't ask me, she just wants you."

"I… all right…"

Raiya knelt down and extended her arms to the girl. Miranda quickly stepped forward and threw her arms around Raiya's scaly neck. Raiya gently extended her arms around Miranda's back and legs. She slowly applied pressure as she lifted the girl off the ground, "Okay… let's put you in the back…"

Drakin
The Story of Raiya

Miranda reached out and grabbed the roll bar of the jeep to support herself. Raiya rested her gently on the seat and let her get comfortable, "There, is that better?"

Miranda adjusted herself in the seat until she could lean back and relax. When she was finally settled, she looked up at Raiya.

"Are you... comfortable?" Raiya asked.

Miranda looked at her and nodded. Raiya forced a smile as she went around to the other side and got into the jeep. Jagger was already in the driver's seat waiting for her. Raiya sat down, huffed, and turned her head so that she was facing away the other way.

"You okay?" Jagger asked.

No response.

"All right... This is going to be a quiet trip."

Raiya wasn't about to answer. It was a stupid question. Of course, she wasn't okay, what in the world made him think otherwise. She was still toiling with her own fears that all of this was her fault.

Raiya just stared out at the ruins as the jeep picked up speed. Her eyes fluttered as she watched the damage and debris pass by. She quickly wiped the tears away and let out a pained breath. She didn't want to look behind her. Doing so would mean having to face the stare of a child she was likely responsible for hurting.

"Do you want to put the seatbelt on?" Jagger asked.

No response.

Drakin

The Story of Raiya

"Great… two people who don't talk. I can't believe I'm saying this, but we need to get Eric back here now. He'll pick up the slack."

Chapter 14

The jeep arrived back at the center of town within a few minutes. The breaks screeched as it came to a stop. Jagger jumped out as soon as he put the truck in park, "Doc... Andy!"

Andy poked his head up from a pile of rubbed a few hundred feet from the center, "What is it?"

"We found someone over by the residences. She needs help, now!"

Andy jumped up and ran to the back of the jeep. Miranda looked at him without any sign of emotion. Andy's eyes narrowed as he reached for her. She immediately backed up on the seat and shook her head.

Andy smiled warmly, "I just want to look at your wounds. I'm here to help you."

She turned and looked at Raiya as though asking her if Andy was safe.

Raiya looked back at her and nodded, "It's okay, he's a friend. You can trust him."

Miranda hesitantly moved forward to the edge of the seat and leaned out to him. Andy gently began to work on her bandages, "Thank you... you're a very brave little girl."

As the bandages fell away, Andy went pale. He did the best he could to hide his concern from the Miranda, but he doubted that his friends didn't see it. This was bad, very bad.

Andy reached into his case and grabbed a spray bottle, some gauze, and bandages. He quickly shook the spray bottle and showed it to Miranda, "This is disinfectant. It's going to

Drakin
The Story of Raiya

prevent your cuts from getting worse, okay? It may sting a little."

Raiya quickly took her hand as Andy went to work, "It's okay..."

Miranda flinched but didn't cry as Andy sprayed her with the chemical. He was certain that it stung, but she barely seemed to respond. Once he was finished, he quickly dabbed her eye with the gauze and then rewrapped the wound in fresh bandages.

"Hey, guys!" Eric said as he appeared from the nearby brush behind them.

Jagger turned to face him, "No luck?"

"Sorry..." Eric replied. "All corpses... no one could have survived this kind of onslaught."

"One person did..." Raiya said in a glum voice.

Andy finished the bandage and looked over at the group, "Eric, can you come here and keep an eye on... —What's your name, little girl?"

No response.

"Can you hear me?"

Miranda just stared blankly at him.

"Hmm... blink twice if you can understand me."

Her eye immediately blinked twice as Andy had asked.

"Okay good, thank you for helping me. We're going to get you fixed up, okay?"

Again, Miranda just stared at him.

Eric leaned on the side of the jeep, "Hey there, are you hungry?"

He reached back into the trunk and pulled out some dried meat that had been given to them by the nomads, "Here, try it. It's really good."

Miranda grabbed it and ripped it apart vigorously with her teeth. Eric frowned, "You must have been down there since the attack. You were starving, weren't you?"

Andy stepped away as Eric continued talking. A look of concern was on his face as he turned to Raiya and Jagger. Jagger frowned and spoke in a low voice, "Bad news, Doc?"

Andy looked back at Miranda to make sure that Eric was keeping her attention before speaking. Miranda looked like she was perfectly distracted by the food, so he turned back, "It's not good. That cut needs to be stitched up, but that's not the worst part…"

"What is it, Andy?" Raiya asked.

"Her eye… whatever happened, it looks like it was gouged. There's no way to repair it. Even if I had an ophthalmology team… I doubt we could save that eye."

Raiya turned away with an angry look on her face, "Is she going to make it?"

Andy shrugged, "If I had access to my lab… she'd have a better chance if I had somewhere to perform the surgery to remove her eye. I don't have the right tools or the proper environment."

"So, we'll have to find one then," Raiya replied. "Maybe Eric knows something."

"That's not the only concern here though…"
"What else?"

Drakin
The Story of Raiya

"The girl seems to be suffering a rather advanced case of PTSD… she's showing symptoms of psychological trauma, including almost no reaction to pain or outward stimulus, and elective mutism. Even if she does survive, it'll be a hard road for her."

"PTSD?" Raiya asked.

"Post-traumatic stress disorder. It's just what it sounds like," Andy replied. "She's experienced a traumatic event that has affected her psychological well-being. We saw it all the time with soldiers who were coming back from heavy fighting."

"What happens?"

"There are several symptoms… flashbacks, nightmares, depression, emotional detachment… only time will tell which ones she's going to live through."

"What's the cure?" Raiya asked.

"Cure?" Andy asked in surprise. "No, there is no cure. This isn't like simply administering medication and it immediately goes away. There are medications that can treat her… and therapy, but… it's just something she'll have to live with. This is considering she survives at all."

"She'll survive… she has to…"

"I hope so."

Eric smiled at Miranda as he tried to get her to speak, "Come on little girl, just one word? I've got a nice piece of candy for you if you'll just say your name."

Drakin
The Story of Raiya

Miranda just stared at him blankly. She showed no sign of any interest in the offer of candy.

"I'm Eric, what's your name?"

Miranda just turned away, clearly uninterested. Eric frowned, "Now that's just cold…"

The rest of the group returned to the jeep. Jagger climbed behind the wheel. He didn't even get a chance to start the truck before a shrill scream came from the back seat. The cry sent chills down his spine and caused him to flip around. Miranda had gone completely pale and was shaking violently.

"What the hell?" Eric asked.

Andy grabbed her arm and squeezed right at the wrist, "Her pulse is through the roof… what in the…"

The mighty sound of a hollow roar cut Andy off. A massive object appeared out of nowhere and blocked out the sun. It was so large that the resulting shadow covered the entire town.

Raiya's eyes adjusted to the difference in lighting as the object took shape, "Dragon!"

Andy picked Miranda up out of the jeep and hid her behind some debris while Jagger and Eric scrambled to get their weapons. Jagger grabbed his bolt gun and tossed the U.S. assault rifle to Eric, "You ready for this?"

A nervous grin appeared on his face, "Are you?"

Raiya quickly rummaged through the back of the jeep, trying to find something to use as a weapon. She pushed a few shirts out of the way to reveal her nomadic knife resting underneath them, "Yes!"

Jagger peered through the scope on his gun, "God… look at the size of that thing…"

Raiya stepped out in front of them, "Jagger, what kind of scales does it have?"

"What?"

"The scales, damn it! Tell me what the fucking scales look like!"

Jagger peered into the small tube as the dragon slowly came closer, "It's black… darker than any dragon I've ever seen before. It's almost like a shadow…"

"Does it have red tips on the scales?"

Jagger moved the gun to the right to get a better view. There was a brief moment of silence before he lowered the gun. His face was almost as pale as snow. There was a quiver in his voice as he spoke, "Yes… and it has yellow eyes."

Eric stepped up next to Jagger with his rifle aimed at its chest, "No… It's the dragon lord that sacked Richmond!"

Raiya turned back and glared at it, "My father…"

Andy peaked out from behind the rubble, "Raiya, if that's true then you need to be careful! That dragon has killed more people than any of the other ones combined!"

She clenched her teeth and stepped forward. The look of determination in her eyes was unmistakable, "Not anymore… not if I have anything to say about it."

Drakin

The Story of Raiya

The dragon slowly lowered itself to the ground. One thrust of its wings created a massive burst of wind that sent ash and debris flying. Raiya blocked her eyes with her right arm as Jagger pressed his back against the jeep, "Let him have it!"

Both Jagger and Eric unloaded their weapons on the dragon. The bullets from Eric's gun just seemed to bounce off its scales, while the bolts were merely absorbed into its armored body. It barely even seemed to notice the attack.

The impact of the dragon lord's feet caused the ground to shake underneath him. Raiya bent her knees to keep from losing balance as she took another step towards the massive beast.

Jagger stepped forward, "Raiya, get away from there!"

Raiya raised her hand, signaling him to stay back, "Not this time. This is my fight. Jagger, do not interfere!"

"But Raiya!"

"Promise me! I don't want you getting hurt!"

"But…"

"Jagger!"

Jagger lowered his eyes, "I refuse to make that promise. As long as you're doing okay, I'll let you have your fun… but…"

"I can survive dragon's fire, you can't. Stay back!"

"Raiya… ugh, fine!"

Its eyes were as bright a yellow as Raiya's. Its smile was hideous, "I thought Raki'Agr was

Drakin

The Story of Raiya

making up stories… now I see that he was telling me the truth. What manner of abomination are you?"

The thunder of the dragon lord's voice was deafening. Jagger had to cover his ears when it spoke, but it didn't seem to bother Raiya. She took a step forward with her eyes fixed on the dragon. She still had a small limp but was clearly trying to hide it. "You destroyed Richmond."

"Heh… that city to the south put up the best fight I've ever seen. It was almost a shame to crush them."

Raiya pulled her dagger off the back of her shirt, "You killed my mother…"

"I have killed many humans," the dragon lord replied. "I don't remember specific ones. Do you remember every single insect you've ever stepped on?"

"You won't be stepping on anyone else."

The dragon lord laughed, "Have I lived through so many uncountable eons…? Have I traveled and survived the challenges of the Cosmos? Have I bested the warriors of this world, only to fall under the blade of an insignificant whelp? I knew killing these people would draw you back out… now I can finish you myself!"

Raiya didn't move. Her eyes met those of the dragon lord. It returned her gaze and regarded her for a few moments, "Raki'Agr was right about you… your eyes are quite striking. Too bad they have to be destroyed."

The dragon lord arched its neck and then thrust its head forward. A massive spray of fire emanated from the dragon's mouth. It immediately consumed Raiya and continued to spray past her until it impacted on a piece of debris that was large enough to stop it.

The screeching sound from the dragon's mouth was beyond tolerable. Jagger dropped to his knees with his hands pressed against his ears as the fire continued to spread. It didn't help much, but it was better than nothing.

Eric was in no better shape, "You've got to be kidding me… is this really what we've been hunting for?"

Jagger couldn't see Andy or Miranda, but he was certain that they were probably no better off. All he could do now was watch Raiya get pummeled by the flame. There was no way to stop the vicious attack. He quickly grabbed a water bottle out of the back of his jeep and hoped he'd get a chance to use it.

The dragon lord's mouth slowly closed as the flame died down. The beast arched its neck and smiled as it watched the massive wall of flame it had created die down. Clearly, it thought that Raiya had been disintegrated.

As the flames weakened, the dragon lord's yellow eyes became wide, "It can't be…"

Raiya was still standing where she had been previously. She was surrounded by the flame wall, but this time, not even her clothes were harmed. She was completely stiff as steam poured off her body. The expression on her face was stoic, as though she were fighting back pain.

Drakin
The Story of Raiya

Jagger breathed a sigh of relief as Raiya continued to stare down the dragon lord. Eric was in complete disbelief, "How…? I heard about Raiya, but how did her clothes survive?"

"They were made at Fort Charleston… maybe they have some flame-resistant material?" Jagger theorized. "What I want to know is how did her dagger survive? The last one didn't!"

Eric smiled, "Dragon bone…"

"Oh, all right."

"What are you…?" the dragon lord asked.

Raiya panted as she looked up into his eyes, "Don't you recognize your own daughter…?"

The dragon lord recoiled its neck again and looked down at her, "What madness are you speaking?"

"Your blood infected my mother… she gave birth to me… nine months later… We've confirmed it."

"That's impossible."

"It's not… how else do you explain me? How else do you explain my eyes? They're the same as yours… father!"

The dragon lord looked closely at Raiya and inspected her eyes carefully, "Could it be…?"

The flame around Raiya was extinguished by the breath of the dragon lord as it moved in close. Its nostrils sounded like the roar of a jet engine as they sucked in each breath, "There is a familial odor about you… could it really be possible?"

"It is… father… somehow… it happened."

A look of disgust appeared on the dragon lord's face, "Kin or not… you are a disgusting abomination. Dragon blood must never be watered down like this…"

The dragon lord recoiled its neck again, ready to unleash more flame. At that moment, Raiya noticed a terrible scar right near its head. Likely that was where the blood had spilled from that resulted in her birth. The beast had no other visible scars.

The dragon lord sneered, "It's sickening just to look at you. I'll kill you, and then your friends. No one will ever remember that you ever existed!"

As before, the flame was relentless and almost knocked Raiya from her feet. It was excruciatingly painful, but she faced it and did not scream. *I won't let you… hurt anyone… else!*

Remembering what Dr. Castillo had told her, and observing dragons use flame, she immediately rolled back her tongue, tense the muscles of her mouth and dropped her lower jaw, "No!"

To everyone's amazement, flame flowed in the opposite direction. The fluid that Raiya shot from under her tongue caught the dragon lord's fire and ignited. It grew in strength as she opened her mouth wider.

Within moments, her flame rivaled that of the dragon lord. She was holding her own, despite being hurt. Her flame pushed back against the dragon lord's with surprising force and power.

Eric's eyes widened as he watched, "Holy shit…"

Drakin
The Story of Raiya

Raiya thrust her head forward, forcing the flame to go even further back towards her father. The dragon lord strained its neck as it pushed back against the unexpected force of Raiya's flame. They were both getting worn down quickly.

Raiya realized that she couldn't hold her flame any longer. Her whole body still burned from the previous attack. She was spent and her strength was gone. The flame died out, leaving her defenseless. To her surprise, the dragon lord had been unable to maintain his either.

Raiya had one chance and only one; the scar on the dragon lord's neck. The scales that used to protect it had fallen off when the injury healed, leaving a thin layer of skin that might be vulnerable. She used her last ounce of strength and lunged forward with her knife.

The blade plunged into the small scar, spewing blood in every direction. The dragon lord roared as it shook its head from side to side. It thrust its head out violently, trying to dislodge the dagger.

Raiya was knocked backward by the force of the dragon's head. She lay on the ground watching as her father made one more hard thrust and the blade came shooting out. It clanked on the ground and was immediately covered in blood.

A quick thrust of the dragon's massive wings elevated him over a hundred feet off the ground, "You... you will not be so lucky when next we meet. Blood or no blood, you are not my child. When next we meet, I will kill you!"

Drakin
The Story of Raiya

Raiya breathed heavily as she watched her father fly away, "Coward…! Come back… I'm not… finished!"

Splash!

Cold water poured down Raiya's skin. It steamed as liquid cooled her down. She looked up to see Jagger kneeling over her, "Thank you…"

ༀ

Raiya's eyes closed as she lost consciousness. Eric shook his head, "If I hadn't seen it myself…"

Jagger picked her up and brought her back to the jeep. He placed her gently on the passenger's seat, "I'll never forget the first time…"

Andy carried Miranda over from the debris, back to the jeep. "That was the dragon we were looking for?"

Jagger lowered his eyes and nodded, "How the hell are we ever going to beat something like that? It took Raiya everything she had just to fend it off."

Before Andy could say anything, Miranda slowly walked over to the passenger's side of the jeep and looked at Raiya. She grabbed her unconscious friend's fingers and squeezed them tightly in her right hand. Though there was no emotion on her face, it almost looked like she was trying to say 'thank you.'

The rest of the group watched the bittersweet moment unfold as the sun slowly began to drop on the horizon. Jagger didn't want to interrupt, but he knew that there was little choice, "Raiya is going to need rest, and Miranda will need help. We have to get out of here. Likely that dragon will send more after us."

"Where are we going to go?" Andy asked.

Eric beckoned to the group, "Come on guys, let's head back to my place. You can rest up for the night and we can take Miranda to our clinic."

Jagger looked at him oddly, "You guys have a clinic?"

Eric nodded, "Yeah… an old walk-in clinic from before the war. It wasn't badly damaged when the dragons attacked. A lot of the equipment was left behind, so our medicine men use it whenever one of us gets injured. We had to relearn a lot of it, but most of the stuff still works. I'm sure it'll have everything you need to help save Miranda.

"All right," Andy replied. "I'd rather have a full clinic, but I'll take what I can get. As long as they have the necessary equipment, I can work with it."

"So, we're heading back to Natick?" Jagger asked.

Eric jumped into the back of the jeep, smiling. "Yeah, sounds good. I could use some good food for a change anyway."

Chapter 15

The jeep pulled up outside of the nomad hideout as night fell. Jagger got out and picked up Raiya while Eric spoke to the guards. He couldn't make out what Eric was saying but assumed that he was explaining the situation.

A few minutes later, Eric turned around and nodded to the group, "All right guys, come on inside. Jagger, you and Raiya can have the room you had before. I'll take care of Miranda and Andy's arrangements as…"

"We need to get her to the clinic," Andy insisted. "Any longer and we risk infection or blood loss."

"All right," Eric replied. "It's not too far from here. —Jagger, can we borrow the jeep?"

"Yeah, keys are still in the ignition. Just bring her back in one piece."

"No worries, get a good night's sleep… and keep an eye on our hero there."

Jagger chuckled, "I'm sure she'd resent such a title, but I will."

"All right. See you in the morning."

Jagger turned back and carried Raiya past the guards. The massive bonfire was once again lit. It was almost as bright as the flame from the dragon lord himself, but not quite. The low crackling sound gave the building a sense of serenity.

Raiya needed rest. Her body had no doubt been strained beyond reason and needed time to repair. Her skin temperature had thankfully returned to normal as had her breathing. She was alive, but she still hadn't regained consciousness.

Jagger touched her cheek and then suddenly remembered the bullet wound in her hip. He quickly pulled back her pants to assess the damage. The bandage, gauze, and even the stitches were completely gone. The bullet wound was black, but not bleeding. Apparently, the intense heat from the dragon lord's breath had instantly cauterized the wound.

"Getting a little familiar, aren't you, partner?"

Jagger immediately let go of the waste of her pants, letting them snap back into place. He looked up to see Raiya staring down at him. She winced as the waistband struck her skin, "Ow, that wasn't nice!"

"Sorry."

"I'm sure you are… had you been a little gentler, I might have let you stay down there a little longer."

Jagger rolled his eyes, "Yeah right."

He moved up and looked into her eyes, "How are you feeling?"

"Better now that I'm not burning up… I guess…"

"You guess?" Jagger asked.

Raiya rolled over on her side, refusing to say anything else. Jagger placed his hand on her shoulder, "Look, I think it's time that you and I talked."

Raiya didn't move, "All right, what do you want to talk about?"

"You."

Drakin
The Story of Raiya

"I'm not that interesting."

"Even so…"

"Fine, what is it?"

Jagger sat back, bracing for an argument, "You've been moping around ever since we got to New Framingham. Something's been eating at you."

"Figure that one out on your own?"

"Very funny."

"I thought so…"

"Come on!" Jagger shouted, getting annoyed. "Talk to me, we're partners…"

"So, what? You think that means that you automatically get access to my every thought?"

"Well no…"

"All right then."

The room fell silent. At first, it seemed as though Raiya had successfully avoided an annoying argument. Jagger didn't move. He sat on the bed next to her and watched as she shifted, trying to get comfortable.

After a few moments, she sighed, "You're not going to let this go, are you?"

"No."

Raiya rolled belligerently back over to confront him, "Fine… you want to know what's wrong, buddy? I'll tell you. I killed those people! I killed them all."

"Who?"

Raiya gave him an annoyed look, "Don't act dumb. Just because you look the part, doesn't mean you can pull it off. I'm talking about the people of New Framingham. Jerry, Miranda's

Drakin

The Story of Raiya

family, Mariam… and the rest of your people… They're all dead because of me. I stood up to that Dragon Lord and brought my father down on them. He confirmed it. I should have been there to protect them… Why wasn't I?"

"They didn't want you there," Jagger replied. "They threw us out, remember? It's their own fault, not yours. You could have been there to defend them."

"I'm sure that'll be a lot of comfort to Miranda…" Raiya said, sharply.

"It looked like she understood. She seems to have become attached to you."

"If that's true… then she's a pretty stupid kid. She should hate me."

"Raiya…"

"I can't protect her. She needs to know that. What good am I?"

"You did a pretty good job of it," Jagger said. "You kept her safe from the biggest fucking dragon I've ever seen."

Raiya didn't respond.

"Look, you can't blame yourself every time a dragon attacks. You're going to wind up carrying the weight of the world on your shoulders. That's no way to be. New Framingham was not your fault, Richmond was not your fault… your grandparents and your mother were not your fault."

"Wish I could believe that…"

Jagger frowned, "Well, in the end, you're going to have to come to terms with it. So, what do you want to do? We can keep going, or we can find you a place to hide away from everything."

Raiya bent her legs and huddled herself together on the bed, "I'm getting tired, can we just get some rest now?"

"Sure, if you want…"

Jagger got up and walked over to the other bed. He slowly got comfortable and began to fall asleep as the mattress kneaded his skin. His mind was racing with everything they'd found out. It was all one gigantic mess that he needed to sort out.

"Jagger?"

He turned over to see Raiya looking at him, "Yeah?"

"Thanks… you're a good friend… I'm lucky to have you around."

That was all he needed. One weight had been lifted from his heart and it seemed like he'd finally gotten through to her, "You're welcome… I'm glad you think so."

"Good night."

"You too."

What is going on in there?

Eric was pacing back and forth in the destroyed waiting room. He and Andrea had arrived at the clinic about two hours ago. It was a small building, but it was of enough value that Mason kept it guarded at all times.

Eric stared blankly at the door. He wanted to go in and try to help, but what could he do? Did Andy need help holding Miranda in place? Given her reaction so far, he somehow doubted it. The sense of uselessness was infuriating.

That wasn't Eric's only problem. He'd seen what they were up against. Raiya barely survived the encounter. If she lost her fight, what chance did the rest of them have?

That dragon lord… her father was the stuff legends were made of. He literally wiped out whole armies, destroyed major cities, and murdered countless innocent people without provocation and without mercy. What chance did they really have? All their hope rested with a single half-breed and a small scar on the dragon lord's neck.

There was no way around it, she'd need all the help she could get. If he left and she wound up getting killed, he would never forgive himself. Every city, every settlement, every person that died would be on his conscience. He couldn't live with that.

"Eric, can you give me a hand in here?"

Finally.

Eric ran into the next room. Miranda was sitting on the table, completely motionless. The wound on her head was now clean and held together by steri-strips. Her eye was now covered by a makeshift patch.

Eric saw small pieces of flesh on the table next to where Miranda was sitting. He recognized it almost immediately. This was what was left of her left eye. It was a grotesque site, especially given the amount of damage. Even in one of the cities, there was no way that could have been saved.

Andy brought new gauze and bandages over and dabbed the wound on her forehead. Once the blood was gone, he wrapped the bandage around her head. He tied it tightly and stepped back, "That's it… we're done. I can't really do any more. It's not exactly a work of art or anything, but it'll heal."

Eric nodded, "I think it looks good, she's in a lot better shape than she was when we found her."

He looked at Miranda and smiled, "What do you think?"

Miranda just stared blankly at him. Eric couldn't be certain, but he could have sworn she'd smiled at him just a little. Maybe it was just in his head, but he didn't care. He liked to think that he'd gotten through to her in some way.

Andy stepped out in front of her, "Can I talk to you for a minute?"

"Sure. –We'll be right back, Miranda."

Andy took Eric back out to the lobby where Miranda couldn't see them, "Eric… there's more that we didn't know about."

"What's that?"

"She's… sick…"

"What?"

"I tested her blood for infection. Thank God you guys kept this equipment up. I'm not sure how it happened, but she has dragon's bane."

Eric's jaw dropped, "What?"

"Yeah… it's in its early stages, but it's definitely there."

Drakin

The Story of Raiya

"So that means…?"

"It means she's only got a few months to a year at most… then she'll start to deteriorate. It'll be painful."

"But there's something you can do, right? I mean there has to be. We have treatments for this kind of thing now."

Andy frowned, "Sorry… no… there is no treatment after the infection takes place."

"Nothing?"

"No… everything Dr. Castillo created was to prevent the disease. It's too late for that now."

Eric scratched the back of his head. He didn't quite know how to process it, "So… what do we do? Do we tell her?"

Andy shrugged, "What good would it do? I'm not even sure she knows where she is right now. I think maybe our best bet is to tell Raiya."

"Why?"

"She seems to have attached herself to Raiya. Maybe she can help."

"Or maybe she'll claw our eyes out for the trouble."

"Also possible," Andy admitted with a faint smirk, "but I'd rather not be the one to destroy what little life the poor girl has left."

"Yeah, I can understand that… all right, we'll tell Raiya. God help us…"

Eric turned and headed back into the operating room where Miranda was waiting. She hadn't moved an inch. Her body was like a statue, watching over the messy floor of the clinic.

Drakin
The Story of Raiya

Eric leaned on the table next to her, "You look tired, ready to get going?"

No response. Miranda got down from the table and looked up at him. Eric nodded, "Well that's something. Come on, we'll get you a bed back at the main compound."

"..."

"Maybe get you some food?"

"..."

"Yeah, I think that's a good idea too. We could all use some food."

"..."

God, this guy never shuts up. Andy thought to himself.

🦇

The black and red dragon lord landed on his roost atop Mount Whitney. Using their intense flame, the dragon lords had melted the rock into a defensible fortress and meeting chamber. To the eyes of a human, the fortress looked like a burnt ruin, but it served the dragons' purpose and was easily defended from any attack.

Large black spires of dried molten rock sprung up from the ground. They served as citadels where younger dragons could perch and launch fireballs at incoming armies. There was no wall surrounding it. The dragons didn't see the need for one.

Below the fortress, the woods parted to reveal crashed jet fighters, bombers, and a few scattered vehicles that had attempted to scout the area. They were little more than skeletons on the scorched earth.

Drakin
The Story of Raiya

He let out a mighty roar that shook the entire mountainside. Immediately, four other dragons appeared around him and landed on the other spires. Each one had distinct scales of various colors. The first to land had long gray scales, "You summoned us, my lord?"

The black and red dragon nodded, "I did Entharis. Thank you for responding so quickly."

The massive dragon spread his wings and roared as the others touched down, "The rumors are true!"

The yellow dragon lord hissed, "You have found the girl who wears the skin of a dragon, Eutherys?"

Eutherys hissed, "This girl doesn't wear dragon's skin at all... it is her own skin! The blood of a dragon runs through her veins... my blood!"

"How is that possible?"

"I don't know, Amzer'ial. All I know is that Raki'Agr's insane ramblings were proven right after all."

Eutherys looked around quizzically, "Where is he anyway?"

The all-black dragon lord spoke up, "Brother... it would appear that he is as unreliable as you thought. We don't know where he went, but he was rambling about the end of our kind."

Eutherys lowered his eyes, "It matters little... we need to take down this girl. I've seen what kind of a threat she possesses."

Drakin
The Story of Raiya

"Is that allowed?" his brother asked. "You would be killing a member of your family… our laws forbid such…"

"Our laws are obsolete, Auirn! You know this. Those laws are what lost us the first war. We were bound by honorable thought and action. As such, traitors and weaklings infiltrated our ranks. I will not have a repeat of that! If word of what she can do gets out, the humans will have a symbol to rally around. We can't allow that to happen. Like it or not, they still outnumber us! We had the advantage before in that their world was still divided by culture and territorial borders. By the time they attempted to rally, we'd already pushed them back. They can still rally together…"

Amzer'ial lowered her head, "No… no, we can't have that… We have all but broken their spirits. Their forces are fragmented and only loosely organized. They just fight to survive another day. A symbol to rally behind would change all that."

"I am curious…" Auirn said in a low voice. "Why did you let her live? You knew what kind of a threat such a creature posed, yet she was allowed to survive your encounter. Perhaps you aren't as willing as you let on to kill someone that carries your blood?"

Eutherys roared as he turned to his brother. The massive dragon clamped its jaw shut, narrowly missing Auirn's wing. The snapping sound of its teeth echoed against the mountainside.

Drakin
The Story of Raiya

Auirn backed away slightly. Challenging Eutherys was not a good idea. He was no match for his elder brother and he clearly knew it.

"I will not be questioned or challenged, not even by my own brother," Eutherys hissed. "I have kept our people alive, but more than that, I have fought with them. I know our enemy and how to fight them. If it wasn't for me, we'd all be extinct by now! You will know your place if you plan to remain with us!"

Auirn lowered his eyes, "Forgive me, brother. As a lord, I am tasked with the safety and security of my brethren."

"And you have held that position with honor," Eutherys replied. "I would not have gotten this far without you. Don't ruin such a prestigious reputation now, when we are so close to claiming this world for ourselves."

Auirn looked up at his brother, noticing the dried blood from Raiya's attack, "Brother, you're wounded!"

"Just a scratch."

"Did she do this?"

Eutherys growled softly, "I admit I didn't anticipate her being impervious to my attack. I underestimated her and she seized the opportunity. I will not make that mistake twice."

"That is disconcerting," the green dragon hissed.

"Perhaps Kazrai'em," Eutherys replied, "but I assure you that I am still as fit as I ever was. She got lucky, nothing more."

Drakin
The Story of Raiya

Auirn moved closer and looked at the wound, "That is more than a scratch, brother."

"There is no need for concern. This will heal quickly and that… daughter of mine will pay for what she did."

Eutherys turned his attention back to the group, "However, as my brother stated… under our laws, I can't kill a family member… even if it is a disgusting abomination, not without the approval of the council. I take it we're all in agreeance as to what needs to be done?"

The four dragon lords looked at one another. Muttered growls and groans echoed through the small tower. Eutherys nodded, "Then let us put it to a vote. I vote in favor."

"In favor."

"In favor."

"In favor."

Eutherys looked at his brother, "The final vote falls to you, brother."

Auirn hesitated for a moment, as though in deep thought. How much of a threat was this girl?

Eutherys's eyes narrowed, "Brother?"

"In favor."

Chapter 16

"What do you mean she's going to die?"

Andy looked like a deer in headlights. He adjusted his glasses and took a step back as he spoke, "I'm really sorry, Raiya… For some reason, Miranda must not have been inoculated when she was born."

"But isn't there a cure? Please, you have to help her!"

Jagger stood quietly off to the side. The rage in her eyes told him that this was one time where he did not want to get involved.

Andy's arms fell to his sides, "I'm sorry… I could have tried some advanced treatment had we gotten to her sooner, but even that might have been risky. At this point… I'm afraid that not even one of Dr. Castillo's radical procedures could help her. There is no way to neutralize all of the dragon cells without killing her."

Raiya looked away angrily, "It's not fair… she's a little girl… she's already been through so much. I know what dragon's bane does. There really isn't anything we can do?"

The look on Andy's face was pained. It looked like he was fighting a battle in his own mind as he spoke, "Euthanasia…"

Jagger's eyes widened, "What? Andy, you can't be serious!"

"Unfortunately, I am…"

Raiya's eyes narrowed, "What does 'euthanasia' mean?"

"It's another word for mercy killing," Jagger replied. *Here it comes…*

The yellow in Raiya's eyes flared up. In a flash, she grabbed the collar of Andy's white jacket, "Are you fucking kidding me?"

Andy stuttered as he spoke, "L… look… um… I'm sorry. I wish I knew how to make this all better. I wish I could say something that would take away the pain, but all I can do is treat injuries. I don't like it any more than you do… but if you know what Dragon's Bane does, then you know how painful it can be. Euthanasia may be more merciful than letting the disease run its course."

"This is my fault…" Raiya said in barely a whisper.

At that moment, Jagger came to life, "For the last time, you can't blame yourself. You had no idea that the dragon was going to attack. Even if you had, they didn't want you there, remember? That wasn't a peaceful town meeting at the gates. That was a lynch mob! They condemned themselves."

"It wouldn't have mattered anyway," Andy cut in. "This case is too advanced. It's still in its early stages, but there is no way she's only been infected for a few days."

"What?" Raiya asked.

"Miranda's symptoms are too advanced. She would have to have been infected months ago. Unfortunately, there is nothing more I can do for her. Even attempts to ease her symptoms wouldn't work."

Drakin
The Story of Raiya

"How long…?" Raiya was about to finish her question when she noticed a small hand clinging to the doorway behind Andy.

Jagger followed her gaze and saw the little girl standing behind the door, "Oh shit…"

Miranda looked like her spirit had been crushed. She took off running as fast as she could. Raiya blew past Andy and gave chase, "Miranda… please wait!"

Jagger quickly followed behind Raiya to catch the little girl, "She's heading outside, quickly!"

Miranda blew through the entrance and ran past the old jeep. The sun was just coming up, spreading an orange hue over the clouds. It would have been beautiful had the circumstances been different.

Raiya picked up speed and pulled away from Jagger. As they reached the top of a small grassy hill, Raiya caught up with Miranda and scooped her off her feet, "I got you…"

Miranda put up a fight, kicking and pounding on Raiya's chest with her small fists. Raiya dropped to her knees as she carefully struggled against the injured child. She flinched against the girl's relentless attacks. From the look on her face, these seemed to hurt her more than any dragon attack ever could.

Raiya quickly threw her arms around the child, trapping her fists. Before Miranda could squiggle free, she pressed the little girl's head against her own, "I'm sorry… I'm sorry… this shouldn't be happening to you. I wish I'd never come to your town. I'm so sorry…"

Drakin
The Story of Raiya

The fists and elbows were losing strength with each impact. Miranda slowly began to calm down. Raiya's words seemed to be taking the fight out of her. Unable to do anything to break free, Miranda buried her face in Raiya's right shoulder.

Jagger knelt down next to Raiya and touched her arm, "You okay?"

Raiya looked up with tears in her eyes. She shook her head and didn't say anything. Her jaw quivered as more tears escaped her eyes. Jagger nodded that he understood. *She's still blaming herself. This isn't right...*

Raiya opened her mouth as though she was about to say something when a dark shadow passed overhead. Jagger looked up and immediately jumped to his feet, "Drakes, shit! We're under attack!"

Ten drakes with twice as many wyverns came plummeting out of the sky towards them. "Shit, where'd they come from?"

Raiya jumped to her feet and grabbed Miranda's hand, "Come on, we've got to get you inside. Quickly!"

Raiya led Miranda to safety inside the compound while Jagger ran back to his truck. He called to the guards as he moved, "We're under attack, get whatever weapons you can!"

Jagger grabbed the bolt gun out of his jeep as Eric appeared next to him. The young nomad grabbed the assault rifle and immediately opened fire, "Watch it!"

A wyvern fell from the sky just in front of the jeep. Eric dashed to the other side, stepped on its

Drakin
The Story of Raiya

neck, and put two rounds into its skull through the eye, "Die!"

Jagger nodded, "Thanks!"

"You're welcome!"

WREEEEEEE!

"Two more coming at you!" Jagger said as he whirled around.

He aimed the bolt gun and discharged two rounds into the nearest drake. The beast fell to the ground, as the shock dulled its senses. The drake let out a low moan as it struggled to get back on its feet.

Eric took the opportunity, threw the rifle on his back and drew his daggers. Before the drake could react, Eric plunged the blades into its temples. The dragon let out a high-pitched whine before falling lifelessly to the side.

Raiya appeared followed by Mason and twenty more nomads. She grabbed the bolt pistol out of Jagger's holster and started shooting at anything that came near her. One wyvern landed nearby. She clenched her teeth as she reached behind her back. The beast lunged at her, intent on claiming a death blow.

Raiya's dagger appeared in her hand. In a quick flash of orange light that reflected off the blade, the dragon was immediately decapitated.

🜚

A second drake flew close and smacked her with its claw, sending her flying backward. She hit the ground hard. Pain shot through her cheek and neck. Her entire body hurt, and she struggled to get back on her feet.

Drakin
The Story of Raiya

Her cheek was bleeding as she aimed the pistol at the drake that attacked her and fired three rounds into its belly. The lizard fell from the sky and landed on its back. It let out a shrill screech as it hit the ground.

Raiya jumped on it, pinning its wings to the ground with her feet, "Die you fuck!"

She plunged her dagger into its chest, using an incredible amount of force. The blow killed it instantly.

Jagger's eyes widened, "Whoa…"

Raiya quickly withdrew her blade and turned as Andy appear on the scene. He ran to a nomad that had been badly scratched across his stomach.

The man cried out in pain as Andy worked to patch his injuries with some steri-strips he'd taken from the clinic, "Take it easy, you'll be okay. It's just a flesh wound."

The nomads came out equipped with everything from spears, rifles, pistols, daggers, and anything else that they could get their hands on.

Raiya caught sight of them dodging flame and claw attacks with ease. One of the nomads back-flipped out of the way of a claw that certainly would have cut him in half.

Another nomad ran towards a wyvern and launched himself into the air by pushing off his knees mid-stride. He landed on the dragon's back and began stabbing it mercilessly in the head. They put up a good fight, but they were slowly getting cut down.

Drakin
The Story of Raiya

Raiya took out another wyvern as a larger shadow appeared over her head, "Watch it, alpha!"

The dragon landed a short distance away from the battle and breathed fire on the large compound. Within seconds, the entire building was engulfed in flames. It was as though a massive incendiary device had been detonated inside.

The fire was so hot that anyone standing within fifty feet of the flames was badly burned. The flames lit up the land around them, roaring as it burned.

Eric looked up in a panic, "No!"

A berserk look came over him as he charged at the dragon. The alpha turned towards him and curled its body around behind it. The beast was clearly gearing up for a fight.

Eric drew his blood-covered daggers as the dragon opened its mouth and unleashed a blast of flame. He quickly darted out of the way, bent his legs, and launched himself sideways at the dragon's neck. His arms reached out with the daggers as his body went airborne. The daggers impacted on the dragon, but its scales were too hard for the blades to penetrate.

The impact of Eric's body against the dragon wasn't enough to knock it off its feet, but he was able to grab hold. The alpha shook its head as hard as it could, trying to free itself from Eric's grip.

Drakin
The Story of Raiya

Eric was not about to give up. He closed his eyes and kept his arms and legs wrapped tightly around the large beast. His head began to spin as he was tossed back and forth. Between thrusts, he quickly moved up the dragon's neck. He inched up slowly as the dragon recoiled and then held on tight for the imminent impact. What felt like an eternity had passed before Eric felt the back of the dragon's head.

The moment he was close enough to the head, he squeezed his legs tightly and let go of the alpha's neck with his arms. Eric was so fast that his arms blurred as he went to work. He brought his daggers around and jabbed them into the beast's eyes, "Murderous son of a bitch! You die now!"

Blind, the alpha dragon screamed and threw itself against the wall. Debris fell as the side of the building shook from the strike. Eric impacted against the hard concrete, having the wind knocked out of him. The dragon pulled away and wound up for another blow.

Eric only had seconds. He knew that if he got struck a second time, he'd likely pass out. There was no time and he only had a little strength left. He used what he had and plunged the daggers deeper into the beast's eye sockets. The dragon roared one last time and lowered its head as it stopped moving.

The mournful death cry of the alpha caused the remaining wyverns to cease their attacks. Their ranks had become disorganized and panicky. Leaderless, the dragon horde quickly devolved into chaos. As the wyverns scattered, one of them let out a thunderous roar and turned away from the battle. Immediately, all the other dragons turned and headed back the way they came.

Eric wiped the blood off his face. He was shaking and breathing heavily. The moment he realized what was happening, he pulled the assault rifle off his back and aimed it at the retreated cloud of dragons, "No, come back here and fight!"

He squeezed the trigger until it was pressed against the grip. Two more wyverns fell from the sky as Eric spent his entire magazine. The moment it was empty, Eric threw the rifle to the ground and grabbed a pistol from one of the fallen nomads.

He aimed the gun at the group of fleeing dragons and screamed as he unloaded another magazine, "Cowards!"

Click... Click... Click...

Raiya watched from a distance. Tears filled his eyes. He brought the hand that was holding the gun back, wound up, and threw it in the direction where the dragons had gone. It wasn't going to hit, Raiya was certain that he knew that. Likely it was more of a symbolic gesture.

She could see the intense level of hate in his eyes. She could have understood him being mad about the destruction of his home, but this kind of thing happened all the time. In this case, casualties were fairly low. No, something else was going on there. What she saw in him was blind rage and hatred. What could have caused that?

Eric dropped to his knees and pounded the ground with his fist. His breathing was irregular and his face was turning red. His eyes were wet and completely bloodshot.

Jagger ran up next to him, "Hey buddy… you okay?"

"Fucking dragons… kill them all if I could… someday…"

Jagger nodded, "I know how you feel."

"I doubt it."

Raiya turned back and looked at the building while Jagger spoke to Eric. A cold pain entered her chest as though someone had just stabbed her with a thick icicle, "Miranda…?"

Jagger looked up towards Raiya and quickly got to his feet. He gave chase, but was unable to catch up to her, "Raiya, stop! You can't go in there!"

Raiya was too far ahead and too fast. Her legs moved so quickly that they could barely be seen, "Miranda, no!"

She reached the doorway to the compound and looked in. A wall of flame blocked her path. She was about to charge through it when someone grabbed her and knocked her to the side, "No, the whole place could come down at any moment!"

Raiya turned over and tried to fight Jagger off, "She's still in there! We've got to get her out!"

"If she's still in there, then she's already dead!"

Drakin

The Story of Raiya

"No, shut your mouth! She can't be gone! She can't be!"

Raiya put up a fight, straining every muscle she could to try to get out of Jagger's grip, "Let me go!"

The sound of rubble being disturbed nearby made them both stop struggling. Miranda appeared out from behind a piece of debris. A look of relief appeared on Raiya's face. The expression was almost one of joy, "Miranda, you're alive."

Jagger let go of her and sat back, "She must have gotten out just before the dragons attacked."

Raiya knelt in front of Miranda, "Are you okay?"

Miranda nodded and pointed off to the side. Another doorway stood open that hadn't been consumed by flame. A wide smile appeared on Raiya's face, "Smart…"

As Raiya dealt with Miranda, she glanced at the scene around her. Of the twenty nomads that had come out to fight, only three remained standing. Five more had been wounded. The screams of pain pierced her ears.

Jagger's eyes darted around the field, "Where's Mason."

"Over here!" another voice called.

Raiya turned to see one of the surviving nomads kneeling beside a pile of debris. A bloodied old man lay on the ground behind it. It was the same man that had welcomed them several days ago.

Drakin
The Story of Raiya

Jagger ran over and was soon joined by Eric, "Father, no!"

Mason looked up at Eric, "Eric… I'm sorry."

"Don't be sorry, live!"

Mason smiled as he laid back, "I don't think so… not this time…"

Mason turned and looked at Jagger, "Eric brought me up to speed on what happened in Charleston. Raiya… if there is any hope, it may very well rest with her completing her mission. She may be the world's last best hope…"

Jagger nodded, "You have my word, I'll do everything I can."

"Good."

Mason looked at the sky, "This is it for us… tell my people… find refuge where ever they can… tell them…"

Mason's eyes closed. Eric leaned down close to his father's face, "Father… no…"

Raiya moved up next to Mason as tears dripped down Eric's cheeks, "I can't… Dad… why?"

Raiya lowered her eyes, "They came looking for me…"

At that moment, it was as though something snapped in Eric. His eyes flared as he looked up at her, "You…"

"No way," Jagger replied. "You took on a dragon lord. You can't possibly think…"

"They sent them to wear you down," Eric said through clenched teeth. "We were just collateral damage…"

Drakin
The Story of Raiya

He stood up and glared at her, "My Dad... all of these people... we survived... and now..."

Jagger stood up and stepped in front of Raiya. He looked straight into Eric's eyes, "Back down, Eric. You know this isn't right."

Andy came running up after giving one of the wounded nomads a shot of morphine, "Eric, you're angry right now and that's normal, but blaming Raiya won't solve anything. These attacks happen quite often. It was only a matter of time before they came after you."

Eric kept his gaze directly in Raiya's eyes, "Bullshit."

He immediately turned and walked back over to the side entrance of the compound. Jagger turned and placed his right hand on Raiya's shoulder, "I'm sorry, Raiya... he's wrong."

"No... he isn't," Raiya replied softly. "No matter where I go... I'm a danger to everyone around me. We need to leave here... today... right now."

Jagger nodded, "All right, where do you want to go?"

Raiya's eyes darted back and forth as she thought about it for a moment, "I don't know... we need to go somewhere safe... or at least somewhere that the dragons wouldn't find us."

Jagger scratched his head for a moment as he thought about it. "The dragons seem to congregate in the northern areas. Their original hiding place was in Siberia... maybe they don't like heat?"

"You want to go south?" Raiya asked.

"It might be the best way to go. We can take the heat off the cities until we figure out our next move."

"Right then let's get moving."

Jagger frowned, "Let's give Eric some time, first. His father just died."

"If we hang around here, the dragons could come back at any moment."

"Raiya…"

"Ugh… fine…" She groaned. "A few hours… no more. Doubt he even wants to come with us now."

Drakin
The Story of Raiya

Chapter 17

The bonfire was as bright as ever against the night sky. Eric and the other three unwounded nomads carried Mason's body to the flame. A few women and children stood nearby in silent respect. Their eyes lit up orange as the flame danced. The looks on their faces ranged from stoic to complete sorrow. Their leader was gone and with him, much of their hope for survival.

The nomads carrying Mason's body stopped right in front of the flame. Eric had an emotionless look on his face. He made no move as he stared into the fire.

Raiya and Jagger stared attentively to see what he was going to do. It was an uncomfortable silence, but no one was willing to speak up. This was Eric's last farewell to his father and no one wanted to interfere.

Raiya stood back in the shadows with a nervous look on her face. She hung her head in shame.

Jagger placed a gentle hand on her shoulder, "This wasn't your fault."

"Bullshit," she replied. "First New Framingham and now this. I brought the dragons down on them. We know this now. Look around you, everything they built here is gone. The whole place has been burnt out. They'll all need to pack up and find new homes now."

"That's the life of the nomads. I think you know that."

"Don't tell me what I know," Raiya hissed softly. "I know there are groups of nomads out there that just want a permanent home and go through a lot to try to build one."

"So, we're to blame you for just existing? The dragons killed these people, just like they killed the people of New Framingham, just like they killed everyone I cared about."

Raiya's eyes flared up as she watched the flame. Jagger was certain that the fire had nothing to do with glow in her eyes. She sucked in a deep breath and spoke through clenched teeth, "I want him… I want his head, Jagger."

"We'll get him, don't worry."

"Never stop telling me that… even if it's a lie."

Jagger nodded as he turned his attention back to the funeral procession. Eric lowered his eyes after about five minutes. He made no effort to hide his sadness as he began to speak, "We're gathered here this evening to bid farewell to my father, Mason Fausten. This was a man who gave everything he had and then some. A man who would have given the shirt off his back for the asking. Most of us would not be here right now if it weren't for him. He had to watch my mother and sister die in an inferno. He watched his countrymen be slaughtered by the thousands, but throughout it all, he remained calm and always lent an ear to anyone who needed it. His demeanor was always kind and open. In a world where our numbers are dwindling to extinction, people like my father, people who are kind and

Drakin
The Story of Raiya

accepting, are nearly impossible to find. We need more of them."

Eric wiped his eyes with his free hand, "Father... you guided us here... and you made your last stand keeping us safe. You will never be forgotten until the last of us is gone."

He reached down and gripped the white cloth that his father was wrapped in, "You made me promise you that when the time came, we'd burn your body. You didn't want any scavenging dragons to find anything to eat... so now we commit your body to the flame."

Eric sucked down a deep breath as he and the three nomads lifted the wrapping over their heads, "Dad... I love you... and I'm going to miss you... every day..."

With one push, the four men threw Mason's body into the massive flame. The fire decreased momentarily before flaring up with a vengeance. The body quickly disappeared under the flame, "They'll never have you now."

Eric sighed and turned to his people, "This is it for us... It's time we all go our separate ways. Staying in large groups is no longer safe."

One of the other nomads stepped forward, "But... where will we go?"

"I don't know," Eric replied. "Try to make your way to the other nomad groups in the area. Scatter and go into hiding. Go as far south as you can... You'll be safe there."

Jagger nodded and headed back outside to his jeep, sensing that it was time for them to leave. Raiya followed a few minutes later. She

Drakin
The Story of Raiya

approached the jeep without a word and began helping Andy get the last of their supplies in the trunk. Miranda was sitting in the back seat, watching the sky.

"So where are we going?" Andy asked.

"South-southwest," Jagger replied. "We need to find a place to hide out for a little while until we can figure out our next move. The dragons are obviously looking for us now and we don't want to put anyone else in danger."

"You think turning and running is the answer?"

"I prefer to think of it as a tactical retreat."

Andy nodded, "All right."

Raiya grabbed the last couple of ammo magazines they had and shut the trunk, "Not much left... hopefully, we'll be able to hold out. Are we ready?"

Jagger nodded, "Yeah... I think it's time."

"What about Eric?" Andy asked.

Raiya shrugged, "His people need him now, more than we do. We can't expect him to come with us on this one. Probably for the best."

"Oh gee, thanks!" a familiar voice yelled in annoyance. "So, you're all just going to leave me behind? After everything we went through? What am I, chopped dragon liver?"

"Eric, your father was the elder... maybe you should stay behind and keep your people safe. Isn't it kind of your job to carry the torch?"

"No way," he replied. "I'm no leader... I never have been. I know myself and I'd likely lead my people off a cliff. Jagger, you heard my father. Raiya may be our last, best hope for survival. He told you to protect her, but frankly, I don't think you can."

Jagger's eyes narrowed, "What's that supposed to mean?"

"Nothing negative!" Eric said defensively. "I mean look, you're one man. You've seen what we're up against. You can't protect her alone, no one could. You need help… and that's why I'm here."

"That is true," Andy replied. "You'll need as much help as you can get."

He then turned to Raiya, "Look… about what I said…"

"You don't need to say anything," Raiya replied.

"Yes, I do. You didn't do anything wrong. This wasn't your fault, nor was New Framingham. None of it was your fault. I'm sorry I got mad at you. The dragons are the real enemy. They are the dealers in debt here. If killing them brings an end to this, I'll go with you and help Jagger keep you safe… If I'm still welcome, that is."

Raiya nodded, "You're annoying, but you're all right."

"Hey what about Miranda?" Jagger asked.

"What do you mean?"

"We're pretty much going to war against the dragons, shouldn't we leave her here? I'm sure some of the nomads would take her in for us if we asked."

Raiya frowned, "No… I'd rather drop her off behind city walls somewhere. If we come across a settlement that's under the protection of the coalitions, that would probably be safer. She'll stay with us for now."

"We may not come across a city... are you sure?"

"Yes. I'm looking after her."

"You know, that might not be a bad idea," Andy added. "I'm still not done treating her, so it might be best if she stays with us for the time being. If her wound reopens or her dressings aren't properly cared for and switched out, she could run the risk of an infection."

"All right, if that's what everyone wants," Jagger replied.

Eric hopped in the Jeep behind Jagger. Andy slid in behind Raiya while Miranda sat between them. It was a bit of a tight squeeze, but they managed to get comfortable enough to continue.

Jagger started the jeep and backed it out, away from the building. It rattled as he put it into drive and pushed forward down the road. They began their journey south on the remains of I-95. Raiya looked back at Miranda as it got dark, "How are you?"

As expected, Miranda smiled but said nothing. Raiya smiled in return, "We'll find you somewhere safe to stay. Don't you worry... We'll put you with good people. They'll look after you."

Miranda frowned, reached forward and touched Raiya's cheek. She knew what the little girl was trying to say, "I'm sorry, you can't stay with me. Why would you even want to? I'm a wanderer, a nomad. My life is way too dangerous.

Drakin
The Story of Raiya

You need to be raised by a family somewhere quiet and peaceful."

Miranda didn't look convinced. She removed her hand from Raiya's cheek and resumed her statuesque state. Raiya turned back around and looked at Jagger, "As if such a place existed... honestly, I wouldn't have much objection to just keeping her with us if we weren't a moving target."

"Right..." Jagger replied. "You've really grown attached to her, huh?"

"No... I just..."

"Raiya..."

She looked at him with an irritated expression, "Jagger, her family is dead because my father came looking for me, okay? You can tell me I'm not responsible until you're blue in the face, but it doesn't change that fact. I... I just don't want her left alone... not like I was."

"I see..."

"What?"

"That's why you're drawn to her. You were in a similar boat. Your family died when you were really young and you were left alone."

"So, what's wrong with that?" Raiya demanded. "I don't want her out there starving to death."

Jagger nodded, "Yeah... I can understand that."

Raiya lowered her eyes, "Look, I'm sorry if I've been difficult over the last few days... it's just a lot to take in."

Drakin
The Story of Raiya

"You don't need to apologize. It's not every day you find out that you're a half dragon hybrid and your father is the massive dragon lord responsible for the deaths of countless millions."

"Yeah… that about sums it up."

"It's not like you asked for any of this. It all kind of just happened and you were thrown in the middle of it. Believe me, we all get it."

Raiya forced a smile on the right side of her mouth, "Thanks… partner."

The light on the roll bar flashed on as Andy leaned forward, "So I couldn't help but notice that we're now on the run without a game plan. I think we need to come up with something… we've only got four bolt gun power cells left, and three more magazines for the assault rifle."

Jagger nodded, "And I'm down to my last mag for each of my pistols as well."

"Can we get more?" Raiya asked.

"Traditional ammo mags and rounds are hard to come by… only the U.S. remnant force still uses them consistently. The Westcon uses bolt weapons almost exclusively. We can trade for more power cells, but they're expensive."

"We still have all those dragon teeth, don't we? I thought they were worth a lot."

"Sure," Jagger replied, "but those will only get us a few power cells and we need some money for food too. There are now five of us. The rations we have won't last long."

"So, we need to find a safe harbor and somewhere to find supplies," Andy said. "Any thoughts?"

Drakin

The Story of Raiya

Raiya shrugged, "Don't look at me, I did my best to stay away from populated areas... for obvious reasons and I never got that far south... I didn't like the heat."

Jagger looked into the rear-view mirror, "Eric?"

"Don't look at me..." Eric said. "I don't know much about the south either. You may be able to find an underground or traveling trade post. They don't come out during the day, but at night a wagon will flash a red light periodically to let nomads know they're nearby. The underground ones are marked with special red paint. Dragons don't know what it is and typically don't even see them. There's never been a report of one being attacked."

"All right, well at least we know what search for. We'll keep an eye out."

Eric sat back and stared out the side of the jeep, "You gotta love this... of all the cars out there, you pick the one with an open roof. How easy would it be for a dragon to swoop in and take us out?"

Jagger shrugged, "About as easy as it would be for us to bail out if we came under attack. Or would you rather be trapped in a baking steel oven?

"Okay good point."

Southern Frontier
Unclaimed Territory
Formerly Arkansas

Drakin
The Story of Raiya

Chapter 18

"Can we please stop?" Eric asked. "We've been traveling forever."

"It's only been two days!" Jagger replied in an annoyed tone.

"Exactly, two days! We haven't had a break and my back is killing me... I need to sleep on solid ground for one night! We haven't stopped for more than a few minutes for a bathroom break."

"I think that might be a good idea," Andy agreed. "We're all tired. We've been cooped up in this small jeep for days... One night on solid ground could be a huge difference for us. It'll also give Miranda a better chance to heal."

"Yeah it could also make us open targets for a hungry dragon," Raiya shot back.

"Not really... not much more than we are during the day. Besides, we haven't seen a dragon in over a day."

Jagger sighed, "All right... I see some ruins up ahead. We should be able to hide out there for the night."

A few shattered buildings stood off to the side of the road. One large wall with rectangular holes that had once served as windows, provided decent cover from anyone who might pass by. It was the only settlement nearby that could be seen in the darkness.

Raiya's eyes scanned the ruins, "It looks... defensible. I suppose that will work for now."

Jagger nodded, "Good. We'll stop there."

Drakin
The Story of Raiya

Jagger pulled the jeep over behind the wall and powered it down, "All right, let's set up a campsite. —Eric, see if you can grab something to burn."

"Will do," Eric replied.

"You're lighting up a fire?" Raiya asked. "You should know better than that!"

"Like we've both said; dragons don't typically come out at night. Besides, I'll take my chances with the dragons over the cold."

Raiya rubbed her arms and looked back at the setting sun, "I guess I can't really argue with that. Fine… just keep it low. There are other things to worry about besides dragons."

"Will do."

Andy hopped out the other side, being careful not to wake Miranda. He grabbed a couple of pieces of cloth out of the back. As Eric went to work building a fire pit, he unrolled them around it. These would serve as beds for the evening.

Once he'd gotten what he needed, Raiya pulled the guns out from underneath the other supplies. Andy looked at her oddly, "Planning on going to war? I thought you guys said that dragons don't attack at night."

Raiya sat against the wall with the bolt gun, "They don't, typically… but this isn't a typical situation. Besides… there are things out here that are just as dangerous as dragons, make no mistake about that."

Andy looked at her oddly, "What are you talking about?"

Drakin
The Story of Raiya

"This isn't like city life, Andy. Out here, you eat, you find things to barter with, you take refuge somewhere out of sight, or you die. I know that life all too well. If the dragons don't get you, then raiding parties that are looking for food or provisions might... and if they don't..."

Raiya's face froze. She looked down at the scar on her wrist and then out into the distance. Her eyes scanned the horizon a few times before she returned her attention to the guns.

"What is it?" Andy asked.

"If they don't... The canbans will."

"Canbans? I've heard of them, aren't they a feral group of humans?"

"Feral? Yeah, I guess that's one way of looking at them... They're not like wild animals or anything... not really..."

"Then what are they?"

Raiya sighed, "Just trust me... they're bad news."

"All right... if you say so..."

The clicking sound of two rocks being smashed together echoed off the building and a small fire sprung up from the pit. It illuminated the wall and the surrounding area for about a hundred feet.

"Just in time," Raiya said. "The sun is almost gone."

Eric and Jagger settled down on their beds. Miranda leaned against the jeep while Andy stayed up and worked on her bandages, "Do you think there are any canbans nearby?"

Drakin
The Story of Raiya

"Hard to say," Raiya replied. "They're nomadic, but unlike the others, there is no real sense to the way they move. They basically just spread out in hunting parties looking for food."

Andy finished retying the bandages as the sounds of light snoring eminated from the campfire. Miranda stepped away from Andy and rested on her own bed.

Andy also laid down nearby, "You aren't sleeping?"

"No."

"Why?"

"Someone needs to stand guard."

"You're really that worried?"

"Better safe than sorry."

Andy laid back and stared up at the stars. Raiya looked out into the darkness. The light from the fire polluted her view, making it hard to see anything. She rested her head in her hands and slowly sat back.

The sound of light footsteps made her jump. She quickly grabbed the rifle and stood up. Her ears scanned the nearby surroundings.

Andy looked up at her oddly, "What is it?"

The sound grew louder. Raiya's ears picked up at least three sets of feet moving, maybe more. They were coming from all directions, making it impossible to get an exact count.

Raiya eyed the darkness, "Andy… get back in the jeep…"

"What?"

"Get back in the jeep, now… take Miranda and go."

Drakin

The Story of Raiya

"What about you guys?"

"I'll get them up… you need to go, now!"

Andy got up and slowly nestled Miranda in his arms, "What's going on?"

"We're being stalked…"

That was all Andy needed to hear. He immediately ran back to the jeep and slid into the driver's seat.

Raiya reached down to wake Eric and Jagger, "Guys, get up now!"

Andy reached down to start up the truck when he felt something sharp against his hand. He looked down to see that the ignition was being blocked by a blade. He looked back up to see a hideous bald man smiling at him.

The man's teeth were brown and green, he looked like he hadn't bathed in months, and his clothes looked like they had been crudely cut from animal skin, "Raiya…"

"I said go, Andy!"

"Raiya… I can't…"

"Why not?"

Raiya was about to turn around when three large knives appeared at her throat, "Shit… Jagger, Eric, run!"

A fourth dagger appeared on her neck, this one pressed against her skin, telling her to shut up. Three torches appeared from the other side of the stone wall, revealing a crowd of thirty men.

Raiya clenched her jaw when she noticed that Jagger and Eric had both been captured. They lay on the ground with their eyes closed, but she could see that they were still breathing. Her yellow eyes burned into the group of filthy, imp-like, men that stood in front of her, "We're no threat to you. Let us go."

"Well now I don't think so," the bald man in the jeep replied. "What's say you, boys? Looks like meat be back on our menu."

The men cheered as Miranda was picked up, and Andy was guided over to Raiya's side. He looked at her in terror, "Are these…?"

"Yeah," Raiya replied. "These… are the canbans. They're cannibals…"

Before she could say anything else, a blunt shock entered the back of her head. Pain spread across her skull, causing her sight to vanish. She quickly lost consciousness and fell forward.

My arms… Raiya woke up to find that her arms were restrained over her head, as were those of her companions. She tried to reach the ropes with her fingernails, but her wrists had been tied low enough that she was unable to.

Jagger was hanging next to her, still unconscious. She tried to move her legs only to find that she'd been tied at the ankles too. Using her right hip, she thrust to the side and tapped him.

"Jagger…" she whispered. "Jagger, wake up."

"Huh… what's going on…?"

"We've been captured by canbans."

"Ugh… what?"

"My arms are tied. I can't reach the ropes. Can you get free?"

"No… where is everyone?"

Drakin

The Story of Raiya

"Look around."

Raiya beckoned to her left. Andy and Eric were tied on that side. Miranda was lying in front of them, strapped to a wooden table. The entire group was standing in a circle in a hut that looked as though it had been constructed of animal skins. Though Raiya didn't even want to think about which animal.

"What are they going to do to us?" Jagger asked.

"What do you think?"

"Oh, God…"

Raiya struggled against her restraints as she desperately tried to free herself, "Eric, Andy, wake up!"

The two slowly began to stir as the bald canban appeared from outside and jumped in front of them, "Well now, who would have that this would be our lucky day, praise be to God."

Raiya clenched her teeth as he looked at her, "What do you want?"

"I'm here to give you a final prayer before you meet God."

"Final prayer?" Raiya asked.

"Sure, even an ungodly abomination like you deserves to be cleansed of its sins before it dies."

'Abomination.' Raiya knew that word all too well. She'd grown used to it and didn't let it get to her. Jagger, however, had only been around her for a little while and clearly took exception to it, "You think God would approve of what you're doing? First capturing us, then taunting her, and then you're going to kill us?"

Drakin
The Story of Raiya

The bald man frowned, "Young man, I speak for the almighty God as his ordained minister."

"Ordained minister?" Raiya scoffed.

"Yes ma'am, Reverend Archibald Duwalt, at your service. You can call me Reverend," the bald man replied with a bow. "My charge was a small congregation of faithful before the satanic beasts attacked. After they did, I realized that the dragons were little more than God allowing the devil to test our resolve. Only those willing to do anything it took in order to survive were deemed worthy. So here we are today."

"In other words, only people willing to give up their humanity were worthy?" Andy demanded.

"We're still as flesh and blood human as any one of you," the reverend replied with a hurt look. "We've simply found a new way."

Raiya growled as the reverend pulled out a small cross and spoke a short prayer. "Oh lord, we thank you for the bounty that you have bestowed upon us. We ask that you take these poor souls away from their mortal coils that they may feel no pain in their passing. If, however you feel that these sinners may deserve their fate, we will bow to your wisdom. We ask always for your love and forgiveness in your name. Amen."

"Pray all you want!" Raiya hissed. "No one up there is waiting for you. I'd be more worried about another direction!"

"Sorry you feel that way, little miss. In any case, what's done is done. Now it's time for the celebration."

Drakin
The Story of Raiya

"Celebration?" Raiya asked.

"Oh yes indeed. Whenever the good lord grants us such bounty, it merits jubilation. You are to be the guests of honor."

"Somehow I don't feel very honored," Jagger said softly.

"Well, you should. In any case…"

Seven men entered the hut. Each one was as disgusting as the man that had come before him. They were all filthy, their teeth were either missing or so rotted that they were green. Andy grimaced and turned away in a futile effort to avoid the smell.

The ropes that bound their hands were tied to hooks hanging from the ceiling. The canbans went to work unhooking them and dragging them forward by their wrists.

"Are we putting her with the womenfolk?" one of them asked, referring to Raiya.

The reverend looked at her for a moment, "Well now she does seem young enough to be re-educated to our ways, but look at her. She has the eyes of the satanic beasts that have been plaguing our land. No brother, I believe that God had us find her for the sole purpose of cleansing her corrupted body. She'll join the others on the stakes."

The man shrugged and tugged at Raiya's rope, "As you say, Reverend."

Raiya could feel the ropes twist around her wrists, causing irritation and a severe burning sensation. She could only wonder how bad it was for her friends with their soft skin. Despite the

Drakin
The Story of Raiya

pain, it took everything the canbans had to force her forward. Her legs locked in place, refusing to move until the rope squeezed her wrists so tight that it was cutting off her blood circulation. If they were going to turn her into a meal, they were going to have to work for it.

She lurched forward as her feet compensated for the canban tugging. A second canban pushed her from behind, making it harder for her to resist. She clenched her teeth as she was led outside.

It was still dark. Clearly only a few hours had passed since they'd been captured. The scene outside was the stuff nightmares were made of. The men dragging her were ugly enough, but the women and children were equally as horrific. Many ran around with little to no clothing. They danced around Raiya and her friends. Some pulled at their clothes, others pinched their skin as though they were inspecting it. Raiya tugged away as they were continuously pulled forward.

On either side of the large crowd were massive tents that looked more like huts. These did not look like ones that could be disassembled quickly. Raiya closed her eyes when she realized what they were dealing with. These were not nomadic canbans. This was a canban settlement.

Stories of these people had made their way around nomadic groups. While most canbans were small groups that mostly kept to themselves except when they needed food, these ones were much worse. Not only did they not just take what they needed, they practically bathed in the blood of their victims in a ritualistic manner. These ones

Drakin

The Story of Raiya

didn't see the dragons as a threat and didn't care if they survived. They relished their lifestyles for however long they would last.

Raiya eyed the makeshift racks that sat next to many of these tents. They held everything from old swords to large meat cleavers. A few of the larger ones even had rifles. Impish-looking children could be seen running around with clubs. Pools of blood and stacks of bones littered the ground all around them.

If Raiya somehow managed to get out of this alive, the scene would haunt her memories for years to come. She closed her eyes and tried to drown it out, but her other senses betrayed her. The smell around her made her throat seize. She tensed her muscles, struggling to keep from throwing up.

"Keep moving!" Raiya's captor shouted.

Raiya lurched forward and tripped over a small pile of wood. She was led up another stack of wood to a post with another hook. Several other stacks stood nearby.

Raiya eyed the post that she was being attached to. It was almost completely black except for several scratch marks a few inches under the hook. This hook had been used before.

Raiya could almost see the scenes of others being burned right in front of her by just looking at the post. Her mind echoed with the sounds of screaming.

Miranda was carried out behind them and placed on a nearby table. Her arms were tied next to her and her legs were bound together. She didn't appear to be conscious, something Raiya was grateful for, "What are you going to do to her?"

"Don't worry, she'll be well cared for," the reverend replied. "We're going to raise her like one of our own, starting with her sampling a piece of you."

Raiya lurched forward, "You sick fuck!"

Her teeth were clenched as she pulled against her bonds. It was no use. No matter how hard she pulled, they were too strong. She couldn't break free.

The reverend ignored her and turned to the crowd. He raised his arms like a priest delivering a blessing. The crowd quieted down as Raiya and her friends were fastened to their posts. It was almost surreal how quickly the wild crowd fell into order.

The look on the reverend's face was one of pure euphoria, "Brothers, sisters, on this blessed night, let us bow our heads and give thanks to our almighty creator. For it was he, with his guiding hand that brought us these bountiful sacrifices. It was he who gave us the foresight to find and receive them… and it is he who continues to protect us from the dragons."

The crowd cheered, "Amen! Amen!"

The reverend nodded. He was clearly enjoying the scene. No doubt he'd given this speech before, but he seemed to relish it. He took his time and lavished every cheer and every round of applause. "With this feast, we will survive the dragon onslaught for yet another day. We will persevere

Drakin

The Story of Raiya

and we shall survive as we always have! Let the godless fools of the Westcon and the U.S. Remnant fight themselves into oblivion. Let us give thanks, my friends!"

Raiya spat at the back of his head, "When I get out of here, I'm going to kill all of you... filthy degenerates!"

The reverend wiped the spit away and turned to her. He pulled a knife from his jacket and quickly slashed part of her shirt, making the neckline larger. It wasn't clear if he was aiming for the shirt or skin. He then reached inside her shirt with his right hand and cupped Raiya's left breast for a moment, "It does seem somewhat of a shame to toast something so fine... even if it is an abomination!"

The crowd laughed as Raiya struggled against her restraints. A quick flash of teeth forced the bald man to withdraw his hand and back away. At that moment, Raiya's eyes were filled with rage. Anyone who didn't know her would likely have assumed that she was as wild as the canbans.

Jagger jolted forward, struggling against his restraints, "Hey try that on me, you son of a bitch! Come on!"

The reverend turned back to his people, "Unfortunately such things are not for us to decide. Our benefactor has long stated that ours is to exterminate any and all sins against nature! This is as glaring an example as any. What we..."

Grrrooooaarr...

A loud roar from behind the crowd interrupted the bald man's speech, "What I mean is..."

Drakin

The Story of Raiya

Rrrrrrr...

Jagger narrowed his eyes and looked out into the darkness, "An alpha?"

"I don't think so," Raiya replied. "Sounds bigger!"

Finally, the reverend put it together, "Men, to arms! The beasts of Hell are upon us!"

There was a massive flapping sound as another growl emanated from nearby.

Rrrrrrrrrrrrr...

Andy's eyes darted to the side. The growling was immediately followed by a bright trail of flame. Half of the canbans standing in the group were either immediately killed, or quickly became human fireballs.

One of the victims fell onto the stack of wood, igniting it. Raiya could feel the flame quickly spread. She'd never seen fire spread that quickly, not even from a dragon's breath. It must have been coated in some kind of flammable liquid.

Raiya knew that it wouldn't hurt her, but her friends must have already been feeling its effect. Jagger was struggling more fiercely against his restraints, as was Eric. Miranda remained unconscious on the table nearby.

Raiya waited for the flame to get close enough before rolling back her tongue and spraying liquid the same way she had against her father.

It worked. The saliva immediately caught fire, allowing her to direct the flame as she pleased. She quickly threw her head back and burned away the rope that was holding her hands in place.

Drakin

The Story of Raiya

The moment she was free, the flames ceased and she went to work on her friends. Jagger was already sweating from the flames as Raiya dug in with her nails, "Take it easy, partner. I'll have you free in a moment."

"You're timing is spot on," Jagger replied.

Snap!

Jagger's arms fell to his side as the rope hit the ground, "All right, get Andy, I'll take care of Eric."

Raiya nodded and quickly ran over to Andy. His eyes were closed and he wasn't moving. It appeared as though he had passed out, "Andy?"

The young doctor opened his eyes and looked at her, "Raiya, you escaped?"

"Yeah… you okay?"

"Yeah… I was just trying to block out the pain. It's one of the techniques we're taught during training."

"Did it work?"

"Not really…"

Raiya cut his hands free, allowing him to escape. As Andy jumped away from the flame, Raiya immediately dashed off the pile of wood. She ran to Miranda's side and went to work on her restraints, "Come on sweetie, it's time to wake up!"

Miranda didn't respond. She was breathing, so she was still alive, but she wasn't moving. "Miranda, we've got to go, come on!"

Miranda's eyes fluttered open as Raiya cut her ropes away. She sat up when she saw the flame in front of her. Her eyes quickly shifted to Raiya and

Drakin

The Story of Raiya

focused on the rip in her shirt. The little girl placed her hand on the rip and looked up into Raiya's eyes.

Raiya flashed a reassuring smile across her lips, "I'm okay, honey. No one hurt me."

Miranda frowned.

"It's okay, look…" Raiya said as she pointed to the other side of the encampment. "Do you see our jeep? It's parked over by those tents."

Miranda nodded.

"Good. Go get in. Wait there, I'll come get you in a little while."

Miranda froze in place with a look of concern.

"Miranda, sweetie, I promise I'll be right there, but I have to make sure we can get away safely first. If you stay here, I'll have to worry about you too!"

Miranda jumped off the table and ran off into the night. Raiya watched and waited until she was sure that the little girl was safe. There were still twenty or so canbans to deal with, any one of which could have stopped and grabbed her. Luckily, they all appeared to be distracted by the creature that was attacking them under a veil of darkness. The distraction was all Raiya and her friends needed to escape.

As they began to slowly make their way into the darkness, Raiya noticed the reverend attempting to slink away. He was leaving his people to fend for themselves.

Raiya clenched her jaw and turned back, "Pathetic…"

Drakin
The Story of Raiya

Jagger stopped in his tracks and beckoned to her, "Raiya, we've got to go now. That dragon has the canbans distracted!"

"Go on," Raiya growled. "I'll be just fine."

She marched toward the man, intent on ripping him apart. He turned in enough time to see her and pulled the dagger back out, "Well now, you're looking to get payback? The Lord sayeth, seek not revenge, lest you prepare your own grave as well."

Raiya clenched her jaw, "I don't know if there is anyone looking out for us or not... but if there is, I highly doubt you're the one they want to deliver their message. You're dead!"

Chapter 19

Jagger and Eric ran back towards the tent where they had been kept. Out of the corner of his eye, Jagger caught sight of his jeep. Apparently, some of the canbans knew how to drive and had taken it. Thankfully it didn't appear as though they'd had a chance to remove anything of value. Miranda was already sitting in the back, waiting to go. Andy hopped into the front seat and started the car.

The engine roared as it came to life, but it was quickly overpowered by the scream of burning canbans. Though it may not have seemed possible, the scene around them was now even more horrific.

Andy's eyes darted around the darkness, "Where's Raiya?"

Jagger shrugged, "She went hunting."

"Hunting?" Eric scoffed. "She went after the dragon?"

"No... not the dragon..."

"Then what...?"

Raiya appeared before Eric could finish his question. She was covered in blood but had a wide smile on her face.

"What happened to you?" Eric asked.

The look on Raiya's face was one of extreme satisfaction as she raised her left arm. In her hand, was a severed limb, still dripping blood.

Andy grimaced, "Do I even want to know?"

Drakin
The Story of Raiya

"What?" Raiya asked, feigning surprise. "Hey if you're going to cop a feel, it's going to cost you."

Eric smirked as he looked at Jagger, "Better watch yourself, buddy."

"Shut up," Jagger replied.

Raiya smiled as she wiped the blood from her face, "One more monster down."

"Satisfied?" Jagger asked in an annoyed tone.

"Very much so. Come on, let's get out of here before..."

In the darkness, Raiya could see the canbans fighting something very large. She squinted to see what it was. Another blast of flame illuminated the fight enough for her to see what they were dealing with, "Shit!"

"What is it?"

"That... it's another dragon lord."

"Is it...?"

Raiya shook her head, "No... it's not my father... It's big, but it's not that big. Still... that thing is larger than any of the other dragon lords I've ever seen."

Jagger and Raiya quickly jumped into the jeep. Jagger nodded as he hit the seat, "Floor it!"

The tires shrieked and squealed as the old truck pulled away from the burning tents. The fire and explosions quickly began to shrink as they made a quick getaway. The screams also quickly faded into silence.

Jagger turned away as the jeep sped off into the darkness, "Is everyone all right?"

Drakin
The Story of Raiya

Eric looked back from the front seat, "Yeah we're good."

Raiya looked back as the jeep continued to pull away "Sounds like the fight's over."

"I wonder who won," Jagger quipped.

"It's not funny, Jagger! You know damn well who won and you know who it'll be coming for next!"

"I know…"

Jagger didn't even get a chance to respond when the sound of flapping wings appeared overhead, "Aw shit…"

The ground shook as a massive black wall appeared in the jeep's headlights. Andy immediately hit the brakes, "Whoa!"

He pulled the wheel hard right. The jeep swerved as it slowed to a halt. A giant wall of flame appeared in front of them, blocking their escape.

There wasn't enough time to turn around. The dragon would be too quick for that. Jagger grabbed the bolt gun out of the backseat and turned it upwards towards the dragon that now appeared in front of them.

The dragon was right on top of them and looked down at the jeep menacingly. They were mere inches away from his face. The heat of his breath almost matched that of the flame wall.

Jagger let out a deep sigh. If the beast decided to attack them, they were dead. There was no way out.

Raiya jumped in front of Jagger, intent on at least trying to block the dragon fire that she knew was coming. She knew it wouldn't make any difference, but it was still better than doing nothing.

The red-eyed dragon lord watched them for a few moments without moving. Jagger got tired of waiting and aimed his gun at the massive beast's head. He was about to pull the trigger, when it finally began to speak, "Peace between us this night, young travelers."

Raiya looked at it oddly, "Peace? Never thought I'd hear a dragon call a truce."

"Yeah, especially when it just viciously massacred an entire colony of people," Andy added.

The dragon scoffed, "People who were going to eat you. Those creatures earned their fate a hundred times over."

"Even so…" Raiya replied.

"I would think you'd be more grateful after I saved your lives."

"My gratitude is contingent on your next move."

"Your skepticism is well met," the dragon replied. "My name is Auirn. As a token of good will, I saved you from those… disgusting creatures that aren't even fit to eat."

Jagger stepped out of his jeep and looked up at Auirn, "Okay… you have our attention… what do you want?"

The dragon gently thrust its wings downward, propelling itself into the air. It quickly landed on the other side of the jeep, "To meet my niece."

"Your niece?"

Drakin
The Story of Raiya

"Yes," Auirn replied.

Raiya stepped forward, "So the red and black dragon lord... is your brother?"

"His name is Eutherys, and he is no ordinary dragon lord. Unlike the five of us, he leads our council."

Raiya froze in place, "The Dragon's Dread Lord? The rumors were true?"

Auirn nodded, "Yes... I believe that is what your stories call him."

"My father... I don't believe it."

"You've seen him. Is it really so far beyond belief?"

"No, I guess not," Raiya admitted. "So, we've met... now what? I suppose you're here to kill me?"

"That is what Eutherys decreed, yes."

Jagger again raised the bolt gun, ready to shoot. Auirn looked at him with scorn, "I offered peace this night. I will not break such a vow of non-aggression until our business is concluded. You may rest easy, boy. I mean you no harm."

"Then what do you want?" Jagger demanded.

The dragon lord lowered his eyes, "I need your help."

Raiya wasn't expecting that. A dragon asking for help from a human? It was next to impossible to believe. Even in distress, the younger dragons never begged for mercy or asked for help. They lashed out, even as they were about to die. They'd rather the humans kill them. So why now was a dragon lord asking for help? "Okay, now you've

Drakin
The Story of Raiya

got my attention. What exactly do you need help with?"

"Our people are dying," Auirn replied.

"Yeah so?" Eric chimed in. "Your 'people' have been killing ours for over three decades. You've reduced our population from the billions down to scattered groups and desolate wanderers."

"Yes…" Auirn admitted. "What you say is true… though I opposed the attack on humans and wanted to find a way to coexist, I carried out the Dread Lord's will, as was expected of me. For that… I am truly sorry."

"Easy to say now that you're winning."

"Eric!" Raiya scolded. "Stop it, let's hear him out!"

Eric crossed his arms and turned his back, "Whatever."

Raiya shook her head and turned back to Auirn, "So why this sudden stab at diplomacy? My father has tried to have me killed twice."

"The council of lords has voted that eliminating you is a priority. This is why you've been under continuous attack. You were wise to head south."

"Uh huh…"

Auirn sighed, "What is your name?"

"… Raiya."

Auirn curled his neck back slightly. He appeared deep in thought as he looked away from the group, "Hmm…"

Drakin
The Story of Raiya

Finally, he turned back, "A fitting name for a dragonling. Eutherys may want you dead, but to me… you are a drakin, kin to drakeas-kind."

"How did you find us?"

"Finding implies that I lost you. Since I learned of your existence, I have been watching you. Your fighting style, your skill in combat, and your actions lately have earned my respect."

Raiya let out a deep sigh, "Auirn, you're still not answering my question. Why are you here? What do you want?"

"Forgive me," Auirn replied. "I don't get to speak very often and I do enjoy it. My kind favors growls and… more physical forms of expression. It doesn't befit us. I often find myself off track. I need your help."

"So you said, what with?"

"Recently, I've noticed that our females have had a harder time producing young. Many eggs do not hatch. Some of those that do are either lame or extremely lethargic. They aren't significant numbers, but when you factor in how rare such events used to be… it gives me pause. I believe your atmosphere is slowly poisoning us," Auirn said softly.

"How?"

"The high nitrogen content… our bodies have not adjusted to it as well as we'd hoped. I've noticed a lot of my brethren becoming considerably weaker. Several of the eggs I told you about… the fetuses were too weak and died in their shells."

Drakin
The Story of Raiya

"It's been thirty years," Raiya replied. "This just started happening?"

"The difference in your atmosphere is somewhat small. The poisoning would take considerable time."

"How long do you think you have?"

"Dragons are resilient creatures. It is difficult to say. It may be a hundred or several hundred years, but for a species that has a lifespan as long as ours, it's not far off."

"What do you want us to do?"

"Kill Eutherys."

Raiya's eyes narrowed, "You want us to kill your leader?"

"Yes… I have brought my concerns to him many times. I have tried to tell him that we are in danger, but he refuses to hear me. His mind has become too twisted and deranged by a lifetime of war. First, he led us during the war to save dragon kind on our world… now he leads us in our struggle for dominance here. At one time, he was a reasonable, honorable creature… you would have been proud to call 'father.' Sadly, that is not so anymore. He refuses to see the problem at hand. When he does acknowledge me, his solution is simply to attempt to terraform the planet. How he plans to do this is beyond me."

Auirn sighed, "It gives me no pleasure to ask this of you. The dragon council majorly shares my concern, but none of them will speak out against my brother. Out of respect, but more so out of fear, they support him. If he were to fall, I could call for a cessation of hostilities between our two peoples. In exchange for ending the violence, we'd ask for your assistance in getting off this planet."

"Oh great… that should be easy," Jagger said snidely.

"How could we help with that?" Raiya asked.

Andy stepped forward, "The United States at one time was able to launch rockets into outer space. We've kept that technology secured in an archive and even laid down the blueprints for massive colony ships in the event of an evacuation of Earth. We don't have the manpower to build such ships anymore, but an end to the war could allow humanity to come together to build them. In theory, they should be large enough to support dragons."

Raiya frowned, "This whole plan is pretty weak. You're assuming that the council will support you and that humanity would accept such a deal."

"True…" Auirn replied. "It is a long shot, but it is our best chance for survival… If either side refuses, we'll all likely be dead in short order. Are you willing to help us?"

"I could really care less about the fate of your species… and it's been made clear to me long ago that I'm not human either. That said, I planned on killing Eutherys anyway. I want his head for everything he's done. This doesn't change anything. For now, we have a shared interest. Once I have my father's head, you can do what you want. Just don't think for a minute that I'm willing to trust you."

Drakin

The Story of Raiya

"That was the most I could hope for. You have my support. Anything I can do to help you… I will."

Raiya nodded, "Fine… I need you to keep the dragons off my back. We've been on the run because wyverns and drakes seem to follow us."

"I will make sure they are given false information on your movements."

"Thanks… one other thing…"

"Yes?"

"I need to learn how to breathe fire," Raiya replied.

Auirn looked puzzled, "Do you believe that you possess the ability? Such things take dragonlings years to master."

"She's already done it," Jagger replied. "She used it against your brother."

"Did she? Fascinating… –Show me your mouth."

Raiya stepped forward and parted her jaws. The dragon lord brought his head down close to her, turned it to the side, and brought his left eye to level with her lips, "Hmm… lift up your tongue."

Raiya did as she was asked. The dragon's yellow eye darted up and down as it inspected her, "Yes, it does appear that you have the ability. Tell me, how did you use it on my brother?"

"He attacked me. As his flame hit, I just unleashed my own spray."

"You used his flame against him… impressive."

Drakin
The Story of Raiya

Auirn turned his head so that both eyes were looking at Raiya, "Try clicking your front teeth together."

Raiya quickly snapped her jaws together. Nothing happened, "Hm… Try scraping your teeth together as you reopen your mouth."

Raiya pressed her teeth together and slowly scraped the back of her front incisors against her lower teeth. A momentary spark lit up her mouth. The flash in the dragon's eye surprised her.

"Is that?"

Auirn smiled, "Yes…"

The dragon backed away and dug his claws into the ground, "Now, roll back your tongue and spray as you click your teeth together. Hit me with your best shot."

Raiya curled her tongue back and tensed the muscles in the floor of her mouth. Clear liquid shot out, prompting her to quickly clench her teeth. As her jaws parted, a small fire appeared.

Jagger watched as the small flame puffed out in less than a second. Raiya frowned, "I can't do it…"

"You can," Auirn said in a stern voice. "Push harder and be faster with your teeth."

Raiya glared at Auirn as she tensed the muscles even more. Her mouth snapped shut. Jagger heard a faint click as her mouth reopened.

Raiya was nearly blown off her feet by the massive fireball that shot from her lips. Auirn's eyes went wide as the flame impacted on his hide, knocking him to the side. The flame broke on his scales and quickly vanished.

Drakin

The Story of Raiya

Auirn got back to his feet and smiled, "Well done! You are truly drakin!"

Raiya smiled faintly, "I… I did it… I can't believe it."

Auirn nodded, "You did well."

"Am I ready?"

"To take on Eutherys? Hardly…"

Jagger stepped forward, "Then what do we need to do?"

"Eutherys still has the loyalty of the entire drakeas horde. You've proven yourselves formidable, but I can't imagine that you could take on the thousands of dragons that stand between you and your father."

"That's true," Raiya admitted. "We can't possibly get through them all… Taking a few at a time is one thing, but not the entire horde."

"We'll find a way," Jagger insisted.

Jagger's words caught Auirn's interest. He shifted his gaze from Raiya to Jagger. The dragon's eyes shifted as he inspected his niece's companion, "You… So, you are her protector then?"

Raiya looked at Jagger curiously as he stood eye to eye with her uncle. Jagger glanced at her momentarily before turning back to the massive dragon, "I am…"

She smiled as Auirn looked him over. The dragon huffed as he spoke, "Hmm… It is unlikely that even one with such a strong heart could protect her against such a force. Even so, I feel better about her chances now."

Boom!

Drakin
The Story of Raiya

A massive firebolt struck the ground right next to Auirn. Everyone looked up to see the red dragon almost on top of them, "I knew it! Auirn, you are tul'zethian! Your brother will not show you mercy this time… blood traitor!"

Auirn took to the sky, "Raki'Agr, what are you doing here?"

"Long have I suspected that you would betray us. Your radical ideas about our survivability here would only have led you down this path. It was inevitable."

Auirn immediately took to the air, "Raki'Agr… you've never been able to see beyond the bounds of your own lust for power. Our people are in trouble, but you would rather see our people meet their end than ask for help! I cannot allow this."

Jagger quickly raised the bolt gun and fired four shots into the air. Raiya glared at him, "What the hell are you doing?"

Jagger peered through the scope, "If Auirn dies, we may lose our only chance to end this war. We can't let that other dragon escape!"

Raiya forced a half-smile, "All right… let's try to get him on the ground!

Eric grabbed the bolt pistol from under the seat of the jeep, "We're going to need more than bolt guns to bring him out of the sky!"

"I know…" Raiya replied. "–Auirn… can you knock him out of the sky? Then we'll take over!"

Auirn let out a mighty roar as he charged at the other dragon lord. The two twisted around

Drakin
The Story of Raiya

each other. Auirn grabbed Raki'Agr by the throat and jerked his arm violently.

Raki'Agr screeched in pain as the two dragons hit the ground with a loud boom. Auirn landed a few feet away on his back. The stunned dragon struggled to get back on his feet. He was definitely sore but didn't appear injured.

Raki'Agr recovered much quicker and immediately turned to his opponent, "I'll kill you for this!"

Raki'Agr drew back his head and lurched forward, spewing a massive stream of flame at his old friend. Raiya saw what was happening and immediately moved into the flame's path. She curled her tongue back and let her own flames fly.

The two streams impacted against each other. There was a loud boom, followed by a large explosion between them.

Raki'Agr's eyes widened when he realized what was going on, "What…?"

Jagger watched from a hundred feet away, "This isn't going to end well."

He raised his bolt gun and fired four shots into the dragon's wing. The bolts struck the rough hide and disappeared. There was no visible effect. The dragon lord didn't even have to shrug them off.

Jagger dropped the gun, realizing that it was useless and ran back to the jeep. He grabbed one of the larger power cells out of the back and turned it on. The power indicator rose to full strength as it came on. A high-pitched ringing entered his ears as the lights activated.

Jagger set it to maximum output when it reached full strength. Red lights flashed and a warning indicator beeped that something wasn't right. The newer models had a kill switch that would automatically turn the power off if they weren't plugged in. These, however, were much older. Though they all had the same universal hookup, the originals were considered dangerous and banned in most cities.

"What are you doing?" Eric asked. "You're going to get yourself killed. Turn it off before it explodes!"

"No way, that's exactly what I want it to do!"

"What? You want to get yourself killed?"

"Not me…" Jagger replied as he charged forward.

Raki'Agr ceased his flame attack in order to catch his breath. He glared at Raiya with utter malice, "I remember you… Your skin is that of a dragon. I made a mistake letting you live that day… I won't make that same mistake twice!"

Raiya's eyes were full of hatred as she stared down the dragon lord, "You set my father loose on New Framingham… didn't you?"

Raki'Agr smiled and began to chuckle, but did not respond. That told Raiya everything she needed to know.

Auirn was back on his feet, ready to pounce between them when Jagger dove in front of Raki'Agr. The dragon lord opened his mouth, about to fire another blast when something impacted in his throat.

Drakin
The Story of Raiya

Raki'Agr closed his mouth as he choked on whatever had been thrown at him. Raiya looked at Jagger, "What did you just do?"

Jagger immediately got to his feet and grabbed Raiya's hand, "Fucking run!"

Jagger and Raiya turned and ran towards Auirn. Raki'Agr swallowed hard to clear his throat. He was about to give chase when a high-pitched ringing emanated from his insides. Raiya looked back to see the mighty beast's neck explode in a massive blue flame. It didn't even have a chance to cry out in pain as the carcass collapsed on the ground.

Drakin
The Story of Raiya

Chapter 20

Andy and Miranda appeared out from behind the jeep. Eric looked on in disbelief as bits and pieces of burning flesh dropped around him, "Jagger... I can't decide if you're my hero or the worst kind of crazy!"

Jagger stood up as he was joined by the rest of his group, "Did we just...?"

Raiya nodded as she looked at the corpse in a state of shock, "We just killed a dragon lord..."

Andy stepped forward and touched the headless carcass, "I was beginning to think that it wasn't possible. Their hide is impenetrable by any weapon I've seen so far. Even the high energy stuff couldn't do it. Their hides were just too dense."

Auirn growled softly as he looked at his old friend's remains, "Except you didn't attack his hide... you destroyed him from within. Our bodies' scales are solid... but inside, we're as vulnerable as you are."

"You don't sound too happy," Raiya said as she turned to look at her uncle.

Auirn lowered his head, "What do I have to be happy about? He was my friend. For many years, he was someone I could always commiserate with. It brings me no joy to see any of my brethren fall, even Eutherys."

"So..."

The old dragon huffed, "You may rest easy. I do not hold what you've done against you. He was a necessary loss. I just hope that this will not have to be repeated once Eutherys is gone."

"What will you do now?"

Auirn looked to the north, "I will need to return to my people before anyone else sees this. If they realize that I had any part in Raki'Agr's death, it will cost me my life."

Dust kicked up, causing a large black cloud as Auirn thrust his wings. He slowly lifted himself into the sky and hovered over the group, "You'd best find a safe harbor. When word of what happened here reaches Eutherys, his response will be relentless. I will be watching you, as much as I can. The dragon roost is to the north... I believe you call it Mount Whitney. Do not proceed there until you have a plan... and absolutely do not go alone!"

Auirn thrust his wings downward one last time and disappeared into the clouds. A faint roar in the distance was the last they heard of him.

"So, what now?" Eric asked.

Raiya looked back at the group. Her eyes darted between each of their faces. They were looking to her for an answer.

Raiya wasn't a leader. She'd never even wanted to be one. All she ever wanted was to wander the land and be left alone, "I... I don't know... what can we do now?"

"We're going to need help," Jagger replied. "The dragons protecting their base have to be drawn out... It's the only way we're going to get in."

Drakin
The Story of Raiya

"So, who do we turn to? We've successfully pissed off pretty much everyone we could consider an ally."

Jagger nodded, "I know… but what choice do we have?"

Raiya sighed, "All right… so what's our plan then?"

"I think we should start with the Westcon."

"You think they'll listen to you?"

"Who knows?" Jagger asked. "It's worth a shot."

"Wait, wait, wait…" Eric cut in. "So, our plan involves going to one of the major powers and asking them to send their army out as bait?"

"Yup… pretty much," Raiya replied.

"Well, that's crazy!"

"You got a better idea?" Jagger asked.

When Eric didn't respond, Jagger nodded, "Didn't think so."

Raiya looked back at the jeep for a moment before responding, "All right, where are we going then?"

"The capital of the Westcon is Denver, Colorado. The U.S., Mexican, and Canadian forces that merged met there for a final showdown with the dragons. They dug in and fortified themselves with everything they had. The dragon attack never came, so the countries formed together into the Western Coalition, similar to what was going on in Europe and Asia. They've held out there ever since and attempt to aid in the establishment of fortified colonies all over the Western Hemisphere."

"New Framingham being one of them," Raiya replied.

"Yeah, that's right. Some have been a lot more successful than others."

Andy nodded, "So we're going to Denver then?"

"Yeah," Raiya replied.

"We'd better bundle up; it's going to be cold up that way."

Raiya lowered her eyes and looked at her arms, "Oh great…"

Eric yawned as he looked at the dragon lord's body, "Can we start out in the morning? It's still dark and we have yet to have a break."

"Yeah… that's not a bad idea," Raiya replied.

She turned and walked over to the body of Raki'Agr. Her jaw clicked and a large stream of flame left her lips. She moved her head back and forth, covering the body in flame.

Andy quickly grabbed an odd device out of his pocket. He quickly started pressing a red button on the back, causing tiny flashes of light.

"What is that?" Eric asked.

"It's a camera," Andy replied. "If you're going to try to get help from any of the factions around here, you're going to need proof. Trust me, they're going to want to see evidence that we killed a dragon lord."

Jagger nodded and turned to watch as Raiya went to work, "Hey, is that really safe?"

Raiya ceased her fire breath and looked at Jagger, "We need to keep warm... Call it a calculated risk."

Drakin
The Story of Raiya

"All right…"

The group settled in for the night next to the burning body. Their makeshift campsite wasn't much, but it was cozy enough for everyone to relax.

Raiya sat up on the edge of the site, opting to keep guard instead of sleeping. Jagger laid back and looked up at the stars, "Eric, can I ask you something?"

"Sure," Eric replied. "What's up?"

"You seemed a little hostile when Auirn spoke to us. Any reason?"

Eric frowned, "Those dragons have taken so much from us, do I really need a reason?"

"I guess not," Jagger admitted. "It just seems like you have much more of an ax to grind with them, and I mean even before your father died."

"Yeah…"

"Look if you don't want to talk about it…"

"They took Riley from me."

"Riley?"

"My wife…"

"No shit, you were married?" Jagger asked.

"Yeah."

This isn't going to be pretty. Jagger thought. *The same story as the rest of us…*

Eric kept his eyes on the stars as he spoke, "We grew up together and got married pretty quickly when we came of age. Some in our group thought we were too young, but we didn't care. We knew everything about each other, shared

Drakin
The Story of Raiya

everything… We couldn't imagine a life without one another."

"What happened?"

"We were expecting our first child. She was six months pregnant… When the dragons attacked, she had trouble getting away… They caught her… two drakes and three wyverns. I was out on a hunt when they attacked."

Jagger noticed tears coming out of Eric's eyes as he spoke, "When I got back… I found her… in pieces. The dragons took their time and ripped her to shreds for us to find. She never even had a chance."

"Oh… I'm sorry."

"I went from getting ready to start a family, to being completely alone in a matter of hours."

Raiya kept silent on the side of the group. Her eyes were focused on the sky. Her expression remained stoic, but every few moments her lip twitched into a frown.

"It's been five years," Eric huffed. "I've… come to terms with it about as much as I'm ever going to. Just don't expect me to be happy about working with dragons… in fact, if it comes to that, don't expect much out of me at all. I came with you to kill dragons and prevent this from happening again. That's it."

Jagger was beginning to wish he'd kept his mouth shut, "No problem buddy, whatever you say."

The camp fell silent. No one knew what to say after that. Jagger knew that he was responsible for the mood. If his group was going to get any rest, he needed to change the subject if he could. What could he say after that? *Come on Jagger, think of something. Sitting here feeling bad isn't going to help anyone.*

"I wonder if they'll have pizza in Denver." *Really? That's the best you could come up with?*

Raiya turned and looked at him, "What?"

"Pizza? You've never tried it?" Jagger asked.

"No…"

"It's cheese, tomato sauce, and usually some kind of meat and vegetables on baked dough. I haven't had one in years. It's so good!"

"If you say so," Raiya replied.

Eric shook his head as a smile slowly returned to his face, "Nah man… I'd kill for a plate of nachos. My group stumbled across a destroyed caravan with a ton of food when I was a kid. My dad made us this massive plate of nachos with all kinds of stuff on them. It was the best thing ever."

Jagger looked above his head as he lay back, "What about you Andy? What do you miss?"

Andy was nearly asleep when he heard his name called, "Me? Oh… well… I still remember my dad grilling hot dogs before the food shortage hit."

"Hot… dogs?" Raiya said in a disgusted tone.

"Yeah, they were great. Put them on a bun, coat them in ketchup, mustard, relish, or cheese and chili, and they were delicious. My mouth waters every time I think of them."

"You… actually ate dog… willingly?"

Drakin

The Story of Raiya

The group burst out laughing as they watched the stars. Raiya frowned, "What? What's so funny?"

"Hot dogs aren't actually made from dogs," Jagger replied. "They were usually some combination of beef and pork."

"Then why were they called hot dogs?"

"Hell if I know…"

"What about you?" Eric asked Raiya. "Any particular food you'd like to dig into?"

Raiya leaned forward, looking into the flame, "Not really…"

Eric frowned, "Oh come on, there has to be something?"

Raiya sighed as she thought back to her grandparents, "Well… I don't remember much about it… but my gramps used to make something on his stove called pancakes. They were these doughy little circles and he'd pour this sweet syrup on them."

Eric pointed at her, "Flapjacks, yes! God… I haven't had those in years!"

He then turned over and looked at Miranda, "What about you, little darling? Would you like a nice big cone of ice cream?"

Miranda looked at him oddly. Eric tried to illustrate with his hands and some ash, "It's like frozen milk, except it's made in all different flavors. I bet you're a strawberry girl, aren't you?"

Miranda smiled and nodded vigorously.

"Yeah, I thought so."

Drakin
The Story of Raiya

"I wonder if we'll ever get those things back," Jagger said in a sad voice. "We lost so much… It's hard to say if any of the old world will survive this awful war."

"They'll be back," Andy replied. "The U.S. Government created a time capsule. It's currently hidden under the command center. It's basically a massive drive containing as much of our history and culture as we could store on it. History, sports, food recipes, city construction layouts, scientific achievements, everything. If we can beat the dragons… it'll all come back in some form."

"Hear that Raiya? You may get to try hot dogs after all."

"Yeah… I'll pass," Raiya replied, despite a tiny smile momentarily flashing across her lips.

"What do you mean he's dead?"

Eutherys's roar echoed across the mountains. The ground shook with a mighty boom as he growled. The other dragon lords backed away and lowered their heads in submission. Eutherys quickly turned and slammed his tail against the side of the mountain. The resulting boom echoed for miles.

Amzer'ial stepped forward with her wing-muscles tensed. If Eutherys was to become violent again, she didn't want to stick around to see the result, "It would appear that your daughter is far more powerful than we originally expected."

"Can you be certain that it's him?"

Drakin
The Story of Raiya

Amzer'ial nodded, "We found Raki'Agr's bones. They were too big to be from any other dragon. It was him, we can be sure of this."

"Even so, he has been missing for many weeks and we've lost track of the girl," Auirn said. "How can you be certain it was her? We've been fighting against the humans for decades. Could it be possible that the human forces got lucky and found a way to take him down? He was never the smartest of us…"

Eutherys slammed his claw into the ground, causing another loud boom to ripple across the mountain, "Do not speak ill of our brethren. He was one of us and a fine warrior."

"Forgive me, brother," Auirn replied. "I did not intend any disrespect to our fallen comrade."

Eutherys nodded, "And none will be implied from your words."

Amzer'ial turned and snapped her jaws shut in a threatening manner, "His hide had been burnt away and his bones were charred. Only the breath of a dragon could do that."

"Which means she's mastered fire-breathing," Eutherys said.

"We also saw footprints and tire tracks. How many humans do you know that have the ability to breathe dragon's fire?"

Entharis stepped forward, "This is bad… very bad. If word spreads about Raki'Agr's fall, it will boost morale amongst the human forces."

"It would be worse than that…" Eutherys said, having finally calmed down. "This could bring together the coalitions, nomads, and the nationalist forces."

"What are your orders?" Amzer'ial asked.

"The city they call Denver. It's the capital of their forces… Entharis, take whatever force you need with you. Go there and wipe them out… all of them."

Amzer'ial looked concerned, "Attack the coalition's capital city head on? Is that wise?"

"Are you questioning my orders?"

Amzer'ial shuddered a little under Eutherys dark stare, "Normally no, but you're asking us to attack a heavily fortified city. The humans are not going to just roll over and die. We're going to take heavy casualties trying to take them down."

"Desperate times call for desperate measures. We can no longer afford to wait and wear them down. Circumstances have changed too much. I know how you feel about our young, but many more will die if the human forces unify. That is not a risk I can take."

Entharis stepped forward, "I agree. I am not worried about it. I will take our forces ahead and crush the pathetic fools."

"Do not allow your lust for blood to blind you!" Amzer'ial hissed. "Have you forgotten that you are dealing with a species that have proven themselves to be resilient and resourceful many times over? They will not go down as easily as you think!"

"Such dribble," Entharis replied.

"The humans are a formidable foe," Amzer'ial said angrily. "Only a fool would think otherwise."

Drakin

The Story of Raiya

"You sound as though you admire them," Entharis said with a sneer.

"I respect them," Amzer'ial replied. "Their skin is soft and offers almost no protection against the elements. Their brains are nowhere near as developed as ours and they are a pathetically primitive species in every measurable sense. Yet they have survived and here they are offering true resistance to us. Even knowing that they may lose, they still continue to oppose us at every turn. That is a species worthy of respect."

"Amzer'ial speaks wisdom," Eutherys said as he sat on his perch. "You would do well to follow her advice."

"As you wish," Entharis said as he bristled his sharp scales. "I will take my leave of you now to rally my forces."

Eutherys nodded, "Victory to you, my friend… good luck!"

Amzer'ial hissed as Entharis flew down the mountain, "Fool…"

Eutherys turned and looked at her, "Speak plainly my friend. No one will hold it against you."

"I am entirely loyal to the horde… you know that," Amzer'ial replied. "However, this decision to send him… He is blinded by his bloodlust… Years of warfare have clearly clouded his mind."

"You think I made a mistake?"

"I think he's going to get a lot of drakin killed."

Drakin
The Story of Raiya

"Maybe…" Eutherys said. "Or maybe it will rid us of a loose cannon. Only time will tell, I suppose."

Drakin
The Story of Raiya

Denver City
Capital of the Western Coalition
Formerly Colorado

Drakin
The Story of Raiya

Chapter 21

"Watch him!" Jagger shouted as Raiya grabbed the attacking wyvern by the neck.

"Watch out for yourself!" Raiya replied. "I got this."

Raiya tightened her grip and jerked her arms to the left. The wyvern cried out in pain as its neck snapped. It fell lifelessly to the ground with a loud thud.

Raiya turned to see how the rest of the group was doing. Jagger was holding his own with his bolt gun. He'd brought one out of the sky, but a second one came swooping in behind him, "Jagger, watch out!"

Jagger quickly turned and pointed his gun at the wyvern when three bolts struck it out of nowhere. Raiya turned and looked back at the jeep to see where the bolts had come from. Andy was standing next to the truck with a nervous look on his face as he held the pistol.

Jagger nodded, "Thanks!"

"You're welcome," Andy replied as he ducked back down with Miranda.

A loud boom made Raiya turn and look behind him. A drake lay on its back, barely moving. Eric was hard at work trying to pry his knife from its chest, "One less of these!"

"Nicely done, Eric," Jagger replied.

With all the dragons dead, Andy took Miranda by the hand and led her out from the cover of the jeep, "That was the third attack since we started heading north. They're becoming more and more numerous."

Raiya nodded, "My father… He must be getting nervous."

"If that's the case, why hasn't he sent anything bigger after us?" Jagger asked.

"Maybe he doesn't know where we are? He must have patrol upon patrol looking for us and has his forces spread thin."

"That might be to our advantage then… but it won't be for long. We need to get to Denver."

"How far away are we?" Eric asked.

"About an hour," Jagger replied. "That sign we saw said that we were in Colorado Springs. I believe that's only about an hour away… but I've never been here, so I'm not certain."

"All right, let's go," Raiya said as she jumped into the jeep's passenger seat.

⚐

"Is that smoke?" Andy asked.

"That's smoke…" Raiya replied. "Shit, they're under attack!"

Denver quickly came into view. Like every other city they'd visited thus far, it had a large metal wall around it with fortifications every few feet. They couldn't see over it, but the few buildings that still poked out from behind the wall appeared to have been damaged recently. At least two of them had been set ablaze.

Jagger kept his eyes on the sky above them as the jeep approached the city walls, "Holy shit, look!"

Drakin
The Story of Raiya

A massive gray dragon flew down out of the clouds and perched on the taller of the two burning buildings. He let out a massive roar as several static bolts flew past him.

"That's a dragon lord!" Raiya shouted. "No doubt about it… and he's not alone!"

As the cloud of smoke passed, they could see massive groups of wyverns, drakes, and even beta dragons attacking the city. They appeared to be forming into packs as they dipped down to strike.

Jagger watched as the city's defenses attempted to fight the dragons off. They were successfully bringing down some of the smaller ones, but nothing they did had any effect on the leader. As expected, his hide was just too strong for their weapons.

Jagger slammed his foot down on the gas and blew right through the city gates. Eric held onto the rollbar in the back, "Jagger, be careful man! What are you doing?"

"I'm not letting this turn into another Foxborough! Hopefully, no one told them about what I did in New Framingham."

The jeep raced down the surprisingly well-maintained road to the main city square. Like most of the cities they'd visited, this one had been destroyed and rebuilt several times.

They passed by smashed buildings, rubble, and small shanties that had been built as makeshift homes for several refugees. It wasn't the most pleasant sight, but to see that several buildings were in the process of being repaired did instill hope for the future.

Drakin
The Story of Raiya

The jeep finally arrived at the Denver City Hall and County Building. This had once been the capital building of the city but had long since been converted into Westcon Central Command.

The solid gray building was covered in black ash and burns. It had seen several attacks but had stood defiantly against all of them. Even the small clock tower on top had survived everything that had been thrown at it.

Around the massive building was an open field. Where once there were finely trimmed trees and beautiful flowers, now stood only ash and dead branches. Several gunner positions had been dug into the ground around the command center. Soldiers were running to various positions to assist with fending off the dragon attacks.

Jagger pulled the jeep to a halt and jumped out as a group of soldiers passed by. He called out to one of the soldiers, "You there, who's the officer in charge here?"

The soldier stopped in his tracks and looked at Jagger, "Identify yourself."

"Lieutenant Jagger Bishop, Westcon eastern front."

"Identification?"

Jagger pulled his ID out of his pocket and handed it to the soldier, "Here you go."

The soldier looked at the paper and handed it back, "This way, sir."

Jagger followed the soldier as his friends jumped out of the truck and ran to catch up. They were led to one of the gunning positions where an older man stood under a small canopy. The massive anti-air laser array continuously fired at the dragons overhead. It made a loud humming sound each time it fired, making it hard to hear anything else. The soldier had to shout to be heard, "Commander Bhatia, this is Lieutenant Bishop reporting from the Eastern Front!"

Jagger stood straight and saluted the commander. The older man ignored the salute, "Welcome to the fray, Lieutenant. What can I do for you? As you can see, we're a little preoccupied here!"

"At the moment, I'm here to help. We can talk about what I need once the dragons are gone."

Commander Bhatia stepped forward and pointed at the dragon lord, "Do you see that? You know what that is?"

"Yes, I do. It's a dragon lord."

"Then you know that unless we can ward it off, we're all pretty much dead, right? My goal is to hold out as long as we can until we can evacuate."

"Evacuate the capital? Is that even possible?"

The commander frowned, "We've trained for it… but we've also brought in several refugees since then."

"Commander, with respect… abandoning the capital…"

"Will throw the coalition into chaos, I know. This could wind up losing us the war."

Jagger glared at the commander, "Sir, we can kill it."

"Excuse me?"

Drakin
The Story of Raiya

"We can kill it. Give me the chance and I'll save the city."

"How? Nothing's been able to penetrate its hide. There's no way to kill one of them."

"I'm not going to penetrate its hide. If you hit it from the inside, you can kill it."

"How the hell are you going to do that?"

WROOOOOOOAAA!!!

"There's no time to explain!" Jagger insisted. "Please sir, just give me command!"

Commander Bhatia looked oddly at Jagger. He clearly didn't believe a word of any of this, but what choice did he have? Likely everyone was about to die anyway. He scratched the short gray hairs on his head as a fireball took out a nearby gunnery emplacement, "Fine… what the hell… What's the worst that can happen?"

He reached over the radio that was attached to the laser array and tapped the black button on the side. With a look of disgust on his face, he picked up the speaker, "All units not currently engaged in the evacuation, this is Commander Bhatia. I'm relinquishing command of the capital ground forces to Lieutenant Bishop. You are to follow his orders until instructed otherwise."

Commander Bhatia immediately handed the speaker to Jagger, "What are your orders, sir?"

Jagger quickly looked around. He had gone from being a rogue junior officer to the commander of the capital defense force. At least a million people lived in this city. Everything rested with him, "All fighters out of position, get to the wall and keep the citadels firing. All defensive arrays and turrets are to focus on the smaller dragons. Take down as many as you can. Do not fire on the dragon lord, I repeat… Do not fire on the dragon lord."

No one responded over the radio, but clearly, they heard him. The turrets switched targets and quickly began to bring down huge numbers of wyverns and drakes. The guns were so powerful that one quick strafe typically took down five or six wyverns.

Jagger turned to Raiya, "All right, partner. You're clear, get that thing's attention."

Raiya nodded and ran out into the open field with a determined look. Jagger turned back to the commander, "Do you have any G1 medium-sized power cells?"

The commander nodded and opened the case on the side of the laser, "G1s were kept in reserve… I never thought we'd be desperate enough to use them. Each laser has a spare, just in case."

Jagger grabbed it and stepped out from under the canopy, "Commander, get everyone who's nearby to safety. This is going to be a tough fight."

Commander Bhatia nodded and turned to a few of the men that were out in the open, "Roger that… —You men, get inside the command center, now!"

Eric appeared next to Jagger with the bolt gun in his hand, "What can I do?"

Drakin
The Story of Raiya

"Just be ready to be a thorn in that beast's side if Raiya looks like she's losing. We're going to need everything we've got."

Raiya ran out to the open field and clicked her teeth together. She screamed as a stream of flame emanated from her lower jaw. The flame shot into the air and acted as a beacon.

Entharis grinned when he saw it, "So… you actually did come here. I was so hoping you would. It saves me the trouble of hunting you down."

Raiya ceased her flame as the dragon lord hovered close to her. A look of disgust entered his eyes, "Is this it? Is this really what Eutherys has been so worried about? This pathetic creature?"

He quickly landed and rested his tale on the ground, "I find it hard to believe that something so small could cause such problems."

Raiya found herself surrounded. The dragon had curled its tail so that while its face was locked with Raiya, its tail was at her back. She stood with her chin out, defiantly, "I'm tougher than you think!"

"We'll see! I find it impossible to believe that you succeeded in killing my brethren, but I will not be so easily felled."

Entharis raised his head over Raiya and snapped downward. Raiya jumped out of the way of his jaw and darted behind the dragon. It quickly turned, jumped back, and snapped again.

Raiya smiled, "I've seen faster wyverns! You're going to have to try a lot harder than that to make me a meal!"

"As you wish," Entharis replied. "I like my meals cooked anyway…"

The dragon lord opened his mouth as wide as he could and unleashed an intense wall of flame. The heat from the flame felt like a sunburn to anyone standing nearby. The flame moved quickly, but not quick enough.

Raiya dodged out of the way and clicked her teeth together. Now it was her turn. A stream of fire sprayed at the massive dragon, striking its neck.

Entharis looked more annoyed than hurt as he turned into the flame and deflected it, "So it is true…"

He again unleashed his fire breath on Raiya, forcing her own fire back. This was much stronger than any of the other dragons she'd fought so far, apart from her father. She didn't expect it and didn't have time to counter.

As before, a massive fireball appeared between the two flames. It fed off the energy that was being supplied by both streams of fire, but this time it was being pushed back towards her. This dragon was attacking with full force. She pushed harder and harder until her throat became horse. There was nothing she could do. She had lost this round.

She ceased her attack and attempted to dodge out of the way, but the fireball was too close. The sheer force of the explosion sent her flying

Drakin
The Story of Raiya

backward out of control. Her spine struck a piece of metal debris that looked like a telephone pole. Her body snapped back from the force of the impact. She hit the ground with a thud.

"No… –Light him up!" Jagger screamed as he dropped the power cell.

The group attacked the dragon lord with everything they had. Eric used the bolt gun while Jagger unloaded both pistols. Entharis ignored the attacks like they were little more than annoying fruit flies. He was focused on more important prey.

🦇

Raiya lay next to the post where she had impacted. Her back pulsed as she turned and lay on her side. Every movement she made was extremely painful. Her body no longer had the strength left to stand.

As Entharis approached, she sprayed the last of her fire breath at him in a vain attempt to hold her ground. She knew that it would likely do her no good, but it didn't matter. She wasn't about to just lay there and die without a fight.

Entharis shook it off as he stood over her, "I expected someone that even Eutherys feared to put up more of a fight than that… too bad…"

The dragon lord opened its mouth widely and lowered its jaw over Raiya. Time seemed to slow to a crawl as Raiya embraced the fact that she was about to die. After the life she lived, she wasn't scared of death, but she did feel some remorse about leaving her friends behind. *Jagger…*

Drakin
The Story of Raiya

Miranda... I'm sorry... please take care of yourselves.

"No!"

A shrill voice broke Raiya out of her haze and startled the massive dragon. Miranda ran between Raiya and Entharis, holding the power cell. She grabbed the dragon's tongue as its jaw descended on Raiya. She quickly turned and smiled at Raiya as the dragon pulled its tongue back into its mouth, "Goodbye."

Raiya's eyes went wide, "Miranda, what are you doing? Stop!"

She reached out and tried to grab Miranda, but Entharis jerked his head back. His mouth closed with Miranda inside as he appeared to be gagging. "What is..."

Before he could finish the sentence, a shrill ringing sound entered his ears. He didn't have time to think before the object that was stuck in his throat exploded.

Raiya cried out in despair as Entharis's head was blown clear off his body, "No! Miranda, no! Please!"

Boom!

The massive head hit the ground, rolling a few feet from the body. The upper part of the neck was badly singed and smoking. It darted back and forth a few times before hitting the ground.

Jagger dropped to his knees, "No..."

Eric stood with his fists at his side, "Miranda... no... no more babies..."

Drakin
The Story of Raiya

Andy ran to Raiya's side and knelt down next to her, "I'm sorry… she got away from me! I had no idea she was going to do that."

Raiya clenched a fist and tried to hit Andy, but was too weak to make any real impact, "You were supposed to protect her!"

"I tried, she was too quick."

"Why?" Raiya asked as she vainly struggled to get to her feet. "Why would she do something like that?"

Andy lowered his eyes. "She knew that she didn't have long… In the end, she made a choice to give up what little time she had left to save the one person that she cared about… you."

Jagger ran to Raiya's side and grabbed her arms as she tried again to stand up, "Are you okay?"

"No!" Raiya screamed. "What kind of stupid question is that? Miranda's gone!"

"I know…" Jagger said softly. "I didn't even see her grab the power cell until it was too late."

"She's gone, Jagger! I watched her die… I can't believe it… I saw her eyes… She was right in front of me, but I couldn't get to her!"

For the first time since he met her, Jagger saw something he didn't think he'd ever see; Raiya was crying. He quickly absorbed the shock as Raiya balled her fists, "Raiya there was nothing you could have done... This is what she wanted…"

"Don't you say that!" Raiya screamed. "There should have been. I should have been stronger… why couldn't I save her?"

Drakin

The Story of Raiya

Jagger grabbed her, pressing her head against his chest. Nothing he could do was going to prevent the imminent meltdown, but at least she was with friends, "She made her choice… She was already dy…"

Raiya's eyes flared to a yellow fire as she looked up at Jagger, "Shut up! Don't you dare give me that bullshit excuse! I don't care if she was near death. I don't care if she had Dragon's Bane or any other disease. No one deserves that kind of death! Do you hear me? No one!"

"I'm sorry," Jagger replied. "Look… this may have been less painful for her than dying of Dragon's Bane."

"You don't fucking know that…" Raiya hissed.

She didn't say anything else. What could she say? Miranda was gone and nothing was going to bring her back.

Raiya gave up and buried her face in Jagger's chest. It was an odd and uncomfortable feeling, adding to the stress that she was already dealing with. She'd never had to rely on anyone, not since she was a child. No matter how hurt she felt, she'd always dealt with it. However, this time was different. This time she'd lost someone she cared for and she didn't know how to handle it, "Why…?"

"Nothing I can say will make you feel better right now."

"Then why say anything?"

Jagger shrugged, "Because you asked…"

Drakin
The Story of Raiya

"I don't believe it!" a voice yelled from behind. "That was a dragon lord! They killed a dragon lord!"

Jagger looked over to see Commander Bhatia staring in disbelief at the corpse of the gray dragon lord. A large group of soldiers slowly congregated around them.

"I didn't think they could be killed."

"Does this mean we have a chance?"

"An actual dragon lord… dead."

"They are going to be pissed!"

Commander Bhatia smiled as he turned back to his men. He looked up and pointed at the remaining dragons, "Well come on men! Lieutenant Bishop did his part, now let's do ours! Denver won't fall, not today and certainly not on my watch! To the walls!"

Chapter 22

Cheers went up from the men and women defending the city. The last of the dragon army was defeated and its survivors were in full retreat. It was over.

Bullets from old projectile firearms shot into the air, followed by hats and helmets. The celebration could be heard for miles.

The celebration spread through Central Command square. Though the celebration was erupting around them, Jagger's group was completely unconscious of it. They stood together as Jagger pointlessly attempted to console Raiya. His shirt was soaked with her tears. Many soldiers attempted to congratulate them, but quickly backed off when they saw what was happening.

Eric and Andy stood on either side, attempting to give Raiya some privacy. It wasn't much, but she appreciated the effort.

The cheering crowd slowly flowed towards Jagger and his friends. They formed a circle and began clapping for the group. Raiya let go of Jagger and stood cautiously off to the side.

The moment they saw her face, many of the men and women in the crowd froze. A few gasps emanated from the scene as everyone beheld the person most responsible for saving them. For a second, time had completely stopped.

Raiya remained completely still. She'd seen these looks before. This was usually when people either turned into a lynch mob or began running away.

Drakin
The Story of Raiya

"This could be bad," she whispered.

As the initial shock wore off the crowd, one soldier slowly began to clap his hands. One by one, each person in the crowd quickly began cheering again. Many came up to her and either tried to hug her or shake her hand.

"Thank you! Thank you!"

"We owe you one!"

"You're amazing!"

"Hey, can you teach me to breathe fire?"

Raiya didn't know how to handle this. Her eyes teared up. For the first time, she wasn't looked at like a freak or a monster. These people were actually happy to see her, "I... you're welcome!"

Jagger smiled at seeing her caught off guard. It was a short-lived celebration when the large crowd began to part and form a path. A very stylish man in a white uniform, black trousers, and a blue cape stepped forward. His white hair matched his uniform and shined in the sunlight. A large scar covered most of his forehead and the bridge of his nose.

Commander Bhatia appeared next to him, "Attention!"

The cheering immediately ceased as every man and woman in uniform froze in place. The smile disappeared from Raiya's face as she turned to see what was going on. *What now?*

Commander Bhatia stepped forward and beckoned towards the group, "Sir, this is Lieutenant Jagger Bishop of our Eastern Division."

Drakin
The Story of Raiya

Despite a rather cold expression on his face, he spoke in a mild yet welcoming tone, "… or what's left of it. I'm Field Marshal Lavoie, welcome to Denver."

Jagger shuddered as Marshal Lavoie extended his hand, "Sir… it's an honor to finally meet you."

Jagger immediately turned to his friends, "This is…"

"Raiya, Dr. Andrea Wagner, and Eric Fausten, am I correct?"

"Uh… yes, sir…" Jagger replied, clearly caught off guard that Lavoie knew who they were.

Lavoie smiled, "I haven't been in power this long without having eyes in other camps. You all caused quite a stir with the U.S. Remnant Forces. It's rumored that a doctor there tried to put a bounty out on your heads."

"A stir that was of their own making," Jagger replied.

"No doubt. I've heard of Dr. Castillo's fanatical behavior."

The Field Marshal's eyes quickly glanced around the group as he spoke, "On behalf of the city of Denver and of the entire Western Coalition, I thank you for your help. In killing a dragon lord, you've given us new hope that we could actually win back our world."

"This is actually the second dragon lord we've killed," Raiya replied.

Quiet gasps erupted from the crowd. Marshal Lavoie's eyes widened, "You don't say? Which one was the first?"

Drakin

The Story of Raiya

Andy stepped forward and showed the Marshal his camera, "Sir, we killed the red one."

"That leaves yellow, green, black, and the Dread Lord."

"You know about the Dread Lord?" Jagger asked in a surprised tone. "I thought most people regarded him as a myth."

"When you don't see something for a while, it becomes a myth... however, I've personally seen him."

Lavoie pointed to the scar on his face, "Trust me, I know what he's capable of."

Jagger nodded, "We've seen him too... in fact, we believe he's hunting us."

"No doubt you've attracted his attention by killing off his brethren."

"We haven't been able to stay in one place for very long without getting attacked."

Commander Bhatia frowned, "Which means he'll probably send another force after us. You being here poses a great risk to our people."

Marshal Lavoie turned to him sternly, "Enough of that. Remember your place, commander. Do not forget what these people just did for us."

Commander Bhatia lowered his eyes, "Apologies, sir."

Lavoie nodded and turned back to Jagger, "Even so, the commander is correct. I assume there's a good reason as to why you decided to put my people at risk?"

Jagger nodded, "There is sir, a very good reason."

Drakin
The Story of Raiya

"Very well. Perhaps we should speak about this in private."

Marshal Lavoie beckoned them to the capital building. Jagger stepped forward and followed closely behind the Field Marshal.

Raiya held back hesitantly. She was still uneasy about the large group around her. However, she eventually followed them inside when Jagger looked back to her, "It'll be all right."

Andy and Eric took up the rear as they passed by the massive columns of the capital building. The building was so huge that it cast a shadow over half of the field.

The group entered a massive lobby from the first set of doors. What was once likely a luxurious building had been reduced to burnt wood and exposed electrical wires on the inside. While the exterior had held together almost perfectly, the inside had taken extreme damage. Burns from dragon's fire scorched the floor. Glass and debris were scattered everywhere. The few people running around trying to clean everything were obviously overwhelmed. They looked as though they hadn't slept in days.

Marshal Lavoie led the group to the large staircase opposing the entrance, "Sorry about the mess, we've seen an increase in dragon attacks lately and haven't really been able to keep up with the damage."

The marshal proceeded through the first set of doors at the top of the stairs. The next room appeared to be a makeshift waiting area. A large wooden desk lined one side. On the other side of the room were four luxurious leather chairs that had somehow been spared any damage. They were dark brown leather with brass studs in the back. Between them was a dark wooden table with a cracked white vas in the middle.

A young woman with dark brown hair sat at the desk, focused on whatever she was doing. A large terminal computer had something flashing on the screen that was out of their view.

She wore a dark navy-blue suit with a blue shirt underneath it. She had no rank, insignia, or citations of any kind. The only identifying marks were the blue and gold patches on her shoulders just below the neckline. She was likely assigned to Marshal Lavoie as his assistant.

Lavoie stopped at the next set of doors and turned back, "If you'll excuse me for a few minutes. I have to make sure our defenses are ready to handle another attack. I won't be long. – Carole, please see to it that our friends here are comfortable."

"Yes, sir."

The young woman stood up and walked out from behind her desk. She eyed Jagger suspiciously, "Chief Warrant Officer Carole West, at your service."

Jagger stood at attention and saluted, "Lieutenant Jagger Bishop and company."

Carole stiffened up and saluted nervously, "Sorry sir, I didn't realize you were an officer."

"Honest mistake," Jagger replied.

"Well… can I get you anything, sir?"

Jagger looked at his friends. None of them volunteered any information. "No, I think we're okay for now."

"Very well… let me know if you change your mind. In the meantime, please make yourselves comfortable."

Jagger flopped down in the nearest chair. He was visibly exhausted. His eyes fluttered and he moved gingerly as though he was in pain. His head rested against the back and let out a deep sigh.

Raiya sat down and turned away from the group as they took their seats. She was still upset and didn't want to talk to anyone. It was her goal to keep that poor girl safe and she had failed. Her lips quivered, but her eyes remained dry.

"You okay?" Jagger asked.

Raiya barely moved as she spoke, "I'm fine."

"Look, if you want to talk about…"

"I said I'm fine!" she shouted.

Carole looked up from her post to see what the commotion was about. Jagger signaled that everything was okay, "All right…"

Eric sat down in the second chair next to Jagger, "Jagger… who is this guy?"

"You've never heard of Field Marshal Reginald Lavoie?" Andy cut in before Jagger could reply.

"No…"

"He's easily one of the greatest heroes of this war. Even the remnant forces respect him. The man has been credited with more dragon kills than anyone else. It's said that he was able to kill off

Drakin

The Story of Raiya

an elder dragon all by himself! He was a Lieutenant General in command of the Canadian Army when the war began. After the United States, Canadian, and Mexican Governments collapsed, he came forward and helped organize the three militaries into a resistance movement. As they established themselves a foothold in North America, the resistance became known as the Western Coalition."

Jagger nodded, "A similar event took place in Europe and Asia, following the dragon rampage. Everyone that remained standing became part of the Eastern Coalition."

"I see… the man's a war hero," Eric said in disbelief

"Probably closer to a folk hero at this point," Jagger replied. "A lot of those stories are likely exaggerated."

"What you mean like the one where I killed an elder dragon with my bare hands?"

Jagger shot to his feet as Marshal Lavoie entered the room, "Sir!"

"At ease," the old man chuckled. "Actually, most of those stories are badly exaggerated. I lost a lot of good men earning that reputation and believe me… I could do without it. –Carole, another chair please."

"Yes, sir!" Carole replied as she pulled a chair out from behind her desk and wheeled it over to the table.

Lavoie nodded as he sat down, "Thanks."

"No problem, sir."

Drakin
The Story of Raiya

As Carole went back to her duties, Marshal Lavoie sat back and folded his hands together, "So… Lieutenant Bishop, what city do you hail from?"

"Sir, from New Framingham," Jagger replied.

"Terrible loss, that one. I just received the report. Our scouts didn't locate any survivors."

Jagger frowned, "We found one… but…"

"Her name was Miranda," Raiya said. "She was the little girl who sacrificed herself to kill the dragon lord."

"I see…" Lavoie said sympathetically. "I am truly sorry for your loss. It's always tough losing someone you care about, especially when they're so young."

Raiya fell silent. She didn't even acknowledge what Field Marshal Lavoie was saying. There were far worse demons for her to fight in her own mind.

Lavoie turned back to Jagger, "So what brings you to the capital? You said you had a reason for coming here?"

"Yes sir," Jagger replied. "We need the Western Coalition to organize an offensive against the dragon's primary base."

Lavoie looked like he was about to choke on his own tongue, "An offensive? We haven't been able to launch an assault against them in years. None of our bombers have ever been able to get close enough to Mount Whitney to do any damage and they somehow see our missiles coming. What exactly are you hoping to accomplish?"

"We want to end the war," Eric pipped in.

Drakin
The Story of Raiya

"A noble and admirable goal if ever there was one, young man," the marshal replied. "However, there remains the problem of a massive dragon horde. Even if you could take out their base, they'll scatter and regroup somewhere else."

Raiya quickly turned and looked at Lavoie, "Not if we kill my father."

Shit. She didn't mean to say that, but it just came out.

"Your father?" Marshal Lavoie asked.

Raiya lowered her eyes, "My father is Eutherys, the black and red dragon lord... The Dread Lord..."

Marshal Lavoie's jaw hung open as he looked at Raiya. He was completely dumbfounded, "Eh... well... I guess that certainly explains a lot about you, doesn't it? I'm interested in hearing your story..."

"Another time, maybe," Raiya replied. "Honestly, we're not even completely certain how it happened. All I know is that he killed my mother, massacred the people of Richmond... and I want him dead."

"I can understand why, but how will killing the Dread Lord end the war? They still have three other lords that could easily take over."

"They won't," Jagger replied. "I have... assurances... if we kill the dread lord, they'll agree to a ceasefire."

"What kind of assurances?" Marshal Lavoie asked.

"My uncle," Raiya replied.

"Another dragon lord, I take it?"

Drakin

The Story of Raiya

Raiya nodded, "The black one."

"And why would they agree to a ceasefire?"

"Because they're dying. The nitrogen levels in our atmosphere are poisoning them. The dread lord refuses to listen to reason and no one will stand against him. If we can take him out, the dragons will stop fighting us."

"What do they want in return?"

"Help getting off this planet."

"What?" Lavoie scoffed.

"Yes, they want help to return to their homeworld."

Marshal Lavoie shook his head, "How are we supposed to do that? We don't have the technology."

"The U.S. Remnant does," Andy said.

"Oh?"

Andy sucked down a deep breath, knowing that he was committing treason by revealing this info, "Our forces have been devising an emergency evacuation of Earth if we lose the war. We have designs and a prototype of our colony ship ready to go at a secret location."

Field Marshal Lavoie rubbed his forehead as he processed everything they'd told him. Raiya watched his expression change from confusion, to fear, to dismay, and all the way to disbelief. *He's not buying this... I knew it was a bad idea.*

Finally, Lavoie spoke, "Lieutenant, you're asking me to dedicate the last of our forces to a massive assault on a fortified location in the hopes that we can get in close enough for you to kill her father."

Drakin

The Story of Raiya

"Not exactly," Raiya cut in. "The battle will be a diversion. We want you to draw the horde's attention so we can slip into their home on Mount Whitney and take him out."

"And if he decides to join the fight?"

"Then we'll have enough time to get back to you and will probably have an easier time taking him out."

"And all I have for assurances is the second-hand word of a dragon lord?"

"You don't trust us?" Raiya asked with a flare of anger in her eyes.

"No, no, it's not that," Marshal Lavoie replied. "After what I saw you do out front against that dragon lord, I'm pretty much willing to believe what you tell me. That said, it's a big risk asking me to do this. How do you know you can trust your uncle's word?"

Raiya sighed, "Because he helped me kill the red dragon lord."

Marshal Lavoie rested his head on the back of the chair, "Now that is something…"

The older officer sat back in deep contemplation, "I won't ask our forces to abandon our cities. I'll arrange an expeditionary force to proceed to Mount Whitney. It shouldn't take longer than a week."

"How big a force are we talking about?" Jagger asked.

Marshal Lavoie shrugged, "Eight… maybe as much as thousand men… including armored units."

"Air support?"

"Minimal, likely just a few scouts."

Jagger sighed, "That won't be enough…"

"It's all we can afford."

Jagger looked at his friends, "Thoughts?"

Eric shrugged, "This whole thing will be for nothing if the Westcon force gets wiped out. We need more men and equipment."

"The U.S. Remnant Force," Andy replied. "If I can talk to the commandant, I should be able to convince him to send aid."

"But you'd need to get all the way across the country!" Jagger said in a dismal tone.

"I can spare a transport chopper," Lavoie said. "It'll get you there in no time."

"You sure you're up for that?" Jagger asked. "You're not exactly on friendly terms with them anymore."

Andy nodded, "Yeah I know that. Don't worry about it. I've never seen a bad situation that I haven't been able to talk my way out of. Besides, it's my word against Dr. Castillo's and no one takes him at his word for anything anymore."

"I might be able to help too," Eric added. "There should be a nomad encampment not too far from here. If I can get to it, they should have an old CB radio. All nomad groups are supposed to carry them, assuming they still work. I should be able to request assistance."

"You think they'll come?" Raiya asked.

Eric nodded, "You're a nomad, so you must know about the tenants that each clan agrees to in order to stay on good terms with others. If someone calls for help, all the nearby clans are obligated to provide aid. Besides, we've been taking a beating from these dragons for too long. I'm sure some of them are itching for a fight."

Marshal Lavoie smirked, "So if this works, it'll be quite a fight…. Possibly the last fight of the war."

The group rose to their feet with Marshal Lavoie, "All right, well we all have work to do. I suggest we get started."

"Marshal…" Raiya said hesitantly. "I was wondering if you wouldn't mind doing one thing for me before we go…"

Chapter 23

The sun slowly set over the city of Denver as Raiya brought a small case down the steps of the capital building. The case was a small mahogany box with brass latches on either side. She brushed her hand over the smoothly carved wood, "Goodbye."

The Capital building was illuminated by a large fire that danced in the moonlight. The Westcon defense force had arranged for a small funeral pyre. Several of their soldiers had apparently decided to stick around. At least twenty stood in two lines facing one another.

As Raiya walked by, each soldier on either side saluted. Jagger stood next to the fire, waiting for her. Tears welled up in her eyes as she finally stopped a few feet away from the flame.

Field Marshal Lavoie stepped out of the darkness next to Raiya, "Would you like to say anything?"

Raiya looked down at the small box, "I… don't even know what to say… I've never done this…"

"I understand," Marshal Lavoie replied. "Would you mind then if I did?"

"Go ahead."

Marshal Lavoie turned and faced the flame, "We are gathered here this evening to bid farewell to a young hero, a special little girl who helped to show us that virtually anything is possible."

He reached over and placed his hand on the box, "It is truly sad when we must say goodbye to someone we care about; a friend, a loved one, a family member. However, it is even more so when that person is so young... so full of life. The book of Miranda Foster is a short one. There are many pages that will have to remain blank. There are chapters that can never be written and an ending that yet feels incomplete. That said, it is a story that we must be sure will never be forgotten in the pages of history. For it is because of that story that we now stand here, ready to face down an evil that we thought could not be defeated."

"Attention!" a voice shouted from behind.

Field Marshal Lavoie nodded as a loud stomp signaled that his men were now standing straight, "Therefore, under my authority, should we win the day... The field on which she fell will be forever remembered as the Miranda Foster Memorial Field. Let the world never forget her sacrifice."

He turned and looked at Raiya, "We now commit Miranda's remains to the flame, that they may never be fodder for the dragons."

Raiya kissed the box before throwing it onto the flames. Small embers flew into the air as the box impacted against the burning wood. It quickly caught fire and vanished into the flames.

"At least now she's at peace," Jagger replied.

"Is she? How do we know for certain?" Raiya asked. "Have we ever known anything like peace?"

"Not for a long time..."

Raiya let out a deep sigh as she turned to face Jagger. The look on her face was one of pure rage,

"I want him, Jagger. I want his skull as a trophy. I want him dead… My father has gone too far. I can't leave him unchecked any longer."

Jagger nodded, "Don't worry, you're going to get him."

"Keep telling me that, partner. Even if it's not true… just keep saying it."

She then turned to Marshal Lavoie, "So where are we with preparations?"

"We're getting there," he replied. "I've got a chopper prepping for launch to deliver Dr. Fausten back to Charleston. We're also giving your friend Eric an old car. It's not much, but he should be able to at least find his people."

"Thanks…" Raiya replied.

"No problem. I suggest that you say your goodbyes. The chopper is slated to leave within the next hour."

"That's good advice," Jagger said as he turned away from the flame.

ᐦ

Andy was sitting by himself at the makeshift airfield. A pair of aging F-22s and F-18s sat next to the closest airstrip, ready to launch in an emergency. It was a fairly pathetic airfield when compared to the Charleston one. At least Charleston had more fighters on standby and the carrier was always ready to go.

A Sikorsky HH-60 Pave Hawk sat on a small landing pad, roughly two hundred feet away from the fighters. Crews worked to get it refueled and ready for launch. Flashlight beams darted around the Pave Hawk. Unintelligible shouts and

Drakin

The Story of Raiya

arguments could be heard in the distance as the crews worked.

"Great job, Andy!" he said to himself. "Now you're going to be hanging from blades in the sky, completely open to dragon attacks! How do you get yourself into these things?"

"These things?" a voice asked from behind. "You mean this isn't the first time you've gotten yourself into trouble?"

Andy smirked as he turned to face Jagger, "Hardly... I always seem to be stuck in the middle of a catastrophe. It's the story of my life. When I was a kid, I tried to create a fort in my backyard that could survive dragon's fire... and almost wound up burning my house down in the process of testing it. I swear trouble follows me where ever I go."

"Good times," Jagger replied.

"Tell me about it."

Jagger laughed as Raiya approached from behind, "So... it looks like this is it."

"Yup... I'm off to Charleston," Andy replied.

Raiya quickly threw her arms around him, "Thanks, Andy... we wouldn't have made it this far without you."

Andy looked bewildered, like he'd never been hugged before. He quickly adjusted and gently placed his hands on Raiya's back, "Yes you would have. With your determination, you would have torn ass all over the world until you got what you wanted."

"Think so?"

Drakin
The Story of Raiya

"I know so… Your father should be saying his prayers right now."

"If the dragons even have gods."

Raiya pulled back and nodded, "Thanks, Andy… We'll see you again."

"Hope so," Andy replied.

"No, we'll see each other again," Raiya said adamantly. "That wasn't a question. I expect you to survive."

"I'll do my best."

"Hey, we're ready! Come on!" a voice called out as the scream of the chopper engine became audible.

Andy quickly turned to Jagger and shook his hand, "Jagger, it's been a pleasure. Good luck."

"Thanks, buddy. You too," Jagger replied.

Andy smiled and turned away, heading for the chopper. *Be safe, you two.*

Jagger watched Andy throw on a helmet as he boarded the chopper. The gray pave hawk came to life with a mighty whirl and began takeoff procedures. Andy disappeared behind the sliding door as it was closed. Crew members scattered to get out of the way when the chopper slowly lifted off the pad.

Jagger waved as it disappeared into the night sky, "Be safe."

"I suppose I should be off too," a voice chimed in from behind.

"Probably," Jagger replied as he turned to see Eric standing behind him. "You got everything you need?"

Drakin
The Story of Raiya

"Just about," Eric replied. "They gave me a bolt gun and an old land rover. It's in terrible shape, but I get the feeling that they don't plan on seeing it again."

"Do you know where the nearest nomad outpost is?" Raiya asked.

"No, but I know what to look for. Don't worry, I bet you anything I'll find it before Andy gets back to Charleston."

"Good luck," Jagger replied.

"You too. Once this is all over, we'll have a beer to celebrate."

"A beer?" Raiya asked.

Eric smiled and shrugged, "Don't look at me, it's just something my father used to say. I've never actually had one either."

"Right…"

"Do I get a hug?" Eric asked.

Before Raiya could move, Jagger reached out his arms and grabbed Eric. The moment he had a tight grasp on him, he gave the young nomad a quick peck on the cheek, "There you go!"

"That wasn't exactly what I meant!" Eric said, rubbing his cheek.

"You wanted a hug, you got a hug!" Jagger replied. "What's your problem?"

Raiya forced a smile and wrapped her arms around Eric, "There you go, you've been a pain in the ass, but you're all right."

"Thanks, we'll see each other soon."

"We better."

Eric turned and walked off into the darkness, "Take care, you two."

Drakin
The Story of Raiya

Jagger turned back to Raiya, now that their friends were off carrying out their assignments, "Maybe it's time we get started."

"Do you think there's any chance we'll see any of them again?"

"I think we will," Jagger replied. "They're survivors. What's more, they're good people. A combination like that isn't easy to kill."

Raiya frowned as she watched Eric disappear. Jagger turned away and beckoned her to follow, "Come on, it's time we got started too."

"I agree," said another voice.

Field Marshal Lavoie stepped out of the darkness behind them, "You've got a long journey ahead of you. We've refit your jeep with better tires, a new power cell, and installed a fold-out cannon in the back that should knock anything up to an elder dragon out of the sky. We've also given you food and provisions in your back seat for about two days. Do you need anything else?"

"Power cells and ammo, sir?"

"Already taken care of as well."

"Then I think we're good."

"You sure now? You're not exactly going up against a wyvern here."

Raiya nodded, "We should be good, as long as you can draw out the horde."

Marshal Lavoie nodded, "Give us a few more days, we'll throw everything we can at them. I just hope we won't be alone."

"What about the EastCon forces?" Raiya asked. "Why haven't you asked them for help?"

Drakin
The Story of Raiya

Marshal Lavoie frowned, "We have a… tenuous relationship with the Eastern Coalition. We share resources whenever we can, but they don't typically come running when they receive requests for help."

"Why not?"

"A large number of dragons took a liking to Siberia. The EastCon has had its hands full just holding them back. We radioed them for help… but I don't even know if they received the message."

"Andy and Eric will get help," Jagger replied. "They're good people. I have faith in them."

"Hope so… Well good luck, you two… Hopefully, we'll see each other again."

"Likewise."

Jagger saluted and proceeded past the Marshal, heading for his jeep. The Westcon engineers had left her right in front of the capital building. The engine was running as she sat idle.

Commander Bhatia leaned against the driver's side panel, "So what do you think?"

Jagger smiled as he looked at the jeep he'd spent years refurbishing, "Whoa… You replaced the seatbelts and gave it a wash down? It looks almost new!"

"Except for the rust, burns, and bullet holes," Raiya replied.

"You're such a glass-half-empty kinda girl."

"Just how it goes."

Command Bhatia smiled, "Nothing but the best for the people who are going to end the war for us."

Drakin

The Story of Raiya

Jagger frowned, "You don't really believe that, do you?"

"Had I not seen you guys take out that dragon lord, I wouldn't... and I'm still skeptical, but I don't want to spend the rest of my life fighting a war I can't win."

"I see..."

Jagger stepped by the commander and was about to enter the jeep. He was about to turn the ignition when Commander Bhatia placed his hand on the wheel, "You should know... I volunteered to take command of the diversionary force. I will be the forward commander of our ground forces during this fight."

"Really?"

"If we lose, there won't be enough of us left to do anything but stave off the dragon attacks until we're completely spent. No, we'll either win the day or I'll die on the field, as a soldier."

Raiya frowned, "Well don't go getting yourself killed prematurely."

"I don't intend to. I have every hope you'll win. I'm betting on it."

Jagger extended his hand, "Then I hope we'll see each other after the fight."

"Me too," Bhatia said, offering his own hand.

The two stared at each other for a few moments as they shook hands. Neither one seemed particularly confident that they'd see each other again, even if they did somehow win the day.

"Be safe," Jagger said as he pulled away and got behind the wheel.

Drakin
The Story of Raiya

"I won't, but thanks," Commander Bhatia replied.

Raiya slid into the passenger's seat next to Jagger, "We all set?"

"Yeah, I think so."

Jagger put the truck in drive and slowly pulled away from the capital. The road was completely smooth, a rarity where it usually traveled. He looked into the rear-view mirror and watched as the capital slowly vanish.

Raiya kept her eyes on the road as they passed by several buildings and the expected shanty towns set up on either side of the road. Guards with lamps could be seen skulking about, making sure that everyone was safe.

Jagger looked over at Raiya as the jeep passed by the residential areas and began entering the military encampments near the exit, "I wonder if all of this will go away once it's over."

Raiya had a stoic expression on her face, but her eyes were far more revealing. She looked worried. The weight of the world had literally just been tossed onto her shoulders. The fact that she had willingly accepted the job of patricidal assassin didn't change the fact that being humanity's savior was an unfair burden on her.

Jagger slowly and cautiously lowered his right hand to the console where she was resting her arm. Taking a chance, he ran his hand over her claw-like fingers and then threaded his between them.

Her body immediately came to life, causing her to look down and see what had happened.

Drakin
The Story of Raiya

Jagger kept his eyes on the road, pretending that nothing was going on. He quietly waiting for a reaction be it indifference or something more extreme. All he got was a gentle squeeze in response as she gripped his hand.

She kept her eyes focused forward as her mind raced a mile a minute, "Jagger?"

"Yeah?" Jagger replied.

"Thanks… for coming with me."

"You don't have to thank me. Coming along with you meant saving the world. I never thought we'd get this far… but I'm glad we did. Honestly, it's been quite the ride."

"It really has…"

Jagger sat back in his jeep as they slowed near the main entrance. The gates opened, allowing them to exit.

"Good luck, sir!" one of the guards called out.

"To us all!" Jagger replied as he hit the gas.

The jeep roared as it pulled out of the gate. The lights of the city dimmed as the truck picked up speed. They were now on their own.

"So, what will you do when all this is over?" Jagger asked.

Raiya sat motionless in her seat, "Probably go back to what I was doing."

"Being a wanderer?"

"Something wrong with that?"

"No, not really," Jagger replied. "I just figured that once the war's over, you'll have no one left to hunt."

"There are still other evil creatures out there. Dragons aren't the only ones."

Drakin
The Story of Raiya

"You mean the canbans?"

"Why not? Do you really think these people can be reintegrated into your quaint little society?"

Jagger shrugged, "Who knows, maybe? It's worth a shot."

"After what we saw, I doubt it. The ones that aren't feral have apparently become fanatics. You can't reason with fanatics. You kill them or they kill you. Either way, maybe that's what I'll do."

"Rough life."

"I'm used to it. What would you rather me try to settle down in a city? To have kids call me monster and have others look at me like a freak for the rest of my life?"

"I doubt that'll happen," Jagger replied. "If we succeed, you'll be a hero."

Raiya frowned, "I'm not sure being called a hero is much better than being called a monster. In both cases, the names are going to draw attention that I don't want. I still have scales, claws, and dragon's eyes. No matter where I go, I'll still be a reminder of what happened here. I'll still be different from everyone else and there is nothing I can do about it. I'm better off not staying in one place for too long."

She adjusted herself in her seat and turned so that she was looking at him, "What about you? When this is all over, what will you do?"

"Who knows…" Jagger replied. "Maybe I'll carve out a nice little piece of the world for myself. Someplace quiet where I can just settle down."

Drakin

The Story of Raiya

"You won't go back to the Westcon? They're in for a lot of rebuilding if we win. I bet you'd even get a promotion."

"I'm actually all set with that. I've served most of my life. Honestly, it's the only life I've known and I'm ready to start a new chapter. Who knows where I'll go."

Raiya rested her head against the seat, "Anything's possible I suppose."

"We're putting the cart before the horse anyway," Jagger said. "Let's focus on the goal before the reward. There's a pretty massive dragon with an ax to grind standing in the way of any future plans."

"True… but not for long…"

Drakin
The Story of Raiya

Death Valley
Dragon Territory
Formerly California

Drakin
The Story of Raiya

Chapter 24

Amzer'ial cautiously approached the large cavern where Eutherys slept, "My lord?"

"I'm awake," Eutherys replied. "Do you need something? Has Entharis returned?"

"No… he hasn't."

Eutherys stepped out of the darkness provided by the cave's ceiling, "I would have thought that he'd be back by now."

Amzer'ial lowered her head, "My lord… he's not coming back. He's dead… Your daughter beat him to the city."

"What happened?" Eutherys growled, his voice barely a hiss.

"They killed him and burnt his body. All I saw was charred bones when I found him… same as last time."

"Can you be certain it was her?"

"The other dragons who were present on the scene confirmed it. A girl with green skin, scales, and yellow eyes was responsible. They knocked him out of the sky and killed him. There can be no doubt about it."

Eutherys roared and slammed his foot on the ground, "Entharis, dead? First Raki'Agr and now this!"

Amzer'ial timidly recoiled herself, "What do we do now, my lord? Your daughter is proving to be a real threat and now that the Westcon…"

"Even so, she's just a girl… a human girl…"

"It would be unwise to underestimate her, my lord. Entharis and Raki'Agr apparently already made that mistake. They paid for it with their lives."

Eutherys released smoke from his jaws, "Your words are well met. I don't intend to make the same mistake. Send out messenger drakes… as many as you can. Withdraw our forces to Mount Whitney."

Amzer'ial felt a slight chill and shuddered at Eutherys's words, "My lord, we would be halting our advances. Years of progress will be…"

"It's a necessary loss! Are you challenging me?" Eutherys demanded as he took a thunderous step towards her.

"No, my lord… I would never…"

"The humans now have their symbol to rally around. They'll be coming here and she'll be with them. Count on that."

Amzer'ial nodded, "Yes… I can believe that… Very well, my lord. It shall be done."

Eutherys returned to his cave, "Please make sure that I am left undisturbed until our forces are gathered. I have grown weary and in need of rest."

"As you wish."

Amzer'ial took flight and headed for the council roost atop the highest peak of Mount Whitney. Kazrai'em and Auirn were already there. By the look of things, they were busy comparing accomplishments from past engagements.

They both fell silent as Amzer'ial landed. She took a moment to get herself perched before turning to the other two.

Drakin
The Story of Raiya

Auirn could clearly tell that something was bothering her, "What was Eutherys screaming about? Is everything okay?"

"No… Entharis is dead."

"What?" Kazrai'em asked in shock.

"Eutherys's daughter… that homunculus was in the city when we attacked. She's been a thorn in our side for too long."

"Orders from Eutherys?" Kazrai'em asked.

Amzer'ial nodded, "Send out your best fliers, we need to recall our forces. Eutherys anticipates a counter attack from the Westcon."

"How much of our forces and from where?" the green dragon asked.

"All of them. Recall all of our forces to Mount Whitney."

Kazrai'em nearly fell off his perch, "You can't be serious? Recalling everyone would give the coalitions and opening to retake everything we've fought hard for. It'll take years to get back…"

"It can't be helped. With Entharis gone, the humans now have something to rally behind. Eutherys anticipates that his daughter will be accompanying any force that comes here. She is the one person who has successfully posed any real threat to our forces."

"A real threat…?" Kazrai'em asked in a defeated tone. "Now that is something… Very well… I'll send out messengers to recall our people."

Amzer'ial looked down the steep side of the mountain to where Eutherys carved his chamber,

Drakin
The Story of Raiya

"And post guards at Eutherys's dwelling. He's asked not to be disturbed."

Kazrai'em watched Amzer'ial shift uncomfortably in place. She quickly glared at him, "Do it now, Kazrai'em!"

"As you wish!"

Kazrai'em immediately took flight and disappeared into the clouds. Amzer'ial raised her head and watched as the green dragon vanished from view. It took him some time to gain enough altitude, but eventually, his body became shrouded in white mist.

Amzer'ial quickly hopped over so that she was perched on the roost next to Auirn. He looked at her intently, "So?"

"I know what you're going to ask me…" she replied, "but my answer is still no."

"Eutherys now acts out of fear. You must have seen that."

"I have, but that doesn't mean that I'm ready to betray him," Amzer'ial hissed. "He has led us this far… I would personally prefer an amicable solution to our habitation, but that is not what our lord thinks is in our best interest. Unless he says otherwise, we'll continue to carry out our plans to take this world from the humans. We can't trust that they won't continue to damage it."

"You are so incredibly stubborn!" Auirn hissed.

"You love me that way," Amzer'ial said. "You're my lair mate, but don't think for a moment that I'm willing to help you betray your brother. I'll keep your words secret, but that's as far as I'll go. The rest is up to you to figure out."

Auirn nodded, "Then I should hope that my niece arrives here soon… and wins."

"You seem pretty adamant about this," Amzer'ial replied. "Can I ask you though… what if you're wrong?"

"What do you mean?"

"I mean what if you're wrong about what is poisoning us? For all you know it could be the water, the food, or any number of other things. What makes you so certain that it's the air?"

"It's the way the sickest of us are breathing. Even if I am wrong that it's the air… Isn't that reason enough for us to leave this world?" Auirn asked. "If the food is inedible, or the water is poisonous, then we can't stay here anyway. Eutherys thinks he can use dragon's fire to make the world more suitable to our needs. I don't see how. For now, we'll have to let fate decide how this plays out."

"I guess we have no other choice… so we'll wait… for the moment…"

The mid-day sun hit the jeep as they passed into what could only be described as Hell itself. The ground was completely black. Smoke and fire shot out of the dead soil in various locations all around them.

Jagger had to slow his jeep in order to avoid hitting any of the debris they passed. Raiya's eyes fixed on the thousands of burnt corpses and

Drakin
The Story of Raiya

skeletons that looked to be literally climbing over one another, "Is this…"

Jagger nodded, "Yes… this is the site of the Death Valley Massacre. From what I'm told, my uncle died out here."

"So did Teagan…"

"Who?" Jagger asked.

"The people who raised me. Their daughter was named Teagan. She came out here to help the U.S. Military… and never came back."

"No one did," Jagger replied. "When the U.S. scouts reported that the dragons had taken up residence at a secret base out this way, the U.S. teamed up with its allies and launched an attack… they never even had a chance."

"I've only heard stories… what's your version of it?" Raiya asked.

"Probably the same as what you've already heard. They came out here intent on making this a decisive strike. This was supposed to be make or break for the United States. They sent everything they had; soldiers, tanks, armored cars, cannons, fighters, you name it."

Jagger twisted his lips and shook his head, "They never even had a chance. The dragons were waiting for them, in far greater numbers than we originally knew about. They surrounded our forces and attacked from all side. There was no retreat for our people. It quickly turned from an attack to a mass suicide strike. The battle reduced the dragons to less than half their strength, but we paid a much higher cost."

"Did anyone make it out?"

Drakin
The Story of Raiya

"Who knows… it's believed that a few, including Field Marshal Lavoie did, but there is no one to confirm it. Likely it's just a made-up story. I don't think anyone made it out alive."

"How many?"

"Well over a million people died here, not including the civilian losses… which probably triples that number."

"Civilians?" Raiya asked.

Jagger nodded, "When our forces came through here, they saw burnt buildings and people that were either dead or dying. It didn't look like very many people escaped southern California. There were also rumors that several small volunteer militia units showed up to help as well. Pretty much anyone who could fire a gun was given the chance to help."

Raiya frowned, "And after they lost, the United States didn't have enough forces left to protect itself."

"That's right," Jagger replied. "They steamrolled over us, going from city to city, destroying everything in their path. The few of us that stood up and challenged them became the Western Coalition. We salvaged as many of our homes as we could and continued the fight."

Raiya looked on as the jeep passed a downed F-18 hornet. The nose of the fighter had been completely ripped away and the tail had been burnt off. The pilot was nowhere to be found, likely eaten by some scavenging wyvern.

It wasn't long before the jeep entered Lone Pine, California. They soon turned right onto

Whitney Portal Road. Surprisingly, the town was still fairly intact. The roads were a mess and the place was being overtaken by nature, but there were no dragon burns nor had the buildings been smashed.

The structure where the jeep had turned, was tan with red lettering on the side; 'Se..sons.' The letter 'a' had apparently fallen off many years ago.

The next few buildings were small houses with picket fences enclosing fairly small yards. Small trees stood lifeless on either side of the road.

Jagger stopped the jeep next to a small gray building on the corner. The smashed sign laying the ground said, 'Wood Works,' but offered no other information. The view ahead of them appeared to be nothing but dead trees and open fields. As far as they were concerned, this was the edge of town and the point of no return.

Mount Whitney peaked menacingly over several small hills in the distance. Clouds shrouded the top, making it hard to see anything. It stood with an ominous presence, almost daring them to move forward.

Jagger sucked down a deep breath as a dragon's roar echoed in the distance, "Are you ready for this?"

"I've waited years to find him … yeah, I'm ready," Raiya replied.

"You sure?"

Raiya smiled, "You can wait here if you want. I'll be back afterward."

"No way," Jagger replied. "I'm not letting you do this alone. I was… what I mean is that… I was just…"

"Trying to let me know that I don't have to do this. You don't want me to feel forced."

She placed a comforting hand on his wrist, "Relax, I don't feel that way. This is what I want. Eutherys is going to die… for my mother… and for every other person he's ever killed."

"I'm surprised you care about them… given how they treated you."

Raiya lowered her eyes, "My grandparents weren't related to me. I basically fell into their laps, but they never complained. The nomads who took me in, looked at me like I was one of them. I wouldn't be here now if it weren't for them. The care I received from humans who were willing to see past my appearance helped me survive. I know that there are still some of those people out there. I originally just wanted revenge, but… I guess after meeting you… I realized that I also wanted to prevent any more people like that from being killed. I don't want any more Mirandas on this planet… never again."

Jagger nodded, "We'll get him."

"I know we will."

The jeep's engine purred as they moved forward. Dirt roads, downed power lines, and smashed fences were all that welcomed them as the jeep pushed forward. It was a desolate sight, but still an improvement over Death Valley, a name which had taken on a whole new meaning.

Drakin
The Story of Raiya

The road became less and less paved as they drew closer to the mountain. Brush and rubble became the norm as a small brown sign that was miraculously still standing came into view; 'Alabama Hills Information Next Right' was all it said. A small arrow pointed off to the side, directing any would-be traffic.

"We're close…" Jagger whispered.

They quickly passed by a road that was suspiciously in better shape than the one they were traveling on. Soon the brush was replaced by steep hills of gravel, sand, and rock. The skyline was much higher now that they were approaching the mountain.

The road became dark as the sun was blocked out by the hills in the distance. The rocks continued to grow in size as they proceeded further up the road. There were still a few trees on either side, but they were as lifeless as the stones around them.

The road quickly became inclined, making everything feel slightly uneven and heavier behind them. Jagger pushed harder on the gas to keep the jeep going at the same speed. The engine became louder as it compensated.

The sounds of dragon roars in the distance made Jagger pull his foot off the gas and look up nervously, "I think we may need to leave the jeep behind soon."

Raiya stared at the mountains. She was almost hypnotized by the sheer size of what lay ahead of them, "Soon… I agree, but we still have some ways to go. Let's risk it for now."

Drakin
The Story of Raiya

"You're sure?"

"Yeah…"

More telephone poles came into view as the jeep reached a small clearing. The mountains were now in full view ahead of them. This was going to be tough.

"Which one?" Raiya asked as the jeep picked up speed.

"Huh?"

"Which mountain is ours?"

Jagger didn't answer. Did he not know? If not, what was his plan, just to follow the sounds of dragon roars? The mountain range was massive, extending as far as even her eyes could see.

The air became cold as the range grew larger in front of them, "Hello, Jagger I asked you a question. Which one?"

Jagger pointed to a tip in-between two other spikes, "There… that's your mountain."

Raiya's eyes widened, "You've gotta be kidding me!"

The mountain was a massive spire, surrounded by several smaller ones that seemed to jut out as though they were protecting it. Snow covered the land around the massive spire, making getting there much more dangerous.

Atop the mountain, Raiya could see small burnt out caves, and what looked like a hand, seated at the summit. The dragons had been working busily to create a fortifiable base in their new home.

Drakin
The Story of Raiya

"Well, I can see why they chose that one!" Raiya said in an almost defeated tone. "This isn't going to be easy."

"Most things worth doing rarely are," Jagger replied.

"I suppose…"

The road abruptly became a sharp turn and quickly ended in a small parking area surrounded by trees. Jagger pulled his jeep in until it was under the cover of several branches and quickly shut it down, "We're walking from here."

Raiya nodded and hopped out the side.

Jagger touched the side of the jeep and frowned. He looked at it like a friend that he was about to say goodbye to forever.

"You okay?" Raiya asked.

Jagger nodded, "Yeah… just have a feeling…"

"What?"

"I'm worried that I won't see her again."

"Like I said, we're going to win!" Raiya said confidently.

"No, I know that… I just wonder if she'll be here when we get back. I spent a lot of time on her… she's pretty much my prized possession."

"Well if she's not here… I'll help you build another one."

Jagger looked up, surprised, "Really?"

"Yeah."

"All right then, deal."

WREEEEEE!

"Wyverns!" Raiya yelled as she reached for her blade.

Drakin

The Story of Raiya

"Quiet, shh!" Jagger scolded as he quickly pressed himself against the nearest tree. "It doesn't look like they've seen us… they're higher up!"

Raiya followed his gaze until she saw the top of Mount Whitney. Her heart quickly sank, "Shit…"

Perched on the side of the summit was a massive flock of wyverns and drakes. Raiya hadn't noticed them before because the sheer number had engulfed the side of the mountain, but now they were close enough to see just what they were up against.

"How the fuck are we supposed to get by them?" Raiya asked.

"We'll just have to hope that our friends keep their words," Jagger replied. "Come on, we've got a long climb ahead of us."

Drakin
The Story of Raiya

Chapter 25

"This is insane, Eric!"

"What is, Mike?"

Michael, a stout man with a messy black beard and a rather bubbly tone spoke, "You think we have a chance against a horde of dragons?"

"Not alone," Eric replied. "We'll have the help of the Westcons and hopefully some of the remnants too!"

"Assuming they show up!"

Eric grimaced as he looked at his new army. The nomadic clans had responded, just as Eric knew they would. Unfortunately, they had been hunted to the brink by dragon packs. The force numbered about five or six thousand. That number did not include the make-shift tanks and artillery vehicles which had been built out of old cars, trucks, and whatever else they could get a hold of.

The weapons they carried were little more than an assortment of rifles, handguns, knives, and chainsaws. Each of them had seen violence at the hands of the dragons and it was shown on their faces.

It was a motley assemblage of people that seemed either too old or too young to be out there. Eric had no doubt that they would do their part, but if this was the only force that was to be thrown at the dragons, it would be a staggeringly short fight.

"They'll show up."

"I hope you're right."

Drakin

The Story of Raiya

"Trust me."

Eric sighed as he looked west toward the mountain range, "I'd rather be with them right now... I hope they're all right."

"You think that dragon girl you told us about has a chance?"

"You haven't seen her fight... I have. Yeah, they've got a chance. We just need to keep the other dragons off them."

Michael rubbed his chin, "Damn eczema... How will we know when they've killed the dragon lord?"

"No idea."

"So, what then?"

"We just fight until we don't need to fight anymore."

"In other words, we fight until they retreat or until they've killed us all."

"Exactly."

"My kind of strategy..."

Eric sighed. *Jagger, Raiya, you two better still be out there, because after what I've had to put up with here, if you two fail... I'll haunt you to your graves.*

Eric stepped out in front of the army that he'd been sent. He had never been a leader of any kind, but today, it seemed like he had been thrust into that role. For better or worse, he was now in charge.

At that moment, the ground began to shake. In the distance, Eric could see something massive coming towards them. It appeared to be a huge assortment of vehicles, including tanks and other

Drakin

The Story of Raiya

military and civilian transports moving in their direction. They were all moving slowly, keeping pace with the infantry that was with them.

Eric ran over to the old Land Rover that he'd been given and grabbed a bolt pistol out of the driver's side pocket. He ran forward, struggling to set the gun to maximum output.

The gun screamed as it reached its high yield setting. Eric aimed it over his head and fired three blasts. The shots screeched upwards, flashing as they went.

The large force seemed to slightly alter course and head towards the nomads. The rumbling became louder as the army drew closer. It almost sounded like a massive boulder being rolled down a hill.

Eric remained frozen in place as one car that was in the lead, sped up and raced towards them. The car was an old Humvee from the days of the U.S. Military. It had been painted black with blue stripes going up the side.

Eric kept his gun ready until he saw the emblem of the Western Coalition on the door; a hand holding the severed head of a dragon. The car came to a stop right next to him, allowing a tall man in a dark green uniform to step out.

Eric smiled when he realized who it was, "Commander Bhatia, good to see you!"

The gruff-looking commander nodded, "Likewise, we've sent out everything we could spare to assist… and I see you've actually managed to put together a sizeable force yourself."

Drakin
The Story of Raiya

Eric smiled, knowing that he was completely full of it. The look on Bhatia's face was one of disgust. The nomadic army was a fair size, but everything they were using was completely outclassed by what the Westcon brought forward. "We're ready to do our part."

"Indeed," Bhatia replied. "Very well then. We were planning on marching towards Death Valley. That should get us some attention. Our scout planes are going to launch when we're a little closer and attempt to draw the dragons out."

"How many men did you bring with you?" Eric asked.

Commander Bhatia looked behind him as the massive force he led continued to advance on their position. The dust they kicked up made it impossible to even guess how big the force was, "Ten thousand. That includes infantry, armored units, chopper teams, and artillery."

Eric nodded, "Where do you want us?"

"Fall in behind our infantrymen. We'll supply you with what equipment we can spare. When the fighting starts, try to put some distance between yourselves and our heavy armor."

"Understood."

†

"Come on, Jagger!"

"I'm trying… it's just… it's so cold…"

Jagger struggled through snow that was about six inches deep, "You would think a couple of jackets could have been included in the supplies the Westcon gave us!"

Drakin
The Story of Raiya

Raiya sighed as she turned and looked up the mountain and then back at Jagger, "I think we'd better find a place to camp out for the night."

"I'm sorry... it's just..."

"No, I know," Raiya replied. "We're in for the fight of our lives. It's late and it's only going to get colder when the sun disappears. I'm not going to be any good in a fight if I'm half frozen either. Come on, let's find a place to hide out for the night."

"Right..."

Raiya focused her ears and listened for something, anything, that might help them find some shelter. She could hear the wind caressing every rock as it passed by. Her head darted to the left, then to the right.

She'd caught the sound of something, but what could it be? The sound was hollow, almost like an air tunnel or... or the entrance to a cave. *Yes!*

Raiya grabbed Jagger's arm and tugged, "Quick, this way! It's not far."

"What isn't?"

"Just trust me."

Jagger forced his legs to move and pushed forward. Raiya moved like she knew exactly what she was looking for. She pulled him a hundred feet further up, then immediately shot to the left.

They quickly moved behind a large fissure and found a small opening buried deep beside it. The opening was roughly four feet across and seven feet in height. It was just enough for someone to get in comfortably.

Drakin
The Story of Raiya

Raiya went in first while Jagger caught his breath outside the cave. The inside was far different than what she expected. The walls were smooth, and the opening led to a large chamber that was easily almost seven hundred square feet in space, and ten feet in height.

It was dark, but she could quickly fix that, "Jagger, get in here!"

Snow poured through the entrance as Jagger slowly entered the cave, "Well... this is convenient."

"Tell me about it..."

Raiya began feeling dizzy. Her eyesight shifted, causing the world to get blurry. Jagger noticed it and grabbed her before she could fall over, "Raiya, are you okay?"

"The cold... I feel like I'm losing consciousness."

"It must be your blood," Jagger replied. "You said you can't regulate your heat... you must be cold blooded. That would mean..."

"That I'm going into hibernation," Raiya replied.

Jagger nodded and helped her sit down, "I saw a fallen tree outside... I'll be right back."

"You'll freeze."

"Nah. I'll only be gone a few minutes."

"Be quick."

"I will."

Jagger disappeared outside. Raiya rubbed her arms in an attempt to keep warm. It wasn't working. Her eyes continued to flutter, "No... no... not time to sleep... I'm not... hibernating!"

Drakin
The Story of Raiya

She quickly clicked her teeth together and unleashed her fire breath. The floor in front of her lit up momentarily in a bright flame. It didn't last long, but it was enough heat for her to warm her body and stay awake.

She extended her arms as the flame quickly died and warmed her skin. She could feel the heat reinvigorate her body, but only for a moment. It wasn't enough. The fire would need to last longer.

"I'm back!" Jagger called from the entrance.

He had a large stack of wood in his hands, "One sec, there's more."

Jagger brought in two more bundles and set them off to the side. Raiya looked at them oddly, "Where did you find all of this wood?"

"Outside," he replied. "There were several downed trees, broken branches, and a lot of small twigs."

Raiya's eyes began to flutter again, "The wood… it looks wet."

"Light it," Jagger replied. "Your breath should be able to dry it out."

Raiya nodded and unleashed her breath for a second time. The wood immediately went ablaze and lit up the entire cave in orange and yellow light. She closed her eyes as her body became reinvigorated. The heat passed through her skin and slowly revived her.

Jagger had taken a seat close to the flame and was holding his hands over the fire, "How you feeling?"

"Better…"

Drakin
The Story of Raiya

"How did you handle the cold when you were alone?"

"I didn't, I went to warmer climates."

"I think a lot of people did that. How is it you're hibernating but the dragons like the cold?"

"I don't know… maybe it's the combination of human and dragon DNA?"

"Maybe."

Raiya looked over at him, "Jagger…"

"Yeah?"

"I really am glad you came with me on this… I… This is my curse to deal with. You didn't ask to be thrown into it, but you still stepped up without a complaint."

Jagger shrugged, "Yeah I know. I never would complain. Something about you… just made me feel like I could do something awesome as long as I stuck with you."

Raiya slowly got up and moved over to Jagger's side of the flame. She sat down next to him and cuddled up at his side, "I thought you were a careless idiot. You almost got yourself killed. I was actually amazed that you managed to survive as long as you did."

"That so?"

"It is… but as the days went by… well… I don't know."

"Go ahead, you can say it."

Raiya bit her lower lip, "Well… I guess that I've become attached to you. I know it's absurd… I mean we've only known each other for what… a week? Yet like you said… there's something about you…"

Drakin

The Story of Raiya

Before Jagger could say anything, Raiya dug her teeth into the side of his neck. She bit down enough so that he couldn't pull away while she caressed his skin with her tongue.

Within seconds, she could feel his skin break out in goosebumps, "Raiya?"

She released him and moved softly to the side. As soon as he was in her field of view, she sat back on her knees and bit her lower lip. Her figure was menacing in the fire as her yellow eyes stared deeply into Jagger, piercing him, as though they were staring into his soul. It was an intensity that was equaled only by the heat of the flame. It lasted only a moment, but it felt much longer.

Raiya was biting her lip so hard that the skin was at the point of breakage. She slowly reached down to the hem of her black shirt and lifted the top over her stomach. Her hands gripped the shirt as they moved just below her chest. They shook, though she couldn't decide if it was nervousness or anticipation.

Raiya shuddered, this was a new feeling for her. Over the last few weeks, Jagger had seen her naked a few times and she had felt little to no shame from it. She never even gave it a second thought, but this was different. She was undressing in front of him for a different reason now. In the past, when he looked away or tried to ignore her, she didn't care. If he did it this time, it would hurt.

She raised the shirt over her chest, and then over her head and threw it against the wall. She then worked on the tight undershirt that she'd been wearing. Again, she slowly raised the hem of the shirt until it reached her breasts.

Jagger's eyes were dilated. He hadn't said anything. It didn't seem like he even knew what to say, assuming he could speak.

This was it, there was no turning back. Raiya slowly exposed her breasts and lifted the shirt over her head. The chill of the air mixed with the heat of the flame and made her shiver.

Jagger looked at her like he'd never seen any of it before, "Raiya...?"

"Shh... no more words..."

She tossed the shirt aside before slowly undoing her pants and sliding them down to her knees. Her skin chilled as it left the protection of the fabric. It took a little adjustment, given the position she was in, but she managed to quickly wiggle out of her pants.

Her naked silhouette slowly moved towards him like a sleek panther, ready to pounce. She ran her hand up the inside of his thigh until she reached his crotch. His pants were tight and she could feel a stiffness there.

She carefully unbuttoned his jeans and reached her right hand down his waist until she had him in her hand, "You... want me... don't you?"

Her voice was little more than a whisper. A seductive whisper that was closer to the hiss of a snake. Jagger could barely breathe. He sucked down what air he could, but could only utter one word, "Yes..."

Drakin
The Story of Raiya

Raiya smiled as she slid his pants down to his ankles. She felt his hands explore her body as she slowly returned her attention to his face. His hand had discovered her womanhood and had begun to part it. She was now revealed. Her wetness was a complete giveaway.

Wave upon wave of emotion traveled through her body as Jagger's right hand worked its magic. Her whole body began to tremble. Whatever he was doing, it felt good, but it wasn't enough. It was a tease and little more. It couldn't push her anywhere near the edge and certainly couldn't push her over it.

She'd never done this before, but she knew that there was a threshold that she had not yet reached. Above all at that moment, it was something she wanted to experience.

As Raiya looked at the man she'd chosen to share it with, she slowly moved closer to him and lifted her right leg over his waist. She slowly lowered it over him, trying to build up as much tension inside of her as she could.

Her legs were spread wide over him as she lowered herself. She took it slow, unsure of what to expect. At first, it seemed as though Jagger was going to allow her to call the shots, but the anticipation was apparently too much. He quickly thrust upward, burying himself in her.

Raiya's eyes widened as her mouth dropped open. She wanted to cry out, but couldn't find the voice to. Her body had been spread and he was now completely inside of her.

Drakin
The Story of Raiya

Pain immediately shot from her insides all the way through her body. The pain was quickly replaced by wave after wave of intense pleasure. Each was like a gust of heavy wind, beating against her mercilessly. She closed her eyes and ran her claws down his spine as she bit into his neck, desperate for relief.

Raiya's bite was light. She didn't intend to cause harm, but her teeth were sharp and cut through skin like it was butter. A trickling sensation against her lips caused her to pull back. Her eyes widened when she saw a drop of blood fall from Jagger's shoulder, "Jagger... I'm sorry... I didn't..."

A look that was fueled by pure adrenaline appeared on his face. He lowered his hips before quickly thrusting them up again. Raiya gasped as she felt her body being penetrated over and over. Was this revenge? If it was, she wasn't about to let him get away with it. She clenched her jaw and ran her nails down his back, causing red lines on his skin.

Her hips began moving in a circular pattern. Each time her thighs tapped against his hips, another wave of pleasure hit her. She arched her back and ran her sharp tongue over his neck and then kissed the moistened skin.

Jagger leaned forward and cupped her breasts in his hands. Her skin was the texture of fine-grain sandpaper, but he didn't seem to care. He continued to explore her like he'd never seen a woman before.

Drakin

The Story of Raiya

The first thrust into her was slightly painful, but as her lower extremities became more lubricated, it was easier for her to move. He lay back, barely, struggling to breathe, "Shit... you're tight..."

"Shh..."

It was happening. The buildup was becoming too much. Raiya could feel herself losing control of her entire body. The intense pleasure flowed over her until she couldn't take it anymore. Her thighs and stomach clenched in a futile attempt to contain the imminent explosion.

Raiya sucked down a deep breath as her whole body shuddered. Losing control was an extremely unsettling feeling. The idea of allowing someone else control, trusting them enough to give all of that, was foreign to her. Even so, there was nothing she could do. She'd made the decision and had no regrets. Whatever happened next, she'd welcome with open arms.

Her energy was quickly sucked from her body and she became unable to hold herself up. She collapsed forward, forcing Jagger to lay back on the ground. Her body was completely lethargic; even simple movements were burdensome.

Raiya lay on top of Jagger, unable to move, "Oh God... I... I've never felt that before... whoa..."

"Are you okay?"

"Yeah... you?"

"How could I not be?"

Raiya smiled and gently raised her head. She looked straight at him with glossy eyes, "We

Drakin
The Story of Raiya

don't have much time... we should get some rest... tomorrow is going to be a big day."

"I know," Jagger replied. "So, let's just enjoy the here and now for as long as we can."

Raiya rolled off to the side and rested her head on his chest, "Sounds good..."

Chapter 26

Raiya awoke the next morning with her head on Jagger's chest. His skin looked slightly irritated where it had come into contact with her scales, but otherwise, he seemed okay. He looked down at her as she moved away. She was still warm from the few embers that were still burning. The hibernation side-effects had all worn off.

"Good morning," Jagger said as she began to get dressed.

"Morning."

"Ready to get going?"

Jagger looked confused, "Um… sure, I guess."

"What's wrong?"

"Oh, nothing… just… what the hell was that last night?"

Raiya smiled like a school girl and shrugged, "Does it really matter?"

"I don't know, kind of?" Jagger replied.

Raiya let out a deep sigh, "Oh boy… all right look, I care about you. You're my partner and… honestly, the best friend I have. Can't we just leave it at that?"

"All right."

Raiya's face dropped, "What…?"

Jagger shrugged, "I don't know I mean… I guess I kind of thought…"

"Jagger I'm a wanderer, a nomad. What did you think was going to come of that? Do you really think anyone would want us living near them in the city?"

Drakin
The Story of Raiya

"I guess not."

She leaned down and kissed him on the cheek. The affection was anything but welcome and stung when it was meant to sooth. She stepped back as she threw her shirt on. Her heart tugged as she continued, "Right.... You're going to want to settle down someday, you'll never be able to do that with me. So, let's not complicate things any more than they already are."

Raiya took a few steps back and leaned against the opening of the cave, "The sun is out... it's actually warm. We should get going."

"All right."

Jagger stood up and pulled his pants back on, "Ready?"

Raiya quickly turned away, "Sure."

Despite her best efforts, Jagger saw the look on her face, "You okay?"

"I'm fine."

"You sure?"

"Shut up, I'm fine!"

It was a lie. Her words were hollow and she wasn't even sure that she could make herself believe them. The pain she felt from rejecting Jagger cut her deeply. Likely that was worse than any injury she'd get fighting her father. Even so, it was for the best. She was probably going to get killed in the fight with her father, and even if she didn't, there was no way that she'd be able to settle down in one place. On top of that, she didn't even know if her lifespan would be compatible with his.

Drakin
The Story of Raiya

The whole problem weighed heavily on her heart. Though she was convinced that this was the right decision, part of her appreciated Jagger pushing. A selfish part of her wanted him to persist. That part wanted him to fight for her, but she quickly silenced it, "This whole thing is stupid… let's just go."

The look on Jagger's face gave Raiya the impression that he wasn't buying it. She wanted to let Jagger in on her fears, but now wasn't the time to bring it up. If they survived, maybe then she'd get the chance. *He must think I'm a flake… I kind of wish I was…*

They stepped out of the protection of the cave into the sunlight. Raiya could feel a gentle breeze on her skin, but it was considerably warmer than it had been.

Jagger stepped out behind her and looked around, "Let's head back to the trail we were following. It was the smoothest path."

"My thought's exactly."

It didn't take them long to regain their footing and begin climbing the mountain again. Where the path wasn't snowy, it was covered in loose gravel and dirt. The unstable ground coupled with the sharp incline took a toll on Raiya's feet. She did her best to ignore it, but the aching quickly became worse.

"You know… why couldn't your uncle just fly us up here?" Jagger asked as he struggled to keep pace.

"That would be too easy," Raiya replied. "Besides, that would pretty much give any other dragons in the area a clean shot at us."

Jagger frowned, "Uh huh… you don't really trust him, do you?"

"I believe that he wants my father dead… beyond that, only time will tell."

"Right…"

WREEEEEEEE!

Jagger looked up at the summit, "Raiya, the horde is still there! How are we going to get past them?"

"Keep climbing… we'll get as close as we can for now. We may need to wait until nightfall."

⚔

"Central Command, this is Avenger One. We're in position. All units are accounted for. We're standing by for orders."

"Roger, Avenger One. We're prepping the fighters now."

Commander Bhatia sat back in his hummer, "Any word on the U.S. Remnant or EastCon forces yet?"

"None I'm afraid. It looks like we're on our own."

"Surprise, surprise… well, we'll have to make this count."

"Copy that, F-22s are on the way… ETA 30 minutes."

Commander Bhatia turned and looked at Eric, "I sincerely hope you know what you're doing."

Drakin
The Story of Raiya

"Don't look at me," Eric replied. "I'm as much part of the diversion as you are. Our hope rests with Jagger and Raiya."

The commander opened his door and stepped outside, "You think we've got a chance?"

"There's always a chance."

"That's the statement of a dead man if ever there was one…"

Bhatia shut the door as Eric stepped out the other side. A young sergeant approached him and saluted, "Sir."

"Report, Sergeant."

The young soldier removed his helmet, revealing short brown hair. He turned and pointed back to the encampment as he spoke, "Sir, the heavy armor and infantry units are in position. We're having a little trouble with two of our AA artillery batteries. They took some damage in the last attack. The engineers estimate that it'll take roughly two hours to fix."

Commander Bhatia glared at him, "Sergeant, we need all four of those batteries up and running in thirty minutes. Do I make myself clear?"

The young soldier shifted uncomfortably under his commander's gaze, "Yes, sir!"

"Take anyone you need, just get them working. If we don't have a way to bring the larger dragons out of the air, then we're all dead."

"Understood, sir!"

The young sergeant put his helmet back on and ran back into the group. Commander Bhatia nodded as he disappeared, "This is going to be a

Drakin
The Story of Raiya

complete shit show if we don't have those fully functional."

Eric kept his eye on the crowd. Tanks were being moved into formation on the flanks, while MLRS trucks picked up the rear. The soldiers had been divided into groups. Each had various weapons ranging from blades to bolt guns, to assault rifles. The other group carried rocket launchers that would hopefully knock some of the smaller dragons from the sky.

Commander Bhatia was about to say something when one of the scout towers radioed. The sound of his voice was frantic and it was clear from the static that his hands were shaking, *"Sir, we have incoming contacts, ten degrees East! My God... it's a whole lot of them!"*

Commander Bhatia's eyes widened as he grabbed his binoculars, "Dragons?"

"No, sir! They're definitely human, though I can't tell if they're friendly. They're closing fast!"

Bhatia squinted through his binoculars, trying to get some idea of who was incoming, "They're not U.S. remnant forces... who are they?"

In the distance, he could make out several large transport helicopters, gunships, and multiple fighters flying escort around them. Commander Bhatia lowered his binoculars, "What the hell?"

"What is it?" Eric asked.

"Those fliers aren't anything like what we have... if I'm right, we're looking at Mil Mi-26 choppers. The fighters I'd recognize anywhere. Those are Chengdu J-10s."

"Who uses those?"

Drakin

The Story of Raiya

Commander Bhatia quickly returned to the Humvee and switched the radio to the multi-frequency setting, "Unidentified fighters, respond! Identify yourselves and state your intentions!"

At first, his only response was static. He waited a moment for it to clear before speaking again, "Unidentified…"

"Acknowledged, Western Coalition forces. This is Captain Suen, Commander of the Eastern Coalition Expeditionary Force."

Commander Bhatia squinted at the incoming forces in surprise. Captain Suen spoke with an accent he didn't recognize, but could easily understand. He watched as the small specks in the distance grew bigger, "State your intentions."

"We have been monitoring your communications and understand that you are attempting an offensive against the dragons. We would be honored to provide assistance. I formally request permission to join up with your forces."

For the first time since they'd met, Eric saw a smile appear on Commander Bhatia's face, "Well I'll be damned…"

He quickly pressed the button on the side of the radio, "Captain, permission granted. You're a welcomed sight. I owe you a drink after this is over!"

"Roger that, Commander. We'll drink it together. Let's get to work… For Wuhan!"

The massive troop carriers landed a few hundred feet away from the main group. Over a hundred men jumped out of each, carrying

Drakin

The Story of Raiya

equipment and weapons. They began setting up their emplacements right next to the Western Coalition's.

An older soldier in an olive uniform hollered something in a language that he didn't recognize. As his men scattered to carry out his orders, the soldier made his way over to Eric and Commander Bhatia. He stopped a few feet away and saluted, "You command here, yes?"

The man had a thick accent, likely from one of the Russian provinces. Commander Bhatia nodded, "That's me."

"Colonel Nikoli Popov of Eastern Coalition Ground Force, at your service."

"Commander Bhatia, Western Coalition... this is Eric Fausten, commander of the nomadic volunteer force."

"Nomads?" Colonel Popov said as his dark brown eyes widened. "You really are desperate for help."

"As desperate as they come," Eric replied.

The old colonel brushed a few strands of his iron gray-beard, "Surprised you don't have any canbans in your ranks."

"Not that desperate."

⚔

"What do you want me to do?"

Jagger lay against a large boulder with his back to the summit of the mountain, "I didn't say I wanted you to do anything. I just said it was cold up here."

"We're not going to find another cave. You know that, right? Besides, we're so close..."

Drakin
The Story of Raiya

"Too bad…" Jagger whispered.

"What was that?"

"Nothing."

At that moment, the deafening screech of two twin jet engines whizzed by. Raiya covered her ears as she looked up. Two fighters blew by into the distance.

"It's them!" Raiya cheered as the fighters came around for another pass. "The Westcons are trying to drive them off!"

The fighters moved in, fired their heavy Vulcan cannons across the field of dragons, killing several of them in the process. An uncountable number of dragons flew from the side of Mount Whitney, led by an elder.

The path still wasn't clear, but there were considerably fewer dragons on the mountain than there were before. Raiya nodded, "Well that's a start."

"Not enough… we'll never get through them…"

"No, but at least we can move up a little."

Jagger nodded, "All right, let's go…"

🜋

"Watch your six, Wraith Two! You've got wyverns gaining on you!"

"Damn… how can they fly so fast!"

The two jet fighters burned their engines as hard as they could. It was all they could do to get back to the combined forces that were waiting to blow the dragons out of the sky.

Drakin
The Story of Raiya

The elder dragon roared to his squadron, "Take them down… crush the humans in their glass bubbles!"

Three drakes moved forward to try and grab the fighters. Their wings flapped so fast that the pilot could barely see them. It wasn't looking good for him. The dragon was too close.

The massive beast roared and was about to grab the fighter when a red beam appeared in front of it. The drakes were instantly cut to ribbons by laser fire. Red beams shot through the drakes' wings, causing them to fall from the sky. Their screams could even be heard over the hum of the jet engines.

The elder stopped in his tracks when he noticed the massive force below him that was converging on the Mountain, "No… they're already here! All dragons, retreat!"

The cloud of wyverns and drakes pulled back as the human forces opened fire. Several were brought out of the sky as they made their way back to the mountain.

The elder flew as fast as his wings would carry him. In the distance, he could see the large perch where the dragon lords conducted their meetings. He thrust his wings even harder, attempting to pick up more speed. The wind tore at his face and his muscles ached.

Eutherys, Auirn, Kazrai'em, and Amzer'ial were all seated on their perches as the elder dragon crashed down, "My lords… I bring news from the East!"

Drakin
The Story of Raiya

"Breathe brother!" Eutherys replied. "Take your time, now what did you see?"

"Humans, my lord. Thousands of them! Those fighters were just trying to provoke us! They led us into a trap!"

Eutherys growled, "My daughter… – Kazrai'em!"

"My lord?" Kazrai'em replied.

"Take every last dragon, drake, and wyvern on this mountain."

"We're to attack them, my lord?"

"Wipe them out," Eutherys replied. "All of them. My daughter is your primary target. If you see her, kill her!"

"Thy will be done."

As Kazrai'em departed, Eutherys turned to the remaining elders, "Stay close to me. If my daughter somehow makes it here, she will be unable to defeat all of us."

Auirn hissed softly as he looked down the side of the mountain, "You think she'll try to come here?"

"Yes brother, I do…"

"Jagger, look!"

"I don't believe it!" Jagger replied.

The entire mountain was covered in darkness as the horde of wyverns, drakes, and dragons leaped into the air. A massive elder dragon circled the mountain, letting out a bellowing sound. As each dragon heard it, they immediately took to the air.

Drakin
The Story of Raiya

Raiya ducked down each time he passed, "Just a few more…"

The enormous cloud of dragons pulled away from the mountainside, into the air. Raiya looked on in disbelief as a path appeared in front of them, "It worked…"

"You sound surprised."

"I am… I didn't think my father would be so foolish as to send out his entire horde!"

Jagger shrugged, "Calculated risk, maybe? I'm sure they figure that if they can defeat this last band of resistance, then the settlements should be easy picking."

"Well… they're probably right…" Raiya replied. "I just hope this works. If Auirn can't recall those dragons, everyone fighting down there will be completely slaughtered."

"Then we'd better hurry. Are you ready for this?"

Raiya frowned, "Yes. It's what I've wanted for so long… I have to be ready. There is no going back now."

Raiya bit her lip as they began marching towards the summit, "Jagger… go back."

"What?" Jagger asked.

Of all the things Raiya would have asked him, this came as a surprise. The look of fear in her eyes was an even bigger shock, "Hell no I won't go back. Why even ask me that?"

"I… don't want you getting killed."

"I don't plan on getting killed."

"Jagger… you're my friend… I don't have very many."

Drakin

The Story of Raiya

Jagger smiled, "I'll still be your friend when all is said and done. Trust me."

Raiya lowered her eyes, "I won't be able to protect you."

"No need," Jagger replied as he patted the bolt gun on his back. "Got all the protection I need."

"You're an idiot!"

"So you keep telling me, but I'm still going with you."

"Jagger, please?"

"No," Jagger replied adamantly. "If we're doing this, we're doing it together. We're partners, remember?"

Raiya huffed as she turned back to the path, "Just don't die on me!"

"I won't."

Chapter 27

Captain Suen blinked as a drake appeared in her sights, "Wraith leader, this is Daoji One. I've got him in my sights!"

"Roger that, Daoji leader. He's all yours!" Wraith One replied. *"My wing, weapons free. Take down as many as you can."*

Captain Suen let loose with a pair of missiles. One struck each of the dragon's wings. The drake screamed as it fell from the sky, "Woo hoo! Fry dead bastard!"

She immediately pulled her fighter behind another drake when one of the others called out, *"Daoji One, this is Wraith Three... I've got one on my tail! I can't shake him!"*

"Copy that, Wraith Three..."

She pulled her fighter around and attempted to get on the tail of the beta, "I can't get a lock... he's too fast! Hang on, my friend!"

She fired several rounds, hoping something would hit, but nothing did. The dragon dodged her bullets like they were tiny bugs, "No good, Chiyou wing, use your smart missiles, quickly!"

Three Mi-28NM night hunters rose from the dust below, *"Copy that, Daoji leader. Target in our sights!"*

The lead chopper released a single missile towards the beta dragon. The beast saw it and attempted to dive out of the way. The missile quickly compensated and turned to follow it.

The dragon attempted to turn and grab it, but the missile was designed for that exact maneuver.

Drakin
The Story of Raiya

It speared him right in the chest and exploded. The beast didn't even have a chance to scream.

"Another one down!"

Captain Suen nodded, "Good work, Chiyou leader!"

"This is Wraith Three. Thanks, everyone!" a relieved voice came over the com. *"Back to business!"*

Captain Suen turned and looked at the massive horde of dragons still funneling into the battle, "Wraith Three, form on me! We'll take them together!"

"Roger, Daoji Leader!"

Before he could turn and form up with Captain Suen's fighter, three wyvern bodies slammed the fuselage of his plane. The impacts were so hard that they left huge dents in the armor.

Another massive dragon appeared out of nowhere and hit the jet with a fireball. Wraith Three exploded right in front of Captain Suen's eyes. She immediately pulled out of the way to avoid the blast., "Wǒ cào!"

She circled around the battlefield, trying to get a feel for what was going on. The com chatter was almost deafening;

"Watch yourselves, 4 o'clock low!"

"I see him... I see him..."

"I'm hit Chiyou leader, oh my God!"

"This is Wraith Two, I'm going down!"

"Wraith Leader, this is Baker One. We're starting our attack!"

"Mayday! Mayday!"

Drakin
The Story of Raiya

"Chiyou Leader to Wraith Leader, lost units two and three!"

"Copy Chiyou Leader!"

Captain Suen shook her head as she locked onto another drake, "There's too many of them!"

On the ground, things weren't going much better. Eric watched as an elder dragon swooped down and grabbed one of the MLRS launchers and ripped it from its base. He ran towards the center of the fight.

A wyvern jumped out of the horde and landed next to him, "Think you can take me on, filthy human?"

Eric smiled as he drew his blades, "Bring it on, motherfucker!"

The wyvern dove towards Eric, intent on killing him in a single blow. Eric had seen this before. Younger dragons were far more foolish and thus easy to kill.

Eric dropped to the ground, landing on his back. The wyvern dropped in on top of him, ready to deliver a death blow. It stopped dead in its tracks when it realized what he had done. As the wyvern came down, Eric raised one of his blades and allowed the weight of the wyvern to drive it into the beast's chest.

The wyvern went limp as Eric pushed it aside, "Too easy!"

As he got back to his feet, Eric caught sight of Commander Bhatia. He quickly ran through the thick of battle, trying to get to the officer. All around him, the nomads were fighting to the end

Drakin
The Story of Raiya

of their lines. They were good, but there were just too many dragons.

Horrific screams rose from a group nearby. Three wyverns jumped on top of one of the nomadic fighters and began ripping into him with their claws. Eric turned and pulled out his gun, firing several rounds at the nearest dragon. He couldn't save the man, he knew this. However, it might be possible to get close enough to end his suffering.

The largest wyvern turned away from the nomad and charged at Eric. He aimed the pistol right at the wyvern's eye, "Come on Eric, remember what you were taught… breathe, relax, and shoot!"

He pulled the trigger as the wyvern jumped into the air. The bullet screamed from the barrel and struck the beast in the eye. It let out a mournful cry as it hit the ground lifelessly.

Commander Bhatia stood next to his Humvee, firing his pistol at anything that got too close. He had a receiver that was wired into the truck almost pressed against his lips, "Central, this is forward command. We have engaged the enemy, but we are vastly outnumbered! Requesting reinforcements!"

"Negative, Commander. We can't spare anyone. If things are getting too dicey, you have permission to retreat!"

Commander Bhatia sighed, "Where we gonna retreat to? There is no getting away from these

Drakin
The Story of Raiya

dragons. They'll cut us to ribbons if we even try it! We're too far out now!"

"I'm sorry, commander. We have no one to send you!"

Commander Bhatia threw the receiver back into the Humvee, "Useless bastards…"

"No help?" Eric asked.

"Not so much," Commander Bhatia replied. "It looks like we're on our own."

"How bad is it?"

Bhatia shook his head, "We've lost two fighters, a gunship, two tanks, a missile truck, and I don't even know how many men! There's just too many of them!"

Eric nodded, "I know… most of my people that I've been able to find have already been cut down!"

Bhatia made eye contact with Eric. Neither had any words of comfort or confidence for the other. It didn't look like there was any way they were going to survive.

Commander Bhatia extended his hand, "I'm Sai, by the way."

Eric smiled and took his hand, "Good to meet you, Sai."

"Good to meet you too."

The men shook hands as another nomad flew through the air and landed on the back of a wyvern.

"All right, let's get back into this!" Eric shouted.

Sai nodded and picked up the receiver, "All units, this is Commander Bhatia. We could run,

Drakin
The Story of Raiya

and some of us might survive today only to die tomorrow. If we leave, our people on Mount Whitney would quickly be overwhelmed by dragons. We're going to keep fighting… down to the last man!"

"Hopefully it won't come to that!" an unfamiliar voice replied.

Sai looked at the receiver in confusion, "Who is this? Identify yourself!"

Before anyone could respond, the whoosh of three fighters appeared overhead. Eric's eyes widened, "F-22s! I recognize them!"

They were immediately followed by several pave hawk and Chinook helicopters. Each one bore the white star of the American flag on the side.

The lead fighter circled around the battlefield, *"Commander Bhatia, this is Lieutenant Commander Ryan Travers, United States Naval Air Corps. Is there a Jagger Bishop or a Raiya with you?"*

Sai spoke in an excited tone, "No, they're already on Mount Whitney. We need to hold the dragons where they are for now."

"Very well," Ryan replied. *"You all should know that I was against dedicating my men to this… It better be worth it!"*

A cheer went up from the remaining coalition forces as their numbers were replenished by American soldiers. Choppers quickly landed, delivered between thirty to fifty men, and then took off again.

Drakin
The Story of Raiya

Eric waved his dagger in the air, "Come on boys, we're still in this!"

Eutherys growled, "What do you mean?"

Amzer'ial looked up from her perch, "It would appear that the human factions have united against us. The Eastern Coalition has joined the fight, and it would appear that those foolish zealots from the east coast have also arrived."

"Our worst fears have been realized…" Eutherys muttered. "Send all available dragons into battle. Only one side can win today. If the united forces manage to prevail, they'll continue to push against us. We have to stop them here and now."

"Not going to happen, father!"

Eutherys's eyes widened when he heard the familiar voice, "You…"

Raiya stepped forward out of the shadows with Jagger close on her heels, "This is the end. You murdered my mother and destroyed my entire world. Now it's your turn. You're going to feel every pain… every sense of dread, every feeling of despair and hopelessness that I felt. Then maybe I'll show you mercy and let you die."

Eutherys laughed, "Perhaps there is some of me in you after all. Very well spoken… however, today is not my day to die. This will be a day long remembered by all. First for seeing the end of those pathetic resistance fighters down there, then by seeing you die."

Eutherys turned to his brother, "Kill her."

"I will not," Auirn replied.

Drakin
The Story of Raiya

"What?" Eutherys said in surprise.

"Brother, she came here to issue you a challenge. Honor forbids me from killing her… especially given who she is."

"And who is she to you?" Eutherys demanded.

Auirn looked down at Raiya and then back up at his brother, "She is my niece. She is drakin. If you wish to kill her, then you may step forward and fight. I will not."

Eutherys loomed over his brother. The dread lord was at least twice the size of any of the dragon lords. He spread his wings and opened his jaw, "Then you will die!"

Before Auirn could respond, Eutherys shot forward. Hitting him in the torso. The two dragon lords crashed to the ground between the perches. Amzer'ial watched in horror as Auirn struggled to get back on his feet.

He pushed Eutherys off and rolled onto his stomach. The black dragon lord shook his head and huffed as he spoke, "Is that the best you've got? You're getting weak in your old age, brother."

Auirn jumped on his brother's back and bit down hard into his neck. Eutherys roared as blood slowly dripped from the massive dragon's neck. Raiya had to block her eyes to prevent getting sprayed.

Eutherys brought his tail around like a whip and cracked Auirn in the face. Auirn released his grip on his brother's neck and wound up for a second pounce, "Brother, this has to end. Even if we take the planet, our race won't survive. We

Drakin
The Story of Raiya

should go home. With our greater numbers, we could overwhelm the people who wrongfully exiled us. Who knows, they may actually welcome us home after all this time!"

"I will not risk more death on our people. We will take this planet and turn it into the paradise we so deserve. You could have stood with me, brother, but now that will never happen."

Auirn growled, "Brother... these humans have a place called Hell. They believe that the evil among their dead go there. After all the sins I've committed, if that is my destiny then I'm ready. Are you?"

"You'll be there long before I ever am!"

Jagger raised his bolt gun as the two dragons collided together again. Their claws slashed into each other's flesh. Raiya grabbed the gun and forced him to lower it, "No, you could hit Auirn! If I could have, I would've used my fire breath already."

Auirn struggled away from Eutherys and climbed to his perch, "Brother... This needs to end!"

"Yes... yes, it does..."

Auirn lowered his eyes, "I really don't want to fight you anymore. You are also drakin to me. Can't you see that your plan is a pipe dream? You can't challenge nature itself."

Eutherys appeared to have been taken aback by his brother's words, "Why not? Is it too much to ask that our people have a home where they can thrive?"

Drakin
The Story of Raiya

"And how many have to die on your mad quest to find such a place? I'm tired of all the killing. We've lost friends, allies, and we've committed genocide in the process. After everything is said and done in this war, how many dragons have to die before you realize that you've made a mistake?"

Auirn cautiously lowered himself from his perch and extended his claw to his brother, "Let us end this together. We can work with the humans to find ourselves a more suitable world."

"You really think it's possible?"

"I do, brother."

Eutherys let out a deep, defeated sigh and placed his claw on his brother's, "Auirn…"

He slowly closed his claw around his brother. It looked like the fight was over. The two stood together looking at one another for a moment.

Before anyone could react, Eutherys quickly jerked on his arm, pulling his brother in close. As Auirn moved forward, Eutherys jabbed his other claw into his brother's chest.

"No!" Raiya cried out.

Jagger tried to grab her shoulder, but couldn't get a grip as she charged forward, "Raiya, don't!"

She clicked her jaw together and unleashed the most powerful flame that Jagger had ever seen. A deafening scream filled the air as a burst of flame struck her father, knocking him to the side.

Auirn fell limply to the ground, not moving. Raiya stepped between him and Eutherys. Her

Drakin
The Story of Raiya

teeth were clenched as she looked at her father, "Your own brother…"

"Now you."

Raiya once again released a stream of fire. Her father countered with his own flame. The blasts connected and pushed off one another. Raiya pushed her head forward and locked her neck in place to keep her flames stable as she relentlessly attacked the dragon she hated more than any other on the planet.

Both were having a hard time maintaining their flames. While Eutherys's stream was larger, it was not enough to bypass Raiya's. The flames beat against each other for what seemed like an eternity.

The pain in Raiya's jaw was becoming too much. She had to stop and she knew it. Her only hope was to time it exactly right. She needed to push hard with her legs and dodge out of the way.

Seconds passed. The pain in her jaw became intolerable. It was now or never. She quickly relaxed the muscles under her tongue and jumped out of the way.

Raiya propelled herself as far as she could. She landed on her knees off to the side, just in time for Eutherys to bring his head around. His jaws were wide open, revealing teeth that were as long as her arm. This was it. She couldn't get out of the way of his jaw fast enough and she knew it.

All Raiya could see was the tongue and throat of her father as he bore down on her. Maybe she could hit him one last time with her fire breath?

Drakin

The Story of Raiya

Would it even be strong enough to make him back off?

Three glowing bolts hit the side of Eutherys's jaw, turning his attention away from Raiya, "Fool… I'll kill you for that!"

Jagger aimed the bolt gun and fired three more rounds at the dragon that slowly made its way towards him. Eutherys shrugged them off as he charged at Jagger. He wound his neck back, ready to incinerate the human boy in flames when his daughter appeared between them, "No!"

Eutherys stopped in his tracks, "You protect him, now?"

Raiya looked back at Jagger for a moment. The angry expression on her face didn't change, "We protect each other."

"Then you can die together!"

Instead of using his flames, Eutherys quickly spun around. His barbed tail moved like a massive whip. Eutherys's speed was unlike anything they'd ever seen. His tail was little more than a blur as it came towards them.

Raiya had no way to move and no way to protect Jagger. The tail was too fast. She let out an agonized grunt as the end of it slammed into her stomach. Her whole abdomen hurt, but she was forced to ignore it. She was sent flying through the air towards one of the perches.

Raiya focused, she'd only get one chance. If she missed the perch, it would be a long drop down the mountain. She ignored the pounding pain and slowly extended her arms. Her claws scraped the perch as she latched on.

Drakin
The Story of Raiya

Jagger wasn't so lucky. He too had been hit, but he wasn't sent as high. His body slammed limply into the wall just below the nearest perch. His eyes were closed and there was no sign of consciousness. He didn't even try to grab onto anything as he fell to the ground.

Raiya held on tightly to the rocks. Her claws were scraped and bloody. Her stomach was in intense pain. She pressed herself against the rock for a moment as the pulsing slowly dissipated.

Eutherys wasn't going to wait forever, but hiding behind the perch had afforded her some healing time. *I've gotta get to Jagger...*

Still in pain, Raiya jumped down from the perch and ran to Jagger's side. Eutherys snapped at her, giving her another opening. She quickly dodged out of the way and ignited her fire breath. It was a single blast this time. She had only meant it as a retaliatory shot. She hadn't even taken aim when she unleashed it.

The blast left her lips and struck the receding head of the dragon directly in his left eye. Eutherys roared as he fell backward and immediately tried to rub the wound.

It was all the distraction Raiya needed. She ducked down and dropped to her knees next to her fallen partner, "Jagger!"

No response.

"Jagger... no, no, don't do this to me."

His nose was bleeding, his entire face looked like it was about to break out in bruises, and it didn't look like he was breathing, "Jagger... come

Drakin
The Story of Raiya

on! We're partners here, you can't just give up now! You... you can't!"

Nothing she said was making even the slightest difference, "Jagger... I'm sorry..."

To her surprise, a hot tear fell from her eye. She clenched her jaw and stood up. Eutherys stopped rubbing his damaged eye and returned her attention to Raiya, "You've blinded me... you..."

Raiya drew her dagger as she stepped closer to her father, "Ben..."

"I'll kill you for this!"

"Linda... The people of New Framingham..."

"You say those names like they should mean something!" Eutherys hissed.

"Miranda... Mother..."

She clenched her jaw, "And now Jagger... no more!"

"Oh, there will be more, don't you worry about that. Once I'm done here, I'll go finish that pathetic resistance myself!"

"The only way you're done here is when you're dead!" Raiya shouted as she raced towards her father.

Eutherys let out a deafening roar. His flame breath narrowly missed Raiya's ankle. She responded with her own, grazing his right claw. She was now running at him. Her whole body was in pain, but she did the best she could to ignore it. Her mind was too busy focusing on her target.

She quickly dodged around another lash of Eutherys's jaw and jumped on his back, "Die!"

She plunged her dagger into the wound on the side of his neck. Her father unleashed a scream

Drakin
The Story of Raiya

that would have shattered bullet proof glass, "Amzer'ial, help me!"

Amzer'ial was standing next to Auirn's body. She had nudged his head to see if there was any life still in his body. After confirming that he was dead, she'd laid down next to him. When Eutherys called for her, she looked up and growled, "You've earned your fate many times over, Eutherys. How fitting that the daughter you so despise is the one to herald your end."

Eutherys hissed as he jerked his head to the side in an attempt to throw Raiya from his back, "You would turn on me as well? So be it!"

Raiya quickly slid down and grabbed on to the scales next to the wound she was working on. She withdrew that dagger and stabbed it even closer to his head, "Die!"

Eutherys cried out in pain as he put all of his strength into one last jolt, "You will not… end me!"

Raiya could feel the impact coming. She closed her eyes as she waited for it. Even at full strength, she wouldn't be able to hold on.

The impact hit her like a pile of bricks simultaneously striking her. She fell to the ground and rolled a few feet away from Eutherys.

She was badly hurt. Her nose was bleeding, her scales had been cracked and stained with blood, her stomach still hurt, and she was unable to feel her legs. She had no fight left in her.

Eutherys stood over her triumphantly, "I would have expected more of a fight than that.

Drakin
The Story of Raiya

Even with a human mother, you should have been able to do more than this!"

Raiya pushed herself up on her palms. Blood dripped from her lip as she clenched her teeth, "Just get it over with!"

"As you wish…" the dragon replied.

Eutherys growled as he lowered his head to Raiya. She waited and watched as his mouth drew closer. He wasn't going to burn her, he was going to eat her.

Apparently, Eutherys wasn't going to take any chances on her surviving another attack. Seeing the pink inside of her father's mouth gave Raiya an idea. She only had a split second to plan and one chance to make it work. This was it, the next few seconds would determine who walked away from this fight.

Using the last ounce of her strength, she leaped past his teeth. It worked, her feet landed on the fleshy gum inside his mouth. She clenched the dagger in her right hand and drove it up through his upper jaw, into his brain.

Blood rained down from the roof of Eutherys's mouth. Raiya crouched down and waited for whatever was to come next. The beast let out a loud cry and fell to the side. The impact produced a shock that collapsed the council's perches.

Raiya rolled from Eutherys's mouth as she hit the ground. She lay on the cold stone, staring up at the sky, "It's over…"

She let out a deep sigh and closed her eyes. Her fight had finally come to an end. The pain

Drakin

The Story of Raiya

was too much. She'd won, but her victory had come at a heavy price. Her arms and legs would not respond, and her eyes forced themselves closed.

Drakin
The Story of Raiya

Chapter 28

Commander Bhatia watched in horror as a pair of elder dragons attacked their armored units. The tanks fought back as best they could, but the heat was proving too much for them. The shells from the tanks were too slow to hit the fast-moving elder dragons. *This isn't looking good!*

BOOM!

The commander turned to see a massive dragon with green scales land in front of him. Given its size, there could be little doubt that this was a dragon lord, "Oh shit…"

Eric quickly ripped open the hood to the command Humvee and detached the fuel cell, "Good… it looks like it still has more than half a charge."

He quickly jumped between Commander Bhatia and the ancient dragon. It looked at him and scoffed, "Brave… but foolish… You're completely outmatched."

"Think so?"

The dragon jumped towards him with its claws out. The beast was obviously trying to end the fight quickly, "Die!"

Eric tried to jump out of the way, but one of the dragon's claws caught his foot. He cried out as blood poured from the wound. There was no getting away. He was pinned to the ground by the dragon's claw.

More out of spite than attempting to kill the dragon, Eric plunged his dagger into its leg, "See how you like it!"

Drakin

The Story of Raiya

The dragon lord kicked free and turned to face Eric, "You're dead!"

Eric could only watch as the beast lunged at him. His right foot was too badly damaged, so he pushed off with his left. It wasn't enough.

The dragon grabbed him by the leg and sunk his teeth in. Eric's leg went numb as he hung upside down in the dragon's mouth. He was losing blood quickly and his eyes were blurring out.

The dragon jerked its head back, flipping him into the air. Eric closed his eyes, bracing for what was about to happen as he hugged the power cell close to his chest. A barely audible screech left the device as Eric set it to maximum output.

The dragon closed its jaws around Eric. The jubilant smile on its face was hideous. He was about to open his jaws to finish Eric off when his bottom jaw blew clean off.

Commander Bhatia had spent the last of his rounds and could barely move. There was little he could do but watch in complete horror as the dragon gyrated and let out a mournful cry. Eric's remains were nowhere to be seen. The explosion had likely blown him to pieces inside the dragon's mouth.

The dragon lord thrust its head to either side before it collapsed. A massive cheer went up from the soldiers on the ground. Most of them had never seen a dragon lord, let alone heard of one being killed. This was a major victory for them, but the battle was far from over.

Drakin
The Story of Raiya

Captain Suen saw the events unfold from her fighter, "Woo hoo hoo!!! One big boy down!"

Her joy was short lived when the radio chatter picked up, *"Daoji leader, this is Freedom One. Chiyou and Wraith wings are down. I've lost Freedom Three..."*

"Copy that, Commander Travers," Captain Suen replied. "I've lost all but one wingman. I don't know how much more good we're going to do up here. We should commence strafing runs on the ground. If we're going down, at least we'll give our boys down there a better..."

She didn't even have a chance to finish the sentence. A small fireball punched the wing of her fighter. The HUD went red and warning lights flashed all around her, "Fuck... I've been hit! This is Daoji leader... you guys are on your own! I'm going down!"

Captain Suen quickly punched the eject lever on her cockpit. The canopy shot open with a loud hiss and she was propelled up out of her plane. A white and orange parachute shot out of her backpack. The tug on her chest was tremendous, but it succeeded in slowing her descent to the ground.

Three wyverns flew overhead and drove in to attack. The first one missed, the second one barely cut one of her cords, but the third one successfully cut enough away that she was severed from her parachute.

Suen hit the ground hard, but uninjured. The three wyverns landed around her in a triangle formation. She only had a split second to act

Drakin
The Story of Raiya

before they ripped her to shreds. Her wing had trained for this, but it was a totally different feeling when it actually happened.

Captain Suen pressed on the clips, releasing the heavy gear, ripped her helmet off, and pulled a large, scimitar-shaped machete from her back. Her dark hair came loose from the bun on her head and dropped to her shoulders.

Grasping the blade in her right hand, Suen quickly grabbed a 9mm pistol from her pocket, "Want to play?"

The dragons all charged at her together. She drove the machete into the mouth of the first one that got close enough. A second one lunged at her, intending to pin her on the ground. She quickly ducked out of the way and put four rounds into its head. The third one charged at her with its mouth open, but before it could bite, she slashed its lower jaw, severing it.

The dragon roared in pain as it fell backward. Captain Suen couldn't stand the noise and quickly severed its head with the blade. *Just die already!*

As the wyvern's head rolled away, Captain Suen wiped the blade on her sleeve and sighed, "Not over yet!"

She quickly ran through the raging battle, past men and women fighting for their lives, to the Humvee that had been deemed forward command, "Commander Bhatia!"

The commander was struggling to keep his forces together. His mouth was practically on top of the radio, "Central Command, we're getting beaten down badly… we've been surrounded!"

Drakin
The Story of Raiya

"Copy Commander we're prepping more fighters to try to cover your retreat, ETA twenty minutes!"

"I don't think we have twenty minutes!" Bhatia yelled as he threw the radio back into the Humvee.

"Commander Bhatia!"

He quickly turned to see the young Asian running towards him, "Who are you?"

She gave him a quick salute, "Captain Suen, sir."

"What are you doing here?"

"I got hit… I lost my fighter. How bad are things?"

"We've been surrounded, our armored division is gone… most of our fighters are gone… and we've been cut down to a few thousand soldiers. It's about as bad as it can get here!"

The officers watched as their troops were surrounded and quickly forced into a pack. Captain Suen frowned, "I didn't think it would end like this."

"Me either…" Commander Bhatia agreed.

"Maybe it doesn't have to."

"Oh?"

"Our mission was to buy time for your people on the mountain, right?"

"Right."

"Well, we've done that. So, who says we've been beaten? I say we've still got some fight left! What do you say?"

Drakin
The Story of Raiya

At first, the commander looked at her like she was crazy. Then he looked at the worn, tired, and scared faces of his men. Was this really how he wanted to go out? The idea of dying while huddled together with his men in fear was completely unacceptable.

He smiled at Captain Suen and nodded, "I'm Sai, by the way."

Captain Suen smiled, "Luli, Suen Luli."

Sai nodded as he reached into the Humvee and quickly switched the radio to its megaphone setting. He spoke into with as strong a tone as he could, "Everyone, I know it looks like this fight is over. I know you're tired and you've lost friends today... but our job was to help our friends and we've done just that! We bought them priceless time! As far as I'm concerned, we've won the day... now, what's say all of you? Do you want to go out huddled together like cowards or do you want to die putting up a fight that even the dragons will have to remember?"

Cheers went up from the crowd, ending in a resounding 'fight!'

Sai jumped down from the Humvee and turned to Luli, "May I borrow that sword?"

Luli nodded and handed the machete over to Sai, "My honor."

Sai took the sword and pointed it towards Mount Whitney, "Forward!"

The large group of soldiers began running forward. They collided with a line of wyverns and drakes. Miraculously, they managed to break into

Drakin
The Story of Raiya

the line of bewildered dragons and started cutting them down.

Even with the sudden moral boost, there just were not enough of them left to take on the dragon horde. They were quickly getting cut down to nothing. Luli stood with her back to Sai. She quickly grabbed her last clip and loaded it into the pistol, "This is it!"

Sai closed his eyes, ready for the end. He'd fought hard and accomplished what he'd set out to. There was nothing left for him to do.

SHREEEEEEEEEEEEEE!

The blood-curdling cry from Mount Whitney made every dragon's head cock to the side. They immediately looked back to the mountain. The fighting stopped as each dragon's eyes widened.

Sai opened his eyes and looked around the group. The dragons had stopped fighting, despite still being cut down by his forces. Whatever that scream was, it had caught their attention.

One of the elder dragons quickly roared, "Eutherys has fallen! Everyone, back to the mountain!"

The massive horde of dragons took off and flew into the clouds. Gunshots and rockets trailed after them.

"Cease fire!" Sai shouted as a gun went off next to him. "Cease fire, I said!"

Captain Suen Luli looked at him oddly, "What do you think just happened, Commander?"

"I don't know... I think we just won!"

A deafening cheer went up from the crowd. Bodies and debris littered the land. The smoke was so thick that it almost blocked out the sun. A scene of death and destruction surrounded the soldiers, but none of them seemed to care.

The remaining two fighters circled overhead. Lt. Commander Ryan's satisfied voice came over the radio on the Humvee. Commander Bhatia hadn't bothered to turn it off. The megaphone projected across the field, *"Westcon ground forces, this is Freedom One. It looks like the dragon horde is in full retreat. We're low on fuel and requesting permission to fall back."*

Commander Bhatia ran back to the Humvee and grabbed the radio, "Understood, Freedom One. Thanks for all your help."

"Acknowledged, Commander. One hell of a job you guys did down there! This is Freedom One, signing off!"

🦇

Raiya's eyes opened to see a group of dragonlings racing around her. Two of them had bandages in their claws and were carefully patching up her wounds. She tried to sit up, but still didn't have the energy to do so, "I'm still… alive?"

"Better than alive," a voice replied. "You're alive and you're going to be just fine."

Raiya's eyes widened and she forced herself to sit up through the pain, "Jagger!"

Jagger smiled as he placed his hand on her back, "Easy…"

"You should be laying down!" another stern voice said from behind.

Drakin

The Story of Raiya

Raiya turned to see Andy standing behind them, "You've had considerable trauma and your body is going to take some time to heal. Even with that dragon plating of yours, you've taken a beating!"

Raiya smiled as she looked around, "Andy! You made it…"

Then she noticed that someone was missing, "Wait… where's Eric?"

Jagger frowned, "I'm sorry Raiya, he didn't make it."

"What?"

"He fell while taking down one of my brethren. He fell destroying one of the dragon lords," a deep voice said from behind.

The dragonlings quickly scattered as a much larger dragon came into view. Raiya's eyes widened, "You… the dragon lord!"

"The last one, it seems," Amzer'ial said sadly. "Your uncle shared my cave for many years… even before we were banished here. I will mourn his loss for the rest of my days."

Amzer'ial growled as she spoke, "Drakin Raiya… as I look at you, the blood in my veins burns. In my heart, I would kill you for what you did."

Jagger had to help keep Raiya balanced as she struggled to her feet, "Yet you haven't."

"No," the dragon replied. "Killing you now would not bring my people peace, nor grant me any honor. It does me no good to continue this war. It is obvious to me that there will be no winner in the end."

Drakin

The Story of Raiya

"So then… what happens now?" Raiya asked.

"Now… we try for peace, as Auirn wanted it. Our horde is leaderless. We have no council and I am the only remaining lord. We have no direction and no path forward. I do not wish to see my race face extermination… we will agree to a cessation of hostilities if your people will agree to help us get off this planet."

To Raiya's shock, Amzer'ial lowered her head and the other dragons followed suit. This was something that Raiya hadn't expected. It was an uncomfortable feeling. Suddenly she'd been thrust into the role of diplomat.

When she didn't respond, Jagger stepped forward, "On behalf of the Western Coalition, you have my word that I will bring your request to Central Command. I believe that the U.S. remnant still has that technology. We'll work something out."

"Thank you," Amzer'ial replied. "We could expect no more."

Raiya's eyes narrowed as she looked at Jagger, "So now you're back to being an officer in the Westcon?"

"For now, maybe…" Jagger replied. "At the very least, I need to keep being one until this is actually over."

"I see…"

Amzer'ial nodded, "Then I will accompany you back to your command in order to flesh out the final details of our plan."

"First, we should probably get Raiya down the mountain," Andy replied. "She's going to need some time to rest and heal."

Raiya frowned, "I'm fine, really…"

Jagger gripped her arm as she tried to walk, "Sure you are. You've done your part, now let us handle the rest."

"Jagger?"

"Relax," Jagger said with a smile. "It's over now."

Denver City
Capital of the Western Coalition
Formerly Colorado

Drakin
The Story of Raiya

Chapter 29

Loud cheers erupted throughout Denver. It was a day that would be long remembered throughout the land. Representatives of the Western and Eastern Coalitions joined with the U.S. Remnant to sign the Denver Peace Accords.

The entire event took a week to plan and was as big a celebration as either Jagger or Raiya had ever seen. Jagger found it quite fitting that the peace accords would be signed on the steps of the Western Coalition's capital and was happy to see that the city survived.

Countless ceremonies had taken place since Eutherys had been killed. Both Jagger and Raiya were forced to live through diplomatic speeches, heroic welcomes, and citations. It seemed like everyone wanted to be the first to congratulate them.

Today was no exception, before the signing of the accords, Raiya and Jagger were paraded around the city to cheering crowds. Raiya smiled and waved, as was expected of her. She appeared happy, but inside she was a mass of quivering nerves. She'd never spent this much time around people and wasn't used to the attention.

Everyone wanted to shake her hand. Everyone wanted a quote, everyone wanted a piece of her. It was completely unnerving.

All she wanted was to get away. Throughout the entire ceremony, her eyes remained fixed on the city wall. It was as though she was trapped.

Drakin
The Story of Raiya

She wanted to be back outside on the frontier, not there becoming a celebrity.

The signing of the accords was no better. Before the ceremony, Raiya stayed in the suite that had been prepared for her, Jagger, and Andrea. She remained hidden, refusing all guests and requests for interviews.

The suite had been built out of the top floor of Central Command's west wing. It was spacious and clean with rooms for each of them. A large table by the door was completely covered with food for them to enjoy at their leisure. On the other side of the room was a large window that allowed them a view of the field.

Raiya watched as people began filing in. It wasn't as coordinated as some probably would have liked, given the lack of personnel. Several Westcon soldiers were running around, trying to make sure that the final preparations were complete.

A massive table had been set up at the bottom steps of the building. A podium had been placed in front of the table with a microphone hooked into it. Banners displaying the emblems of each faction hung from every flagpole. The capital also had three massive banners draped over the entryway.

Raiya released a nervous breath as Jagger joined her by the window, "They're going to want us there… aren't they?"

"Yup," Jagger replied.

"Are they going to ask us to say anything?"

"Probably."

Drakin

The Story of Raiya

Andy walked into the room from his bedroom, "Hey guys, ready for the signing?"

"As we'll ever be," Raiya replied.

"Shall we?" Andy asked as he beckoned them to the door.

"Fine, let's just get this over with."

The group proceeded out of the suite. A pair of Westcon soldiers stood guard on either side of the door as the group exited. It had been their job to make sure that the 'Heroes of the Red War' remained undisturbed. They nodded as Raiya passed, "Ma'am."

Jagger frowned as they passed the soldiers. Since the fight, Raiya had been the focus of everyone's attention. The rest of the group had been like a footnote. Eric had been all but forgotten in the massive wave of casualties that had come in. Miranda now had a field named after her, but that was it, and Andy was barely a mentioned in the whole story.

Jagger was the only one who ever stood with Raiya and even then, he was off to the side. It made sense. She was the one who killed the dragon. She was the hero of the day, but still, she worried. She didn't want her friends to be forgotten. It was something that kept her on edge.

"So, what are your plans after everything settles down?" Andy asked.

Jagger shrugged, "I never really thought about it."

"Raiya?"

"I don't know either," Raiya replied. "My life has been consumed with killing Eutherys. Now that I've accomplished my work… I really don't know where to go from here. I never really thought about what I'd do after."

She turned so that her focus was on Andy "What about you?"

Andy smiled, "Dr. Castillo is being relegated to the R&D Branch of the U.S. Army. Though rumor has it he'll be quietly asked to retire or face an ethics board."

"You think he'll accept that?"

"I don't know," Andy replied. "To be honest… Despite his problems, he did contribute a lot to the war effort, part of me doesn't want him to. Either way, he won't be anywhere near patients. That's my job."

"Oh?" Jagger asked.

"Yup. You're looking at the new director of Medicine for the U.S. Remnant. I take office as soon as the peace accords are signed."

Jagger frowned, "Be careful, you may not have that job for long."

"Oh, I know," Andy replied. "Politics being what it is. A new world government is going to need to be established. At that time, I'm sure they'll be appointing new people to each position. Honestly, I'm fine with that. If I don't get the job, it's back to treating patients. Maybe I'll even start my own hospital."

Jagger smiled, "If you do, I'll probably wind up being your first patient."

"Consider it a deal then," Andy replied as he adjusted his glasses.

Drakin
The Story of Raiya

A sharp feeling entered Jagger's arm as they reached the entryway and the doors opened to the ceremony. He looked down to see that Raiya was grasping his arm tightly.

The crowd exploded into cheers and applause as the group made their way to the seats that were waiting for them at the rear of the table. Raiya's eyes were wider than he'd ever seen, "You okay?"

"Fine."

"You're lying."

"Yeah? What are you gonna do about it?"

"Do you want to go back inside?"

Raiya frowned, "I doubt that's really an option."

Within minutes, the field was completely crowded. People had come from all across the world to see this historic moment and everyone wanted to make sure that they had a good view.

Field Marshal Lavoie led the precession of faction representatives out to the field. Captain Suen, Commander Bhatia, and Lt. Commander Travers followed closely behind the leaders. They were each dressed in their respective faction's uniforms and were equally adorned in sparkling medals.

Three men carrying a dark wooden box followed behind them and were accompanied by a large group of dignitaries. They lined up on one side of the table and opened the box. Each man removed large documents from the box and placed them at each station.

Jagger couldn't see clearly, but it looked as though they were each copies of the final peace treaty that would be signed by the leaders of each faction. There were four copies in total.

Three chairs had been set up at the table, each one with the emblem of their respective representative. A copy of the treaty was placed in front of each chair. The fourth copy was placed at the end of the table and a large inkwell was placed next to it.

A confused look appeared on Raiya's face, "What's the fourth one for?"

Jagger didn't even get a chance to answer. A massive shadow appeared in the sky over them and circled the field twice to a mix reaction of cheers and gasps. Raiya looked up to see a massive dragon with yellow scales descend on the field.

Amzer'ial folded her feet underneath her at the end of the table where the final copy of the treaty had been placed. Three elder dragons appeared and landed on top of the capital building. No doubt there to make sure their leader was safe.

The crowd fell silent as the rest of the group also took their seats. They each quickly glanced over the document that they would soon be asked to sign.

It was as though time stood still. This treaty had been hastily drafted by members of each faction and few had been given a chance to read it. Would there be any objections?

The tension seemed to disappear as the three leaders placed their copies back on the table. Each was handed a pen by the assistants that had carried the treaties. Amzer'ial couldn't hold a pen and instead dipped her claw into the inkwell. She made the mark of a dragon on the paper.

Once each paper was signed, it was then handed to the right for the next representative. Again, they looked over it and signed their names. This was repeated two more times until all four documents had been signed by everyone.

The moment they were done, the documents were placed inside black coverings and taken back inside. The faction leaders each stood and shook hands before turning to Amzer'ial.

The entire crowd watched as the three men stood silently for a moment and then bowed to the dragon. An appreciative smile appeared on Amzer'ial's face as she respectfully lowered her eyes.

The cheers of the crowds died down as Field Marshal Lavoie stepped out from behind the table and quickly made his way over to the podium. He stood for a moment, straightening out the wrinkles in his uniform before he spoke.

The crowd watched and waited. What was he going to say? What was to become of them and how was humanity going to progress forward.

Marshal Lavoie cleared his throat and spoke into the microphone with a powerful voice, "On behalf of myself, our great allies in the Eastern Coalition, our friends in the U.S. Remnants, and those newfound friends from the nomadic clans that gave their lives… I welcome you all here. Today is a day that no doubt many of you thought would never come. Others may have held out hope against hope. I myself was beginning to doubt… but thanks to our new heroes…"

Lavoie stopped for a moment and beckoned back to Jagger and Raiya. The crowd cheered for a moment before the field marshal turned back, "Thanks to them, we can now rejoice. Ladies and Gentlemen, the war is over. A cessation of hostilities has been agreed to and the fighting will end... While I join you in rejoicing, I must remind all of you not to lose sight of what lies ahead. First, we must fulfill our side of the agreement. We will use what technology we have at our disposal to help dragon kind leave our planet. They hope to return to their homeworld either to be welcomed as friends, or as invaders planning to take back what is there's. I know many of you may have mixed feelings about this. I was also hesitant at first, but in the end, it really is the best course of action."

The crowd applauded as Lavoie paused. He turned and nodded to Amzer'ial who looked on as the speech continued, "Secondly, a new world government will need to come to fruition. I think I speak for everyone around the world when I say that our minor differences can no longer divide us. So many have died… Humanity has been driven to the brink and our world will never be the same… but I promise you, we will survive."

Cheers went up from the crowd as Lavoie raised his voice, "We will survive, and we will come back even stronger than before. Let the world never forget what happened here. Let our children and our children's children sing songs of this day…"

Lavoie once again turned back and looked at Amzer'ial, "And hopefully someday… when our races are ready, we can meet again as friends."

As the crowd died down one last time, he turned back to face them, "But my friends, we must remain vigilant. For our true enemy is still out there. This fight wasn't just about defeating the dragons. It was a fight against the temptation to give up what we are. Every day we survived, we were confronted with a dark prospect. Every day, we had to remind ourselves that we were still human. That great task still remains before us and we must continue to fight for it… and we will fight. Since the beginning of this terrible war, one fear has stood above the rest; losing our morals, our rights, and our freedoms… That scares me more than any canban…"

The volume of cheers increased.

"Or dragon horde…"

The cheers erupted.

"Or any adversary we may yet face ever could!"

Even with the speaker, Lavoie now had to yell just to be heard over the crowd, "Let us overcome these obstacles together, in the spirit of what our forefathers, friends, and neighbors fought and died for!"

Three fighter jets flew overhead, each one left a colored trail of smoke behind them; blue, yellow, and green. Hats, streamers, and anything people could grab was thrown into the air.

Drakin

The Story of Raiya

Jagger, Raiya, and Andy stood in silence and watched as the crowd quickly turned into a party. Food was carted out, music that most of them had never heard before emanated from the speakers.

Raiya looked at Jagger, "So what's going to happen now?"

"Now…" Jagger replied. "The world leaders will likely start squabbling over how to form a new government."

"Sounds fun…"

Jagger shook his head, "I'd rather not be a part of it."

"Why not?"

"Politics was never my thing. It's a lot of fancy speak and weaseling."

Raiya lowered her eyes, "Well… I've been offered a position as goodwill ambassador between the nations."

"Oh yeah? That's awesome, congratulations!"

"Thanks…"

Jagger felt his heart sink. Raiya was about to become a celebrity. It wouldn't be long before she was lavished with all the attention she could ever ask for and more. There was no way around it. Soon he would be forgotten in the mix.

Raiya was about to say something when a crowd of people surrounded her. Some had recording devices, others had scraps of paper and pens. They each spoke at once, each fighting to get a word in, "Raiya, what can you tell us about the peace accords? How do you feel about the treaty?"

Drakin
The Story of Raiya

"Have you been offered a position in the government?"

"Have you considered running for office?"

"What are your plans now that the war is over?"

Raiya had an overwhelmed look on her face. She smiled as she looked at the crowd, "Well… I suppose I never really thought of it…"

Jagger was quickly pushed to the side and soon found himself several hundred feet away. This was exactly what he thought would happen. He was now on the outside looking in.

He felt a hand tap him on the shoulder, "Tough, isn't it? Watching her get all that attention… when you were the one by her side all this time."

"I don't know what you're talking about."

"Oh bullshit," Andy replied. "I may not be an exobiologist, but I can see what's been going on here."

"It's not like that… I don't care about fame… I just…"

"What?"

"I guess I'm going to miss her. She's famous now."

"Ah I see," Andy replied. "Now I get it… you're losing a friend."

Jagger was becoming annoyed with Andy's irritating questions, but he quickly shrugged it off, "I don't care… she'll have a good life now. I'm happy for her."

"What about you? What are you going to do?"

Drakin
The Story of Raiya

"Dunno," Jagger replied. "I've seen a lot more death and destruction than I ever hoped to. Maybe I'll head back east… you know… see what's going on out there. Maybe carve out a little existence of my own, huh?"

Andy smiled, "You sure about this? You'd likely wind up being a general or something if you stuck around."

"I'm good. I joined the Westcon to protect New Framingham. Now that they're gone… well, technically I already resigned."

Andy smiled and extended his hand, "All right… well, good luck my friend."

"And you too," Jagger replied, as their hands came together.

They stood looking at each other for a moment before parting. Andy stepped back towards the crowd, "If you're ever in Charleston again, look me up."

"Will do."

Drakin
The Story of Raiya

Chapter 30

The moment Jagger was free from the crowd, he quickly turned and ran towards the main capital building. He was stopped for the occasional 'hello' and 'thank you,' but otherwise, was able to slip by relatively unnoticed.

The guards that had previously been protecting the suite were now at the front doors to the command center. They both nodded to Jagger as he proceeded inside. He quickly made his way up to the suite, which was now unguarded.

Hoping to make a quiet getaway, he grabbed a few bags and began packing food into one and some supplies into the second. There wasn't much, just a few knives, some cloth, clothes, and some toiletries that would make the trip more manageable.

Flashing lights outside the window distracted him for a moment. He took a peek through the glass to see what was going on. Some of the soldiers launched makeshift fireworks into the sky. Without actually knowing what was going on, someone might have concluded that the city was once again under attack. The lights and loud explosions reminded Jagger of when they arrived in Charleston.

Jagger smiled, "Enjoy it… you have no idea the long hard road that's still ahead of you. Have fun tonight."

His eyes darted over the crowd. He knew that there was no way he could spot Raiya, but that didn't stop him from trying. The largest

Drakin
The Story of Raiya

congregation of people all seemed to be grouping together, focused on something in the middle. That must have been where Raiya was. He placed the palm of his hand on the glass so that it appeared to be right on the center of that group. A deep sigh escaped his lips as he turned away, "Goodbye."

Jagger stepped back and gathered up the remainder of his belongings. It wasn't much, just his two pistols, a few more changes of clothing, and a med pack. Everything else he'd need was already in his jeep.

He opened the door and slowly made his way down the hallway. He felt like he'd been sent on an infiltration mission, slipping into the shadows anytime he heard a noise. Hoping to avoid notice, he took the back stairs to the bottom floor. The guards were too busy tending to the celebration to notice him sneaking out. Thankfully the back exit was completely deserted.

Jagger thanked his good luck that Raiya hadn't seen him leave. He'd always hated long goodbyes. Having to play out a sad scene with her was something he preferred to avoid. She'd probably hate him for sneaking out, but it was for the best. There was no future for them, she'd made that abundantly clear.

What could he have expected anyway? Even if she did decide to settle down in a town, she'd be a celebrity. She'd likely have no time for him. No, it was better to just let her go and move on.

The jeep was parked out by what was left of the city walls. He slowly made his way to the

Drakin

The Story of Raiya

almost-empty parking lot where the armored vehicles had been stored from before the battle.

He passed by the smashed buildings he'd seen on the way in. *This will all be rebuilt soon... just watch. We'll have large cities just like the ones we used to have. It's all going to come back now.*

The sun was quickly setting. Perfect timing. Now he could get away under the cover of darkness.

The jeep came into view, out of the distance. It was the only car in the entire lot. Even the armored transports were gone. To Jagger, it was a welcomed sight. He hadn't had a chance to drive since he'd been carted everywhere in armored trucks, "Hello beautiful!"

He still had no idea how the jeep had survived. They'd fought dragon lords, wyverns, canbans, and even people who later became allies. Yet the ancient jeep had barely taken a scratch that she didn't already have.

Jagger quickly looked behind him to see if anyone was nearby. He could see a few flashlights from patrols in the distance. They were likely looking for looters or inebriated people that had partied too much, not for him. Nothing to worry about there.

He then caught sight of the massive aura above the celebration, resulting from the bright lights. Even the dragons that had been standing guard were hesitantly taking part. Lights of several colors shot into the sky as the sun began to disappear.

Drakin
The Story of Raiya

He began to question his decisions. Was he doing the right thing by leaving? Should he wait and actually say goodbye to Raiya before setting out? He weighed the odds carefully. *No… doing that would only make things harder. It's better if I just get on with things and let her do the same. She'll be mad, I'm sure… but in the end, it'll be easier.*

"Hey, stranger…"

What the…? Jagger froze in place after his personal debate was interrupted. He turned to see a dark figure sitting in the passenger's seat of the jeep. The figure remained motionless, even as it spoke, "Trying to slip out unnoticed?"

Jagger's eyes widened, "Raiya! What are you doing here?"

Raiya leaned over the jeeps center console as Jagger pulled himself into the driver's seat, "We're partners, remember?"

"Yeah, so?"

"So where are we going?"

Jagger sat for a moment with a puzzled look on his face, "Well… um…"

"What?"

"Don't you want to stay here?"

"Why would I?" Raiya asked in shock.

"You're a hero to these people," Jagger replied. "You can have or do anything you want now."

"Yeah and be hounded by people who want an autograph, scale, or piece of my hair? I'll pass on that. I never wanted all that attention. I wanted Eutherys dead, nothing more."

Drakin

The Story of Raiya

"Okay…"

"You know what I want now? I want to see the world. I want to learn about everything I missed and… maybe even cause a little trouble of my own."

Jagger remained silent as he slowly reached for the ignition. Raiya frowned, "Are you my partner or not? I didn't think killing Eutherys meant the end of that."

"It didn't…"

"Good, then where you go, I go."

Jagger smirked, "What about everything you said about this not lasting forever? What about you being a perpetual wanderer?"

Raiya became visibly uncomfortable as he spoke. Her lips twisted as she thought about it for a moment, "Maybe I was wrong…"

"What was that?"

"I said maybe I was wrong, okay? Maybe seeing you almost get killed made me wake up to some things... Look, we can just see where this goes…"

The smirk on Jagger's face became a full-blown smile. He turned and looked into her eyes. A look of urgency appeared behind the yellow flame, "Okay?"

Jagger nodded and started the car, "Okay."

Raiya smiled and enthusiastically sat back in the bucket seat, "So where are we heading?"

Jagger looked out in front of him as he slowly pulled the jeep out of its parking spot, "You know… for some reason, I've had the strangest urge to head to Florida."

Drakin
The Story of Raiya

"You want to go tropical?"

Jagger nodded, "Yeah... rumor has it the dragons didn't spend much time out that way. Who knows, maybe things are more intact down there. Either way, there are still plenty of places to cause trouble."

Raiya nodded, "Southeast it is then."

The jeep picked up speed as it pulled forward, heading for the gates, "You know... they're going to be in a mad panic when they realize that you've disappeared."

"Fuck it. They'll live... and so will we."

The moment they were outside Denver's protective gate, Jagger pressed his foot down on the gas. The jeep's engine roared as the tires kicked up dust, masking their escape.

Drakin
The Story of Raiya

About the Author

James Harrington was born and raised in Boston, Massachusetts. He holds a Bachelor's in History but also studied religion and how it related to his chosen subject matter. It was from those studies that his first book was born.

James has written several essays and short stories but had never gotten a full-length novel published until his big breakthrough with *Magnifica, The Last Enchanter*. Following its success, two more titles were added to the *Magnifica* series.

James currently lives in Massachusetts with his wife and two children.

For more info on James and his books, please visit his Facebook page:

The Creative Works of James Harrington.
https://www.facebook.com/JamesHarringtonsMagnifica/

Or his Blog page for regular updates as well as writing advice:
http://jamesharringtoncreativeworks.wordpress.com/

Drakin
The Story of Raiya

<u>Check out James's other novels</u>:

Magnifica: The Last Enchanter

Magnifica: Tears of the Fallen

Magnifica: Gravestalker

Divinity

Damnation

Soul Siphon: Book One of the Vengeance Doctrine

Drakin
The Story of Raiya